Master of Darkness

K.T. KAYE

ISBN: 978-1-78972-136-2

A MASSIVE THANK YOU

To my big sister Megan for being with me since this idea first began. And to Mum for supporting me every step of the way.

CONTENTS

CONTENTS

PROLOGUE

On the roof of a seven-storey building, in the middle of London, at exactly midnight, a woman was getting all the blood in her body sucked out of her by a very hungry vampire. The vampire's fangs were nestled deep into the woman's neck, her ruby red blood filling his newly found hunger. If the vampire had been paying attention, however, he would have seen the garlic juice-covered wooden dagger before it had stabbed him in the shoulder.

The vampire yelled out in pain as his shoulder and right arm began to burn. He dropped the woman and carefully pulled out the dagger. The vampire looked up as a woman with white feathery wings dropped in front of him and pointed a sword in his direction.

"Now are you going to come quietly, or do I have to kill you?" the winged woman asked.

"You!" the vampire snapped. He charged at the winged woman. She twisted out of the way and quickly pulled a small wooden dagger from her pocket. The woman threw the dagger. It span through the air, making its home in the vampire's side. The vampire groaned as he pulled the dagger from his body. He ran super-vampire fast up behind the winged woman, but she simply turned and stabbed her sword into his belly. The sword was covered in garlic juice. The vampire staggered backwards. The woman punched the vampire's face before stabbing a wooden stake into his chest. The vampire crumbled into ash.

The winged woman smiled.

The sound of a mobile phone vibrating broke the midnight silence. From her pocket, the winged woman pulled out her phone and answered.

"Angel Night speaking. Yeah, the vampire's dead. What? The Master of Darkness? I'm on my way."

1

'BEING SEDATED IS FUN!'

JASON

"Jason Dragonheart!"

"Yes?" I looked up at the sound of my name.

"Mr Dragonheart," my Maths teacher, Mrs Smith, hissed, "Can you answer the question on the board please?"

I looked across to the whiteboard and came face-to-face with my arch enemy...Algebra!

Algebra is one of those things that no matter how many times someone explains it to me, I still don't understand it. I mean what idiot decided to put letters in Maths! Maths is for numbers and English is for letters. The two shouldn't be mixed! My annoyingly smart classmates sneered at me as I stared helplessly at the equation.

"Well Mr Dragonheart? Can you answer the question?"

"No."

"No? Jason this is basic stuff. If you can't get

this…Why exactly are you taking A-Level Maths?"

"Because I failed to make it onto an apprenticeship."

"Mr Dragonheart!"

"I'm leaving," and with that I quickly walked out of Maths. I walked unchallenged out of the school gates, which looking back was probably the first sign that something was wrong. The city was oddly quiet. No one was about, which if I had been paying attention would have been the second sign that something was wrong. I turned a corner and walked through the alleyway which was strangely dark to say it was only one o'clock in the afternoon, sign number three that something was wrong - I really should have paid more attention!

"Hello Jason."

I turned around startled. Behind me, a tall pale man stood. He was wearing a grey suit, which was too smart for this part of town, and had short ginger hair. He began to walk forwards, his large frame towered over me.

"How do you know my name?" I asked, taking a couple of steps back.

"I have a message for you to give to your mummy. Tell her that her dreams will soon come true," the man said softly. The way he spoke made me shudder; his voice was like stepping into a pool of freezing ice.

"Why don't you tell her yourself?"

The man laughed, "Such spirit. But no, I'm afraid it must be you who tells her, for I…must go."

With that, the man vanished.

I stood there and stared at the spot where the man had stood. He had been there one second and then gone the next…how was that possible!? People can't just vanish, can they? No that's not possible, I told myself, it couldn't be possible. The sound of footsteps woke me from my thoughts. A tall pale man with light brown hair raced over to me.

"The man, what did he say?" he asked quickly.

"What?"

"What did he say?"

"None of your business," I pushed past him then ran down the rest of the alleyway.

"Wait!" I heard him call. I turned back to look but the man had vanished. This really freaked me out, so I ran away as quickly as possible. I didn't slow down until I was safely inside my house.

"Jason? You're not meant to be back yet," Josie Dragonheart said as soon as I had come through the door. Me and my mum looked nothing alike. She was small and beautiful with blonde-hair and bright blue eyes whilst I was tall and skinny with brown eyes and hair. I am also rather weak looking and am unable to hurt a fly, while my mum looked sweet and lovely however, she could rip a man to piece in a matter of seconds should she feel the urge to.

"Err I walked out of school," I muttered.

"Jason Dragonheart! I didn't raise you to be a hooligan! Get yourself back in school this instant!" my mum shouted as she whacked my arm and tried to drag me out of the door.

After a brief scuffle, I pushed past my mum and raced up the stairs. Once inside my bedroom, I locked my door and collapsed onto my bed. I was confused. While me being confused is quite a regular occurrence, the situation in the alleyway had taken my state of confusion to the next level. I could feel a panic-attack growing in my stomach as questions began to repeatedly bombard my brain. How had that guy known my name? What was the message? What did the man want me to tell mum? I could barely remember what he had said. What about the other man? Who was he? I groaned into my pillow. So many questions but no answers. I grabbed my headphones and listened to music until I fell asleep. My nap was interrupted, however, by strange sounds coming from downstairs. At first, I thought I was still dreaming, but then I heard what sounded like a scream. I got to my feet and raced downstairs.

"Mum!" I shouted.

There was no answer.

"Mum!" I yelled again as I went into the living room. The room had been ripped apart. Pictures lay broken on the floor and the once yellow walls were now blood red. As I took a step into the living room, I noticed my mum. She was sprawled across the glass littered carpet. Her body had been beaten and, on her neck, there was a deep bloody wound.

"Mum!" I gasped. Her eyes snapped open.

"Jason," she cried, "Run! Leave now! Run!"

"Mum?"

"Run Jason! He's coming for you! Run!"

"Who's coming?"

"Hello Jason," from the shadows stepped the man from the alleyway. Blood covered his lips and his sinister smile revealed a pair of sharp fangs. I stumbled backwards.

"Run Jason!" my mum screamed with the last of her strength. She then closed her eyes and died. I stared at my mum's body then at the strange inhuman creature that stood before me. I ran. I ran out of the house and down the street. I didn't know where I was going or what I was going to do when I got there but I didn't stop running. I couldn't think. My head was spinning. The image of my mum's bloody body kept tormenting my imagination. Suddenly I crashed into a small red-haired woman. I was about to apologise when the woman grabbed my arm and tugged me into an alleyway.

"Get off me!" I yelled breaking free of her grasp.

"Jason, I don't have time to explain this situation to you right now, but I need you to trust me," the woman snapped.

"How do you know my name? Who are you?"

"My name isn't important right now! All you need to know is that I am trying to save your life. So move!" She grabbed my arm once more and hauled me down the street.

"I have the Master," the woman said, placing a hand to her ear, "I'll meet you at the rendezvous point."

"Who are you talking to?" I asked. She didn't answer, instead she continued to drag me through the streets of London. We turned into an alleyway only to find it covered in thick black mist.

"Damn!" the woman muttered, looking around. There was a fire escape on the side of one of the buildings. She dragged me up the stairs, only letting me go once we had reached the top. Going to the side of the roof, she stared down to the alley below.

The red-haired woman put her hand to her ear and muttered, "Stuck in current location. We'll wait for Alex then I'll teleport us all out of here."

"Who are you?" I asked again. The woman had long red hair, that was pulled back in a tight ponytail, and sharp green eyes. She was dressed from head to toe in black and had a rucksack on her back. She looked younger than me.

"I'm older than you, at least I think I am," she said sharply.

"What?"

"You thought I was younger than you. However I don't think I am. I'm pretty certain I must be over eighteen."

"Don't think? Surely, you'd know if you were over eighteen or not. Wait did I say that out loud?"

"No, you thought it."

"Then how did you...?"

"Telepathy."

"What?"

"The ability to read minds."

"I know what telepathy is!"

"Good. To answer your earlier question, my name is Angel Night and I'm the captain of Lightning D.D. Squad. The D.D stands for Demon Disposal; in case you were wondering."

"Demon!? Ha funny! Stop making jokes," As I spoke my mind flashed back to the neck wound on my mum's body and to the man's bloody lips. Could he have been a...? No they weren't real! They couldn't be real. Demons weren't real.

"Demons are real. And your assumption is correct. The man who killed your mum is a vampire, a very powerful one."

"A vamp..." at this point my knees gave way and I collapsed to the ground. A vampire!? A vampire had killed my mum...what kind of sick nightmare was this!? I must be dreaming. I had to be dreaming!

"You're not dreaming," Angel said as she knelt in front of me. She pressed her hand to my forehead.

"What are you doing?"

"Calming you down. I know this is a lot to take in, but I need you to stay calm and not panic."

"Stay calm!? My mum is dead, she was killed by a...she couldn't have been. They don't exist. They don't exist! None of this is real. This has to be a dream!"

"Jason, I need you to calm down. Breathe in, breathe out. Breathe in..."

"That's not helping!"

"Would this situation be more bearable if I turned you into a toad?"

"No! Why? Why would? How would me being a toad make this situation better!?"

"Toads don't suffer from panic disorders for one. I could also shove you in my backpack if you were a toad."

"You're not shoving me into your backpack! And you're not turning me into a toad!"

Angel shrugged, "Suit yourself. I was only trying to help."

"Help? That's not...wait...did we just have a conversation about you turning me into a toad?"

"Yes. Yes we did."

"Wha...what are you?" I stuttered as panic engulfed

my chest. This woman, Angel Night, she wasn't human. She looked like a human, but she wasn't. She was something else. Something paranormal. She could read my mind and she could turn me into a toad…at this moment my panic-attack went into overdrive and I began to hyperventilate.

"Oh don't do that!" Angel exclaimed as she grabbed hold of my shoulders, "Jason! Jason, I know this is a very strange situation, but I really need you to…and you're not listening."

Angel pulled out a wand from her boot and pressed it against my forehead. My body suddenly felt very calm. My mind stopped spinning and became numb as my panic was suppressed. I exhaled heavily as my breathing returned to normal.

"There we go," Angel smiled, "Things don't seem too bad now, do they?"

I shook my head and found myself smiling like a fool.

"Good. To answer your question, I'm a shapeshifter. You know what one of those is, don't you?"

I nodded.

"Good," Angel got to her feet and pressed her hand to her ear, "Alex, where are you? We need to leave. I've just had to sedate the Master of Darkness. Fern stop laughing! This isn't funny. The kid was having a panic-attack. Does anyone know where Alex is? No Fern stay where you are. Araminta find Alex. If he doesn't show up in five minutes, I'm teleporting Jason to the base without him."

"Who are you talking to?" I giggled. Whatever magic Angel had used on me was seriously messing with my brain. Although I was aware that I was in a serious situation, I couldn't process it properly and I kept wanting to laugh.

"Members of my squad. You'll meet them soon. They're also paranormal beings, that won't be a problem will it?"

I shook my head as I stumbled to my feet.

"Good. Nice to see the sedations working."

"Whatever you did to me...it feels funny! See I actually feel very confused and sad, but right now, I really want to laugh!"

"I sedated you, using magic, which means right now you probably feel like you're drunk."

"I'm not drunk! I'm not. I'm not. I want to run away! I want to run far away! All the way to the moon!"

"No you can't run away. We're currently surrounded by death clouds."

"By what?"

"That black mist, that's covering the alley, is called a death cloud. It's very bad. If you touch one, terrible things will happen, do you understand?"

I giggled loudly, "I want to touch it."

"Trust me you don't."

"I want to touch it!" I stumbled towards the fire escape. Angel grabbed my arms and dragged me to the ground. As she did so an old woman with a frame walked down the alley.

"Don't do that!" Angel shouted. But it was too late. The woman stepped into the death cloud. She started to cough. Her hands went to her neck as the cloud burnt her throat. She coughed up blood and stumbled backwards. The old woman fell to the ground. Her body began to tremble and then she exploded!

I laughed hysterically, "The old lady just went BOOM!"

"Yes, she did, and when this sedation eventually wears off, I'm sure you'll realise how horrific the situation you're laughing at is. Now you need to stay very still so that I can teleport us both out of here."

"You're leaving already, what a shame," said a cold voice. We turned to stare as the vampire who had murdered my mum appeared behind us.

"Mr Jet! Is it time for our rematch?" Angel got to her feet and pulled out a long-curved sword, which had been strapped to her back.

"Is that a sword!? How did I not notice that you had a sword!? Wait do I have a sword on my back too!?" I exclaimed as I searched my back for a sword.

"Not now Jason!"

"Ah Jason! What...? Did you sedate the Master of Darkness?" the man, called Mr Jet, asked.

"Yeah. I'm starting to regret it," Angel muttered sheepishly as I pranced across the rooftop in search of a sword. I was having a wonderful time. I was blissfully unaware of how serious the situation was, and the fact that the vampire who'd murdered my mum was stood in front of me didn't bother me in the slightest. I was quite happy searching for the sword that I was certain was strapped to my back.

"Jason!" Mr Jet shouted, I turned towards him, "I did tell you to pass on my message. If you had..."

"You would have killed his mum anyway," Angel interrupted, "That's what you do."

"Still bitter I see. You know you should really learn to let things..." Before he could finish, a sword was pushed through his chest. The man's body steamed. He pulled the sword from his body and swung it at his attacker. But his attacker had vanished. Suddenly the other man from the alley appeared by my side.

"How did you get here!?" I asked, "Are you also magic!? You have a sword! I have a sword too, but I can't remember where I put it."

"Angel what have you done to the Master of Darkness?" the man asked.

Mr Jet laughed. "Did you think your little sword would kill me? I'm disappointed in you Alex. I thought you were cleverer than this. What a shame. Jason take care. I'll be seeing you soon."

The man suddenly disappeared, leaving behind a cloud of black mist.

The mist pushed itself into my chest and out of my back before fading completely. I grabbed my chest. It burned, like there was a fire raging inside my body. I could hear people talking but I couldn't understand what they were saying. I fell to the floor. The pain was unbearable. It was as if a volcano was going off under my skin.

Then the world went black.

2

'WHERE ARE THE GRAPES?'

JASON

Is it weird that the first thing I thought of when I woke up was mint ice-cream? I suddenly got an intense craving for it. Is that weird?

"Hello? Can you hear me?" asked a voice.

"Yes. What happened...?" I groaned. My head hurt. It felt like someone had hit my head with a frying pan multiple times. I blinked continuously until my blurred vision finally settled. I was in a hospital room. Slowly sitting myself up, I looked around and saw Angel Night sat in the corner.

"Do you remember me?" she asked, "How are you feeling? You're not still in search of a sword, are you?"

"You're Angel Night. You're a shapeshifter. And you did something to me!"

"Shhh! Don't say that so loudly. Look I admit I did sedate you without your permission. I was trying to calm you down. I didn't realise it'd make you go crazy and act like a drunk!"

"I…" I paused as the memories returned to me. My mum was dead. She had been killed by a vampire. A vampire. And the woman in front of me was a shapeshifter. Panic gripped my stomach once more.

"This is a lot to process," Angel muttered, "Look I don't really know the best way of explaining this to you but vampires, werewolves, witches, shapeshifters, they're all real. Very real. Jason are you okay?"

I nodded unable to speak.

"Your mum was killed by a very evil vampire. I'm really sorry. He killed my mum too. I don't really know how to help you. I've never lived in the human world, so I don't really know what your level of understanding is. I'm sure everything will become clearer once you've spoken to Willow."

Angel reached forward and picked up a clipboard, "No poison. No internal damage. A clean bill of health, how fascinating."

"What happened to my mum…?" I stuttered.

"We cleaned it up. Josie Dragonheart and her son both died in a robbery gone wrong."

"Her son? I'm dead?"

"Yes but obviously you're not actually dead. Danny created a brilliant illusion. He found an unnamed human corpse and made it look like you."

"He what?"

"He created an illusion, so that if any human looks upon the corpse, they'll see you."

"That's really creepy."

"Maybe but it needed to be done. We had them bury you quickly. It was a simple service. It had a good turnout, admittedly most people who came were your mum's friends, but your classmates turned up too," Angel said awkwardly.

"I'm dead. My mum. Why did…why did he kill her? Who was he?"

"He goes by the alias Mr Jet. No one knows his actual name. He is, I suppose you could call him a terrorist, a paranormal version. He killed your mum most likely for fun."

"Fun?"

"Yeah, that's why he killed mine. He was also trying to get to you."

"To me? Why?"

"That I think would be best left to another time. I have to go. I'm sure Willow will be able to explain things better than I can."

"Willow?"

"You'll meet her soon enough. She's a member of my squad…as are you."

"Pardon?"

"You have been placed as a member of my squad."

"Squad?"

"Demon Disposal Squad."

"But why? I don't want…I'm not…I'm human!"

"No, you're not."

"Excuse me…what are you…this is crazy! I'm dreaming! This is a nightmare! I'm human!"

"You aren't human, you're paranormal. Oh I'll leave that for Willow. Just listen to this and remember, you are a part of my squad now, meaning you do as I say. I am not a fan of rules, so I have only one. If I say run, you run. If I say jump, you jump. If I say fight until you drop dead, you do just that, understood?"

"What? I don't understand."

"Of course you don't," Angel sighed, "But you will soon, so remember what I just said if you want to stay alive."

"You know normally when you get a visitor in hospital you get a 'get well soon' card or some grapes, not a warning," I stared at her coldly.

"It's not a warning, it's a fact. This world you've entered is a hundred times more dangerous than the human world. And you've been thrown right into the deep end. I'm not trying to scare you; I'm trying to save you. I'm your Captain now so do as I say and maybe you'll live a little longer. As for grapes, prove you're worthy enough to be in my squad then I'll bring grapes," Angel stood up and headed down the ward.

I lay back as it hit me. My mum was dead. The woman who had given birth to me, fed me, and cared for me was gone, and she was never coming back. I tried to imagine her happy but all I could think of was her cold dead body lying in our living room. I hid my face in my pillow and cried.

* * * * *

A visitor appeared two hours later, in the shape of a tall black woman with curly hair decorated with a purple ribbon. She wore a big smile on her face and spoke with an Australian accent.

"Hi. I'm Willow Donovan. How are you feeling?" she asked.

I shrugged.

"Do you know what hit you? It was a death cloud, yet somehow you lived through it! You're…it's incredible!"

"Why?"

"Why what?"

"Why did I live through it? That old lady," I shuddered at the memory.

"Because you're the Master of Darkness!"

"The what?"

"Did you not know that you're the Master of Darkness!?"

"I don't even know what a Master of Darkness is."

"How can you not know who the Master of Darkness is!? Oh wait, human world of course! How could you know, you've been living with humans this whole time! The Master of Darkness is the most powerful paranormal in existence, and he also happens to be you!"

I stared at her. This girl was clearly mad.

"I'm not mad. I'm a telepath!"

"Another one?" Were none of my thoughts safe!?

"Angel isn't a telepath, she's a shapeshifter. Don't worry your thoughts are safe. I try not to read people's minds all the time," Willow smiled, "I was being deadly serious about the whole Master of Darkness thing, I assure you. You really are, or will be with some training, the most powerful guy on the planet!"

"That's a lot to take in," I mumbled. I couldn't be powerful! Powerful was not a word that had ever been used to describe me. Idiot on the other hand was a word that had been used frequently over the past eighteen years of my existence.

"Aww you're not an idiot," Willow smiled.

"Stop doing that!" I exclaimed grabbing my head.

"Sorry can't help it. It's because you're new. My powers always go a bit out of control with new people."

"Are you sure you've got the right guy? I'm no one!"

"You were treated unfairly in the human world, weren't you? You were an outsider. Sorry I didn't mean to read your mind. Humans tend to be cruel to people who are different. It's not like that here. Jason, you're the most important person in this world, and we need you."

"That seems like a lot of pressure."

"You did it before, you can do it again."

"What...?"

"Oh damn it! I forgot to mention, you're a reincarnation."

"I'm a what!?"

"Reincarnation, it means..."

"I know what it means!" I snapped. This was quite a lot to take in. My mum had just been killed by a vampire, I had been saved by a shapeshifter and now I was a reincarnation! I felt like my head was about to explode. It was too much. Too much to take in. Too much to process. Panic quickly attacked my chest. I was human. I had to be human. I wasn't a Master of Darkness, whatever that was.

To me it sounded like I was the guy in charge of switching off lights.

Willow laughed, "The guy in charge of switching off lights! Ha that's funny!"

"Stop reading my mind!"

"Sorry, but you seem to be having a bit of a mental breakdown. I swear it's not as bad as it seems. We fight demons that are trying to escape from hell and want to destroy the world, ah I guess it's quite bad actually, I probably shouldn't have started with that!"

"Demons!? Hell!?"

"Yeah, but I promise it isn't as bad as I've made it sound," she laughed, "Come on, Skyjack said you have a clean bill of health. So get up, I'll show you around."

* * * * *

It turned out that I was on the main base of the Demon Disposal Squads. Demon Disposal Squads, like their name suggests, were in charge of disposing of and destroying demons. The idea that demons were real was something that I had a tough time dealing with, so I quickly blocked this notion from my mind and followed Willow like a lost puppy.

Willow briskly showed me round the base. She pointed out several buildings and told me what they were. I, however, was in such a nervous and overwhelmed state that I forgot everything she said the moment the words left her lips. There were only two buildings whose purposes stayed in my memory. The first was the tall dark manor house, which I was told belonged to the man in charge of the base, the Colonel. The second building was a large barn, in which multiple "mythical" creatures were training. I won't lie to you, I almost fainted when a centaur waved in my direction. It wasn't that I had anything against him, I'm sure he was a lovely horse man, but I hadn't expected him to exist so the sight of him gave me a bit of a shock.

Willow led me away from the numerous training buildings and towards eight houses. The houses, I was told, belonged to the eight squads (Thunder, Wildfire, Tsunami, Avalanche, Tornado, Volcano, Lightning, and Alpha) that lived and worked at the base. Willow led me to an old white house that was sat close to the forest and opened the door.

"Welcome to Lightning House," she smiled, "Home to Lightning Squad and your home from now on."

Inside the house was warm and bright. The hallway I had entered had a shining wooden floor and clean white walls. In front of me was a large staircase that split off into two different directions. On the wall to my right were several hooks covered by coats, while to my left a large photograph filled the wall. The photograph was of a group of people smiling happily in front of the house.

"I wasn't in the original version of that photograph. They had to magic an image of me into it," said a voice from behind me. I jumped in surprise. A tanned woman with brown hair and large brown eyes had appeared by my side and was staring at me intensely.

"Jason, this is Araminta Bennett," Willow said with a grin.

"You must be the Master of Darkness," Araminta held out her hand for me to shake.

"Apparently," I answered taking her hand.

"You are. I can smell it."

"That's a little bit creepy."

"I'm a vampire, we're supposed to be creepy," Araminta smiled, "Come on I'll show you to your room."

I followed Araminta and Willow up the stairs. At the top of the stairs was a hallway of doors. Araminta led me to the door at the far end of the hall. The door was black with a golden knocker. Pulling out a black key from her pocket, Araminta unlocked it. Behind the door was another stairway and at the top of this was another black door. Araminta, using the key from earlier, unlocked the door, revealing my room. It was the same as my old one back home; a small desk in the corner, a bed with a blue duvet, a battered grey carpet, a white wardrobe with its paint crumbling off and a pile of well-read comic books stacked on the floor. Two things, however, made this room noticeably different from my old one. The first thing was the massive log fireplace (seriously it was huge and, you know, on fire!) and the other was the scary portraits on the wall. I did my best to avoid the portraits sharp stares as I went over to the open wardrobe.

"I hope you like it, Clover and Fern worked really hard on it," Araminta explained.

"I bet Fern moaned the entire time," Willow laughed.

"Continuously. She never stopped!"

"What are these for?" I asked gesturing to the military uniforms in the wardrobe.

"Ah, right well this base is a unit in the Emperor's army," Araminta began before I interrupted her.

"So am I supposed to be a soldier?"

"No, not exactly. Dinners at six but I'll come get you. Until then," she gave the key to me, before she left with Willow. I sat on my bed dazed.

All I did was walk out of Maths and now vampires, shapeshifters, telepaths, and demons were all real! Not only that but I was meant to be the Master of Darkness, what even was that!? No one had actually explained what a Master of Darkness was. Willow had said I was the most powerful paranormal on the planet, but what did that mean!?

* * * * *

The next few hours consisted of me panicking, having a nap, crying, panicking a bit more, taking another nap before I finally pulled myself together enough to stare at the paintings that covered my bedroom walls. The paintings were all portraits of different men dressed in smart black robes. Each looked as serious and as terrifying as the next. I was so busy staring at one of the paintings that I didn't notice Araminta enter, not until she tapped me on the shoulder.

"Ah don't eat me!" I cried as I ducked to the floor.

"Huh I've not had that reaction before," Araminta laughed.

"Sorry," I muttered as I pulled myself up.

"It's time for dinner."

"Oh. Coming."

"Do you like your room?" asked Araminta, as I followed her down the stairs. I nodded so she continued, "Oh, that's good. If you ever want to change anything just think about it and it should happen. All the rooms are magic, they work on brain patterns, so it knows when you don't like something."

"That's cool," I said although creepy was the word I would have preferred to use. We walked along the hallway, down more stairs and left into a huge room which had a rectangle table in the middle of it. On one side of the room was a door (which I later found out led to the kitchen) and bright white shelves covered in cutlery, whilst on the other side there were two large glass doors that led into the forest. The room was very light and very white…it also gave me flashbacks to my old dentist's surgery, but I quickly shook the terrifying memories of dentistry from my mind and focused my attention to the eight members of Lightning Squad that were sat (stuffing their faces with food) around the table.

"Guys!" Araminta said getting their attention, "This is Jason Dragonheart, the Master of Darkness."

I sat next to Araminta, at the end of the table, as the others stared at me.

"Alexander Laurentius Octavius," said one of the men, breaking the awkward silence. I recognised this man; he had been the person who had ran over to me in the alleyway.

"Ah, yes I remember you," I muttered awkwardly.

"It's nice to see you not sedated. I'm your vice-captain

so any problems come to me," he said, "Oh and I'm a vampire in case you're wondering."

"He's one of the oldest vampires left," Willow explained, "He was born and died in the Roman era!"

"Clover Bramble," a short, pale, blonde-haired lady introduced herself, "Oh and that's my twin sister Fern."

Clover was pointing to a small woman with long brown hair, who wore big glasses and had her nose in a book. Fern looked up at the sound of her name. She looked at me, gave a laugh, then continued reading.

"I know, we look nothing a like," Clover muttered.

"You're not a telepath, are you?" I asked, as I had been thinking the same thing.

"No, but everyone points out that we don't look alike. We're witches. Roxy, however, is a telepath."

"Hey," called a tall black woman from the other end of the table, "I'm actually more than just a telepath! I'm a Mind Witch."

"Which is basically the same thing," Willow muttered to me.

"It isn't. I don't just read minds; I can also control them and…oh never mind! Nice to meet you Jason. I'm Roxy Ash. Yes, I am American, I'm from New Orleans. Oh, you think I'm attractive, thanks sweetie that's cute! Don't be embarrassed, lots of guys think that the first time they see me. You should really learn to block your mind; you don't want the demons reading your thoughts!"

"Right," I muttered embarrassed. I hadn't even realised that I had thought Roxy was attractive. I must have just registered it subconsciously as I had been more focused on the fact that I was sharing a table with a vampire and two witches.

"I'm Roger Night," smiled a tanned man with brown hair, "And this is my younger brother Ethan."

"Hey," waved Ethan, who looked almost identical to his brother, except he was pale and had blonde hair. Suddenly Ethan sneezed.

"Bless you," everyone (but me) said in unison.

"Thanks. Sorry I'm allergic to dogs."

"Right," I muttered, wondering why he had just told me that. There weren't any dogs in the room.

"I'm a werewolf," Ethan explained, "So I'm kind of allergic to myself."

Roger laughed, "No matter how many times you say it, it's still funny!"

"Angel is their adopted sister," Willow explained, "Hence why they have same surname but are different species."

"Oh," I hadn't realised that their surnames were the same, I was still trying to cope with the fact that they were werewolves.

"How old are you Jason?"

"Eighteen."

"Aw cute! Ethan this means you're no longer the youngest!"

"Yes!" Ethan cheered happily.

"How old are you guys?" I asked.

"Our ages range between twenty-one and over two thousand." Before I had chance to process and panic over this information, an Asian woman introduced herself.

"I'm Sue Lee. I'm a selkie. In case you were wondering about my accent, I'm Chinese-Canadian," she bowed her head in my direction.

"Selkie?"

"Ah it means in water I turn into a seal."

"Oh."

"This is Elsa Sunday," Sue gestured to the pale blonde-haired woman sat next to her.

"Vampire," Elsa smiled. She spoke with an accent which I couldn't place but before I could ask where she was from, a ginger haired man with sunglasses on walked into the room.

"Evening all," he said with a Scottish accent, "Oh this must be the Master."

"We're just introducing ourselves. Would you like to…?"

"Sure, I'm Paris Surf, pleasure to meet you," he held out his hand which I shook then he continued, "I'm half-gorgon. I assume you know what a gorgon is?"

"Medusa?"

"Exactly. I have gorgon eyes, which means I have to always wear sunglasses, or I'd turn you all to stone! Luckily I didn't inherit the snake hair!"

"I think that's everyone, oh except Sophie over there!" Willow pointed to the human-sized fairy sat at the end of the table. She had white hair and pale skin that seemed to glitter. Her eyes were a soft purple which matched the colour of her wings. At the mention of her name, the fairy turned invisible. I stared at her, my mouth dropping open. She was a fairy. A real-life fairy.

"Jason stop staring you're making her uncomfortable," Willow muttered, I dropped my gaze quickly, "That's Sophie Day and, as you see, she's a fairy. She doesn't talk much. Ah I forgot someone else. There's also Danny Park. He's an illusionist."

"Angel mentioned him," I remembered.

"He's the guy who made all those humans believe you were dead," Roxy explained, "His powers and fighting skills are exceptional. His personality not so much. He's Korean but…"

"Why are you talking about my nationality?" asked a tall, muscular Asian man as he entered the room.

"Danny, this is Jason the Master of…"

"I know who he is," Danny said, before sitting down.

With the introductions over, we started to eat. They all seemed nice enough but to be honest I just felt overwhelmed by the whole situation. I didn't eat much and was glad when I could go back to my room. As I got to my door, I felt something behind me. I turned and jumped. It was a ghost! A real-life ghost! The ghost was small and sickly skinny. Her hair looked wet (I later found out that this was because she'd died by drowning!) and she wore a long white nightgown. Her large eyes stared at me.

"I'm Helena," the ghost whispered.

"H...h...h...h...hi," I squeaked, this was the first ghost I had ever met, so naturally I was absolutely terrified!

"The Colonel wishes to speak to you."

* * * * *

The ghost led me down a dark hallway inside the Colonel's private manor. She stopped in front of a large wooden door. She turned to me, smiled, then flew straight through the door. I just stood there, unsure what I was meant to do. Then there was a muffled shout of "Come in." I took a deep breath and entered.

"Master Jason welcome! It is an honour. I am so happy to see you alive and well," the man smiled a cold smile. There was no warmth in his piercing blue eyes or his words. He gestured for me to sit. The Colonel was a tall man with white blonde hair and large shoulders that towered over me. Helena was sat floating in the air in the corner of the room, looking miserable. The Colonel's office was smaller than I had expected. It had a large dark wooden desk in the middle, which took up most of the room, and several wooden shelf units covering the emerald green walls. It was a very dark office despite the large stained glass window. Behind the desk was a drinks cabinet, the Colonel was stood in front of it pouring purple liquid into two glasses.

The Colonel turned to look at me and laughed, "Boy you look like a ghost, no offence Helena, here have a drink."

Helena muttered under her breath, "He looks like a ghost! He looks nothing like a ghost, he's too pink to be a ghost!"

I was handed a cup of warm purple liquid. I took a careful sip. The drink was sweet and delicious. It made my stomach feel warm and it battered away my anxiety. The

Colonel sat himself down on the other side of the desk. There was a moment of silence. The Colonel studied me for some time. The expression on his face was unreadable. Just as I was beginning to feel like a fish in a bowl, he began to speak.

"Good that's put some colour in your cheeks. I know this must have been a traumatic experience for you. I am so sorry for the loss of your mother. Mr Jet will be found, and he will pay for what he did to you and to all the others," the Colonel said looking distantly into the air.

"Who exactly is Mr Jet?" I asked, it had been a question I was desperate to know the answer to.

"Who is Mr Jet!? Mr Jet, he's all they ever talk about. Stupid! They're worried about the wrong people. Mr Jet isn't the problem," Helena grumbled.

"That's enough Helena!" the Colonel snapped harshly, before turning back to me, "We don't know. He turned up a few hundred years back and has slowly been getting more powerful. Don't worry boy, we'll get him. Now tomorrow morning," he said, changing the subject, "I have you pencilled in for a sword fighting lesson with Alexander."

Helena laughed, "He's so dead!"

* * * * *

"The first rule of fighting is control," Alexander said to his one pupil. Me. "Anyone can pick up a sword and stab a man but what makes it an art is the swordsman's ability to be the master of his sword."

"Right," I mumbled. I had been pulled from my bed in the early hours of the morning for this sword lesson. I didn't want to be here. I wanted to be fast asleep in my bed. Yesterday I had been in hospital but rather than giving me time to rest and recover, they were making me do exercise. And I hate exercise! Not only that, but which idiot thought it'd be a good idea to give me, with my track record of breaking things, a sword. I hadn't been allowed to touch it yet, but still! The sword looked incredible though. Its handle was gold and its blade jet black.

Alexander explained and demonstrated different fight techniques. While I'm certain everything he said was very insightful and probably very important, I didn't listen to a word of it. I was too busy trying to cope with the fact that I was being taught how to fight by a vampire who had been alive since the Roman era.

"You didn't listen to a word of that did you?" Alexander suddenly asked.

"Yes. No. Maybe," I spluttered.

"Jason pick up the sword." I did so. The moment I did, Alexander swung his sword in my direction. I jumped out of the way and stumbled backwards.

"What are you doing!? You could've killed me!"

"According to records, sword fighting has always come naturally to the other masters, I was seeing if that was the case for you."

"Well it clearly isn't so don't do it!" I exclaimed as I doubled over trying to catch my breath. From the moment I had picked up the sword, my head had started to spin. My body tingled, and a strange shudder ran down my spine. I felt itchy. Really itchy!

"Jason? Are you okay?" I distantly heard Alexander ask.

The sword fell from my hand. A murky mist twisted around my body. My vision blurred, and dark lightning exploded from my fingertips. Alarms sounded as black flames spread across the training room. I suddenly felt a strange craving. A craving for flesh. Before I had time to satisfy this feeling, I felt someone pin me to the floor.

"That's enough Jason," whispered Alexander into my ear.

Then the world went black.

Again.

3

'A LOT TO PROCESS'

JASON

Once again, I was awoken by the desire to eat mint ice-cream. As my vision cleared and I sat myself up, I found myself in the hospital wing. I looked around and found a thing stood at the end of my bed. It looked like a horse. It had white fur and a white mane like a horse. Two things, however, told me it wasn't a horse, and those were the light blue horn that was sticking out of its forehead and the massive pair of wings that stuck out of its back!

"Afternoon," it said.

"H…h…hi" I stammered. It could speak!? I hadn't been expecting it to speak, to be honest I hadn't been expecting it to exist, let alone speak! I couldn't work out if this thing was a unicorn or a Pegasus. I think it must have seen my stare for it gave what I think was a laugh.

"I'm a pegacorn. My mum was a Pegasus and my dad was a unicorn. My name's Skyjack. You've been out cold for four hours."

"What happened?"

"Power overload and you also turned into a demon briefly."

"Pardon? Turned into a…"

"Demon. Oh has nobody told you, a Master of Darkness is half demon. Which means you, my friend, can turn into a deadly monster from the pits of hell. Jason are you alright?" Skyjack asked as I fainted.

When I awoke, Skyjack was staring down at me. The closeness of his face made me jump and fall off the hospital bed.

"How long was I out?" I asked as I got to my feet embarrassed.

"Four seconds," Skyjack replied.

"Oh. Wait you said I turned into a demon!" I could feel my body shaking and I felt faint. I sat myself down on the hospital bed. I had turned into a demon. A demon…no words can possibly describe how massively I was freaking out. A few days ago I had been a normal human being, going to school, failing at algebra and now I had turned into a demon. I bit my lip to suppress my sudden urge to scream.

"It was only briefly," Skyjack said as if those words were supposed to give me comfort.

"That doesn't make me feel better! I turned into a…I feel a bit sick."

Skyjack trotted over to me and pressed his horn against my chest. My sickness vanished and a wave of calmness spread over my body.

"This will calm you down a bit. I have to say boy you're certainly not what I expected. The other masters were so not like you."

"I feel like you're insulting me."

"I am a bit, yes," Skyjack admitted as he pulled his horn away, "Discovering that you can turn into a demon must have been very shocking for you. I'm sure Angel will arrange for you to have lessons with Willow and Roxy, where they'll teach you how to lock your demon self away. So then you won't have to worry about it taking over you."

"I wasn't worrying about it taking over me until you said that!"

"Ah my bad."

"I turned into a demon," I muttered repeatedly.

"I know! I heard you were huge!" Paris said as he walked over to my bed, "And that you had fangs and everything!"

"That won't make him feel better," Skyjack warned.

"Ah, are you feeling a bit weirded out by the whole thing?"

I nodded.

"Don't worry about it. Just own it. You're part demon and that's pretty awesome! Few people can say that. Also panicking isn't going to make your demon self go away. Angel's got you down for some intense telepath training tomorrow, that'll sort your demon self out."

I nodded, not feeling even the slightest bit comforted by Paris' words.

"Is he able to leave?" Paris asked Skyjack, "Angel has arranged for him to have tutoring sessions with me."

"If that's all he's doing then that should be fine," Skyjack then cautioned, "But keep an eye on him. He's prone to fainting."

"I will, don't worry about it," Paris nodded to me to follow him.

"Where are we going?" I asked as we left the hospital wing.

"Library," Paris explained, "Because you're new, Cap has asked me to tutor you, to get you up to date with the way this world works."

Paris led me to the library, which was huge! It had a large glass dome roof and loads of towering bookshelves. The library was filled not only with strange books but with wonderfully weird creatures! Gnomes sat on small wooden stools reading gardening books, a large Minotaur was resting on a sofa enjoying a book on china teapots and behind the information desks sat two grey haired elves! Paris literally had to drag me through the labyrinth of books to stop me from staring. Once we had reached a small quiet area of the library, that was empty apart from a pair of small grey sleeping dragons (at the sight of which I almost fainted!), Paris sat himself down on a battered red sofa. Placing his boots on a small table (much to the annoyance of the elf librarians), he gestured for me to sit opposite him. I did so, feeling rather overwhelmed by the strange world of books and creatures I had walked through.

"So I'm Paris," he introduced, "I know we've already met but I thought I'd give you a proper introduction. I've worked at the base for ten years. I'm also half-gorgon. My mum was the gorgon, my dad was human. He was blind and couldn't really open his eyes, which is why he didn't turn to stone. He also found snakes for hair attractive, not sure why, bit odd really. I'm so glad I didn't inherit the snakes!"

I nodded, not really sure how to respond to Paris' statement.

"Since you've lived in a completely different world to the rest of us, I think it'll be best if you ask me questions. I'll answer them if I can."

"Right," I thought for a moment and then asked, "Where exactly are we?"

"The Headquarters for the Demon Disposal Squads. We are in the paranormal world, a world that inhabits the same earth as the human world. This country, if you want to call it that, is called Transylvania and it is the centre of the paranormal empire."

"Paranormal?"

"Yes, we're actually badly named. We should have been called the supernatural empire, as supernatural is the correct title for the creatures that inhabit the empire. However it just doesn't have the same ring to it.

Supernatural empire. Paranormal empire. See what I mean, it just sounds better!"

"Paranormal?" I asked again.

"Oh right. Vampires, fairies, werewolves, witches; the creatures humans deem as 'mythical'. We're a very diverse bunch. The empire is filled with more species then I can name."

"Empire?"

"Technically we're not actually an empire anymore. We're more like an united kingdom, but that name was already taken. There are multiple kingdoms within the empire, but the ones you need to remember are: Transylvania, Atlantis, the Elf Kingdom, and the Fey Realm. They're the big four. The ones who have the most land and the ones who make the decisions."

"Atlantis is real!?" I exclaimed.

Paris nodded. I collapsed into my chair trying to take all this new information in. I was in an empire of supernatural beings. Beings that should not exist. Vampires, elves, fairies, werewolves, witches, creatures that belonged in movies and stories were real. Not only were they real, but I was sat opposite one. I was one!

"Mate, you're not going to faint on me, are you?" Paris asked.

I shook my head, "Who's in charge? Of this empire. Who's in charge?"

"Good question. Each individual kingdom has their own leader. In fact the elf kingdom has seven, but that's a conversation for another time. Now while these leaders do work together to create peace, they are technically led by one man. The big boss. Emperor Marcus Cloelius Pompeius. And yes he is a former Roman."

"What is he?"

"Ah now he belongs to a species known as immortals. And, as their name suggests, they are immortal! They're a bit like vampires only without the fangs and bloodlust. They are considered the supreme species. The closest one could be to a god," Paris mocked.

"Not a fan?"

"Not really. They're a bit stuck up."

"Vampires…do they…do they…?"

"Bite people's necks and suck out their blood? Nah! Not anymore. Only the bad ones do that nowadays. You can buy bottled human blood at the supermarket, so vampires don't have to go out hunting anymore."

"Bottled human blood!?"

"Yeah, oh don't panic we didn't kill the humans to get it! In fact I probably should have mentioned, paranormals aren't allowed to hurt humans. It's the golden rule. We get the blood from a blood bank. You know, where humans voluntarily give blood."

"What, you mean blood donations?"

"Yeah that! Only rather than going to a hospital, it feeds vampires. Oh I should also tell you that vampires are a very diverse species."

"What do you mean?"

"Right so not all vampires turn into bats, a lot do but not all. Some aren't affected by garlic or crucifixes, and some can appear in photos and can cross running water. Vampires are all very different. They don't all have the same traits."

"Right," I muttered. This was a lot of information to take in, and I was starting to get very confused by it all.

"Ah," Paris continued, "Also vampires have sunlight tattoos. These tattoos are basically spells, that witches attach to their bodies. It allows vampires to walk in the sunlight. Oh and werewolves can transform into large wolves whenever they want, but on a full moon they're forced to transform into the half-wolf half-man monsters you may have seen in movies. Oh also…"

"Wait, wait just, can we take a break for a minute?" I asked, "This is a lot to process!"

* * * * *

I was laid on the floor in one of the training rooms, staring at the ceiling. While this may not sound fun to you, to me it was the most relaxing moment of what had been one of the most stressful days of my life. If you're wondering why I was laying on the floor, the answer is that I was actually doing something extremely important…well I wasn't but Roxy and Willow who were sat next to me were. They were locking my demon self away, deep within my mind, so that it couldn't escape and take over my body. Whilst I relaxed, the two telepaths were hard at work inside my mind. Or at least that's what they said they were doing; I couldn't feel a thing. When they had told me what they were going to do, I had expected it to be a painful process that would emotionally scar me for life, however I couldn't even tell they were doing it. I didn't feel any different. I couldn't even tell they were in my mind. I felt the same way I always did tired, hungry, and confused. As the telepaths continued to work, I found myself falling asleep.

Which was when I was attacked by a rather strange dream.

"Master get down!"

There was a rain of arrows. I raised my hands and a crystal force field covered my body. I pulled Harry under the forcefield, but I was too late. Hit by an arrow, he stumbled to his knees and coughed up blood before falling flat on his face. I knelt and checked his pulse. He was dead.

"Poor soul," I muttered. Getting up, I ran over the bloody muddy battlefield. There were bodies and limbs all around. I jumped as I heard a roar behind me. Turning I found myself face-to-face with a huge demon. It had white scales, deep red eyes and black fangs that dripped with blood. I pulled out my black crystal staff and pointed it at the demon. The crystal glowed. The demon shuddered and then exploded into tiny pieces, its skin falling like snow onto the battlefield.

"Master Robert!" shouted a vampire. The vampire was tall with flowing brown hair and cold eyes.

"Rose," I greeted the vampire "We are running out of men. Where is my sister?"

"She's safe."

"Yes, but where?"

"She's at the camp with Edwin."

"Good. Pull the troops back to the rocks then ah!" I gasped, collapsing to my knees, "What have you done?"

"You have trusted all the wrong people," Rose smiled, pulling the dagger from my back, and baring her fangs.

"What have you done to my sister?"

"Oh, she's bleeding to death in a muddy ditch somewhere."

"You shouldn't have done that," I got to my feet and black mist exploded from my hands, hitting Rose in the chest. Rose stumbled backwards and then collapsed to the floor, as her body slowly crumbled to ash.

Blood dripped from where Rose had stabbed me.

I sat up, my head spinning like a disco ball.

I laid back on my pillow as I tried to calm down. Pillow? I sat up once again and looked around. I was no longer in the training room. I was in my bedroom. I found a note on my bedside table. It read:

You fell asleep, so we brought you to your room. Me and Will have locked your demon away so you no longer have to worry about it. Have a nice nap!

Roxy xx

I calmed slightly and got out of bed. I headed to the chair by the fireplace and sat myself down. Now that I had solved the mystery of how I'd got to my room, I could relax and contemplate the strange dream. It hadn't felt like a dream. It had felt real. The dream didn't make sense. How had I known that the dead guy was called Harry, and who was this Edwin fella? They hadn't seemed like random characters I had created; they had seemed real. When Harry had died, I had felt like I had lost a dear friend. There were other things about the dream that kept bugging me. Like why did they call me Robert? Who was this sister they kept talking about? And why had that vampire, Rose, stabbed me? I'm so loveable! How could anyone stab me!?

I took a deep breath and tried to calm my panic. I was overthinking. The dream had just been a very strange nightmare. That was all. And it was no wonder I was having nightmares. My mum had been murdered by a vampire, I was living in a world full of supernatural beings, and I had turned into a demon! Things don't get much crazier than that! Not unless I found out that I was really Santa in disguise, I think that would top the crazy list! I gazed at one of the pictures on the wall and saw something that sent my insides turning. Under a portrait of a tall man with long black hair was a name plate, which read:

Robert Dragonheart, Master of Darkness.

And that was the moment I began my panicked inner monologue. That man, that couldn't be the same person who was in my dream, could it? No that would be ridiculous, says the guy who just turned into a demon! Why does he have the same last name as me? Are we related? Am I blood related to my reincarnations? Is that how it works? Hang on that's not important, what's important is why have I been dreaming about Robert Dragonheart? Unless it wasn't a dream, what if it was a memory from my past life! No that couldn't be the case, could it? No, no, no that would be too creepy! I can't be dealing with that! It was just a nightmare. I probably saw the name plate earlier and saved it in my subconscious. Yes that sounded like a logical explanation. Okay. Let's just go with that. Come on Jason, take a deep breath. Take a deep breath and just look at the nice calm fire. The nice fire that's just crackling away. Burning wood. Having a great time. Just look at the nice flames…

Then my hand set on fire!

Black flames danced around my fingertips. I jumped to my feet and tried to batter the flames down, but the fire didn't want to move. I hopped around my room trying to put my hand out. However, the flames must have really liked me, as they wouldn't leave my fingertips. I stopped hopping and tried to calm myself, which wasn't easy as I was freaking out! My hand had set itself on fire! I took several deep breaths and realised that the flames didn't actually hurt. In fact it felt like a puppy was licking my fingers. Without meaning to, I closed my hand into a fist, and, to my surprise, the flames disappeared.

I stared at my hand in wonder. What had I done? Could I do it again? How did I do it the first time? I was thinking about fire, and then my hand had burst into flames. Would that work again? I closed my eyes and thought about fire. I thought about the flames dancing around the wood in the fireplace. Then I felt a tingling feeling in my hand. I opened my eyes to see that, once again, my hand was on fire.

"Ha!" I exclaimed, "I can set my hand on fire, that's awesome!"

After playing around with the flames for a while, I began to wonder if I would be able to set other things on fire. I found a crumpled piece of paper lying on my desk and decided that this would be my target. I looked at the flames in my hand and imagined them moving to the paper. As I did so, the flames left my hand and flew onto the piece of paper, burning it into ashes. But then I lost control. The flames spread across my desk. I swore as I raced to my bathroom and grabbed a glass of water, which I quickly threw onto the fire.

The black flames steamed into nothingness.

* * * * *

A week passed in the blink of an eye, and I was beginning to enjoy my time at the base. My average day was made up of training (usually it was fight training with Alexander, but on occasion I'd be taught by Angel), some tutoring from Paris, and then just hanging around the house. I mainly kept with Paris, Ethan, and Roger. Roger and Ethan were nice guys and fun to be around. Paris was cool, he seemed to know everything about everyone. The other members of the squad were nice, apart from Danny (he was a bit scary!), and they helped me settle in quickly. Roxy and Willow regularly checked on my demon self, to make sure it remained locked up, and Araminta introduced me to other people on the base.

The squad (minus Angel who was in a meeting with the Colonel) were training at the shooting range. I was nervous, I had never held a gun before. It was strange, back in the human world, I had never once thought of becoming a soldier. Wars and battles had always seemed so pointless to me, yet here I was, training to fight in a battle I didn't even understand. Sue was up. She aimed and fired. The bullet hit the wooden target's shoulder. Sue exhaled bitterly.

"Stop being a perfectionist," laughed Araminta, "Okay Jason you're up."

Taking a deep breath, I stood in front of the target. Araminta handed me the gun and moved my body into position. She started to explain something to me, but I couldn't hear her. My mind had gone blank. The gun felt cold against my sweaty palms. I felt strange. I felt calm. Really calm. The gun in my hand felt as though it belonged there. Like it was a part of me. Without even realising it, I pulled the trigger. The bullet seemed to fly in slow motion and then bang!

The wooden target fell as the bullet hit its forehead.

Lightning Squad went silent for a moment, then they began to clap and cheer. I stared at the gun in my hand. What had just happened? How had I been able to do that? To be honest I was shocked, and I don't just mean a bit shocked, I mean hit in the face with a dead fish shock level! I had never held a gun before yet here I was hitting the target perfectly on my first go!

"Oh my gods! Jason, how did you do that?" cried Willow.

"Well done mate," Roger nodded impressed.

Fern just smirked as she took the gun from my hands. She fired six times in quick succession, then pulled a knife from her hair and threw it at the target. All six bullets hit the target's chest and the knife landed in its neck. It was clear that Fern was well trained in the art of knife throwing. I made a mental note not to anger her in a kitchen.

The squad then moved into a different training room. Alexander handed me a sword and told me to repeat some basic moves while the others did hand-to-hand combat training. I practiced the moves for a while, okay so I practiced for about ten seconds before I sat myself down and watched the others fight.

First in the ring were Fern and Roger. Fern punched first. She darted forwards and punched Roger in the stomach. Roger went to kick her, but Fern dropped to the floor and kicked him in the leg. Roger fell to the floor but jumped back to his feet quickly. Fern blocked as Roger went to punch her. Fern raced to the side and picked up a bo staff. Roger did the same. The staffs clanged together. Fern spun the staff, but instead of using it, threw it at Roger who went to catch it- he's a werewolf (part of the dog species) so he likes to play catch. As he did so, Fern skidded across the floor and kicked Roger in an *uncomfortable* area. As Roger doubled over, Fern kicked him in the face sending him to the floor. He didn't manage to get up in ten seconds, so the fight was over. Fern had won.

Next was Elsa verses Sophie. Sophie seemed very small next to the tall vampire. She attacked very little and spent most of the time blocking Elsa. Elsa kicked Sophie in the stomach with such force that the fairy was pushed to the floor. She got to her feet only to be kicked in the face. Sophie slumped to the floor as the ten second count ended. My attention was drawn away from the next fight. From where I was sat, I could clearly hear Clover laughing at Sophie's misfortune.

"I know she's good on missions but in training she's

pathetic," Clover hissed.

"She's pathetic!? Have you looked at yourself recently?" asked Fern.

"Are you trying to start something?"

"I don't know, am I?"

To my surprise, Clover suddenly launched forwards and grabbed Fern's hair. She pulled her sister's head backwards and shoved her to the floor.

"Ow!" hissed Fern as she sat herself up and pulled out her wand. She flicked it, sending sparks of green in Clover's direction. The sparks set Clover's hair on fire. The rest of Lightning Squad turned to stare, including Araminta and Alexander who were in the middle of fighting. Clover's hair was covered in green fire. Fern was laughing. I just stared at them. I felt awkward. I wasn't sure whether this was normal, or whether I was meant to try and stop them.

"What the hell happened here!?" asked Alexander.

"Well," grinned Fern, "Ah nothing, grandpa, don't you worry about it."

"Could you put Clover's hair out?"

"I could, technically, but I won't."

"Why not?"

"Because I don't like her."

"And that's a good reason?"

"Yep!" and with that Fern left, via the fire exit.

"My hair!" screamed Clover, "Someone get me my wand!"

Roxy handed it to her. Clover waved her wand and the flames died down, but most of her hair had been burnt to a crisp. Clover screamed as she saw her reflection in her pocket mirror.

"What is going on!?" exclaimed Angel as she entered the room.

"Fern set my hair on fire!" Clover cried.

"Grow it back with magic."

"I can't. She's hexed it!"

"Wonderful," Angel muttered sarcastically, "We don't have time for this. I need you all in the operations room. We have a mission."

* * * * *

I had never been in the operations room before. It was cool! It looked like something from a sci-fi movie! It had a large table in the centre, and the walls were covered in computer screens. I was nervous. Although they had talked about their missions, I had never seen one in action before, so I didn't really understand how they worked.

"The mission is this," Angel stood in front of the touch screen computer that hung on the wall. On the computer screen flashed up images of six nasty looking men.

"In Rio, two days ago, these six escaped the prison they were being held in, killing everyone," Angel clicked on a computer folder and pictures of dead prison guards and prisoners appeared onscreen. I felt sick as I looked at the broken bloody bodies. I think Elsa must have sensed my disgust as she quickly covered my eyes with her hand.

"What are we dealing with?" asked Roger.

"At first the pictures didn't make it very clear until," Angel then (I was told by Elsa later) dragged one picture into the centre of the screen. It showed a dead prison guard with blood running from a very messy bite on his neck. Angel turned to the squad and said seriously, "We are dealing with six deadly fresh vampires."

The room went quiet for a moment as everyone took in this information. Elsa dropped her hand from my face. When I opened my eyes, I found that the pictures had been removed from the screen. Whilst the others quickly read through the mission files (that had been placed at each seat round the table), Angel mouthed to me '*are you okay*?' I nodded back my reply.

"The day before this," Angel then continued, "These men were injured during an inmate fight. I think they got turned when they were being treated at the prison hospital."

"What's the plan then?" asked Ethan, he then sneezed.

"Bless you. I know that most of you have just got back, and with our new member joining us, this mission is very inconvenient. So we're going to make this as simple as it possibly can be. The Colonel doesn't want prisoners, he just wants six body bags, so we go in and we take them out."

"If they're newly turned then it's not really their fault," Araminta pointed out, "Blood lust is uncontrollable. They won't know what they're doing, we can't kill them based on what they've done in blood lust."

"That's what I said at first, then the Colonel told me why they were in prison. These men were arrested because they have kidnapped, raped, murdered and sold over a hundred young girls aged seven to sixteen."

"Bloody hell," Roger muttered "I hate to imagine what these men would do as vampires."

"Which is why, we have been ordered to take them out before they have a chance to hurt anyone else."

"Do we know where these guys are?" asked Ethan.

"These vampires don't really know anything about this world so, my guess is, they'll end up at the vampire hotel," Angel showed a picture of a small metal building that looked to me like a warehouse.

"Who's on this mission?" Paris asked leaning back in his chair.

"Me, Sophie, Danny, Roger, Fern and Ethan. Alexander, you'll act as captain until I get back. People on the mission you need to be down here and ready to go in 10 minutes. Dismissed!"

4

'RIO DE JANEIRO'

The Squad teleported to Rio de Janeiro. They arrived in an empty alleyway which led to a main road. The streets were sticky and filled with people. The midday sun burnt the road as crowds of humans went about their daily business, completely unaware of the fact that six paranormal beings had just entered their world. Angel led the others through the busy streets and down into a dark maze of buildings.

"Question," Fern announced.

"What?" Angel muttered; a question with Fern always turned into dozens of useless questions and comments that made her feel clever, and everyone else feel like headless chickens.

"Are we going the right way?"

"Yes."

"Are you sure?"

"Yes."

"It's just your sense of direction …"

"Fern!"

"Remember that mission in Canada. You thought that the town was…"

"Fern!"

"And then there was that time in Germany…"

"Fern!"

"What!?"

"We're here," Angel pointed to a crumbling old rusty metal building. The building rose from the ground, towering over the street like Vesuvius over Pompeii. The windows were all covered with thick layers of metal. The doors were barricaded, and the roof seemed to crumble inwards.

"I thought it was a hotel," Fern muttered.

"It's meant to be hidden from human eyes," Angel explained, "Which is why it looks…"

"Creepy, abandoned, creepy, ugly, really creepy!"

"So, what do we do now?" Roger asked, interrupting Fern.

"From what I know about this place, there are two different exits; the main door and the roof. Roger, Ethan, and Fern, you will take the roof. Sophie, Danny and I will take the main door."

"How many vamps are in there?"

"I have no idea, a lot probably. So, we need to do this quietly. The last thing we want is a massive vampire fight."

"Do you want us to wait on the roof?"

"Yes, we'll go through the main door then up straight to their room. If we fail to take them out there, or die, you three will be the next line of defence. Sophie, I need you to go find out which room they're in and let us in."

"Can't you just knock?" Fern asked, "Why do you need Sophie to do it?"

"Because, one, I've been here before and the owner doesn't like me. And two, the main door is hexed so we can't bash it down. It needs to be opened from the inside."

"But how will Sophie get in?"

"She'll find a way, right Sophie?"

Sophie grinned and turned invisible.

* * * * *

Quickly Sophie slipped down an alleyway and stared at the endless barricaded windows. She pressed her hand against one of the windows, melting its metal covering with magic. The forcefield surrounding the hotel was strong, so Sophie was only able to melt an entrance the size of a mouse hole. Sophie shrunk down to a fairy's natural size, the size of a dragonfly, and flew inside. The hole she had made vanished by the time her feet had hit the floor.

The room she had entered was luckily empty. The fairy slipped out of the room and into a dark corridor. After upping her pace to a jog, she arrived in the main lobby. Unlike the corridor the lobby was bright, clean and had an extremely gothic style. Sophie darted across to the empty check-in desk. On the desk, there was a thick leather bound book. Sophie had just begun to flick through it when she was grabbed by the neck and thrown across the floor. Her invisibility vanished as she hit the ground.

"Did you think I wouldn't smell you, fey?" asked a red eyed vampire in Portuguese. He had a mock of black hair and a stone-cold face with fangs ready to kill. "What are you doing here, fey? This is a vampire only zone, you know the rules."

Sophie started to explain in Portuguese, "I'm Sophie Day of Lightning D.D Squad. You have wanted criminals staying…"

"Do I? Well not everyone can work on your side of the law. A vampire has the right to live, even if it does mean taking down a few humans," the vampire then smiled, "Or taking down a few fey."

The vampire raced at her. Sophie dived out of the way of the first attack and hopped on top of one of the tables. She back flipped off as the vampire zoomed at her. The vampire threw a table in the fairy's direction, it broke as it made contact with Sophie's back. Sophie picked up a piece of the splintering wood and threw it, like a javelin, at the vampire. The wooden spike hit the vampire's leg. The vampire's leg smoked slightly as he ripped the wood from his body. This gave Sophie time to side kick the vampire's ribs. The vampire twisted quickly grabbing her leg and throwing her to the floor. Sophie scrambled to her feet while picking up another broken piece of wood, which she then threw at the vampire. The vampire avoided the wood and grabbed Sophie by her shirt shoving her into a wall. Sophie kicked the vampire wildly, wrestling against its strength. The vampire grabbed her neck and went to bite her. Sophie's eyes turned a dark purple and she screamed. Her voice became a mighty force which, like the tide pushing against the sand, pushed the vampire to the floor. The room went silent as Sophie raised her hand and spread out her fingers. There was a blinding white light as a scream escaped from the vampire's mouth. The vampire's body began to crumble inwards until only a mummified corpse was left.

Sophie stumbled backwards catching her breath. She looked around, pulled off one of the wooden chair legs and stabbed the corpse with it. Sophie then hopped across the rubble and back to the main desk. She flicked through the book until she found the information she needed. The vampires were in the loft suite, the most impressive and most expensive room in the hotel. After studying the book in more detail, she found that every day and night the vampire guests would have to log themselves in and out of the hotel. The vampires that they were looking for had not logged out, meaning they had to be still inside.

Sophie touched her earpiece, "The vampires are all in the loft suite. Their booking ends tonight, so we need to move quickly."

"How many other vamps are there?" Angel asked.

"There are forty-five other vampires booked in the hotel, but so far there's been no movement from them, so

I think they're all sleeping. I'll open the door for you."

Sophie went over to the main doors and pressed her hand against it. The door glowed purple as it opened. Angel and Danny moved inside; guns raised.

"What happened here?" Angel exclaimed staring at the chaos of broken chairs.

Danny knelt next to the body and asked, "How did you kill him?"

"Stuck the stake in him," Sophie gestured to the homemade stake.

"No, look at his face. It's crumpled inwards like it went under extreme sunlight. Sophie, how did you kill him?"

"I just told you!"

"Don't lie to me."

"Danny," Angel interrupted, "That's not important right now. We have vampires to kill."

Angel headed to the stairs, the other two reluctantly followed. When they reached the loft suite, Angel melted the door handle and the trio entered. The loft suite was a large apartment with seven bedrooms, three bathrooms and a large living room. After signing to the others that they should split up, Angel entered one of the bedrooms, only to find it empty.

"Clear!" she heard Danny yell.

"Clear!" Angel called exiting the room and heading into one of the bathrooms. The shower was running. There was a shadow, but it wasn't moving. Angel tapped on the glass. There was no answer.

"I'll open this door in three, two one," she slowly opened the shower door.

"In here!" Angel yelled.

The others rushed over to the bathroom guns at the ready. In the shower were the bloody bodies of ten skinny children squashed on top of each other. Although she felt sick at the sight, Angel couldn't pull her eyes away from the crumbled deformed figures. Their faces looked so desperate and pleading. On the wall above the bodies was a message written in blood:

Too slow Night, Mr J.

"Mr Jet, he knew we were coming!" Angel exclaimed.

"But that's not possible," Danny muttered.

"Not unless…" then they heard a muffled sound down their earpieces, "Speak up, we can't hear you."

Fern's voice yelled down the earpiece, "Where are you!?"

"What do you mean?"

"The vampires or have you forgotten?"

"Fern, they knew we were coming. Mission failed. They're not here."

"Well, someone might have wanted to tell them that!"

"Hang on, are you fighting right now!?"

"No, I'm having tea and crumpets! Yes of course I'm fighting!"

* * * * *

Fern was not happy.

Not at all.

She was fighting three of the vampires, and the wolf versions of Roger and Ethan were fighting the other three. Fern shot at the surrounding group of vampires, using garlic filled bullets. She could keep them at bay, but she had backed herself into a corner. One of the vampires, who was wearing bright blue shoes, grabbed her neck, and pushed her into the wall. The vampire pulled her gun away and then pulled her head, so the juiciest part of her neck was visible. The vampire then got a pat on his shoulder. He turned to see Angel, who swiftly punched him in the face before throwing him to the ground and chopping off his head.

"You took your time," Fern muttered.

"A thank you would be nice," Angel retorted as she stabbed a wooden stake into the chest of a second vampire.

"Thank you, but next time get here quicker."

Sophie was fighting a rather chubby vampire. The

vampire grabbed her and slammed her into the metal doors that led downstairs. Sophie stumbled and rolled all the way down the small stairway. She cried out as she reached the bottom.

"Oh, is the little fairy hurt?" laughed the chubby vampire in Portuguese, "Did you really think a pretty little girl, like yourself, could kill me?"

Sophie got up; her eyes turned dark purple. The vampire was pulled, by a purple mist, down the stairs and landed at Sophie's feet. The vampire tried to grab her, but Sophie flipped over his shoulder. From her boot, she pulled out a pure crystal dagger, skidding forwards she cut above the vampire's ankles. The vampire yelled then grabbed Sophie by the neck and slammed her small body into the wall. She struggled as the creature's powerful hands began to crush her neck. Sophie placed her hands over the vampire's and dark purple electrical waves ran from her fingertips into his body. The vampire screamed in pain and dropped his hands. Sophie slid to the floor as the vampire stumbled backwards. The vampire fell to his knees. He shook and twisted before turning into a pile of rotting ash.

Danny grabbed the largest vampire. The vampire struggled against Danny's tight grip. The pair had been fighting for a while and Danny was starting to find the situation tiresome. The vampire grabbed Danny's head and slammed him against the edge of the roof. Danny twisted and pulled out a wooden stake. He turned and slammed the stake into the vampire's heart. Danny threw the vampire off the roof as it began to crumble into nothingness.

Roger and Ethan were dealing with two vampires. Ethan pounced on top of the smaller vampire pushing him to the floor. Roger went after the other vampire. The vampire's fingernails grew and became claws. The vampire swung its claws, cutting across Roger's face. Roger howled as blood began to pour from the side of his furry mouth.

Roger growled angrily and pounced on the vampire. He pushed the vampire to the floor and ripped off its head. Ethan still had the smaller vampire pinned against the floor.

Angel shouted, "Don't kill him, not yet."

"Why?" Roger asked transforming out of his wolf form, "I thought we were ordered to take them out."

"I want to ask him some questions," Angel turned to Sophie, "You speak Portuguese, right? I don't want to waste a translator spell on him, so translate for me. Can you ask him about Mr Jet?"

Sophie translated but the vampire didn't answer.

"Sophie, tell him that if he doesn't answer my questions, I will let Ethan rip off his head."

Sophie translated and suddenly the vampire became very talkative.

"He claims not to know anyone by the name Mr Jet."

"Ethan, growl."

Ethan did so and the vampire started speaking rapidly.

"He swears he has never heard the name Mr Jet before."

"Okay," Angel thought for a moment, "Ask him about the man who turned him. A description would be good."

"The man was tall with ginger hair. He was very pale. None of the men had ever seen him before. He just appeared during the inmate fight and then again when they woke up. He brought them to the hotel, got them sunlight tattoos, brought them the children, and then left. He returned earlier today, said people were after them and that they were to head to the roof," Sophie translated.

"Did the man tell them why he had turned them?"

"The man told them that he was impressed with their work. That he liked the way they treated the human girls. That he wanted them to continue their business, only to sell the human girls to vampires as their slaves," Sophie paused as the vampire continued speaking, "He's explaining in detail how they treated the human girls they kidnapped, it's really disgusting."

"This guy deserves to be ripped to pieces," Danny muttered.

"He will be," Angel hissed, "After he answers one more question. Sophie, ask him if he knows where the man is now."

"He doesn't know. The man just said that he had things to get ready for a big event. He didn't tell them what the big event was."

"Okay. Ethan, rip off his head," Angel ordered.

Ethan didn't need telling twice. He ripped off the vampire's head and then ripped its body to pieces. Ethan then transformed back into his "human" form.

"The man who turned them was definitely Mr Jet," Roger muttered, "He's moving fast. He was in London, now Rio, it doesn't make sense."

"No, it doesn't," Angel muttered, "Come on, let's get out of here before the other vampires wake up."

5

'REFLECTIONS'

"Well done, Captain," the Colonel said proudly, "A very well executed mission. Now, I think it is time you and your squad had a break, you've been on five missions in the space of a month."

"Yes sir but…"

"Don't look so glum. Here," the Colonel pulled out an orange folder from one of his desk's draws and handed it to her, "This should put a smile on your face. An old friend of yours has popped up."

"Interesting."

"I thought you might like it. It's a light case but it means you'll not be bored. Now go, relax."

Angel slowly headed back to the squad house, once there she went up to her room. Angel's room was the smallest in the Lightning Squad house. There was a bed in the centre with a small wardrobe, a single set of draws and a large bookshelf which took up most of the space. The room was plain and simple, with little decoration or personalisation. By the side of the bed there was a small table on which sat two photo frames; one which held a picture of Lightning Squad and one that held a photo of Angel's parents surrounded by her six werewolf brothers and the younger version of herself. Angel didn't use her bedroom much (only for sleeping) instead she usually used her office, which was next door. However the mission in Rio had exhausted the shapeshifter so, upon entering the room, she collapsed onto her bed. Before Angel had a chance to rest, she felt a sudden pain in her arm. She sat up and rolled up her sleeve. On the inside of her arm the number 1147512 was scarred into her skin, however this wasn't what Angel was looking at. She was looking at the blood. The blood that wasn't hers. Angel gasped out in pain as the blood twisted and melted into her skin.

"Why are you doing this?" Angel hissed.

"Because it's fun," whispered a cold crisp female voice that Angel knew all too well.

"Where are you?"

"I'm everywhere and nowhere."

"That's great and everything but do me a favour and get lost," Angel muttered bitterly. Then a sharp pain rippled through her body, causing Angel to fall off her bed and onto her knees.

"You need to learn who the master is here," the voice snapped. Angel's room suddenly erupted with sickly green smoke. It clouded Angel's vision and clogged her organs. She couldn't move. Her head span, she fell to the floor, letting the smoke engulf her.

* * * * *

Angel opened her eyes slowly and painfully. She blinked several times until her vision returned. She was in the forest. The smell of wet grass and mud filled her nose. It was a nice smell, a safe smell. Slowly Angel sat up. Only when she was sure she wasn't going to throw up, Angel got to her feet. She walked through the forest nervously. The voice wanted her here for a reason and that was something she didn't like the idea of.

Angel watched as a wild unicorn raced through the thick undergrowth. The creature was beautiful, pure white with a slight blue glow. It ran straight past her then turned back to look. The unicorn walked up to Angel and allowed her to gently stroke its soft coat. It tingled under her fingertips. Most unicorns had evolved to talk, like Skyjack who was a very chatty pegacorn, whereas wild unicorns were silent. The creature slowly pulled away and trotted over to a patch of fresh green grass. Then the creature stopped and looked up, as if it sensed danger. If only it had sensed it a minute before, for just then a large metal spike pushed its way through the creature's beautiful body.

"No!" Angel exclaimed as the wild unicorn fell dead. Where the unicorn had stood was a cloaked woman. She had long blonde hair that was slowly going grey and her eyes were a dark green. Her lips were blood red and smiling. She wore a long old-fashioned black dress and a red cloak.

"Why did you do that?" Angel gasped looking at the poor dead creature.

"Because, Samantha, it was fun," the woman grinned.

"Why are you calling me that? My name is Angel, not Samantha. Why did you bring me here? What do you want from me?!"

The woman moved forwards towards her. Angel transformed into a dragon and roared. The woman simply laughed. The woman flicked her wrist and dragon Angel was hit by a ray of orange light, which caused Angel to involuntarily transform back into her normal form.

"How did you do that!?" Angel exclaimed.

The witch clicked her fingers and a purple lightning bolt hit Angel's chest. Angel yelled out in pain and collapsed to the ground. The lightning raced down her body. Angel could no longer move. The woman dragged her across the undergrowth. Angel could feel each stone and tree root bash into her body as she tried desperately to escape. Suddenly they stopped. Angel pulled herself to her knees and found herself looking into the lake. While most people find lakes pretty, Angel found them terrifying. For as she looked at the water she saw, to her horror, something she had been hiding from herself for many years.

Her reflection.

Her reflection's skin was covered in tattoos. Tattoos of names. The names of the dead. The names of the people Angel had killed since joining the D.D squads. Angel was cursed. When or why she had been cursed, Angel didn't remember. In fact Angel didn't remember anything from her childhood. She had no idea how old she was, who her birth parents were, or why she was found, by the Night werewolf pack, bleeding by the side of a lake.

"Stop it!" Angel screamed, shutting her eyes, and covering her face with her hands.

"Samantha," the woman whispered in her ear. Angel could feel the woman's breath against her face.

"You're fine. You're fine This isn't real," Angel lied to herself.

"You can't escape. You can't run. Samantha," the voice called. Angel was hit by a second orange lightning fork. She shook and wriggled as the pain washed over her body.

"Please just leave me alone!"

"I'm coming for you."

"Just leave me alone!"

"Angel!" a different voice yelled.

"I'm coming for you," the woman whispered.

"Stop it! Just leave!" Angel yelled.

"Angel!" the other voice shouted again.

"I'm coming," the woman hissed once more as her voice faded away.

"Angel!" Angel felt too strong hands grab her shoulders. She jumped and tried to break free.

"Leave me alone!" she screamed.

"Angel, its Alex." Angel opened her eyes and stared at

Alexander who was knelt next her.

"Alex!" Angel grabbed the vampire and hugged him tightly, "You're real, right?"

"Of course, I am."

"Good. Good," Angel mumbled, burying her face in the vampire's shoulder. Alexander wrapped his arms around his trembling captain. The vampire had gone to find Angel but had found her room empty, apart from a lingering dark scent. Alexander had followed the scent into the forest, where it had led him to Angel. The shapeshifter clung to Alexander, squeezing him tightly as if at any moment he would disappear into thin air. Angel wasn't much of a hugger, so her sudden hug not only took the vampire by surprise but also deeply worried him.

Alexander waited for Angel to calm then asked, "What's happened? Why are you like this?"

"Where did she go?" Angel mumbled.

"Where did who go?"

"You didn't see her?"

"See who?"

Angel pulled away from the vampire and pointed to where the woman had stood, "She was right there!"

"Angel, there was no one there."

Angel stumbled to her feet, "She's disappeared again. How did she do it? How did she…how did she get onto the base? How did she…the unicorn!"

Angel ran into the forest.

"Angel!"

Angel found her way back to the spot easily. The unicorn's body was there but there was something wrong with it. The body had decomposed. The flesh had gone and now the bones were rotting before her eyes.

"That's not possible."

"Nasty," Alexander muttered as he joined her.

"But that was alive," Angel span around looking for something that would prove that she wasn't going crazy.

"So was I once," Alexander joked then his tone turned

serious, "Angel what's wrong?"

"This," Angel gestured to the body, "This is what's wrong. Only a minute ago, this unicorn was alive!"

"That's not possible."

"Just listen, only minutes ago, that creature was alive and then," Angel looked at Alexander who was staring at her with a blank expression, "Nothing, it doesn't matter."

Angel tried to walk away but her knees gave in.

"Angel!" Alexander grabbed her before she hit the ground.

"I'm fine," Angel muttered pushing Alexander away and standing up straight.

"You need to go to the hospital wing."

"I said I'm fine."

"You're not fine! You were screaming, by the lake, you were screaming."

"I said I'm fine!"

"It didn't sound that way to me."

"Well maybe you need a hearing test, they do say that hearing goes with age," Angel joked coldly.

Alexander wasn't amused, "Angel what is going on?"

"Nothing, you wouldn't understand."

"Why wouldn't I?"

"Because I don't understand!" Angel muttered, "I don't understand any of it."

"Okay, then what can I do to help?"

"Nothing. Please leave, I think I need to be on my own for a bit. I need to think."

"Angel, at least go to the hospital wing and get Skyjack to give you a check-up."

"I don't need to go to the hospital wing, there's nothing anyone can do for me there. I just need...Roger! That's who I need."

"Roger?"

"Don't tell anyone about what you saw today. In fact it'd be best if you just forgot about it."

"Forget!? Angel you were screaming."

"Yes, Alex, I am aware," Angel then noticed something next to the dead unicorn, "Is that a warlock's card?"

"What?"

"A warlock's card. Covens use them to pass messages in secret. Why would one be here?" Angel walked over to the card and picked it up, whilst Alexander followed close behind. The card was blank, then suddenly it glowed orange and a word appeared:

Samantha.

Angel dropped the card in surprise.

"Samantha. Angel," Alexander asked carefully, "Does that name mean something to you?

"Why does she call me that?" Angel muttered, ignoring Alexander's question, "Why would she call me that? Samantha's not my name, unless, it is."

Alexander grabbed Angel's shoulders and stared at her intensely.

"Angel, who calls you that name? Who was here? What did they say to you?" the vampire asked rapidly, his voice was grave.

"She..."

"Hey, hey what we got here?" Paris grinned walking over to them.

Alexander growled, "What are you doing here?"

"It's my forest as much as it's yours."

Alexander hissed in Angel's ear, "We'll finish this later," then he disappeared.

"What's his problem?" Paris exclaimed.

"When I find out you'll be the first to know," Angel muttered.

"You okay, you look pale."

"I'm fine."

"How was your trip?"

"Trip?" she asked baffled.

"To Rio?"

"Oh that," Angel started to walk back towards the base, Paris followed, "That was interesting."

"That's never good. What happened?"

"That's been classified, I'm afraid. All you need to know is that the mission was a success."

"Ah, then why's it classified? Come on, tell me."

Angel shook her head then asked, "How is Jason's training going?"

"Much better. He has a lot of control already and I think you'll be impressed."

"We'll see?"

"What does that mean?"

"It means the Pied Piper is in town. I think this will be a good opportunity for the Master to prove he's good enough to be in my squad."

6

'SANTA ISN'T REAL'

JASON

"Can I have a break?"

"Jason you had a break less than five minutes ago!" Elsa exclaimed.

"Which means it's the perfect time to have another one," I gasped. I had been training with Elsa all day and I was tired. Exercise really wasn't for me! While I preferred the sword fighting lessons to jogging or press ups, I still found them exhausting. Elsa, being a vampire, didn't understand my pain, so I was forced to fight both the vampire's sword and my desperate desire to sleep.

"Come on Jason," Elsa sighed, "You're getting really good at this. If we practice a bit more…"

"I'll die of exhaustion!"

"To say you're the Master of Darkness, you're extremely pathetic!"

"Rude!"

"But true."

"Your attacks are getting better," Araminta commented as she joined us, "How are you finding your sword?"

"My sword is fine," I explained, "It's a bit strange it feels like…like…"

"Like you've used it before? That's because you have. That sword belonged to the former Master of Darkness."

"The former," I dropped the sword in surprise. The whole reincarnation thing still got to me. It was just creepy to think that I had been other people, or was it that other people had been me? It was very confusing.

"Jason don't freak out."

"I wasn't," I lied, "I don't freak out. Araminta, is that blood on your chin?"

As I had been looking at the vampire's face, I had noticed that there was something red running from her mouth. It looked like blood. I hoped I had sounded cool and calm when I had asked Araminta about it, as in my head I was freaking out. What had she been hunting? Paris said vampires weren't allowed to do that anymore, so what had she eaten!? What if she had eaten one of my long-lost family members? I don't think I have any long-lost family members, but how would I know if they are long lost?

"Jason, relax I drank tomato juice," Araminta laughed.

"Oh right," Damn those mind reading powers of hers! You can never have a private thought in this place, there's either a telepath or a vampire listening in.

"You should really learn to block your thoughts. I can't even read minds well, yet I can hear your thoughts loud and clear. It's like you're shouting down my ear!"

"Yeah, I really need to learn how to do that."

"It's okay for now, you're still new to this stuff but it'll be dangerous if you don't block your mind in the future. Anyway I came to tell you that Angel is back, and dinner is ready."

When we arrived at the Lightning Squad dining room, we found Roger, Ethan and Paris filling their plates. The table was full of food. I had no idea where the food came from but whenever it arrived, it covered the table. Serving plates were loaded with sausages, vegetables, chicken drumsticks, and other mouth-watering delights. One thing I had realised during my time at the base was that Lightning Squad ate a lot! Especially Ethan, Roger, and Angel, they were always stuffing their faces. Even during training, the Night siblings would have snacks hidden amongst their weapons, so that they could start nibbling the moment they had a break.

I sat down next to Ethan as Roger exclaimed, "I never want to be stuck on another stake-out with Fern again! We were there waiting for the vampires and she just wouldn't shut up. And I really don't care about pigeons!"

"Did you say pigeons?" asked Araminta as she sat herself down.

"Yes," Ethan sneezed, "Fern really doesn't like pigeons, remember that if you ever go bird watching with her."

"What's wrong with pigeons?"

"Well I won't give you the whole speech but basically, in Fern's words, they are giant rats that hell has spat out with wings."

"Right. How did the mission go?"

"It went, well we completed it, but it was just weird."

"What do you mean?"

"The mission is classified. Colonel's orders," Angel snapped sharply as she entered. She sat herself down at the end of the table and began to flick through an orange folder.

"I wonder what's wrong? Angel looks a bit out of it," Araminta whispered.

"Well I interrupted her and Alexander in the forest, they seemed pretty intense," Paris whispered with a smile.

"Whatever you're thinking, stop it," Roger warned.

"I wasn't thinking anything. I was just going to say they'd make a cute couple. You and Angel would too."

"She's my sister!"

"Sure she is," Paris muttered sarcastically.

"What's that meant to mean?"

"Well you're not blood related, and you don't really act like siblings."

Roger got up and was about to punch Paris but Araminta got in-between them.

"Paris, Roger!" Angel's voice echoed from the other side of the room, she didn't look up from the folder, "Either take it outside or sit down!"

Roger pushed Araminta off him, moved away from Paris and sat down. Paris sat, with a smirk on his face. The room fell into a heavy silence. Roger's sudden anger had taken me by surprise. The werewolf was normally such a friendly happy guy that I had never expected him to have a violent side. Perhaps it was his wolf instincts kicking in. A need to protect his pack, that caused the wolf to physically respond to Paris' comment.

"Who cooks the food?" I asked, changing the subject. I'm not very good with awkward silences. I always feel the need to fill them. I just don't like silence. I like to talk! And I hate feeling awkward, it's just uncomfortable and awkward silences always make me want to do something weird and spontaneous, like dance an Irish jig, to lighten up the mood again.

Instead of dancing a jig, I took as sip of water as Paris answered, "Ghosts."

I spat out my water, all over Ethan who was sat opposite me. The werewolf was not amused by this.

"What. did you just say!?" I spluttered as the werewolf stared daggers in my direction.

"The food is cooked by ghosts."

"But, but how can they touch it?"

"Good question," Ethan said taking a piece of chicken, "Ghosts are creatures that can't let go of this world which means they can become solid at times. They don't wish to go to the afterlife, so they cook instead. They do it by choice. We don't make them."

"But why?" I asked trying to deal with the fact that ghosts were, not only real but also, cooking my food

At that moment other members of Lightning Squad entered the room, causing my question to get lost amongst the pleasantries. Ethan moved from his seat opposite me to the seat next to me as Fern entered. I was confused by the werewolf's move until I realised that he was trying to keep Clover and Fern separated.

The moment Fern noticed her sister's presence, the witch asked, "Clover, did you do something different with your hair? It looks great,"

"Don't talk to me!" Clover hissed.

"Now that's no way to talk to your older sister."

"I swear you were swapped at the hospital."

"I hope so, that would mean we weren't related."

"You little!" Clover got to her feet and went to pull out her wand, but Sue stopped her.

"Clover don't bother," Sue mocked, "You know she's just jealous."

"Jealous!" Fern scoffed, "Of what?"

"That Clover is more powerful then you."

"Ha!"

"At least I've passed my broom flying exam! You've failed sixteen times," Clover laughed.

"Cut it out," Angel snapped, "If you want to start something take it outside, the rest of us want to enjoy our food."

"I don't know how you can enjoy it, with her ugly face across from you," Fern muttered.

"You little!" Clover exclaimed.

"That's enough!" Angel shouted looking up from the orange folder, "If you don't shut up and sit down, I'll put all of you in the cells for the night!"

The two witches quickly returned to their seats. Fern and Clover were an odd pair. I couldn't work them out. They were sisters, twins, but they acted like they were mortal enemies.

"Are they always like this?" I whispered to Ethan.

"Pretty much," Ethan hissed, "Fern and Clover hate each other."

"Why?"

"I'm not exactly sure but I think something serious happened before they joined the D.D squads. Fern once muttered something about their thirteenth birthday. I think they haven't gotten along since then, and that was like, fourteen years ago," Ethan said before devouring another piece of chicken.

"Fourteen years that's a long time to hold a grudge. It must have been something serious. Hang on so the twins are twenty-seven?"

"Twenty-six, it hasn't been their birthday yet."

"I thought they were closer to my age."

"Really? I guess they do have quite young-looking faces. Apart from us two, Danny and Roger, everyone else is over twenty-five."

"Danny isn't twenty-five yet?"

"No he's twenty-two."

"I thought he was older! How old are you and Roger?"

"Roger is twenty-three but it's his birthday soon. I'm twenty-one so, until you came, I was the baby of the group."

"What about Angel?"

"We don't know," Ethan muttered.

"You don't know?"

"I suppose I should tell you before you hear it via the rumours. You know how Angel is my adopted sister? Well my Pops, that's what we call our dad, found Angel when she was a kid, all beaten up, so took her in. It turned out Angel was cursed. She had been cursed by a memory wiping spell, so Angel doesn't remember anything from before my Pops found her."

"Damn. So you don't know who beat her up or who cursed her?"

"No idea. We also have no idea how old she is or who

her parents are or her birth name. Roger named her Angel."

"Why Angel?"

Ethan paused for a minute then whispered, "You may have noticed that Angel nearly always wears long sleeves."

I hadn't but I nodded so that the werewolf didn't think I was completely oblivious to my surroundings.

"Well, Angel has numbers burnt onto her arm. We don't know why she has them, how she got them, or what they mean. When he was younger, Roger really loved puzzles and riddles, so he though the numbers might be a puzzle. He converted the numbers into letters, and they ended up spelling a name. So the first number on her arm is one so that became A."

"Because A is the first letter of the Alphabet."

"Exactly. Roger looked after Angel a lot when we were younger. He taught her how to speak and read and stuff. They're really close because of that and that's also the reason why there are a lot of false rumours about them."

"Ah, you mean what Paris said about them being a couple."

"Angel is the first female captain the base has ever had. Lightning Squad, under her orders, now has the highest mission success rating, which sadly means that a lot of people have it out for her. So you will hear lots of ridiculous rumours, Roger and Angel being in love with each other is perhaps the most common. Though some people believe that me and Angel are secretly married and have three kids!"

"That's just…"

"I know, it's gross. And that's not even the worst rumour around. The worst one, and if you hear anyone say this, I want you to punch them, is that Angel killed our mum."

"Why would people say that? That's awful! Angel said that Mr Jet killed her."

"He did. It was pretty nasty," Ethan trailed off sadly.

"What was your mum like?"

"She was great. Slightly terrifying at times, but she was brilliant. In fact it was kind of funny, because my mum had always wanted a daughter, but she got six sons instead. So mum was so happy when Pops found Angel."

"Six sons!? You have five brothers!?"

"I did have, I only have three now. Mr Jet killed them as well."

"Oh. I'm sorry."

I wanted to ask more but at that moment Alexander, Danny, and Sophie arrived. Sophie was the only member of the squad I had never spoken to. The fairy went and sat down next to Angel. They talked quietly.

"How come Sophie only talks to Angel?" I asked Ethan.

"She doesn't only talk to Angel," Ethan answered.

"But she mainly does."

"Okay yeah that's true. Angel and Sophie were roommates when they went through training. They've always been together. They've always been promoted at the same time and always get put on the same missions. they just work really well together."

"Also they got really close," Roger interjected joining in our conversation, "After they went on this mission that went horribly wrong."

"Oh yeah the zombie mission!"

"Zombies? Zombies are real?" I asked as I felt the panic pit at the bottom of my stomach begin to rumble.

"Yeah they're real and absolutely terrifying!"

"Zombies!?"

"Yeah. This mission, it was an absolute nightmare. Fourteen people were sent on it but only Angel, Sophie and Jin (he's captain of Wildfire Squad) survived. The others had their brains eaten!"

"Brains eaten!" I squeaked, "Did you just say that their brains were eaten!?"

"Ethan stop," Willow hissed, "Jason will have a

meltdown if you continue."

As I tried to calm myself down, I heard Fern ask, "What you got there?"

I looked up, thinking the witch was talking to me, only to find that her question was directed at the orange folder in Angel's hands.

"It's a case," Angel muttered not looking up from the folder.

"A case? We haven't had one of them for ages," Elsa exclaimed.

"Didn't you just get back from one?" I asked Ethan confused.

"What? Oh, no that was a mission."

"What's the difference?"

"Cases are the police jobs," Elsa said as Ethan had shoved his mouth so full of sausages that he couldn't answer, "We do a mix of police work, military work and undercover work. A case means it's police work, like a murder or something along those lines, whilst a mission refers to military work. And if it's undercover work, which is like spy stuff, then it's referred to as an assignment."

"So, what's the case?" asked Ethan after sneezing.

"Bless you. An old friend of ours has shown up," Angel smiled, "The Pied Piper is back."

"The Pied Piper! As in the rat guy from the fairy tale!" I spluttered.

"Yes, he was sighted three days ago, in the city centre."

"Hang on, just back up a minute. Are you telling me the Pied Piper is real?"

"Yes, the Pied Piper is real."

"Zombies, ghosts, the Pied Piper, is there anyone else I should know about!?"

"Well," Fern paused then continued, "There's Neptune, the other gods, Big foot, Jack Frost, Mother nature, Nessie…"

"The Loch Ness monster is real?"

"Yes, but never call her that, she gets very angry if you

do."

"Right," I muttered, "Santa and the Easter bunny aren't real, are they?"

"Don't be an idiot Jason, of course Santa and the Easter bunny aren't real."

* * * * *

The battlefield spat out its bloody children at us from all directions. The demons crawled through the mud, biting at the horses' legs, pulling them down into the dark pits of hells mouth. The smell of rotting flesh and burning metal seemed to grow with every minute. The battle was only ten miles or so from the camp. We had been hit before we had even reached the border. The demons were everywhere and with each passing moment there were more of our allies' bodies on the ground.

My sword clanged against the creature's sword. The creature was tall and seemed to float just above the ground. Its only facial feature was a pair of milk white fangs. The creature held a long thin sword and fought with the grace of a ballet dancer

Our swords sparked as they drew apart. I tried to attack but was blocked. The demon's speed was almost impossible to counter act. It never tired. I pulled out my crystal staff and slammed it into the demon's chest. The crystal glowed but the creature did not crumble. Instead it stumbled backwards and roared angrily. I cursed, kicking the creature backwards. The creature grabbed my leg and threw me to the floor. The creature pounced on top of me and dug its fangs into my neck. I yelled and slammed my sword into what should have been the demon's heart. Black mist escaped from its heartless body. I coughed and choked as the toxic mixture was pushed into my face...

* * * * *

I woke, headfirst, on the floor coughing and spluttering. I rolled onto my back and took a deep breath. I felt dizzy and sick. There was a pain in my neck and my ankle felt twisted. Slowly I pulled myself to a sitting position, placing my head between my legs to stop myself from passing out. That wasn't fun. Another creepy dream...seriously! Wasn't one bad enough? I looked at the painting of Robert Dragonheart; I was half sure that this dream was also about him. It was so strange. Was it a memory?

No it couldn't be. Or could it?

No that'd be too weird for me to deal with. It must be, I reassured myself, my body's reaction to finding out that the Loch Ness monster and other legendary beings are real. Yeah that must be it! That was a logical, and not completely terrifying, explanation. I got back into bed and fell back to an uneasy sleep.

7

'THE PIED PIPER'

JASON

The arrow flew and landed perfectly hitting its target.
Bullseye.

Angel took a step back, smiling she turned to me, "See nothing to it."

It had been three days since I had found out that the Pied Piper was real, and I was stuck in an archery lesson with Angel and Paris. 'Nothing to it' she says, nothing to it! If there was nothing to it then how come I hadn't been able to even get close to the target! I thought to myself. While my sword fighting and shooting skills had improved massively during my time at the base, my archery skills were still practically non-existent! Angel handed me the bow.

"Do I have?"

"Yes," Angel interrupted, cutting me off before I could finish. I took the bow and pulled an arrow out of my quiver. I pulled back the bow then released the arrow. I watched in dismay as it hit the ground faster than a dead bird.

"Err, not bad," Angel gulped down her laughter.

"Don't lie Cap," Paris laughed.

"Paris! Jason, it wasn't that bad, but your form was off."

"How come I can shoot a gun perfectly without trying but I stink, worse than mouldy cheese, at archery even with hours of practice!?" I exclaimed.

"Try again but this time straighten this arm and look at the target not at your hands," Angel instructed. I tried again. I pulled the arrow back and released it. The arrow flew and hit the ground, far from the target.

"That was better," Angel said looking at the arrow, "Again."

Ten unsuccessful tries later I threw the bow to the ground.

"I give up!" I exclaimed.

"Would it sound cruel if I say I'm glad," Paris laughed, "This has been painful to watch."

"Paris! That is not helpful," Angel snapped, "Everyone in my squad must have at least four weapons that they're trained in. So far all you have is a sword and a gun. Gun, that's it!"

Angel ran off into the weapons shed then returned moments later, with a cross bow. Angel handed it to me, "Try this."

I looked at the cross bow. I had never used a crossbow before, in fact I had never even seen a crossbow before, so I had no idea what I was supposed to do with it! Whilst I was inwardly panicking, my body started to work on its own. I lifted the crossbow up, without realising it, and aimed it at the target. Before I was even aware that I had done it, I pulled the trigger. The dart flew and slit Angel's perfect arrow in half.

"I knew it! You work best with weapons that belonged to the former Master of Darkness. Both your sword and this crossbow belonged to your past reincarnations."

"What about the gun? That wasn't a former weapon, was it?"

"No that was new, but the former Master was known for being an excellent marksman. You must have retained your skills."

"So, I work best with the weapons that once belonged to the former Master of Darkness because I am the former Master of Darkness just reincarnated so they're technically my weapons."

"Jason, are you alright mate?" Paris asked.

I was the complete opposite of 'alright'. I used to just be a nice boring human but now I was the Master of Darkness. A being who was supposed to be all powerful, yet I felt as powerful as a ran over hedgehog! Not only that but I was a reincarnation! Did that mean that the former Master of Darkness was me or was I him? It was very confusing and hard to understand. I was a reincarnation, but I look nothing like the other Masters. Robert Dragonheart was small and well-built whereas I bare a strong resemblance, I've been told, to a stick insect!

"Captain!" Elsa yelled as she raced over to us, "The Piper has been spotted in the city."

Angel smiled and turned to me, "I think it's time for your first case."

* * * * *

Transylvania was not what I had expected. I had been expecting everyone to be wearing dark cloaks and for the streets to be dark, lit only by candlelight, however that wasn't the case. The streets were bright, and the people wore a colourful array of clothing. Some people wore cloaks and long old-fashioned dresses however most wore denim jeans and t-shirts. And by people, I mean vampires, werewolves, witches, griffins, hippogriffs, giants (yes you heard me correctly I did say giants! And guess what, they really are giant!) as well as other creatures I couldn't even begin to name. There were cars sharing the road with carriages pulled by horses and large elephants that had three trunks (one almost killed me as I was too busy staring at it that I forgot to move out of its way- luckily Angel dragged me away just in time). The shops were an odd mix as well. There were wand shops, werewolf grooming salons and vampire blood banks standing next to pizza takeaways and chip shops. It was certainly less gothic then I had imagined.

Me, Angel, and Elsa walked through the crowds towards a tavern called 'The Unicorn and the Griffin'. The couple who owned the tavern, Freddie, and Bertie Johnson, had called the squad that morning saying they had spotted the Piper. Freddie was a tall skinny werewolf with a mock of brown hair. He was cleaning tables by the doorway as we entered.

He looked up and smiled, "You're here. Look at you Angel, I swear you get prettier each time I see you."

"Hi Fred," Angel smiled, "Any sign of our friend?"

"He booked a room here under the name of Donald Smith. He's on the first floor in room five but he normally comes down around lunchtime. If you could arrest him then it would be best as we have some vampires in the room next door who get very grouchy if they're woken before dusk."

"Okay, will do. How's things been?"

"Well last week two of our customers were murdered before they had a chance to pay, we should really start making people pay in advance! Every day you hear these stories about dead and missing people, gives me shivers just thinking about it! Me and Bert are seriously thinking of setting up fresh in the human world. Transylvania is just so dangerous at the moment."

"That's not a stupid idea."

"The problem is we'd need someone to cover our shifts on a full moon and it'd be too dangerous to hire a human."

"Well if I get fed up of being a captain, I'll come work

for you."

"I'll hold you to that," Freddie grinned, "Look, what am I doing? I should have these tables cleared by now. Stop distracting me and run along to the bar, tell Bert drinks are on me, just don't get drunk."

"We're on duty!" Angel called as we headed towards the bar.

"Like that's ever stopped you lot before!" Freddie laughed.

The tavern was a mix of old-fashioned and modern. It's wooden furniture and large ale barrels made it look like something from a pirate movie, however its large bright pink drinks sign, and its glamorous array of weird cocktails quickly reassured me that I hadn't stepped back in time. The tavern was quiet, only a couple of people were inside. There were a group of half-men/half-pigs sat round one table, a fairy couple at another as well as a, very drunk, satyr (half-man/half-goat) who was flopped, a drink in hand, on a sofa. Elsa pushed me through the tavern to stop me from staring. Behind the bar was Bertie. He was small, large, wore a pink shirt and had a scruffy ginger beard. He had his back to the door, so Angel tapped him on the shoulder.

"Angel!" he exclaimed pulling Angel into a hug across the bar.

"Not breathing," Angel gasped.

"Oh right," Bertie let her go, "It's been nearly three months young lady, I was beginning to think you had dropped off the face of the earth."

"That's scientifically impossible."

"Shut up," laughed Bertie, "How have you been?"

"Busy. Elsa Sunday, you know, and this is Jason Dragonheart," Angel gestured to the two of us.

"Lovely to meet you," Bertie smiled shaking my hand.

"Jason is the Master of Darkness," Angel explained quietly.

"I thought I smelled something different about you.

There have been rumours going around saying that you had returned. It's an honour to meet you."

"Thanks but really it's nothing," I stuttered.

"Just embrace the honour," Elsa smiled.

"Listen to fang-girl here," Bertie said with a knowing smile, "When people find out you're back well, expect people to act differently around you."

"Why?"

"Because it always happens," he answered mysteriously, "Now what can I get you?"

"Anything that isn't alcoholic, we're on duty," Angel muttered as she looked around for the Piper.

"What did he mean? About people acting differently?" I asked Elsa.

"There are lots of myths and legends about the Master of Darkness. People say you're a god," Elsa explained.

"I'm not, am I?"

"A god? Well I'd imagine you'd know if you were a god or not."

"True but I didn't know that I was the Master of Darkness."

"You're not a god Jason," Angel interrupted, "You're far too stupid."

"Hey!"

"If you were a god, the entire world would be in danger, it's bad enough that you're the Master of Darkness."

"Hurtful!" I exclaimed but Angel merely smiled.

"Don't mind her," Elsa laughed, "Angel only teases people she likes."

"Oh, well I guess that's okay then," I paused for a moment then asked, "Okay I'm sorry this might be a strange question but what is your accent?"

"I'm French."

"Really? Huh, you don't sound French."

"That's because I died during the French Revolution."

"You weren't, you weren't, how do I put this nicely?"

"I wasn't beheaded! I thought that'd be pretty obvious! I was shot in a riot."

"Elsa Sunday isn't exactly a French name."

"My birth name was Gwendoline Dominique Beaumont."

"That's a name."

"I changed my name as Gwendoline makes me sound old."

"You are old! No offense but your like over two-hundred years old."

"I know but I died when I was thirty, so I sometimes forget that I'm actually two-hundred."

"You're not looking bad for someone who's over two-hundred."

"Well those anti-wrinkle creams really work," Elsa joked.

"Okay," Angel hissed, she was clearly bored of our conversation, "You two stay down here I'm going to do a sweep of the building and lock any backdoors."

"What's up with her?" I asked as Angel walked away.

"I don't know, she's been strange since Rio."

"Paris said that Angel and Alex were, err, having an intense conversation the other day."

"That's nothing unusual. Those two often argue."

"I heard that Alexander has been at the base longer, so why is he vice-captain and Angel captain? Not that I'm saying that I don't want Angel to be captain or anything!"

"On paper Alexander is more qualified but Angel is just...she's just better. She cares about all the members of the squad and she knows how to get the best from us. She goes on every mission, unless she's ordered to stay behind and, when that happens, she stays in the operations room and oversees everything."

"Also Alexander disappeared for almost nine months," Bertie added, bringing us our drinks.

"Oh yeah," Elsa exclaimed, "I totally forgot about that!"

"What happened?" I asked.

"Alex just disappeared one night. No one saw him go. The Colonel wouldn't talk about it. It was really weird."

"Yes then Angel went on that horrific zombie mission," Bertie continued, "And Alexander came back."

"What exactly happened on that zombie mission?" I asked, "Ethan mentioned it the other day."

"Are you sure you want to know?"

"I'm not going to freak out."

Well I might, I added internally.

"Okay so this mission is considered the worse mission in the base's history," Elsa explained, "This happened when Angel and Sophie were in Wildfire Squad. The mission was to rescue a group of humans who had been taken by a cult of vampires as blood slaves. The squad arrived and freed the humans."

"Then out of nowhere the squad gets attacked by zombies. Six of the squad die in the first five minutes. Jin (have you met Jin yet, he's a lovely lad) got badly injured, so Angel had to literally drag him away from danger, while trying to save the humans," Bertie continued.

"At this point Jin noticed that the zombies are wearing execution tags. Ah, zombies must be executed. It's the law. So these zombies should have been executed but they hadn't been, they had been purposely let lose."

"Why would someone do that?" I asked.

"Well it turned out..." but before Elsa could tell me more Angel appeared behind us.

"Piper at your three o'clock," she whispered.

After working out which way was 'three o'clock', I watched the Pied Piper as he sat himself down at a small table in the far corner of the tavern.

"So how are we playing this?" Elsa asked.

"Elsa 'zoom' over there and sit on that seat next to him. I'll go opposite and Jason you at the end. Keep your guard up, he may be old but he's fast."

Angel nodded to Elsa and they both zoomed over to

the Piper. I followed, sitting down next to Angel. The Pied Piper was not what I had expected. There was no brightly coloured outfit or army of rats behind him, there was just a deflated looking man. He wore all black and although his face was battered, he still looked young. His sad cold eyes stared at me.

"Piper, you're under arrest," Angel announced firmly pulling out her ID badge, "Jason, time to make your first arrest."

Angel nodded to Elsa. Elsa took hold of the Piper and pulled him to his feet. Angel handed me a pair of chains. Now I won't lie to you, I was very excited about making my first arrest. Police officers always look so cool when they arrest the bad guys in movies! I took the chains and placed them over the Piper's wrists.

"With the power the Emperor has given me, I place the Pied Piper under arrest for crimes against the paranormal empire," I locked the chains, "You have the right to remain silent and the right to legal representation."

The moment I finished speaking, the Pied Piper broke the chains and escaped. I ran after him not wanting my first arrest to end in disaster. The Piper was fast, and I was in danger of losing him. The Piper turned left and headed down a small alleyway. I followed him. The alleyway seemed to come to a dead end but the Piper, being a fey with magic and everything, just decided to run up the side of the wall, as you do!

I looked up as the Piper ran across the roof tops. I sighed and looked around. There was a box on the opposite side of the alleyway. Standing on the box, I pulled myself up onto the roof. No one else had decided to take the roof that day so it was easy to spot the Piper. Despite being slightly concerned that I might fall through someone's roof, I ran after the Piper. However I quickly realised that I was extremely bad at running. I stopped, out of breath and exhausted.

"I need to start going to the gym," I panted, "Ah he's

getting away. Someone stop him! Oh wait there's no one around. Great. What am I going to do!? We have doctors at the base right? I think I might need one. Whoever said running was good for you, was lying! Who am I talking to? Oh I'm talking to myself, that's not good. Right I really should do something as he's getting away."

Then an idea popped into my tired mind. I pulled out my crossbow and with shaking hands, I pulled the trigger.

The world seemed to move in slow motion. The small dart zoomed through the air and hit its target. The Piper fell. I ran (well to be honest it was more of a fast paced walk) over to the Piper, locking him in chains the moment I arrived.

"With the power the Emperor has given me, I place the Pied Piper under arrest for crimes against the paranormal empire," I gasped, "You have the right to remain silent and the right to legal representation."

"Well done Master," the Piper nodded, "You win."

"Great," I muttered, although I wasn't sure what game we had been playing.

I then realised that shooting the Piper may not have been my best idea, for now the Piper couldn't walk. With some difficulty, I gave the injured Pied Piper a piggyback. Getting down from the roof with the Piper on my back was much harder than I had anticipated however, after twenty minutes of failure, I managed to get both myself and the Piper safely off the rooftop. Once my feet were firmly planted on the ground, I headed, with the Piper on my back, to the tavern. I was surprised to see Angel and Elsa sat at the bar looking totally relaxed.

"I told you he would do it!" Elsa exclaimed as I walked over to them. Elsa held out her hand and Angel handed her a fifty-pound note.

"What is that?" I asked.

"Oh, we had a bet on if you would catch the Piper or not."

"What!?"

"It was a test stupid," Angel muttered as she grabbed the Piper and put him on the floor. She glowed white then pulled the dart out of the Piper's leg and began to heal his wound.

"What do you mean it was a test?"

"When I visited you in hospital what did I say?"

"Err you warned me that this world was really dangerous and said some other scary things."

"Well...okay fair enough I did say that, but I also said you had to prove yourself worthy of being in my squad. That's what the test was for. To see if you were good enough to be in my squad. Luckily you succeeded."

"So if I hadn't caught the Piper I would have failed?"

"Correct."

"Then what would have happened?"

Angel didn't answer. She just smiled and handed me something. I looked down and in my hand was a Lightning Squad ID badge.

"Welcome to Lightning Squad."

8

'THE POWER OF THE PIPE'

Although he had caught the Pied Piper, due to his lack of training Jason wasn't allowed to take part in the Piper's interrogation. This task fell to Angel and Alexander. The pair had dragged the Piper into the interrogation room, which had a table and two chairs in the middle of it and a one way window on one wall. Once the Piper was securely chained to the table, Alexander joined the Colonel in the next room where they could oversee Angel's interrogation. Angel sat down opposite the Piper. She flicked through an orange folder and then, after five minutes of painful silence, she spoke.

"You have lived a very interesting life," Angel placed the folder on the table and studied the Piper.

"Do not believe all the things you read," the Piper muttered.

"Your name is Jamison Pied, correct?"

The Pied Piper smiled, "I have not been called that for a long time."

"But it is your name?"

"Correct."

"So Jamison, let's talk about your crimes. There's so many, I'm not sure where to begin."

"The very beginning, I hear, is a very good place to start."

"Indeed. Let us go back a few hundred years then, to your most famous crime. You went to Hamelin to help with the town's rat problem, correct?"

"Correct."

"You, and your magical pipe, succeeded in getting rid of the rats. The Mayor of the town refused to pay you, so you enchanted and kidnapped the town's children, correct?"

"No."

"No?"

"It is correct that I succeeded in getting rid of the rats. It is also correct that I enchanted and kidnapped the town's children."

"So you confess that you are guilty of abducting?"

"But I did not kidnap them because the Mayor refused to pay me!"

"Then why did you take them?"

"Because he tried to kill me!"

"Who did? The town's Mayor? The town's Mayor tried to kill you?"

"That is correct."

"Why?"

"Because I am fey, and he was human. Do you know who the Mayor of Hamelin was at that time?"

"No, I don't. Who was he?"

"His name was Nikolaus Achterberg."

"That name sounds familiar."

"When the fey realm and the human world were at war, that man led the battle of High Rock Hill, that battle I am sure you have heard of."

"Yes, I've heard of it, hundreds of fey died in that battle. But the human world and the fey realm were no longer at war when you got rid of the rats."

"Just because we were not at war does not mean we were at peace."

"So, the Mayor used you. He made you get rid of the rats then he tried to kill you, so you abducted the town's children?"

"Correct."

Angel paused for a moment then asked, "Why were the children returned? You returned all of the children, but one, after almost a month, why?"

The Piper smiled sadly, "Because she asked me to."

"By she, you mean the girl that wasn't returned. That girl, was the Mayor's daughter, correct?"

"Correct."

"Why wasn't she returned?"

"Because she did not wish to leave."

"You and her, were a couple?"

"Miriam, she became my wife."

"I see. So you ran off into the sunset together. Happily ever after," Angel mocked.

The Piper laughed, "Happily ever after! If only it was that simple. He followed us."

"The Mayor?"

"He followed us, and he stole her away. To catch me, he claimed that his daughter had been bewitched and the only way to free her was to have her executed."

"He killed his own daughter!?"

"He was going to."

"But you saved her?"

"Correct but there was a price. I was a child during the war between us and the humans. The human army came to our village one night and killed many of our people. I was injured. My injury affected my ability to use magic."

"The pipe, is that the only magic you can do?"

"That and a couple of basic spells. I knew that my minimal powers would not be enough to take on Achterberg. So I got help. There was a witch that lived close to Hamelin. She gave me some of her magic, however in return I was supposed to give her my pipe once I had rescued Miriam."

"Given that we have your pipe in lock up, I assume you didn't live up to your side of the deal."

"It was not intentional. In order to escape, we ran far from Hamelin, things were so chaotic that I just forgot."

"What was the price?"

"The witch cursed me. No matter how hard I try, I cannot die. The curse, I believe, is called 'Undying Misery'. Have you heard of it?"

Angel nodded, "So the great Pied Piper of Hamelin cannot die and must live forever in misery. How tragic."

"I watched Miriam and my children all die. I watched my grandchildren, my great-grandchildren, my great great-grandchildren..."

"All die? Yeah, we get it. I am sorry. Watching that, must have been awful. However, it doesn't excuse the crimes you committed after their deaths!"

"I did not care. I did not care what I did or what I used my powers for. I had lost everything. I was alive, but I was not living. When you have lived for as long as I have you realise that this world is filled with cruel and horrible people."

"So what? If you can't beat them, join them? How pathetic," from the folder Angel pulled out a piece of paper, "Here's a list of all the crimes you have been accused of. Cross out the ones you didn't do."

Angel got up and was about to leave the room when the Piper asked, "Finished already, Samantha?"

Angel turned quickly, feeling sick to her stomach. She stuttered, "What did you call me?"

"Your name."

"What?"

"You know a lot about curses, don't you?" the Piper smiled.

"What are you talking about?"

"You were cursed by a memory loss spell, correct?"

"How did you know that!?"

"Because I was there when it happened?"

"What?"

"I was there when you were cursed."

"This is..."

"You do not believe me," the Piper smiled then softly started to hum.

"No, I don't. I have no idea how you found out I was cursed but...can you stop humming!?" Angel snapped.

The Piper simply started to hum louder. The hum scratched the inside of Angel's ears. The tune made Angel feel dizzy. There was something sickly sweet about it. It sounded familiar.

"What are you doing to me?" Angel gasped, "Alexander!"

"Relax Samantha. I am not here to hurt you."

"I need to get out," Angel tried to get to the door, but her legs felt as though they were sinking into quicksand. Angel fell to the ground. The world around her spun. The tune was getting louder and lounder.

"Alex!" Angel tried to shout but the words died on her tongue.

Angel looked up at the Piper and noticed that between his lips was a small musical reed.

"The pipe," Angel gasped.

The Pied Piper smiled.

And Angel fell into darkness.

* * * * *

Angel awoke in a room she didn't recognise. It was dark, lit only by candlelight. Angel pulled herself to her feet. The room was filled with shelves that were stacked full of old books and jars filled with eyeballs. Angel headed to the door but found that it wouldn't open. At that moment she heard talking behind her. She turned and found the Pied Piper sat at a round table with a woman. The woman had her face covered by a long purple cloak and spoke in a soft voice.

"Hey Piper, what do you think," Angel went to grab the Piper only to find that her hands fell straight through him.

He wasn't real.

"This is a memory," Angel realised, "He's trapped me in a memory. Okay. Okay Piper I'll play along, what do you want to show me?"

"Seer," the Piper in the memory whispered to the woman in the cloak, "Have you found one?"

"You still wish to die?" the seer asked slowly.

"Yes. Have you found one cursed like me?"

"Yes and no."

"What does that mean?"

"I have found one who will be cursed like you, but she has not been cursed yet."

"Where is she? When will she be cursed?"

"Soon. In a couple of days. Poor child."

"Child? It is a child?"

"A child with a great destiny. One that she cannot outrun. This child is different to the others. She is not only cursed but powerful. She is the…"

Suddenly someone banged on the door.

"Open up! This is Captain Hardwick of Thunder D.D Squad," came a shout from behind the door.

"Damn it!" the Piper hissed, "This girl, where is she?"

"In three days, she will get cursed in the Night Forest."

"The Night Forest, thank you," and with that the Piper and the memory faded.

The next memory took Angel to a place she knew well. The Night Forest. Home to the Night werewolf pack. Angel's home. Angel followed the Piper.

The Piper was also following someone.

He was following a young girl with long blonde hair. The girl hadn't sensed his presence. She was covered in blood and bruises. The number 1147512 had been recently burnt onto one of her arms. The girl was limping and stumbling. She was also crying. The Piper felt sorry for her but didn't dare get any closer. The girl finally collapsed. The Piper was about to go over to the child when the girl's body started to tremble. The girl glowed white as her body started to twist out of control. She transformed into a lion and then a bear, then a rabbit, then a dragon, then a unicorn and then she started transforming with such speed that the Piper could no longer tell one creature from another. The Piper followed at a distance as this hurricane of creatures rampaged through the forest.

Deeper in the forest a small human child was playing by a lake. The constantly transforming girl headed towards the human child. She transformed into a vampire and bit down into the human child's neck. The child yelled in pain and fell to the floor. The girl let the child go and watched as the human ran. She then transformed into a large white tiger. The tiger raced through the forest. It pounced on top of the human child and dug its claws into the child's thin flesh. Breaking the skin, the blood spilt across the floor. Then the girl transformed again, and again, and again. It was a blood bath. Only when the human child was unrecognisable did the girl stop.

The girl changed back into her original form and stood looking at the destruction she had caused.

The girl sobbed, "I'm so sorry. I didn't mean too. I'm so sorry."

Angel watched as the Piper pulled out his pipe. He brought it to his lips and began to play. The soft deadly tune reached the girl's ears. She swayed to the music slightly then stumbled to the ground. Her body began to glow once more but this time she didn't transform.

"What is he doing to that kid?" Angel wondered aloud, "Who is that kid anyway?"

"Samantha!" someone suddenly shouted.

The Piper quickly stopped playing and the girl returned to her senses. She ran towards the lake but before she could reach it, a fork of red lightning hit her back. The girl fell to the ground, gasping for breath. She crawled across the mud.

"Where are you going Samantha?" from behind a tree a woman stepped into the Piper's view. She had long blonde hair that was slowly going grey and her eyes were a dark green. Her lips were blood red and smiling. She wore a long old-fashioned black dress and a red cloak. The woman hit the girl with a second red lightning fork. The girl screamed, as she did so the ground shook.

"What is she doing here?" Angel stuttered, "Who, who is that kid?"

"I'm impressed Samantha, I really am," the woman laughed walking through Angel as she did so, "You're more powerful than I had expected. You can even kill people now."

"I didn't. I didn't mean too," the girl whimpered.

"That doesn't matter. The fact that you can kill, that's what matters," the woman smiled, "You're a murderer now Samantha, just like me."

"I'm not like you." The woman walked over to the girl and grabbed her by her hair, pulling it back so that the woman could see the girl's face.

"How pathetic. It's time to go home, don't you think? We can use you now."

The girl laughed, "You can't use me, if I'm dead."

With that the girl grabbed a dagger from the woman's belt and stabbed it into her own stomach. The woman dropped the girl in surprise as the girl began to bleed.

"You stupid girl!"

"Samantha!" a male voice shouted.

The woman knelt next to the girl and whispered, "I can just heal you."

"And I can just stab myself again," the girl hissed.

"If you're not going to work with me willingly then I'll just…"

Before the woman could finish, she was grabbed and thrown across the forest. A man had appeared. Neither the Piper nor Angel could see his face. It was carefully hidden behind a hood. The man went over to the girl.

"Samantha.," the man muttered in a low tone.

"Get away," the girl hissed.

"I'm not going to hurt you. I'm going to save you, let me take…" the man went to remove the dagger, but the girl stopped him.

"No! Let me die. Please."

"Sam," the man was thrown into the air and then crashed to the ground.

"What do you think you're doing here prince!?" the woman shouted.

The man got to his feet, "Leave the kid alone."

"Why would I do that? She's finally ready. She's finally perfect! She can kill now!"

The man punched the woman's face. The woman stumbled back. She raised her hand and tree roots rose up from the ground, wrapping around the man's legs.

The woman then turned to the girl. With a click of her fingers, the dagger flew from the girl's stomach into the woman's hand. The woman then hit the girl with two massive black lightning forks. The girl screamed, and her body trembled. She was lifted into the air. A black mist twisted around her, covering her body from view. Then with a crash the girl slammed to the ground. The blood on the forest floor began to move. It slid over to the girl's hair and dyed it blood red.

"What did you just do!?" the man shouted.

"I saved her life," the woman then added, *"Oh and cursed her."*

"Cursed? What did you do?"

"When Samantha awakes, she won't remember anything, not even her own name. A clean slate, I will be able to make her do anything I want."

"Why is her hair?"

"Oh, that's a little extra something I've added to the curse, to make sure she does what she's told. The colour will fade as the curse settles."

"I won't let you take her," the man crashed out of the roots that were holding him back.

"Why are you being like...Oh, oh this is funny!" the woman laughed.

"What is?"

"You can't see it! You don't know why you're protecting her, do you?"

"Enlighten me."

"She's..."

"Get off my land!" came a shout. The woman and man turned to find themselves surrounded by werewolves. Only one was in human form.

"Pops," Angel gasped. The man stood in front of her was David Night. Her adopted father, *"Wait then that means that kid is..."*

"Wolves," the woman hissed, "This doesn't concern you and your puppies, Night!"

"I disagree," David snapped, "This is my land. Anything that happens on my land is my concern. I will not have demon worshippers here, so leave now before I let my wolves rip you to pieces."

"Please rip her to pieces," the man smiled, "You'd be doing the world a favour."

"You!" David exclaimed in recognition.

"Tell your pack to kill this woman. Me too, if it makes you feel better but leave the girl. She has nothing to do with this."

"How cute," the woman hissed. The woman then raised her arms and sent lightning forks in multiple directions. The werewolves charged, and chaos followed.

Not wanting to get caught in the middle of it, the Piper ran away, and the memory faded.

* * * * *

Angel opened her eyes and found herself on the cold floor of the interrogation room. She could feel tears running down her cheeks. The Pied Piper was still sat chained to the table. Angel could hear Alexander banging on the door behind her.

"Alex!" Angel shouted.

"Angel, are you alright? He's done something to the door, we can't get it open," Alexander shouted.

"What have you done? You said you didn't have any powers!" Angel turned to the Piper.

"I do not," he replied.

"Then what have you done to the door?"

"That," he smiled, "Is just a little trick I picked up."

"How much power does your pipe have?"

"More than you can possibly imagine."

"You didn't get caught, did you? You let us catch you. Why?"

"Finally, you start asking the important questions."

Angel sat down opposite the Piper once again.

"What did you just show me?" Angel asked.

"How you got cursed."

"That girl, that was..."

"You? Indeed, it was."

"No way!"

"Ask your father if you still do not believe me."

"This is mad," Angel laughed, "This is...when you played the pipe to the kid in your memory, what were you doing?"

"I was implanting a tune into her head. A tune I could then reactivate when I needed to. That's how I made you enter my memories. The tune allows me to have complete control of a person's mind. The enchanted party becomes a slave to the music of the pipe."

"Is that your fancy way of telling me that right now I am completely at your mercy?"

"Correct."

"What do you want from me!? You obviously got caught for a reason, what was that reason?"

"I came here so that you would kill me."

"What?"

"I will only die if someone who has been cursed, by a witch of the same bloodline as the one who cursed me, kills me."

"So, the woman who cursed me, was of the same bloodline as the witch who cursed you?"

"Correct."

"This is madness! This is," Angel laughed, "I'm not going to kill you!"

"What you just saw must have been difficult to watch. If you have any questions about that memory, please ask?"

Angel paused then asked, "What happened after? After the wolves came?"

"I quickly left as you saw. I was originally planning on returning to the forest and making you kill me, however that wolf pack tighten their security making it impossible for me to enter. Years later I saw a newspaper article about the D.D squads first female captain, I recognised you."

"And started planning this?"

"Correct."

Angel dropped her head to her hands and muttered, "I stabbed myself."

"Indeed, you did."

"What did they do to me?"

"I do not know but clearly it was not something pleasant."

"My hair colour, it was dyed with actual blood, she said it would fade."

"Clearly the curse never fully settled, which must be why your hair never returned to its natural colour."

The door to the interrogation room suddenly began to glow purple.

"Ah, it seems that we have run out of time," the Piper sighed, "For showing you that memory and for what I am about to make you do, I am truly sorry."

"Make me? What are you talking about?"

The Pied Piper once again brought the pipe reed to his lips and began to hum. Angel's head felt like it was going to explode.

"What are you doing!?"

"Please stop resisting me and relax, this will all be over soon," the Piper whispered. The hum got louder and the tune more painful. Angel's body shuddered and trembled. Her hand moved, without her permission, towards her gun.

"No, I am not going to kill you!" Angel shouted as she tried to fight the power of the pipe.

"You do not have a choice."

The tune got louder and louder to the point where it was suffocating. Before she could stop herself, Angel grabbed her gun, aimed for the Piper, and pulled the trigger.

There was a deafening sound of a gunshot.

Then it went silent.

And the Pied Piper of Hamelin died.

Angel stared at her hand and then at the Piper's blood

that wallpapered the interrogation room. Angel cried out as she fell to the ground.

"What have I? What did he?" Angel gasped. She didn't even register that Alexander had kicked the door down or that the Colonel had charged into the room.

"What did you think you were doing!?" yelled the Colonel. He grabbed Angel by the neck and pushed her up against a wall.

"I didn't…"

"You! You are supposed to be a captain, yet you allowed your mind to be controlled by a damn flute!" the Colonel banged Angel's head against the wall then he let her go, she slid down to the floor.

The Colonel looked at Angel then turned to Alexander, "Take her to the lock up."

9

'WERE-MAIDS'

The lock up was a square white room with a small bed (on which Angel was laid) and a glass roof, so guards and on watchers could look in on their prisoners. Angel used to think the lock up's design was perfect for housing prisoners, however after being locked inside it for several hours, her opinion of the lock up's design swiftly changed. Staring at four white walls was incredibly boring! Not only was it boring but it also offered Angel no distraction from the whirlwind of thoughts that echoed around her mind. She couldn't stop thinking about the memory the Pied Piper had shown her.

"That girl was me. If that girl was me then that means that I killed a human child. No. That can't be true, I would never do that! That woman, that witch! Who is she? What does she want from me? Samantha, is that my name? If it is, I hate it! It's a horrible name! Who was that man? His voice, his voice is so familiar. Ah! I need to get out of here. I need to talk to Pops! He was there, he will be able to tell me, whether this memory is real or not," Angel thought aloud.

Then one of the walls opened and someone walked into the cell.

"Am I being released?" Angel asked.

"No," Alexander answered.

"Fantastic. How is this situation my fault? It's not like I asked the Piper to implant his pipe's tune into my head!"

"What exactly happened?"

"The Piper implanted the pipes tune into my head. Which meant that all he needed to do was hum the tune with the reed in his mouth and I would become enchanted. Why did he have a reed? The pipe doesn't even need a reed!" Angel ranted.

"When did he implant the tune?"

"In a time I don't remember."

"Before you were cursed?"

"Exactly, the Piper has had this planned for over a decade."

"The Piper showed you something, didn't he? Something from before you were cursed."

Angel remained silent.

"Angel," Alexander spoke softly, "What did you see?"

"Something," Angel muttered, "Alex, do you have your phone on you?"

"No, I had to hand it in before I came in here."

"Of course, you did, damn, I really need to ask Pops something"

"I see," Alexander mumbled as he sat down on the end of Angel's bed, "The Piper said, what he showed you, Angel, what you saw, was it you getting cursed?"

Angel nodded. There was a moment of silence before Angel asked, "Alex, if you had lost your memories, and you found out that those memories might be painful, would you still try to recover them?"

"I'm probably the worst person you could've asked," Alexander muttered, "I have a lot of memories I'd like to forget. What exactly did you see?"

"Once I've confirmed it's real, I'll show you."

"Angel, some memories are forgotten for a reason. If these memories are painful then maybe its best that you don't remember them."

"I used to think that too, however now I just get this feeling that there's something important hidden amongst those lost memories."

"Maybe there is but there also…"

"Alex what is it? The other day, that warlock's card, does the name Samantha mean something to you?"

"No."

"You reacted to it."

"No I reacted to you," Alexander turned to face Angel, "That name. That name scared you. When I found you that day, you were in pain and you were screaming, then you saw that card and got scared."

"That was…"

"I'm worried. Angel, I'm worried about you. I don't want to see you like that again and if these memories are painful, I don't want to see you in pain. I don't want to see you hurt."

There was silence. Alexander stared at Angel. His eyes softly traced Angel's face, studying her tired expression. Alexander and Angel had an odd relationship, one that could not easily be defined. A strange tension hung in the air whenever they were alone, it often felt like at any moment one of them might burst. Yet strangely this tension wasn't uncomfortable. If anything the pair were most relaxed in each other's company.

"I'm your captain, remember?" Angel smiled breaking the silence, "It's my job to be worried about you, not the other way around, but thank you."

"For what?"

"Just, for everything. The Pied Piper situation, what's going to happen?" Angel asked, changing the subject.

"I'm not sure. The Colonel is furious and so is the fey court."

"Great," Angel sighed. A bell sounded.

"Times up. I'll try to talk to the Colonel," Alexander got to his feet, "I'm not sure when I'll be able to visit again, I'm being kept pretty busy."

"How are you finding being captain?"

"Tiring," the bell sounded a second time, "I'm going to have to go, before they try to drag me out. I'll see you soon."

With that the wall opened and Angel was once again left alone.

* * * * *

After several days of staring at white walls alone, Angel received another visitor.

"What mess have you gotten yourself into this time?"

Angel looked up and smiled, "Jackson!"

Jackson Night was tanned and muscular with a mock of brown-hair and a pair of friendly brown eyes. He was dressed in a pair of denim jeans and a crisp white top with a pair of battered sandals covering his feet. The captain of Alpha Squad stared down at his sister.

"How are you pup?" he asked.

"Bored. Extremely bored!"

"Well, luckily for you, I've managed to persuade the Colonel to let you out of here," Jackson smiled.

"Really?"

"You're free to go. Well, free to leave this cell anyway. You can't leave the base."

"That's fine, if I can get out of this room, I'm happy."

* * * * *

As Angel and Jackson stepped out into the crisp morning sunlight, they both transformed into their wolf forms. Angel was a medium-sized white wolf and Jackson a large grey and brown wolf. As the pair raced towards the forest, they were pounced upon by two more wolves. Ethan, in wolf form, was small with grey fur and sneezed continuously whilst Roger was large and had light brown fur. In wolf form, the Night pack had the ability to talk to each other using a telepathic link, known as the wolf bond.

'*Angel! You're alive!*' Ethan telepathically exclaimed, then sneezed.

'*Yes, obviously,*' Angel thought to him.

'*How are you feeling?*' Roger asked.

'*I need a good run.*'

'*Then why are we just standing here like lemons?*'

Roger ran into the forest. Ethan howled then followed his brother happily. Jackson and Angel quickly followed. There was no feeling Angel could compare to running through the forest. The wind running through her fur seemed to blow all the twisted cobwebs in her mind away. The smell of the rain on the leaves and the tiny footsteps of squirrels in the trees became beautiful music that awakened Angel's tired body. After a while the wolves stopped in a clearing and transformed back into their normal forms.

"I had to explain to Jason yesterday why werewolves transform back into their normal forms fully clothed," Roger stated breaking the silence.

"Did he think we ripped off our clothes and ran around naked?" Ethan laughed.

"Yeah!"

"How did you explain it?"

"I said, transformation is all about imagining yourself as the being you want to transform into. When a werewolf thinks of their 'normal' form, they tend to imagine themselves fully dressed."

"Did he understand?"

"He claimed he did but the dazed expression on his face made me think otherwise."

"Who's Jason?" Jackson asked.

"The Master of Darkness."

"Is the Master of Darkness stupid?"

"Nah, he's just grown up in the human world."

"How long have I been in lock up?" Angel asked.

"Twenty days," Roger answered.

"I didn't realise it had been that long, I just meditated through most of it."

"Well while you were meditating, we had Alex going all Roman on us," Ethan grumbled, "His training is ten times harder than yours."

"Do any of you, oh no you wouldn't have."

"Wouldn't have what?"

"Your phones. I really need to call Pops."

"Why?" Ethan sneezed.

"Because the Pied Piper showed me something, one of his memories,"

"And Pops was in it?" Jackson asked.

"Yes, so was I."

"You were in one of the Piper's memories? What was this memory about?"

"It might be easier for me to show you."

The pack's telepathic link also allowed them to share memories. Angel opened her mind and allowed the three wolves to enter. She showed them the memory the Piper had shown her. Once the memory finished, the wolves returned to their own minds. The four of them were silent.

"That was," Jackson started but he couldn't think of the right words to describe how he was feeling.

"I know, it's messed up," Angel muttered.

"I remember when Pops and Tobias brought you home. Pops said he'd found you by the lake and that there were bad people after you. Tobias wanted to leave you at an orphanage, but Mum insisted that it was our destiny to protect you."

"The woman, in the memory, is that the same woman who haunts you?" Ethan asked Angel.

Angel nodded, "She appeared on the base."

"What?" Roger exclaimed, "When was this?"

"When we got back from Rio. I was in my room. My arm started to hurt. When I looked at it, it was covered in blood, which then burnt and dissolved into my skin. Then the woman started talking and this smoke entered my room. Next thing I know, I'm in the forest."

"She moved you? Who the hell is this woman!?" Jackson exclaimed, "How did she get onto the base!?"

"That is the question," Angel mumbled. They fell into silence. Angel's mind wandered back to her oldest memory, waking up in the Night pack's living room. She had woken up surrounded by strangers, in a place she couldn't recognise. She hadn't been able to speak. She had forgotten how to get the words inside her head to leave her lips. Roger had helped her regain her ability to talk. He had also taught her how to read and write as well as how to interact with other people. As Angel skipped through her reel of memories, she thought back to when she had first seen the woman. It had been on her first night with the Night pack. Angel had awoken from a nightmare. She had run outside only to find the woman standing at the forest border. The woman had smiled at Angel and had beckoned her to come closer. But Angel had remained still. Even though her memories had been lost, Angel had known, from the moment she saw her, that the woman was evil.

"What are you thinking about?" Roger asked, waking Angel from her thoughts.

"I was thinking about the first time I saw her. When she turned up at the border."

"On the first night? Yeah, I remember that. She just stood there, staring at you. It wasn't until Pops came that she left. You were really odd when you first joined the pack. You had nightmares all the time, you were so skinny, and you hated being inside, if anyone shut a door, you'd open it straight away. I can remember it was hard for Pops to get you to come into the main house. You used to just sit and stare at the sky, all day and night."

"I remember," Angel mumbled, "I need to find the seer. From the Piper's memory. She knew that I was going to get cursed so maybe she also knows where I came from.

The problem is I'm not allowed off the base."

"I'll see if I can persuade the Colonel to let you leave," Jackson assured, "If I'm with you, he might allow it."

"Because you're the Colonel's favourite," Roger muttered.

"The thing is, I don't even know if I want to find out," Angel sighed, "How awful must my life have been for me to stab myself and beg to die?"

The Night quartet fell into silence once more. The werewolf brothers had been thinking the same thing. Whilst they were curious as to what kind of life Angel had before she had joined their family, they were also terrified of finding out. They each clearly remembered how badly broken and bruised Angel had looked the first time they had seen her. It had taken their mother and Roger weeks to get Angel to interact with the rest of the pack. Before that Angel had simply sat by herself, staring at the sky for hours on end.

Ethan sneezed breaking the silence.

"Bless you," Roger turned to Jackson and changed the subject, "How was Italy?"

"Great, don't think we could have picked a better honeymoon spot," Jackson smiled.

"How did Rowan's 'lovely' royal parents take it?"

Jackson went silent.

"You didn't tell them!?"

"What do you think? Or are you forgetting the small stabbed with a trident incident?"

"It's still funny," Roger smiled at the memory, "So Rowan's parents don't actually know that you two are married? Oh Jack you're in trouble!"

"What do you think they'll do, stab him with another trident? Or do you think they'll have him executed?" Ethan laughed.

"I can't believe you got caught kissing the Princess of Atlantis," Angel laughed.

"I can't believe the Princess of Atlantis would want to

kiss you, let alone marry you! I mean, no offence Jackson, but Rowan is like a badass mermaid and you're, well you're pretty pathetic," Roger teased.

"Hey!" Jackson exclaimed.

"I still think it's funny that the King stabbed you with his trident. That thing is the crown jewel of Atlantis and now it's got your blood all over it!" Angel joked.

"I'm glad you guys find the fact that my parents-in-law almost killed me so hilarious!"

"It is hilarious! The great captain of Alpha Squad broke perhaps the most sacred rule in Atlantis…"

"What rule is this?" Ethan asked.

"A princess of Atlantis isn't allowed to be touched by an air breather."

"Really!? I didn't know that, I thought they just stabbed him because he was kissing Rowan."

"You know there's one thing I've seriously been wondering," Angel smiled mischievously, "Jack, if you and Rowan have kids…"

"Don't say it," Jackson muttered.

"Are they going to transform into dog-fish?"

"You said it!"

"Dog-fish are a type of shark, aren't they?" Roger asked.

"I hope so, it'd be cool to have sharks in the family," Ethan laughed.

"Or would the kids turn into half-wolves, half-mermaids? Mer-wolves or were-maids?" Angel joked.

"I vote were-maids," Roger laughed.

"Me too!" Ethan smiled.

"Were-maids it is," Angel turned to her oldest brother, "Jackson if you and Rowan have kids, they're going to be Were-maids.

10

'THE PAST'

ROBERT DRAGONHEART

"Master get down!"

There was a rain of arrows. I raised my hands and a crystal force field covered my body. I pulled Harry under the forcefield, but I was too late. Hit by an arrow, he stumbled to his knees and coughed up blood before falling flat on his face. I knelt and checked his pulse. He was dead.

"Poor soul," I muttered. Getting up, I ran over the bloody muddy battlefield. There were bodies and limbs all around. I jumped as I heard a roar behind me. Turning I found myself face-to-face with a huge demon. It had white scales, deep red eyes and black fangs that dripped with blood. I pulled out my black crystal staff and pointed it at the demon. The crystal glowed. The demon shuddered and then exploded into tiny pieces, its skin falling like snow onto the battlefield.

"Master Robert!" shouted a vampire. The vampire was tall with flowing brown hair and cold eyes.

"Rose," I greeted the vampire "We are running out of men.

Where is my sister?"

"She's safe."

"Yes, but where?"

"She's at the camp with Edwin."

"Good. Pull the troops back to the rocks then ah!" I gasped, collapsing to my knees, "What have you done?"

"You have trusted all the wrong people," Rose smiled, pulling the dagger from my back, and baring her fangs.

"What have you done to my sister?"

"Oh, she's bleeding to death in a muddy ditch somewhere."

"You shouldn't have done that," I got to my feet and black mist exploded from my hands, hitting Rose in the chest. Rose stumbled backwards and then collapsed to the floor, as her body slowly crumbled to ash.

Blood dripped from where Rose had stabbed me.

I placed my hands over the stab wound and slowly began to heal myself. I stumbled across the battlefield.

"Robert!" yelled a blonde-haired vampire.

"Edwin, where is Victoria?"

"Rose took her."

"Rose is a traitor and dead."

Edwin and I ran across the battleground, desperately trying to find Victoria. Suddenly Edwin stopped. He remained still for a moment, sniffed the air, then turned and slid down a ditch.

"Robert!" he yelled from the bottom. In the ditch was the limp body of a small blonde-haired woman.

"Is she...?" I started to ask but the words died on my tongue.

"She has a pulse," Edwin whispered as he pulled Victoria into his arms, "But it is weak."

"We must get her to the camp."

* * * * *

Once we had gotten Victoria inside the warm tent, Skyjack quickly got to work. The poor creature had blood on his horn and mud coating most of his body. Victoria's condition was harder to heal than anticipated. More healers were called in, and me and Edwin swiftly kicked out. I paced outside her tent as the moon began to rise into the blood red sky.

"I should have never allowed her to come," I muttered.

"It was not your fault," Edwin reassured calmly, "None of us could have foreseen Rose's betrayal."

"Master," Skyjack called as he trotted out of the tent.

"How is she?"

"Weak but she will live," Skyjack announced before walking over to another injured soldier.

"Thank you Skyjack."

Edwin and I then entered the candle-lit tent. Victoria lay, eyes closed, on the small bed inside. Discarded on the floor around her were blood dyed bandages. Edwin tensed at the smell but quickly composed himself. He walked over to Victoria and gently stroked her hair. At his touch, she opened her eyes and smiled softly.

Victoria looked over to me and sighed with relief, "You are well."

"Indeed," I muttered.

"Rose is a…"

"Rose is dead," I snapped sharply. There was a pause then I asked, "What did she do to you?"

"I am not sure exactly."

"Did she stab you or bite you or…"

"She stabbed me but the knife," Victoria paused, "It was strange. It was thin and crystal."

"The knife of the Order," I muttered to Edwin who nodded.

"The Order?" Victoria asked.

"Nothing you need to worry about."

"Robert, I have just been stabbed! I think I have the right to know who by."

"The Order is a group of paranormals that want to open the gateway between the worlds permanently," Edwin explained, "They believe spilling your blood will do so."

"Is my blood capable of such a task?"

"Of course not!" I snapped, "It's a story, it's never been proven."

"Eddie?"

Edwin sighed, "It is true that there are properties in your blood that are different to others, and it is believed that a past Mistress of

Light did indeed open the gateway with her blood."

"She did?" I turned to the vampire surprised.

"It was a long time ago. About three Masters back. She was able to open the portal, but something went wrong, and it closed."

"Master!" called Tin, the Minotaur leader of the Emperor's private guard, as he entered the room, "The Emperor wishes for you and Sir Edwin to lead a guard of five hundred men over the north border."

"The Emperor wishes what?" I asked getting to my feet. I led Edwin and Tin out of the tent.

"Orders Master," Tin proclaimed, "The Emperor believes that we can advance further into enemy grounds if we go over the North border. He wishes for you to leave at daybreak."

"Yes, but five hundred men…"

"Lord David is taking the same over the South border and Sir Williams the East."

"And yourself?"

"The Emperor and his guard will make a full attack on the demon camp to keep them distracted."

"But that is suicide! Surely the Emperor knows that."

"He does however this is the only chance we have."

"Yes. Tell Sir Holmes to get the men together. He can explain the situation to them. I need to see to my sister."

"Yes Master. Will the Mistress of Light be joining you?"

"Not if I can help it. Goodnight," I nodded to the Minotaur then turned back to the tent.

"Are you truly not taking Victoria with you?" Edwin asked.

"You think I should?"

"She is the Mistress of Light. She is just as powerful…"

"She is only a child."

"She is only three years younger than yourself."

"I thought you loved my sister so pray tell me why you seem so desperate to see her killed."

Edwin hissed angrily, *"Believe me, Victoria dying is the last thing I want! However, I have been around in the times of other masters and Mistresses, so I know exactly what power she possesses. It is time you stop treating her like a child and let her fulfil her destiny."*

"*She is not going. I am sending her home.*"

* * * * *

"*Home? You are sending me home?*" *Victoria exclaimed.*

"*It is for your own good,*" *I tried to explain.*

"*Is it? Robert, you know full well that you cannot do this alone.*"

"*I am hardly going to be alone with five hundred men fighting next to me.*"

"*Robert that is not what I meant, and you know it! It is my duty as much as it is yours to protect this world!*"

"*Enough! You are going home and that is the end of it.*"

"*I am the Mistress of Light!*"

"*I said that is enough! I am ordering you, go home.*"

"*I do not take orders from you! What do you expect me to do? Just go home and sew while you fight in a war that needs us both!*"

"*Victoria, I do not wish to argue with you.*"

"*You would not have to if, for once, you actually listened to me!*"

"*Victoria please just do as you are told.*"

"*Robert!*"

"*You will be leaving in the morning,*" *I stated firmly,* "*You will be under guard until then.*"

"*You cannot…*"

"*That is final!*"

* * * * *

The cold air rippled through my thin shirt as I watched my soldiers prepare themselves for the bloodbath which was to come. As Edwin saddled his horse, Victoria rushed over to him. I turned away as Edwin bent down and kissed her. I watched as the morning sun rose and wondered whether I would live to see it set. I felt a tap on my shoulder, I turned to find Victoria behind me.

"*Robert,*" *she sighed,* "*Be careful.*"

"*When am I not careful?*" *I joked.*

"*Robert.*"

"*I know,*" *I pulled my sister into a tight hug and muttered,* "*I know.*"

"*Just come home.*"

"*I will I promise.*"

"Do not make promises you cannot keep."

"I love you, my little sister," I pulled away.

"I am not that little...love you too."

"Now go to Sir Lance, he has the portal open for you."

Victoria looked as if she was going to argue with me, however she remained silent. Instead she simply smiled before walking away.

"This is the worst part," Edwin muttered.

"Pardon?" I stuttered startled. I had not realised Edwin was stood beside me.

"Parting with a loved one. It is the worst part of every battle."

"You can leave with her if you wish. No one will think any less of you."

"We are stuck in this mess together my friend, as much as you would like to get rid of me," he joked.

"I am serious, I know that she would be more upset if something happened to you then if something happened to me."

"I doubt..."

"You can read her mind as well as I can. I have not been the best of brothers."

"I am not leaving you, after all who else would watch your back."

"Then we ride as brothers," I smiled as I got on my horse.

"Brothers."

* * * * *

The battlefield spat out its bloody children at us from all directions. The demons crawled through the mud, biting at the horses' legs, pulling them down into the dark pits of hells mouth. The smell of rotting flesh and burning metal seemed to grow with every minute. The battle was only ten miles or so from the camp. We had been hit before we had even reached the border. The demons were everywhere and with each passing moment there were more of our allies' bodies on the ground.

My sword clanged against the creature's sword. The creature was tall and seemed to float just above the ground. Its only facial feature was a pair of milk white fangs. The creature held a long thin sword and fought with the grace of a ballet dancer

Our swords sparked as they drew apart. I tried to attack but was blocked. The demon's speed was almost impossible to counter act. It never tired. I pulled out my crystal staff and slammed it into the demon's chest. The crystal glowed but the creature did not crumble. Instead it stumbled backwards and roared angrily. I cursed, kicking the creature backwards. The creature grabbed my leg and threw me to the floor. The creature pounced on top of me and dug its fangs into my neck. I yelled and slammed my sword into what should have been the demon's heart. Black mist escaped from its heartless body. I coughed and choked as the toxic mixture was pushed into my face...

I twisted and pushed myself out from under the beast, only for the creature to grab my ankle and drag me back into its clutches. Its long fingernails dug into my shoulders. I could feel my body tremble.

My head fell backwards, my skin twisted and changed. I could feel myself falling and then it arrived. My hands clawed the floor and sweat poured from my forehead. Lightning forked in the sky, lighting up the whole battle ground. My demon had taken over. I grabbed the creature and dug my fangs into its hellish flesh. I ripped the creature apart as if it was nothing more than a carrot stick. The creature's black blood warmed my mouth as I swallowed the rest of the creature whole.

Then I felt claws dig into my back. I twisted my head and looked into the red eyes of another beast. The beast roared before biting into my neck. I screamed, threw the beast to the ground then pounced on top of it. We rolled across the mud, biting, and clawing at each other. Blood dripped from my chest as I slammed the beast against a cart. The beast jumped on top of me and bit hard into the back of my neck. I stumbled and flopped to the ground. I struggled to my feet, throwing the beast off my back. The beast roared and cut into my stomach. Blood poured, I twisted and grabbed the beast between my claws. I bit into the beast, then pulled it into tiny pieces.

After devouring the beast, I sank down into the muddy ground before transforming back into my normal self.

I was covered in blood.

"Robert!" Edwin rushed to my side, "The enemy has retreated."

"That is good," I whispered. I felt weak and I could not move.

"What...how can I help you?"

"There is nothing."

"Surely there is something."

"No…I have fought my last," I winced in pain.
"No let me get you to…"
"It will not work…look after Victoria for me."
"Robert…"
"You have been a loyal friend…thank…"
I died before I could finish my sentence.

11

'A CHAT WITH A VAMPIRE'

JASON

I woke and found myself lying on my bedroom floor. A burning sensation ran down my back as I sat myself up. What had just happened? Had I been dreaming? Since coming to the base, my dreams had started getting really weird. I used to have nice safe dreams about kittens playing violins, not bloody battles, and demons! I fumbled in the darkness until my hand found the light switch. It was only once the light was on that I realised that my hand was covered in blood. I raced to the bathroom and stared in the mirror to find that my entire body was coated in blood. I turned on the tap and washed the blood away. I searched my body but there was no wound. So where had the blood come from?

I stumbled from the bathroom as panic began to take over. I had to escape. I needed to be far away from Robert Dragonheart's piercing portrait eyes. I raced downstairs to the kitchen and got myself a glass of water.

I jumped as a voice behind me asked, "Dream or

memory?"

Alexander was sat at the kitchen table, watching me.

"Dream or memory?" Alexander asked again.

"I...don't know..." I muttered.

"You're a reincarnation Jason. Which means, sooner or later, your old memories will start to come back to you," Alexander explained, "Sit, tell me about it and I'll try and help."

I sat. After a moment of awkward silence, a jumble of words left my mouth, "It was this battle. They were calling me Robert. We were fighting these demons. That pegacorn, Skyjack, from the hospital wing was there! And I think I died!"

"Robert Dragonheart, he was the tenth Master of Darkness. It sounds like you dreamt of his last moments. He was killed in battle," Alexander calmly explained.

"Tenth? How many have there been?"

"You're number thirteen."

"Thirteen."

"Which means you're also the last."

"The last?"

"According to the legends, the Master of Darkness will reincarnate only thirteen times."

"Oh."

"Yes, the thirteenth reincarnation happened sooner than expected."

"What do you mean?"

"Well technically speaking a Master of Darkness should live for at least a million years, however the longest lasting Master only lived for a hundred and forty-two years. Most of you have died before you've even reached thirty-five!"

"Oh."

"Yes, your past reincarnations have not been very lucky."

"Oh," was all I could say as dread and panic had captured the rest of my vocabulary.

"Ah, sorry I probably shouldn't have said that. I didn't

mean to worry you."

"It's fine."

"Jason my mind reading skills are not the strongest, yet I can hear your internal panic-attack so clearly it's as if you are shouting down my ear."

Why was everyone in this world telepathic!? Okay, I admit it, I was internally freaking out. Alexander had just told me that most of the former masters had died before reaching thirty-five, that means that the likelihood of me surviving the next seventeen years was very slim. Now I'm not saying I want to live for a master's full million-year lifespan but, you know, I would at least like to reach a hundred!

"He has the same last name as me," I muttered, "Does that mean we're related? Blood related, not just reincarnated related."

"Possibly. Dragonheart is an unusual surname. We'd have to run some tests to check. Tell me more about this dream of yours."

"In the dream, I had a sister. Victoria. They called her the Mistress of Light."

"I was wondering when this would turn up. Every Master of Darkness has had a sister. This sister, known as the Mistress of Light, is just as powerful as the Master of Darkness but their powers are polar opposites. While a Master draws his powers from darkness, a Mistress draws hers from Light."

"Every Master has had a sister?"

"All but you."

"Is me not having a sister a bad thing?"

"To be totally honest with you Jason, we're not sure. This has never happened before. Currently there is a team of investigators trying to work out why you've reincarnated without your sister."

"Oh." There was silence, "What happened to her?"

"To who?"

"Victoria, Robert's sister, and Edwin."

"Oh, when she found out about her brother's death, she created an army that won many victories until she became ill and died. Edwin married Victoria and became a general in her army. However, after her death, he lost his way. He's still alive, well as alive as a vampire can be. If you want, I can take you to meet him, he might have some useful information."

"Oh," I muttered. The idea of meeting Edwin again gave me mixed feelings. Part of me thought it'd be nice to see the vampire again while the other part of me hated the idea. I mean, what would I say to him? 'Hi, I'm the reincarnation of your best friend/ brother in law, I've been having dreams about you, do you fancy having a cup of tea and a catch up?' Just the idea of saying that sentence aloud made me shudder.

"Do you know anything else about the past versions of me?" I asked.

"I don't know much. I only know that you have always turned up whenever the world needed you. Normally before a great war or disaster. I feel like Jet and his demon worshippers, I don't know, maybe they're the reason for your return."

"Why did he kill my mum?"

"Most likely, he did it for fun. To him killing people is a game. It's entertainment. Jason what did he say to you in the alley?"

"Err he said I have a message for you to give to your mum. Tell her that her dreams will come true or something along those lines."

"Interesting. Jason did your mum sometimes get headaches, like really bad ones or suddenly daze out of a conversation?"

"Err…I guess, sometimes. She'd sometimes get a bit weird. Like her eyes would roll back and she'd start talking about stuff that was apparently going to happen…"

"Jason, I think your mum was a seer."

"A what?"

"I think your mum had the ability to see the future."

"Wait…wait…what?" I stared, opened mouthed, at the vampire, "My mum was a what!?"

Now this was just too much! My mum was human. A nice simple human who liked to listen to music from the eighties whilst doing the dishes, not a supernatural being! She couldn't have been a seer, could she?

"This is just my guess of course," the vampire continued, "I might be wrong. Your mum was called Josie, right? I'll check the hall of records next time I'm in the city."

"The hall of what?"

"The hall of records. It's where all official records are held. If she entered the paranormal world, then there should be a record of her. Was Dragonheart her married name?"

"No, she was never married to my dad. Her surname is Dragonheart."

"Your dad, who was he?"

"I don't know much about him. I think his name was William. Mum never said much."

"Is he alive?"

"I haven't a clue. Oh, that reminds me of a question about my dream, the unicorn thing, was it the same one as in the hospital?"

"Skyjack's a pegacorn and yes it's the same one. Skyjack's been a healer for years. That was his first battle, straight out of training."

"Pegacorns live for a long time."

"Most people in this world live a long time. I've been around ages."

"Is it…I know this may sound strange but, living for forever, is it nice?"

"It's interesting. You meet a lot of people; you lose a lot of people. I suppose I've managed it because I've never got attached to people. I've never loved a person enough for their death to haunt me and make me regret living forever."

"Sounds lonely."

"I suppose it was."

As the silence began to feel awkward, I changed the subject, "I hear Angel got released from lock up."

"Yes. How Jackson managed to convince the Colonel to let her out, I don't know."

"Who?"

"Jackson, Roger and Ethan's older brother, he's captain of Alpha Squad. That's the top squad."

"Oh, I've heard of him."

"He must have convinced the Colonel to let Angel go."

"Why did Angel get locked up? I heard the Piper enchanted her."

"He did. Technically speaking Angel did nothing wrong. The Piper's pipe was more powerful then we realised. However…"

"However?"

"The Colonel was supposed to hand the Piper over to the fey courts. The Piper was number one on their most wanted list."

"Ah, so the fey courts aren't happy?"

"Exactly. This is the type of incident where there needs to be someone to blame and the Colonel has decided that that someone is Angel."

"Yet you were the one in charge of confiscating the Piper's pipe. Surely if someone needs to be blamed, then it should be you for letting the Piper walk into the interrogation room with a weapon," Danny muttered as he walked into the kitchen.

"Danny what are you doing here?" asked Alexander coldly.

"Getting a drink, sorry have I interrupted an important meeting?"

"Aren't you meant to be on night duty."

"Don't remind me. Who am I patrolling with?"

"I thought you didn't want to be reminded?"

"Don't get clever."

"Sorry I forgot your primitive mind can't keep up," Alexander smiled.

"Look just coz your vice-captain doesn't mean I have to take any of this sh…"

"Sophie Day."

"What?"

"That's who you're patrolling with."

"Oh brilliant," Danny muttered sarcastically.

"Something wrong?"

"Sophie Day that's what's wrong! There's something not right about her."

"There's something not right about you, but you don't hear us complaining."

"Shut it, grandpa."

"Enough. Your patrol should have started by now."

"Since vamps never sleep, why don't they just do night duty?"

"Patrolling is part of your training. It helps…"

"Whatever! When's Angel coming back?"

"She's out of lock up. Whether the Colonel will let her come back as captain, I don't know."

"He better," Danny muttered and with that he left.

"Do Angel and Danny get along?" I asked Alexander.

"Yes, surprisingly. They've been friends since their training days."

"I can't imagine it."

"I know, they're an odd combination."

"Do you think the Colonel will let Angel come back as Captain?"

"I hope so, I really hope so."

"Don't you enjoy being captain?"

Alexander laughed, "I hate it. I absolutely hate it."

12

'THINGS GO BUMP IN THE NIGHT'

Sophie Day leant against a tree. Her purple eyes wondered around the dark shadow covered courtyard as her wings softly fluttered against the night wind. Sophie zipped up her jacket as the coldness of the night hit her.

"Let's get this over with," Danny muttered as he walked over to her.

The pair began to walk towards the forest. For patrol, they would have to go through the forest and then walk around the border of the base.

"Okay I'm bored," Danny muttered, "I know you can talk so start."

"I don't want to talk to you," Sophie whispered.

"Why did you lie?"

"I don't know what you're talking about."

Danny grabbed Sophie's arm, pulling her around so that she was forced to face him.

"I know you lied about how you killed that vampire in Rio," he growled, "How did you do it? It's a simple question, so why are you lying about it?"

"You can hardly talk to me about lying. What about you?"

"What…?"

"I know who you are."

"No, you don't."

"Are you sure about that demon boy?"

"Shut it," Danny dropped Sophie and began to walk away.

"You complain about me keeping things hidden yet you're lying about something much more important!"

"I said shut it!"

"You're terrified, aren't you?"

"That's enough." Danny grabbed Sophie's neck and slammed her body into a tree. His grip was painfully tight, if he pushed any harder Sophie's neck would snap in half like a toothpick.

"Get off!" Sophie struggled.

"What are you hiding? And how do you know about…me?" Danny hissed.

"I'll tell my secret when you admit yours."

"Don't make me hurt you."

"When did you get so interested in my life anyway?"

"Well your life is *very* interesting princess," from behind them a cold voice called. Danny dropped Sophie and quickly span around, pulling out his gun as he did so. Sophie grabbed her bow and pulled an arrow out of her quiver as the pair came face-to-face with Mr Jet.

"How did you get here?" Danny asked.

Mr Jet smiled, "I was invited."

"By who?"

"Really Danny, do you think I'm going to answer that?"

"How do you know my name?"

Mr Jet just smiled then turned to Sophie, "Now I believe we have something to discuss, don't we princess?"

"How…?" Sophie stuttered.

"You should have been more careful. That vampire you left in Rio. You should have disposed of the body better. I was quite surprised. Who would have thought it, a fairy girl with the unseelie king's…?"

Before he could finish, Sophie released her arrow, it hit Mr Jet in the shoulder. The vampire winced as the garlic juice sank into his skin.

Mr Jet looked up and smiled, "Take her."

Suddenly Sophie and Danny were surrounded. Out of the darkness of the forest appeared figures, dressed in black cloaks that covered their faces. They pulled out swords that shined in the moonlight.

"Now might be a good time for an illusion," Sophie muttered to Danny.

Danny nodded, his body began to glow and suddenly where there once was one now stood twenty versions of Danny. It was impossible, even for Sophie, to tell the real one from the illusions. The illusions fought against the hooded figures, fading out of existence the moment they were attacked.

Whilst his illusions were hard at work, the real Danny was fighting a vampire. The vampire was quick, disarming Danny in a matter of seconds. It then grabbed Danny by his shirt and threw him into a tree. Danny pulled himself up, picking up his fallen gun as he did so. Danny shot at the vampire, but the undead creature avoided each bullet with great speed. The vampire jumped onto Danny's back, causing the pair to roll across the ground. Blood began to pour from Danny's nose as the vampire's fist beat against his face. Before the undead creature could cause any serious damage, it was hit by a purple lightning fork. The vampire shuddered and trembled before exploding into tiny pieces. Danny looked up and saw Sophie standing close by.

After successfully defeating a witch, Sophie had been attacked by a vampire. This vampire, much like the one that attacked Danny, fought quickly and with much aggression. The fairy was forced to the ground.

The vampire pounced on top of her and pressed down

on her neck, choking her. Sophie's eyes glowed dark purple and the vampire was lifted into the air. The fairy dropped the vampire. The undead creature fell into a bush where it was impaled by branches.

At that moment the sound of a horn could be heard echoing around the forest. The hooded figures moved their heads towards the noise. There was a pause. Then the figures disappeared into the forest, taking Mr Jet with them. The twenty Danny's faded back into the one, who was badly beaten up and tired.

"What was that all about?" Danny panted.

With her fey eyes, Sophie noticed the flicker of a cloak as it headed into the night.

"Get the others."

"Sophie don't…" but it was too late for Sophie had already disappeared. Soundlessly and invisibly she made her way through the forest. Sophie could hear the trees whisper to each other and the ground under her boots groan. The sound of voices ahead interrupted the soothing song of the forest.

In front of Sophie appeared a clearing, inside which a large smokeless bonfire burned. Around the fire stood the hooded figures who had attacked Sophie only minutes before. The figures, however, were not the focus of Sophie's attention. Sophie was more interested in the huge dogs that guarded Mr Jet. Hell hounds. Creatures that were as deadly as their name suggested.

"My friends," began Mr Jet, "We are so close now. Our plan shall soon be put into motion."

The figures clapped and cheered.

"Oh and as expected, we have a guest," Mr Jet smiled, "Hello Miss Day."

Sophie's insides turned cold as two strong hooded figures grabbed her and pushed her to her knees in front of Mr Jet. The vampire grabbed her face and forced her to look into his cold dead eyes.

"Did you really think I wouldn't smell you?"

"What do you want from me?" Sophie asked.

"That's simple, I want your powers."

"Yeah well that's not going to happen."

"Oh princess," Mr Jet leant next to her ear and whispered, "All I have to do is bite you. Your blood is all I need."

Mr Jet grabbed Sophie's hair, pulling her head backwards. He stroked her neck thoughtfully.

"Such a small little thing," he whispered, "Young and juicy."

The vampire then sank his fangs into Sophie's neck.

Sophie screamed.

* * * * *

Angel hadn't slept. She sat in the armoury, her phone in her hand. She pressed the call button again and placed the phone next to her ear. The call went straight to answer phone, so Angel left a message.

"Hi, Pops it's Angel. I've tried calling you five times, but you've not answered, obviously. Err I really need to ask you something. It's important. If you can call me back that'd be great," Angel then hung up.

"Why aren't you answering? Is there a werewolf council meeting on today? Or he could be on a run or asleep? Ah, this is annoying," Angel muttered to herself, "I should go to bed, he probably won't call back tonight. Okay, I'll go to bed after I check my weapons, why am I talking to myself!? Twenty days in lock up has broken you Angel. This is annoying, this is the Pied Piper's fault! Why am I still talking!?"

Angel unlocked her weapons locker. Her locker was filled with her guns, her bow and arrows, her wand (for when she transformed into a witch) and numerous other weapons. One weapon, however, was missing.

"Someone's stolen my sword!" Angel exclaimed, "No one touches my sword!" Angel locked her weapons locker and then headed out of the armoury. She was about to head upstairs to find Alexander, when she heard his voice coming from the kitchen. She followed the sound to find Alexander as well as Jason, who was stuffing his face with mint ice-cream.

"Hey," Jason greeted.

"Why are you up?" Angel asked.

"Well I decided to remember how I died…and I also wanted a snack."

Angel, unsure how to respond to Jason's answer, turned to Alexander and asked, "While I was in lock up did anyone take out my sword?"

"No. What's wrong?"

"Someone's stolen my sword!"

"What? Are you sure?"

Angel nodded.

"That's not…Danny?" Alexander's focus turned to the doorway as Danny ran in to the room. Danny was a mess. His face and hands were bloody, and his clothes wore a coat of mud.

"Mr Jet's in the forest. Sophie ran after him," Danny gasped. Angel opened one of the kitchen cupboards which was filled with weapons and quickly passed them to Alexander and Jason. Once armed, the three of them followed Danny out into the night.

"What happened here?" Angel exclaimed as Danny came to a stop at the spot where the figures had attacked him.

"They came to get us," he looked around trying to work out where Sophie disappeared to.

"Angel!" Alexander called as he unmasked one of the figures, "It's Joe Long of Wildfire Squad."

"That makes sense. Mr Jet claimed that he was invited here. I bet they're all from the base," Danny was cut off by a scream.

* * * * *

Mr Jet sucked the blood from Sophie's open neck. Her blood was sweet and powerful. The magic tingled on his tongue. She struggled but the vampire was stronger than she was. Sophie grew pale as her wings went limp. Mr Jet smiled as he filled a bottle with the fairy's blood. The vampire was then shot in the shoulder.

"You can either let her go," Angel aimed her gun at the vampire's forehead, "Or I can shoot you and take her from your cold dead corpse."

"Wouldn't you already be doing that," Jason pointed out.

"Good point," Angel fire two shots at the vampire. Mr Jet zoomed out of the way dropping the lifeless Sophie to the ground.

"Captain Night, I take it you got my message in Rio," Mr Jet hissed, Sophie's blood dripping from his chin. The vampire turned to Jason. His gaze was strong and made Jason want to crumble into the earth. "Jason, how nice to see you again."

"Can't say the same," Jason muttered.

"You're starting to remember things, aren't you? Yes, I can tell. You're going to get more powerful soon. You're going to need someone to guide you…"

"That's enough! Now you have a choice; surrender, or die," threatened Angel. The cloaked circle laughed.

"You do realise you're outnumbered," Mr Jet laughed.

"Are we though?" Angel nodded to Danny.

Once again Danny put his illusionist powers to work. Danny illusions sprang into existence, surrounding the hooded figures and terrifying Jason.

"Correct me if I'm wrong but aren't you now the ones outnumbered?"

"A simple illusion," Mr Jet laughed, "My hell hounds will be able to sniff out the real one in an instant!"

"Hmmm, good point, Danny you and some of your illusions might want to start running."

Danny and four of his illusions ran into the forest. The hell hounds followed. A hooded figure ran at Angel. Twisting quickly Angel avoided the first attack and was able to block the second. The figure fought with a sword and was, much to Angel's annoyance, an extremely good swordsman. Angel dived out of the sword's way, as she did so she realised something.

"That's my sword!" Angel exclaimed, "No one touches my sword!"

Angel clicked her fingers; her magic sent her stolen sword clattering to the ground. Just as Angel was about to be reunited with her beloved weapon, the hooded figure rugby tackled her to the ground and then succeeded to punch her in the face. Angel yelled out in anger causing the figure to be thrown into a tree. The figure pulled out a gun and fired it five times. Angel dodged four of the bullets but the fifth made its home in her shoulder. Angel picked up her stolen sword and threw it at the figure. The sword would have stabbed the figure's stomach, had the figure not disappeared into a cloud of smoke.

"Well that's just cheating," Angel muttered as she glowed white and transformed into a vampire.

Jason was in trouble. Despite being the most powerful man on the planet, Jason lacked both the training and the hand-eye coordination to deal with this situation. Although Jason's sword fighting skills were good, his attacker's skills were better. Much better. Jason was quickly thrown off balance and shoved to the ground. The figure then, after some struggle, kicked Jason's sword away and sat on top of him. The figure went to stab Jason but was stopped by the throwing knife that landed in its forehead. The figure fell dead on top of Jason. Jason pushed the dead body off him and crawled through the mud.

"I nearly had him," Jason muttered as Angel pulled him to his feet.

"Of course you did," Angel muttered unconvinced.

As Alexander headed over to the unconscious Sophie, a ray of white light hit his chest. Alexander stumbled backwards. He then raced towards the warlock that had attacked him and, in one swift movement, broke its neck. At that moment Alexander was shot in the back. Irritated rather than hurt, the vampire pulled out his old Roman sword and attacked the hooded figure that had shot him. After three slices, the figure fell to the ground dead.

"I'm impressed," Mr Jet held the limp Sophie against his chest.

"Let her go," Alexander ordered.

Mr Jet, his eyes red with blood lust, muttered, "Her blood gives me power. I'm not just going to let you walk away with that."

Angel ran and jumped on top of Mr Jet, pushing him to the floor. The vampire had been so engrossed in his blood lust that he hadn't noticed the shapeshifter sneaking up on him. The pair exchanged blows before Mr Jet twisted out of Angel's grasp. The vampire grabbed Angel's fist, as she went to punch him, and slammed her against the ground. While Mr Jet was distracted Alexander rushed over to Sophie and moved her out of harm's way.

As Mr Jet got to his feet, Jason decided that it was time he helped. The slight issue was that Jason had absolutely no idea what to do. His eyes darted around the clearing, looking for inspiration. That's when Jason noticed the bonfire. Jason smiled as he placed his hands into the fire. Rather than burning his skin to ash, the flames danced on Jason's fingertips. Jason threw the fire at Mr Jet. The flames twisted and ripped at the vampire's skin. Jason, who had no idea what he was doing, somehow managed to make the fire grow and spread all over the vampire's body. Mr Jet then quickly disappeared into a cloud of smoke, taking his hooded followers with him.

"Danny," Angel muttered.

"Yes," the illusions said in unison.

"Not you guys, the actual Danny," Angel transformed into a wolf and raced into the forest.

Angel could smell Danny's scent. She could also smell the Hell hounds. Wolf Angel followed Danny's scent until she came to the lake. Angel transformed into a healer as she caught sight of Danny who was covered in blood.

"Danny!" Angel tried to shake him awake, "Wake up! Danny! Wake up!"

"No need to shout," Danny muttered.

"You little…" Angel cursed as she pressed her hands against Danny's chest and sent a healing spell across his body. Once the spell was finished Danny pulled himself into a sitting position.

"You look a mess."

"So do you."

"Do you still need the illusions?"

"No."

"Good as I can't keep them going any longer," Danny sighed, and the illusions faded, "Six died…I thought so…That's going to hurt in the morning."

"What happened to the hell hounds?" asked Angel.

"I'm not sure. My illusions and I just kept running, trying to confuse them. Those damn hounds didn't fall for it though, they knew which was the real me. I outran them for a while, then they caught me and…err…we fought it out a bit…then they disappeared."

"You fought against two hell hounds and you're still alive? That's not possible."

"Well when I say 'fought' I mean they totally used me as a chew-toy. What happened to Mr Jet? Sophie?"

"Sophie is alive, and Mr Jet has vanished."

"So have his supporters I take it?"

"Apart from the dead ones."

"I bet the dead ones are all from this base."

"I guessed we had a leak, Rio made that obvious, but I didn't expect this," Angel muttered, "The base is filled with terrorists."

13

THE CAPTAINS' MEETING

"Carrying corpses is really hard work!" Jason panted.

After dragging the bodies of Mr Jet's fallen followers into a small private room in the hospital wing, Jason finally had a chance to sit down.

"I'm exhausted," he sighed as he flopped onto an empty hospital bed.

"I can't believe you're the most powerful guy in the world," Angel muttered as she stared at Jason in wonder.

"What? What did I do?" Before Angel could answer Jackson crashed into the room. He raced over to his sister.

"Are you okay?" he asked as his eyes scanned Angel's body.

"I'm fine. A bit bruised but other than that I'm fine. Did Alexander explain the situation?"

"He did. I can't believe it. Mr Jet's followers at the base."

"And not just one or two, there were at least twenty of them."

"This is a disaster!"

"It makes sense though. Rio. It all makes sense now."

"I think I've missed something."

"In Rio, Mr Jet left a message, he knew we were coming."

"All the missions have been compromised," Jackson scratched his head and mumbled, "We have a leak."

"A bit more than a leak," Alexander muttered as he entered the room.

"The base is filled with terrorists," Angel sighed.

"Angel," called Rowan Night, Jackson's ginger-haired mermaid wife (who was also a healer at the base), from behind the curtained bed that hid Sophie. Angel walked behind the curtain. Skyjack was on one side of the bed, his horn glowed as it was gently pressed against the fairy's heart.

"It's not looking good," Rowan muttered, "She's lost a lot of blood, but I can't replace it."

"Why not?"

"I think she lied on her report. Look at this," Rowan passed Angel a clipboard. Angel flicked through the results before handing the clipboard back, "Her blood type doesn't match anything."

"Will she make it?"

"The thing is we have no idea how quick her body will heal."

"Skyjack?"

"She's right," Skyjack agreed, "I've calmed her as much as I can, but there's not much else we can do for her."

"Damn it! Okay, do whatever you can. What about Danny?"

"He's fine. Actually he's looking extremely well to say less than an hour ago he was fighting a hell hound. Most people would have died."

"Danny's stronger than most people."

"That he is. I imagine that he'll be back to his usual self in a day or two."

"Alright, keep me up to date," Angel then turned to

Rowan, "Oh, and it's lovely to see you again. Though this isn't exactly how I was expecting to welcome my sister-in-law into the family."

Rowan smiled, patted Angel's shoulder affectionately, then returned to her patients. Angel re-joined the others on the other side of the curtain.

"What's wrong?" asked Jackson.

"Sophie's condition isn't good," Angel paused, "We've got to keep this quiet. If we make a big fuss, we'll never work out what Mr Jet's plan is. We need to be careful with how we play this, does the Colonel know?"

"Not yet. He wasn't in his office. I've told Alpha to patrol around the base. I've told them nothing of this, I just said that there have been some disturbances by the border."

"Seems we can do nothing more tonight. There's enough beds here, we should just try and get some rest," Alexander suggested.

"Good plan," Angel agreed, "Jackson, me and you will go to see the Colonel in the morning."

* * * * *

"This is a nightmare," the Colonel exclaimed as he sank into his chair, "We have no idea how many of these terrorists there are."

He was sat in the conference room; a circle turret on the main building of the base. The Colonel and all eight of the captains were seated around a large circular table. To the Colonel's right was the Captain of Thunder Squad. William Hardwick was a ginger-haired English vampire who had been stuck in the body of a seventeen-year-old since the nineteen-sixties. Next to him was Lu Jin the Chinese Captain of Wildfire Squad, he was a telepath. To his right sat Jonathan Phillip, the Captain of Tsunami Squad, who was a brilliant warlock from Jamaica. He was next to the blonde-haired American elemental Axel Freeman, Captain of Tornado Squad. Ambroise Deniel, the Captain of Volcano Squad, sat next to him. Ambroise was a skinny black banshee from France. After him was the Japanese Captain of Avalanche Squad, Kato Hiroshi, a kitsune (a nine-tailed fox) who was currently in his human form. Angel was sat next to him with Jackson sat in-between her and the Colonel.

"What I want to know is why?" Captain Ambroise Deniel asked, "Why last night? What was the purpose of it?"

"To cause panic," Captain Lu Jin suggested, "Now we know, we realise we can't trust anyone, and this fear starts growing into paranoia."

"That must not happen," the Colonel snapped firmly.

"What about missions?" Captain Kato Hiroshi lent back in his chair, "In Rio, Jet just left Angel a message, what if next time he leaves a bomb?"

"What are we doing about the bodies?" Captain William Hardwick asked.

"That's something we're debating," Jackson explained, "We could play it two ways. We could either announce that they were followers of Mr Jet or we get rid of them quietly. Personally I feel that the second option is our best move. The last thing we need is panic."

"Who are the dead?" Captain Jonathan Phillip asked. Jackson lent forward and pressed the computer touch screen that was situated in the middle of the table. After a few moments of fiddling he pulled up the personnel files of ten people. Four were from Tornado Squad, two from Wildfire, two from Volcano, one from Thunder and one from Avalanche.

"There's also one in a coma in the hospital wing," Jackson pulled up another photo of a woman from Tsunamis squad.

"It would have been better if you'd told your squad not to kill first and ask questions later," Captain Axel Freeman snapped at Angel, "If you had, we'd be able to interrogate them rather than bury them."

"I'll remember that next time I'm being shot at," she retorted.

"How did she get in a coma?" asked Jonathan.

"She couldn't handle Sophie Day's magic."

"Why did he bite her?" Ambroise wondered aloud, "Vampires don't tend to drink fey blood."

"He has a point," William agreed, "It is highly unusual for a vampire to drink fey blood. Angel maybe you could look into this. There may be something about Day's blood that has attracted the attention of Mr Jet."

"Is anyone else confused over what Jet's plans are?" Hiroshi asked.

"I think that's the point," Angel muttered, "Nothing links. Rio, London, Tokyo, Germany. All the places he's been spotted recently, the events that have happened there, they don't link. I think he's just playing with us."

"Perhaps," the Colonel continued, "Tell your squads that these traitors have been sent on a training mission in Romania. In a few weeks we'll announce that there was an accident and they were killed. This way we won't have to deal with a panic. Is there any chance of the coma patient waking up?"

"It seems unlikely," Jackson explained, "Even if she does her brain could be so messed up…"

"Okay, ask Skyjack to prepare a mind take. We may get some answers that way. Make sure it finishes her off."

"Yes sir."

"Sir, what about the missions? All future missions are at risk and our current undercovers are in serious danger," Hiroshi pointed out.

"How many undercovers do we have in operation?" asked the Colonel.

"Three. All mine," Jackson said.

"Pull them out."

"Even the unseelie court mission?"

"Hmmm, keep that agent in but pull the others out."

"Yes sir."

"What about the cases and missions?" asked Angel.

"Cases, for now, you will have to handle yourselves. As for missions, don't reveal any mission details until you've arrived at the mission location. If there's a leak, you hold any of the returning members under lock down," the Colonel got to his feet, "I think we can call this meeting to a close. I'm going to meet with the Emperor to let him know of our situation. You are dismissed!"

With that the Colonel left.

"Well this is a fine mess you've got us into," Axel spat at Angel.

"I hardly asked them to be terrorists," she snapped.

"No but it would be on *your* patrol, wouldn't it?"

"What's that meant to mean?"

"It means that everything always goes wrong when you're involved! The Colonel should have never promoted a girl to captain…"

"Are you trying to start something?" Angel's hand went to her sword.

"That's enough both of you," Jackson snapped.

"Angel," William paused before asking, "Do you think Mr Jet came to the base purposely to get Sophie's blood?"

"I don't know," Angel muttered, "It's a possibility. Jack, do you really think it's safe to leave Mia in the fairy realm?"

"Safe? Definitely not, but we can't lose that assignment."

* * * * *

Angel and Jackson left the conference room and headed to the hospital wing. Alexander was sat on a chair, leant against the wall, his eyes closed, whilst Danny slept in a hospital bed. Sophie's bed was still curtained off from the rest of the room.

"How did it go?" Alexander asked, eyes still closed, as Angel and Jackson entered the room.

"How do you think?" Angel muttered before taking a seat next to him.

The vampire opened his eyes, "That bad huh?"

"No, it wasn't that bad," Jackson explained, "The Colonel is having a meeting with the Emperor…"

"The Emperor?"

"This situation could put the empire in danger."

"I thought I heard you come in," Rowan smiled as she joined the trio.

"How's Sophie?" Angel asked.

"It's strange. She is healing with incredible speed. Whatever blood she has certainly makes her stronger than the rest of us," Rowan then turned to her husband, her smile faded slightly as she saw his face, "Jack what's wrong?"

Jackson sighed, "How's the coma patient?"

"Very little change, why?"

"I need you to do a mind take."

"Are you serious?" Skyjack exclaimed as he trotted over to them.

"What's a mind take?" Rowan asked.

"It's exactly what it sounds like. Using magic you completely wipe a person's mind. You remove all their memories, their feelings, everything that makes them a person."

"But that could kill her! We can't kill a patient!"

"I don't think we'll have to," Skyjack looked at Jackson who nodded.

"I feel like I've missed something here." There was an awkward silence.

"If she lives through it, Jackson has been ordered to finish her off," Angel said bluntly, everyone stared at her, "What? Someone had to say it."

"Neptune's beard," Rowan cursed under her breath.

"Look we have little choice here," Jackson sighed, "We need to get the whole situation covered up as quickly as possible."

"And you're okay with this?"

"No I'm not okay with it but an order is an order. So

can you please just get the equipment ready."

Skyjack turned to Alexander and Angel, "You two leave. Alex, make sure Angel rests."

Before Angel could respond, Alexander had shoved her out of the door.

Once the pair had left, Skyjack headed into a cupboard. Using magic, Skyjack lifted an odd-looking device into the air and gently placed it on the table next to the coma patient's bed. The device looked like a crystal ball only it had two long wires attached. At the end of the wires were two sharp needles. By magic, the wires rose into the air and the needles stabbed into either side of the comatose girl's head. Skyjack placed his horn on the girl's forehead. It glowed and a ripple of pink floated along the girl's body. At the same time, different coloured waves floated up into the crystal ball. Rowan watched the monitor as the girl's heart rate began to drop. There was a long-held beep as her heart stopped all together.

"I think it's done," Skyjack nodded to the crystal ball. The wires removed themselves from the girl's head. Rowan picked up the crystal ball and handed it to Jackson.

"I hope the Colonel gets what he wants," she muttered, "What does he want done with the body?"

"Does she have any family?"

"You're worried about that now!"

"Rowan," Jackson said in a low tone.

"No she doesn't."

"Then…"

"I'll have her cremated with the others tomorrow."

14

'SALTY!'

"Today's going to be a long day," Angel sighed as she and Alexander walked back to the Lightning Squad house.

"It's going to be difficult," Alexander agreed, "To keep this from the rest of the squad."

"As long as we keep Jason away from the telepaths, we should be fine. Do you think one of them is a terrorist?"

"I think, it's highly likely that one of them might be. There's one other thing, you better prepare for questions about the Pied Piper."

"I'd forgotten about that!"

"Shall we go in the back way?" Alexander asked, "You're less likely to bump into anyone."

"Also it means we'll enter through the kitchen and I'm starving!"

"What do you fancy eating?"

"Food."

"I guessed that," Alexander laughed, "What kind of food?"

"The edible kind," Angel smiled as she unlocked the backdoor into the Lightning Squad house. The kitchen was a large clean silver room that was filled with ovens, vegetable-covered worktops, fiery frying-pans, and ghosts. The eleven ghosts, who had been hard at work preparing Lightning Squad's next meal, looked up as Alexander and Angel entered.

"Angel, you're back," smiled a beautiful female ghost wearing a hijab.

"Sara! Have the squad been behaving while I've been away?" Angel asked sitting down at the table.

"For the most part yes. Sue and Clover made a complaint about one of the meals..."

"How dare they complain about my food!" exclaimed a rather large French ghost, "There's nothing wrong with my food. I used to be a professional chef you know!"

"As you can see, Jacob wasn't too impressed."

"They said it tasted salty! Salty! How could it taste salty? Rude! Just because they're alive they think they can complain about my cooking!" Jacob cried.

"He's been like this for five days," Sara whispered to Angel.

"Jacob," Angel interrupted the ghost's rant, "I'll speak to Sue and Clover and get them to apologize."

"Apologize, yes they should apologize! Those girls wouldn't know good cooking if it slapped them in the face..."

"That's enough Jacob!" Sara snapped at him then turned back to Angel, "What can I get you dear?"

"I can cook something for myself, you look like you've got enough work to do." As Angel got up, Alexander pushed her back down.

"Sit down," Alexander ordered, "I'll cook."

"You can cook!?" Angel and Sara asked in unison.

"Why is that such a surprise?"

"Because you're a vampire. You don't exactly need to

eat," Angel explained.

"Doesn't mean I can't cook," and with that the vampire started cooking.

"If it tastes awful," Sara whispered to Angel, "I'll find you some leftovers."

"I heard that!"

"I don't know how you managed in lock up," Sara began as she chopped vegetables "Given how much you and your brothers eat."

"We don't eat that much." To that all the ghosts and Alexander laughed.

"Those werewolf boys eat ten meals a day!"

"That's a bit exaggerated."

"Hardly. These last twenty days they've eaten double that! Your brothers always eat more when they're upset."

"Jackson used to be the same," Jacob reminisced, "When he was in this squad, he'd eat everything…I used to find him in the kitchen in the early hours of the morning stuffing his face."

"You eat just as much as your brothers do."

"I don't, do I?" Angel asked sheepishly.

"You do and you don't even have the excuse of being a werewolf."

"I like food!" At that moment Angel's phone started ringing.

"Oh it's Pops. I've got to take this, come get me when the food is ready," Angel got off her seat and headed to the hallway. When she was alone in the operations room, Angel answered her phone, "Pops."

David Night answered, "Sorry I couldn't answer your calls, I was at a werewolf council meeting with Tobias. What's wrong?"

"Well, it's a bit, I don't even know where to start. Did Roger or Ethan tell you that I, err well, I…"

"That you killed the Pied Piper and were locked up. Yes, the boys told me about it. I had to talk them out of breaking you out of there."

"Did you? Ah, they were more upset by it then they let on."

"Of course they were, what happened?"

"What happened, well, that's a bit complicated," Angel collapsed onto a chair and told her father everything. Her thoughts came out at a rapid speed. Tears ran down Angel's face as she recounted the memory once again. The emotions she had bottled-up spilt into every word. Her father didn't speak. He remained silent as Angel explained every detail.

"Pops, is it true? The Piper's memory, is it true?"

"Well," David sighed, "Yes. I think it is. Obviously, what happened before me and Tobias arrived, I can't vouch for, however the rest is accurate."

"Right, so I really did stab myself."

"Angel stay calm. Remember this is all in the past."

"Pops that doesn't really help! Sorry. What happened next? What happened after the Piper left?"

"Well, me and the pack fought against that witch woman. She was strong but she didn't fight for very long. She could have done and given her powers she could have won. But she didn't, she just disappeared. I don't know why."

"And the man?"

"He…he…disappeared as well."

"You knew him, who was he?"

"I think Angel, it might be best for us to talk about this in person. Can you come home?"

"Err, not at the moment, there's kind of, I'm not sure I can."

"Angel is something going on?"

"No! I'm just, because of the Piper incident, I'm not allowed to leave the base."

"Ah, I see. Perhaps it'd be better for me to come to you. I have a meeting in Transylvania in a few days' time,

I'll come see you then. When we meet, I'll…"

"Angel, food's ready," Alexander shouted from the hallway.

"Who was that?" David asked.

"My vice-captain, Alex, I'll introduce him to you when you come visit."

"I see. I'll let you go. I don't want to get in-between you and food."

"Okay, I'll see you soon. Love you. Bye," and with that David hung up. Angel put her phone in her pocket and quickly wiped the tears from her face. She took a deep breath and went back into the kitchen, a smile painted on her lips. She sat down as Alexander placed a bowl of pasta before her.

"Trust the Italian to cook pasta," Angel joked.

"I'm not Italian. I'm a Roman."

"Rome is in Italy."

"Rome came before Italy."

"Whatever," Angel took a mouthful of pasta, "Oh, this is good!"

"Why do you sound so surprised? I told you I could cook."

"Hmmm, not bad," Sara muttered examining the pasta. Alexander smiled and sat down opposite Angel. He grabbed a napkin and gently stroked it against her cheek. She looked up in surprise.

"Your eyes were watering," Alexander explained, "Must have been the steam."

Angel nodded, she sniffed back any remaining tears and focused her attention on her food. She didn't mind crying in front of Alexander, it was the gossiping ghosts that bothered her. As Angel ate, she could feel the vampire's eyes scanning her. She looked up as he mouthed *'are you okay?'* Angel smiled and nodded before returning to her food.

"Pops is coming to the base soon," Angel then

whispered after a moment of silence, "After that, I'll explain things."

Alexander didn't get chance to reply as at that moment Fern crashed into the kitchen and hugged Angel's back. The witch grinned as she crushed her captain against her.

"Angel! You're alive!" Fern exclaimed.

"Get off," Angel pushed Fern off with a smile, "Anyone would think you've missed me?"

"I have. Well mainly I've missed how laid back you are compared to Alex when it comes to training."

"And here was I thinking you missed my sparkling personality."

"Sure, let's go with that," Fern joked.

"What's wrong with my training?" asked Alexander.

"Everything, grandpa, everything!"

"Stop calling me grandpa!"

"He made us get up at 5am and go for a run…a run! You know how I feel about running!" Fern exclaimed, collapsing into a chair.

"You hate running," Angel said.

"Exactly! Then we had to do hand-to-hand combat training, then train at the shooting range, then run back to the house to have breakfast. He made us do exercise before breakfast!"

"It's good training," Alexander muttered.

"No, it isn't! It's cruelty to Fern's that's what it is! You're lucky I didn't turn you into a frog!"

"You should have turned him into a frog. That would have been hilarious!" Angel laughed.

"Don't encourage her," Alexander hissed.

"Why? You'd make a cute frog."

"Anyway, how are you Angel? You're back properly, right?" Fern asked.

"I'm fine and yes, I'm back properly," Angel answered.

"Good! Perhaps now I can get some sleep."

"Sleep?"

"Roger's room is above mine and while you've been in lock up, he's been pacing back and forth instead of sleeping. And it's not like he paces quietly! I tried using magic, but that werewolf is still so noisy!"

"I'll tell him to stop."

"Good. Oh! That reminds me..." Fern continued to talk as Angel ate. While Angel admittedly was only half listening to Fern's rant, she was glad of the distraction. For Angel's mind was racing. The memory the Piper had shown her, and Mr Jet's attack echoed around her head. She didn't know what to do. She didn't know how to keep her squad safe. They had gotten lucky in Rio. Mr Jet could have easily left a bomb or, worse, a zombie instead of a message. It was her job, as captain, to keep her squad safe but how was she supposed to do that when the danger was amongst them. Angel had never felt the pressure of being captain as strongly as she did in that moment. Fern's rant was interrupted by the sound of Angel's phone ringing.

"Hello?" Angel answered, "Jin. What's...I'll be right there."

"What's up?" Fern asked when Angel hung up.

"Just a captain thing. I'll see you guys later."

As Angel sprinted out of the door, she heard Fern exclaim, "What's up with her!? Angel doesn't run...not unless free food is involved!"

* * * * *

Sadly Angel wasn't running for free food. Instead she ran over to Hiroshi, Jonathan and Jin who had been waiting for her by the base's border. The border was on the other side of the forest. It was a small field of green on which two white security buildings stood. The buildings were empty, and the grass was dry and brown. The area, which usually gave off a friendly welcoming vibe, felt cold and deserted. Angel stared at the large dome forcefield that covered the base. Interrupting its glittering waves of purple and blue was a large black crack.

"So this is how Jet entered. What exactly is it?" Angel asked.

"That's the question," Hiroshi sighed, "We don't actually know. The border isn't cracked. We've checked, we tried throwing something at it and it just bounces back."

"If that isn't a crack then what is it?"

"Our best guess is that it's a portal. A portal that has been attached to the border."

"If it's a portal, then why aren't we overrun with demons?"

"I don't think it's that strong. It's perhaps strong enough for one or two journeys but not much more," Jonathan explained, "The magical energy this thing is giving off, it's dark but not powerful."

"Do the other Captains know about this?"

"Ambroise is at prayer so William has gone to the mosque to get him. Jackson is telling the Colonel. And we all hate Axel, so we haven't told him yet," Hiroshi explained.

"Fair enough," Angel muttered, "We're going to have to guard this."

"Speaking of guard, over here," Jin led them away from the crack to where a coat was covering something on the floor. Angel knelt and pulled back the coat.

"Joseph."

Under the coat was the body of one of the centaur guards (the one who had waved to Jason on his first day) that oversaw the base's border. His face was covered in blood. His horse legs were broken, his human upper body bruised, and his tail had been ripped off. His cold dead blue eyes stared up at Angel, who was trying to decipher the demonic symbols that were painted around the centaur's body.

"It looks like it was a team effort," Jin sighed, "At first

we thought that he'd been killed by a hell hound, but it seems it was actually a group attack. If you look at the ground, you'll see they used Joseph's blood to paint those symbols."

"They killed Joseph together," Angel hissed bitterly, "As some kind of ritual?"

"That's what it looks like."

"The symbols aren't a spell," Jonathan explained, "I've checked. There more of a…I suppose you could call it a warmup."

"A warmup!?"

"To prepare for battle."

Angel swore under her breath, "We need to up the security. Ask the dragons to guard this border. We'll get the sea beings to guard the docks and have the Griffins and Phoenixes watch from above."

"Good plan," Hiroshi agreed, "Make sure they're paired up as well."

"What do we do about Joseph?" Jonathan gestured to the centaur.

"Once the Colonel has seen and cleared this, we give him a proper funeral," Angel sighed, "Even if we have to keep it quiet, we give him the send-off he deserves."

"This border," Hiroshi muttered, "It's the entrance all new recruits take. I remember when I arrived meeting Joseph at the gate on the other side."

"It's also the only entrance that leads into the forest. Mr Jet must have known he wouldn't be spotted if he entered here."

"Why do they make the new recruits enter here? This entrance is so unprotected. Why don't they enter near the main gate?"

"It's because this entrance has the best view of the base," Jonathan explained.

"Really?"

"Yes, it was designed so that the new recruits see the

base's 'best side'. If they entered at the main gate, one of the first things they'd see would be the entrance to the cells, which might put them off signing up."

"Ah, so they enter here so they think the base is cool."

"What they don't know," Angel muttered, "Is that it's actually filled with demon worshipers."

15

'SECRETS'

Hell hounds.

Large dog shaped creatures that live to serve the devil.

The hell hounds were hunting a fairy. She was quick, but they were quicker. They caught her easily. They pounced onto her back and knocked her to the floor. She rolled over and shot at one of the hell hounds. Although a deadly beast from the deepest pits of hell was crushing her, the fairy's aim was surprisingly accurate. The bullet made its home in the hell hound's forehead. This, however, didn't kill it, for they couldn't be killed by anyone but the Master.

The hell hounds' bit into the fairy's skin.

The fairy screamed.

* * * * *

Sophie sat up suddenly. Her forehead dripped with sweat and her vision was blurry.

"Sophie can you hear me?"

"Yes," Sophie muttered, as her eyes refocused, she found that Skyjack was stood in front of her.

"You've been unconscious for almost a day," Skyjack

147

explained, "Are you okay? I could hear you screaming."

"I was screaming?"

"Yes. Sophie are you okay?"

"I need to get some fresh air," Sophie felt quite faint. She went to get off the bed but the pegacorn stopped her.

"Not without a full examination."

"Please I'll only be a few minutes."

"No."

"Please Skyjack!"

"Oh, I'm such a softy. Okay, but only for a few minutes."

Sophie was quick to leave the hospital wing. The sky was pink as the sun had not yet set. Sophie walked over to the grassy grove that stood between the hospital wing and the surrounding buildings. The fairy lent against a tree taking in the cold crisp evening air.

"Not dead then," Danny got up from his spot behind the fairy. Danny had recovered from his injuries earlier that afternoon and had been dozing in the shade, before Sophie's appearance had interrupted him.

"Clearly."

"You okay?"

"Don't pretend to care, demon-boy, it doesn't suit you."

Danny's face turned colder than usual. "How do you know that?"

"You told me. I read your mind. That's how I found out that you're half-demon."

"I have a barrier against mental attacks."

"Doesn't matter, unlike others I can still get through."

"How long have you known?"

"Since the day we met."

"Who else knows?"

"Well I've told no one, but that doesn't mean others don't know. Angel doesn't know yet. That's what you were worried about right?"

Danny cursed under his breath then, after a long pause, he hissed, "Well since you know my secret, you can tell me yours. Why did Mr Jet call you princess?"

"I have to go," Sophie muttered, she quickly tried to leave but Danny grabbed her arm.

"I don't think so. Start talking."

"I really have to go I promised Skyjack..."

"Stop making excuses and start talking. What's wrong, don't you trust me?"

"Is that a trick question!?"

"See I don't trust you either. Yet I'm currently stuck...no I'm not. I can just kill you. I can just kill you then I won't have anything to worry about."

"You wouldn't."

"If you believe that then you really don't know me at all," Danny pulled a dagger from his belt and pushed it against Sophie's neck.

"Angel won't forgive you if you do."

"I'll just tell her that you were killed by one of Mr Jet's followers."

"Do you think she'll believe that?"

"Why do you think I care what she believes?"

"Because I've been in your head. Angel is the only person whose opinion matters to you. She's the only person you care about."

"You know I preferred it when you were a mute," Danny dropped Sophie to the ground and hissed, "If you don't want me to kill you, start talking."

Sophie stared at Danny. Although he had threatened to kill her, Sophie knew he wouldn't do it. Angel would never forgive him if he did, and that was something Danny wouldn't risk. Sophie didn't have to tell him, yet she wanted to. For over two decades she had carried this secret with her, never daring to speak it aloud. But she had wanted to. She had desperately wanted to tell everyone. To get rid of the heavy burden that rested on her shoulders.

Now she had the perfect opportunity. For while Sophie hated Danny, she knew full well that he'd never breathe a word of her story, not when his own secret was in jeopardy.

Sophie contemplated her situation for a moment more before she began, "Where to start?"

"The beginning would be nice."

"The beginning? Well I suppose the best place to start would be to tell you that I wasn't born, I was created."

"Created? How?"

"What's the easiest way I can explain this? Right, you know how two negatives always equal a positive in maths. Well it's the same in magic. And that's how I was created, two deaths spells hit each other exactly."

"And the equal opposite to death is life. Okay, but this still doesn't explain why Mr Jet called you princess."

"It does if you think about it. Which two fairies hate each other enough to try and kill each other?"

"Well there could be loads."

"That are royal?"

There was a moment of silence as Danny realised, "You're the daughter of the Seelie queen and the unseelie king!"

"Don't say that so loud," Sophie hushed.

"Wow, you're really not what you seem."

"Look who's talking, demon-boy."

"Don't call me that! Why are you here anyway? Shouldn't you be in a palace somewhere?"

"So technically speaking, a child born of both Unseelie and Seelie blood could unite the fey courts however..."

"The courts don't want to lose power."

"Exactly."

"But why did they leave you alive? Wouldn't it be easier for them if they got rid of you?"

"They did or they thought they did," Sophie muttered. She watched the sky as a phoenix flew above their heads.

"They think you're dead, don't they?"

"At first the courts were interested in me. Interested in the powers I possess. Each side wanted to use me as a weapon. But then they realised that I have a mix of both their powers and that if I wanted to, I could take over."

"So they decided that it'd be better for both of them if you died."

"Exactly. To be honest I'm not sure how I survived. The courts were about to execute me when there was a flash of white light and I ended up in Portugal."

"Portugal?"

"Yeah."

"A fey princess, no wonder Mr Jet came to the base. Tell Angel who you are. Mr Jet came here because of you. He knows who you are which means he's going to keep coming after you. You're currently putting us all in danger!"

"I'll tell Angel when you do."

Danny hissed, "My secret isn't putting anyone in danger!"

"Really!? We have a demon in our squad. What happens if one day you decide that one of us looks like a tasty snack?"

"Jason is also..."

"Jason is the Master of Darkness, you're just a demon."

"Maybe I should just kill you."

"I would like to see you try."

"Just how powerful are you?"

"I'm more powerful than you can imagine."

"Prove it," Danny smiled, "Take your best shot."

"You're kidding, right?"

"Scared to show what you can do?"

Sophie smiled slightly and her eyes glowed dark purple. A lightning bolt hit Danny's chest. His chest began to glow, and a ripple of pain spread down his body. He winced but remained strong.

"Not bad," Sophie walked around him, "Most people are screaming by this point."

"I'm not most people."

"Indeed," Sophie clicked her fingers again. The pain intensified. Danny stumbled to his knees. Sophie clicked her fingers again and the lightning bolt returned to her. She knelt beside Danny.

"Not bad," Sophie whispered, "But that was just a warmup."

"Warmup? Ah!" Danny rolled over clutching his head as he felt his body burn from the inside outwards.

"It's normally the aftereffects that kill people rather than the actual process," Sophie clicked her fingers once more and the pain stopped. For a while Danny just lay on the ground, trying to catch his breath. Once his body calmed, he sat himself up.

"You are definitely more powerful than I had expected, you alright princess?" Danny asked as Sophie dropped to the ground.

"I shouldn't have done that. I haven't been examined yet," Sophie gasped.

"If you haven't been examined, then why are you out of the hospital wing?"

"I just needed some air. I had a dream. It was of a fairy getting killed by hell hounds.

"Your head sounds like a lovely place."

"But it was me. I was the fairy…and I don't think it was a dream."

"Can you see the future?"

"I don't know!"

"Well surely you would know if you could see the future or not."

"There isn't exactly a guide to being the daughter of the two most powerful fairies in existence! I have no idea what I can do. Paris?"

"Evening," Paris greeted the pair as he walked over to

them, "I've just been told to bring Sophie back to the hospital wing."

"Sure," Sophie got to her feet.

Danny watched as Sophie and Paris turned a corner. Then it hit him. How did Paris know that Sophie was in the hospital wing? Everyone had been told that she was on an assignment in Russia. Danny got to his feet and ran after them.

"Sophie get away from him," Danny ordered.

"Dude, what's your problem?" Paris asked.

"You are. Sophie get away from him."

"What's wrong with you Park? Do I need to turn you to stone? Sophie needs to get back to the hospital wing."

"How did you know that she was in the hospital wing? You were told she was in Russia."

"I've just seen Rowan..."

"Rowan is with the Colonel."

"Well done," Paris clapped, he took off his sunglasses. Danny and Sophie turned their eyes away. One look and they would be turned to stone. Paris grabbed Danny from behind and dragged him to the ground. Danny struggled against him, keeping his eyes firmly shut.

"If you have a plan princess, I think you should get on with it," Danny shouted as Paris began to repeatedly punch his face. Sophie opened her eyes, raced forwards, and placed her hands on either side of Paris' head. A purple glow surrounded him. Paris yelled as the magic sank deep into his soul and ripped out his most important weapon. His powers. Sophie cried out as she staggered backwards, covering her face with her hands. She stumbled to the wall and sank to the ground. Danny pushed the dazed Paris off him.

"Danny you can open your eyes," Sophie gasped.

"What did you do? What did you do to me!?" Paris yelled.

"I took away your powers."

Paris turned to Sophie; she was blind unable to open her eyes as she had no control over Paris' powers. The former gorgon grabbed her, shoved her into the wall and then punched her in the stomach. Danny stumbled to his feet. He grabbed Paris by his ginger hair and dragged him away from Sophie. Paris pulled out a knife and attempted to stab Danny. The attempt failed. Danny swiftly disarmed Paris, punching him in the face in the process. Paris stumbled backwards, blood dripping from his lips. Danny kicked Paris in the chest and threw him into a tree where he slumped to the ground, lifeless.

Danny panted, "You okay princess?"

Getting no answer he turned around to find Sophie slumped against the wall.

With an iron dagger stabbed into her stomach.

16

'A MAMMOTH SIZED PROBLEM'

JASON

I vaguely remember someone calling my name.

At least I think someone did. To be honest I wasn't listening. I was too busy trying to deal with the fact that Mr Jet had been on the base. Last night Mr Jet, the man who had murdered my mum, had been right in front of me and he had got away. I hadn't been able to stop him. In fact I hadn't really been able to do anything. I set him on fire, by accident, but during the fight I had been useless. If it hadn't been for Angel, I would be dead. That thought had plagued my dreams. I had almost died, again! During the last three weeks, I had lost my mum, come face-to-face with a terrifying vampire (twice), had turned into a demon, had carried corpses (which was really gross and awful by the way) and had suffered from more panic-attacks then I had during the eighteen years I had lived in the human world! I was not okay! My head was a mess. I wanted to scream, and shout and cry. Cry a lot! Preferably whilst stuffing my face with a tub of ice-cream.

But I couldn't do any of this. I had to act as if nothing had happened. Like there was no problem. This wasn't easy as Mr Jet being on the base wasn't just a problem, it was a huge mammoth sized problem! No it was more than that. It was a problem that was double the size of a mammoth, what's double the size of a mammoth?

"Jason?"

I looked up. Araminta and Clover were staring at me.

"Yes, no, that depends on the question," I stuttered coming back to my senses. I was sat, with Araminta and Clover, in the Lightning Squad living room. It was a cosy room with multiple chairs and sofas (in multiple colours) scattered around a large fireplace. A TV hung on one of the light pink walls whilst a large shelf unit, that was covered in tattered old books, hung on another. A battered rug lay in front of a second smaller disused fireplace that was now the home of the blue fairy spirits that danced around the lightbulbs. At first, I had been surprised by the small fey beings that seemed to live in the woodwork of the house, however Araminta later told me that these fey were friendly house fairies who loved organising and tidying-up homes. There were loads of them at the base. Practically every building had a couple.

"Are you okay?" Araminta asked, turning my attention away from the house fairies.

"Me yeah sure why wouldn't I be?"

"You've been staring at your drink for over twenty minutes."

Damn it! I had been outsmarted by a glass of water!

"I'm fine, just tired."

"You look tired, have you…?"

"He looks like he's been shoved headfirst into dragon dung," Fern exclaimed as she entered.

"No one asked your opinion," Clover muttered to her

sister.

"Maybe not but I'm going to give it anyway. What's up demon-breath?"

"The sky," I muttered sarcastically.

"Clever!" Fern mocked.

"Why are you here?" Clover hissed.

"I live here."

"I know that! I meant why are you in this room?"

"Because I want to be. Don't worry I'm not going to interrupt your flirting."

"I'm not flirting," Clover said turning pink.

"Whatever."

"Anyway," Clover turned to me, "I hear that your sword fighting has improved a lot recently."

"Err, yes I suppose so," I muttered.

"That's great, perhaps me and you could train together sometime."

"Flirting," Fern coughed.

"I was just…" Clover started but was interrupted.

"Dinner is on the table," Ethan announced as he stood at the door.

We got up and followed him into the kitchen.

"Anyone know where Sophie is?" asked Ethan as we sat.

"I haven't seen her since last night," Clover answered.

"Have you guys heard?" Sue asked as she entered with Roger and Elsa, "Angel's back as Captain."

"Really?" Clover exclaimed, "That's a surprise."

"She was let out of lock up, and now she's back as Captain!" Sue explained.

"Have you got a problem with that?" Roger asked coldly.

"No, it's just a little strange."

"Angel is strange though" Clover exclaimed, after seeing Roger's harsh stare she quickly added, "I mean her powers are strange."

"What do you mean?" I asked confused.

"Oh of course you don't know! Normally shapeshifters can only transform into animals or humans, they can't transform into other paranormal beings. However Angel can transform into a vampire and into a werewolf in human form!"

"How come Angel can transform into paranormal beings when other shapeshifters can't?"

"No one knows," Ethan answered. At that moment, Willow and Roxy entered, they were chatting about some big scandal involving lords and ladies I had never heard of before. I quickly drowned out their conversation and returned to a more important matter, what was bigger than a mammoth?

"Have any of you seen Sophie?" Ethan asked again.

"Oh, haven't you heard?" Roxy didn't wait for an answer, "She's on an assignment in Russia. Angel told me earlier."

"I wonder what's going on in Russia. It's not often people just disappear in the middle of the night," Sue muttered.

"Speaking of disappearing, where have you been?" asked Fern as Angel and Alexander arrived.

"Nothing for you to worry about," Angel muttered before sitting herself down next to me.

"Sounds interesting," Fern smiled, "So where have you been?"

"I'm sure I just said, it's nothing for you to worry about."

"Normally when you say, 'it's nothing for you to worry about' it ends in you getting either yourself or, more importantly, me shot."

"Not this time."

"So, where were you?"

"I was at a captain's meeting. There, you happy?"

"See that wasn't so difficult, was it?"

"I wish you weren't so difficult."

"Love you too cap," Fern muttered sarcastically, "Love you too!"

"Oh you're getting really good Jason!" Roxy suddenly exclaimed.

"At what?" I asked confused.

"At blocking your mind, I can't read it at all."

"You shouldn't be trying to read his mind in the first place!" Angel snapped.

"Lock up has clearly done nothing to fix your attitude."

"Has anyone seen Paris? Or Danny?" Araminta asked trying to change the subject.

"I saw Paris earlier, he said he might be a bit late," Elsa replied.

"Danny is doing a job for me," Angel explained, "He'll join us later."

While the rest of the squad were distracted with food, Angel turned to me and whispered, "I want you to switch out with Danny. He's been watching over the hospital wing all day, he could do with a break."

* * * * *

Once I had finished eating, I quickly headed to the hospital wing. I arrived to find Paris unconscious and handcuffed to a bed, whilst Rowan and Skyjack were trying to remove a dagger from Sophie's stomach. Danny was stood in the corner of the room, a grave look covering his face.

"What the hell!?" I exclaimed, "What happened?"

"Paris, he's a terrorist or traitor, whatever it is we're calling them," Danny muttered, "He just tried to kill Sophie."

"He's a...Bloody hell!"

"Exactly. Do you have your phone?"

"I...yes...why?" Danny didn't give me an answer, instead he grabbed my phone and quickly called Angel. I could hear Danny speak but I didn't take in anything that he said. Paris was a terrorist. He had tried to kill Sophie. He worked for Mr Jet. These three sentences bounced around my brain. How could this be? How could? I thought Paris was my friend but, all this time, he had been working for the man who had killed my mum.

Angel arrived moments later, and I could see Danny explaining the situation to her but, once again, I couldn't hear what they were saying. I didn't know what I was supposed to do. How was I supposed to deal with this situation? What was I supposed to feel? What was I supposed to do? Was I supposed to feel angry? Angel looked angry. She ran her hands through her hair and paced the hospital wing. She had known Paris for longer than I had, was that why she was able to get angry so quickly? I couldn't do it. I couldn't muster up any anger. I couldn't muster up anything. I wasn't upset. I didn't feel upset about Paris being a terrorist. In fact the only feeling I felt was confusion. I couldn't understand. I couldn't process this situation.

"She stole his powers!?" I heard Angel exclaim as my hearing returned.

"Yeah, I'm not sure how. We have to keep her eyes covered as she can't control his powers," Danny muttered.

"This is a mess. Is Sophie...?"

Rowan walked over to us, "She's alive. We've taken the dagger out, now we just need to wait and see. Have you informed the Colonel?"

"Alex went to tell him. Rowan make sure you give Danny a full check-up."

"I'm fine, just a couple of bruises," Danny muttered.

"Just do as I say," Angel pleaded.

"Yes Cap."

"Come with me," Rowan took Danny to one side.

"I can't believe Paris is a..." I couldn't finish my sentence. I really couldn't believe it. Paris had taught me all about this world, he had trained me, he had been my friend, but that had all been a lie.

"I should have seen this coming!"

"How…?"

"I don't know!" Angel exclaimed, "I just…I should have seen this. I've trained with him every day for the last…how could I have not seen this!"

"None of us saw this coming," Danny called from behind a curtained off bed, "So stop blaming yourself."

"I…" at that moment Alexander and the Colonel arrived. The Colonel studied the situation for a moment then turned to Angel.

"This is a disaster. I'm putting the base under lock down. No one leaves. The ghosts will patrol at night and all alarm systems will be activated," the Colonel snapped sharply, "The whole base is under house arrest."

"What do we do about Paris?" Angel asked.

"Well this is the first one we've got alive and awake; we need to get him talking."

"That won't be easy to break him. Paris is…was one of the best."

"Everyone breaks eventually. For now take Paris to the cells."

"The cells, is that a good idea? You do want him to talk, don't you? It's going to be a bit hard to get him talking if he gets eaten by a demon."

"The guards will intervene if it tries to kill him."

"Well it's hardly going to try to start salsa dancing with him, is it?"

"Captain!"

"Yes sir," Angel hissed. The Colonel stared at Paris for a moment, then turned quickly and left.

"Paris won't break easily," Alexander stared at the unconscious Paris, "It would be better to do a Mind Take, we'd get more from him that way."

"Then we should just…" at that moment Angel's

phone began to ring, she answered, "Ambroise, you're on speaker, what's up?"

"The Colonel sent me and the other captains a message, he just ordered us to take our squads to the drill field."

"Why?"

"I'm not sure but he said it was important."

"Okay, I'll bring my Squad."

"See you there," then Ambroise hung up.

"What does the Colonel want all the squads for?" I asked.

Angel muttered, "There's only one way we're going to find out."

* * * * *

All the squads gathered at the drill field and waited. It wasn't until that moment that I realised just how many people (and creatures) lived at the base. I had spent most of my time at the Lightning Squad house, so I hadn't really encountered the other squads before. I tried not to stare as I found myself face-to-face with dragons, griffins, centaurs, and other incredible paranormal beings. At the end of the field was a stage on which the Colonel was stood. Once all the squads had gathered the Colonel began to speak.

"I stand before you all with a heavy heart," the Colonel began, "Last night, the base was attacked by followers of the terrorist known as Mr Jet."

"He isn't," Angel muttered under her breath, "He wouldn't."

"These followers killed the Centaur Guard Joseph. Joseph was a good friend who has worked at this base for many years. He will be missed. Mr Jet and his followers entered the base but were stopped by brave members of Lightning Squad. I would like to thank Sophie Day, Danny Park, Alexander Laurentius Octavius, Jason Dragonheart and Captain Angel Night for their hard work," the Colonel paused.

The Colonel then continued, "Mr Jet and his followers had help getting onto the base. Paris Surf, a member of Lightning Squad, was arrested today on charges of attempted murder and terrorism. Until the prisoner is moved, I am placing the base under lock down. We shall not let this defeat us. We shall stand strong. This Empire belongs to the paranormals, and we shall defend it. Demons have no place in this world, and we shall ensure that they go back to the underworld where they belong. Dismissed!"

With that the Colonel left and the drill field became incredibly noisy.

"He didn't mention that the other followers were from the base," Alexander pointed out.

"I noticed," Angel muttered, "He's made out it was just Paris on his own, saves us from paranoia and panic at least."

"He said 'until the prisoner is moved', where exactly is Paris moving to?" I asked.

"To the court and execution house," Alexander explained, "I think the Colonel is planning to have Paris publicly executed."

Executed! I felt my stomach drop. Alexander had just said executed. He had just said that Paris would be executed! How could he say that so calmly!? Executed? How could someone be? What crazy world was this!? Executions were things of the past. They belonged in the "dark ages" not now. Not in the twenty-first century! How could Paris be...? And publicly!? The vampire had said publicly, that meant that people were going to watch! People would watch Paris be... I felt sick. I couldn't deal with this. I didn't want to have anything to do with this. This wasn't right. This wasn't...Angel grabbed my arm as my knees gave way. She helped me over to a bench where she sat me down.

"Deep breaths Jason," Angel whispered, "Nothing's been decided yet. Alex shouldn't have said that."

Angel pulled out her wand and pressed it to my forehead. Her wand glowed as I felt the soft reassuring bliss of magical sedation take over my body. Suddenly the fact that Paris was going to be executed didn't bother me in the slightest. The rest of the squad quickly joined us. They asked Angel numerous questions, speaking loudly and on top of each other. I didn't take in a word they said. I was too busy thinking about my earlier extremely important question, what was double the size of a mammoth?

"Angel," I vaguely remember hearing Araminta ask, "What have you done to Jason?"

"I sedated him. He was freaking out and I didn't really know what else to do," Angel replied.

"You sedated the Master of Darkness! That's hilarious! Aww he's smiling, he looks tipsy!" Fern laughed.

"This isn't the time to be laughing Fern," Clover snapped, "Paris is a terrorist!"

"I knew there was a reason I never liked him!"

"Fern! Mr Jet got onto the base. This isn't the time for you to be acting like a..."

"Why didn't you tell us!?" Roxy interrupted, "About Mr Jet, about Paris!?"

"I've only just found out about Paris," Angel explained, "And the attack on the base was classified."

"Of course, it's always classified," Clover muttered.

"What's that supposed to mean?"

"It means we're always kept in the dark. We never get told anything! The Colonel expects us to fight and die for him, but he never tells us what's going on!"

For some reason I found Clover's outburst amusing, so I started to giggle. The squad turned to stare at me, but I didn't mind, I was happily sedated. Their annoyed gazes were highly entertaining or at least I thought so at the time.

I then began to talk about how watermelons and cabbages were planning to take over the world and that we needed to pray to the holy cheesecake for protection. I laughed and continued to talk absentmindedly, until Angel slapped the back of my head and I fell into a disgruntled silence.

"I know this is a big shock, but I need you all to pull together," Angel said softly, "Things are going to start getting a lot harder for us. The fact that Paris was in our squad means that all eyes will be on us. We need to show them that Paris hasn't broken or converted us. I expect that we will all get called into questioning at some point."

"Questioning? Why?" asked Willow.

"To make sure none of us are working with him."

"Captain Night," the Colonel suddenly appeared behind me. I jumped, falling off the bench and landing heavily on the ground, at the sound of his voice. Fern laughed at me, which I thought was rather rude.

"Yes sir," it was hard to hear Angel over my nonsensical rant about how Fern was rude and if she wasn't careful a giant carrot called Steve (not sure why the carrot was called Steve, not the most carroty name I could have come up with) was going to eat her.

"I thought I told you to take Surf to the cells."

"Yes sir, I'll get right on that sir."

"Good," the Colonel then added, "And stop sedating the Master of Darkness, it's embarrassing."

"Yes sir," Angel bowed her head in apology as the Colonel walked away. She stared daggers in my direction before turning to the rest of the squad, "Go back to the house and rest. Alexander, make sure they do that. Danny, I want you to go to the hospital wing and guard Sophie."

"Guard Sophie? What happened to Sophie?" asked Roger.

"Alex will explain when you get to the house. Jason, you come with me."

"Me? Why?" I asked stumbling to my feet.

"So I can keep an eye on you!"

INTERLUDE

Hidden by a forcefield, in the middle of a dark and dangerous wood, stood an old manor house. The house had a regal look, with grey stone walls and a large well-kept garden decorating the front. Gargoyles sat on the rooftop, scaring pigeons and unwelcome sparrows with their grotesque faces. Inside the manor house was dark and gothic. Its furniture belonged in centuries past and candles were the only source of light. In a large old-fashioned living room (decorated with leather chairs, a piano, and a large crackling fire) a record player was playing classical music. The room was covered in high bookcases and on the only remaining wall sat a large portrait. In one of the brown armchairs sat a vampire. The vampire was sipping human blood from a wine glass. Having been bottled two-hundred years previous, the blood had become rich and succulent. Just as the music was reaching its crescendo, someone knocked on the door.

Mr Jet sighed, "Enter."

The door opened and an old thin man entered. He had a hunchback and wispy white hair. His skin was wrinkled and his grey eyes fading. He walked over to Mr Jet and bowed his head.

"What is it Jeeves?" Mr Jet asked.

"Well Master Jet sir, there was a call for you on the telephone," Jeeves, the vampire butler, stuttered.

"Who was it?"

"The Miss from the base." Mr Jet flicked his wrist and the record player paused. The vampire beckoned his butler closer and gestured for him to continue.

"The plan is in motion. The gorgon boy has been captured."

"Excellent."

"Master Jet sir, I don't quite understand."

"I don't pay you to understand Jeeves."

"You don't pay me at all sir!"

"Well, I give you blood don't I!? And... what don't you understand?"

"I don't understand why you wanted the gorgon boy to be caught?"

"Really Jeeves! Do I have to explain the entire plan to you again!?"

"It'd be appreciated sir."

Mr Jet hissed angrily, "Why do I keep you alive!?"

"Because everyone else would rather die than work for you sir," Jeeves answered honestly.

"That's," the vampire sighed, rubbing his head as a migraine surfaced (this regularly occurred whenever Jeeves spoke), "He got caught so that he would tell them about the warehouse."

"But they'll execute him!"

"That's the point Jeeves!"

"But why did you have to choose him? I liked that lad, he was a nice chap, very friendly and he owes me..."

"Because he will have the biggest impact on Angel."

"Her again!" Jeeves exclaimed, "It's always that Angel. She's all you ever talk about. I'm setting this trap to catch

Angel. I'm killing these children to send a message to Angel. Will this manor be expecting a mistress soon?"

"Jeeves!"

"Sorry Master Jet sir. I didn't realise you were still obsessing over the shapeshifter. I thought you'd moved on to the fairy."

"The fairy? Oh the princess! Ah no, I just needed her blood. Apart from as a blood slave, the fairy is of little use to me. If it wasn't for our friend, I wouldn't keep her alive."

"How did you know she was a princess? I can't understand how you worked that one out!"

"Because of the body Jeeves! I explained this to you before! The body at the vampire hotel! He was killed by the powers of the Unseelie King."

"Why would the fairy king go to a vampire hotel?"

"He didn't! His daughter did! Really Jeeves, has your memory faded with age!?"

"Well I am seven-hundred and seventy-three, sir."

"Yes, well there has been a rumour, rattling around the changeling trade for years, about the Seelie Queen and Unseelie King having a child, which is how I knew she was a princess."

"Ah," Jeeves nodded, "But wouldn't such a powerful fey be of use to you?"

"The girl herself is of little importance, her blood, if we were to drain her, would be of use."

"Is the shapeshifter of use?"

Mr Jet smiled, "Indeed."

"Are you sure you don't just have a crush on her?"

"Jeeves!"

"I was only asking sir! You just seem a little bit obsessed with her."

Mr Jet gave his butler a hard stare then asked, "Has the forcefield been set up at the Polar Base?"

"Yes sir however they still require the final ingredient."

"Tell them I shall bring it to them shortly."

"Ah so you'll be paying her another visit then?"

"Indeed. Her memories have started to return. I could sense it when we last met. It'll be intriguing to see how she copes, and how he copes."

"I'm surprised you left him alive, he'll cause you problems later on! Him just being there, if he kills you, don't say I didn't warn you. It'll be your own fault after all, you shouldn't have made him so powerful!"

"Yes well I didn't expect him to break free from the enchantment! And he may be more powerful than his peers, but he is certainly not more powerful than me!"

"Master Jet sir, you know none of this would have happened if you hadn't started experimenting! You had all of them in the palm of your hand. The Master, the shapeshifter, the prince, but you got too excited and started messing around with your tools, if you hadn't ruined the Mis…"

"Jeeves!" Mr Jet shouted, throwing his bloody wine glass at his butler. The wine glass smashed into pieces as it hit the floor. The blood staining the old carpet rug.

"Sorry Master Jet sir. I didn't mean to say that!" Jeeves apologised, staring at the blood stained rug, "No need to waste good blood though. And look at that stain, that'll never come out!"

Mr Jet sighed, "What about Atlantis?"

"Our spies tell me that Atlantis is prepared."

"And they're certain that there aren't any teleporters in the city?"

"They've been removed, as have our allies. But Master Jet sir, how are you so sure that Angel will do as you plan?"

"Because she's predictable. She cares about others so naturally she'll attempt to save as many people as possible. She won't let others get hurt in her place, so she's bound to remain behind."

"But Master Jet sir, what if she dies?"

"That won't happen! I'll make sure of that," Mr Jet got to his feet and walked over to the fireplace. The vampire watched the flames for a moment then placed his hand into the blaze. Instead of turning into ash, the flames bounced across the vampire's fingertips.

"That's mighty impressive that is, sir," Jeeves complimented as he stepped away from the fire.

"Indeed," Mr Jet smiled, he rolled his hand into a fist and the flames extinguished. He then turned to his butler, "Tell the Miss at the base to be prepared. Remind her to collect as many souls as possible. And contact the witch. Tell her to visit. She's been acting up recently, she needs to be reminded who the boss of this operation is. Oh and make sure you feed the hell hounds, you forgot yesterday so they ate one of the maids."

"Maids? Oh you mean the possessed human girl! She wasn't that bright anyways sir, and her blood was horribly bitter!"

"Still the maids are our dinner Jeeves, not the hell hounds. I especially don't want Timothy eating them. He's meant to be on a diet!"

"Yes Master Jet sir, I'll see to it sir," Jeeves bowed his head and quickly headed out of the room.

As soon as he was out of Mr Jet's earshot, the vampire butler muttered, "Ungrateful twit!"

17

'JUST FOLLOW THE PROCEDURE'

Angel pushed Paris down into the cells. The cells were dark and dirty. Guarded by vampires, the cells were a place that few dared to tread. It was a cold place. A deadly place. Filled with demon prisoners awaiting execution. Angel hated the cells. The stench of the place messed with her senses. With every step she took, shivers ran down her spine. Paris, on the other hand, was surprisingly calm to say that he was about to be locked up with a demon.

"I bet this must kill you," Paris muttered, "Having to lock up one of your own. The great Lightning Squad crumbling under the leadership of a stupid little girl. You're going to die you know."

"Yes, well most people do," Angel shoved Paris towards a cell, "Look in there. Remember her?"

Inside was a giant three stinger scorpion. Its body was black, and its eyes bright red. It was chained to the wall. As the pair got closer, it scrambled as far as it could towards them. Angel unlocked the cell door and stood Paris in the doorway.

"Because look, she remembers you. You killed her children."

"Is this meant to scare me? Are you trying to get me to talk? Because this isn't going to work," Paris snapped.

"We'll see," Angel pushed Paris inside the cell and chained him to the wall.

"You'll die Angel! On Halloween you'll die."

"Looking forward to it," Angel began to walk away.

"You'll regret this Night!" Paris yelled.

"Oh, I doubt it."

* * * * *

Jason was sat on a bench waiting for Angel. The sedation had finally worn off and the Master of Darkness had returned to his usual confused self. The magic Angel had used to sedate him had suppressed his panic-attack, so now Jason could clearly think through the situation. Paris was a terrorist. He had tried to kill Sophie and because of this he was, most likely, going to be executed. These were the facts. However whilst Jason knew these facts to be true, he still found them hard to understand.

Paris hadn't seemed evil. He had seemed normal, well as normal as a half-gorgon could be. It wasn't like Mr Jet. Mr Jet looked evil. He looked cold and his eyes held little emotion. Paris hadn't been like that. Paris had been fun and cool; he had always worn an inviting smile and Jason had enjoyed being in his company. It was this that Jason found hardest to deal with. Jason had been friends with Paris, however Paris worked for the man who murdered his mum. Jason scratched the back of his head as he stressed over how to cope with this situation. In the space of a few weeks Jason had lost his mum, had found out that he wasn't human, had joined this crazy paranormal world and had fought against a monstrous vampire. Not only that but his friend and tutor had turned out to be a terrorist! This was a lot for Jason to deal with!

"The sedation has worn off," Angel muttered as she walked over to Jason.

"Yeah, sorry about the nonsense."

"You mean Steve the evil carrot?" Jason nodded. "You know normally people, when they're sedated, just get a bit tired and tipsy, they don't normally think that vegetables are going to take over the world."

"Sorry, in the cells did everything go okay?"

"I guess," Angel shrugged as she sat down next to Jason.

There was silence until Jason finally mustered up the courage to ask, "Why did Paris do it? Why did he work for Mr Jet? I can't understand why he would want demons to take over the world."

"I don't really understand it myself. I think many of Mr Jet's followers don't actually want demons to take over, rather they think that they can use the demons to take over themselves, if that makes sense?"

"Ah I see," the pair fell into silence once more.

"I need your notes from your tutoring sessions with Paris," Angel explained, "I want to check what Paris has been teaching you. I should have tutored you myself. I put a terrorist in charge of teaching the Master of Darkness! In your tutor sessions, did Paris ever say anything that looking back seems suspicious?"

"I don't think so. He once mentioned that he wasn't a fan of the Emperor but that's it."

"Okay," Angel paused for a moment, "We're going to have to take it in turns to watch over Sophie. I will work out a timetable. We're going to have to be careful from now on, the other squads are going to be watching us closely."

"Thunder, Wildfire, Tsunami, Tornado, Volcano, Avalanche and Lightning," Jason muttered, "Why are all the squads, apart from Alpha, named after natural disasters?"

"I was told that the squads have these names to remind us that some things are out of our control. No matter how great your plan is, no matter how hard you might prepare, things can happen that we have no control over, like a natural disaster. The missions we go on, things can go wrong, things can go horribly wrong, however no matter how awful or bloody the mission might end up being, we have to pick ourselves up and come back fighting, like humans do after a natural disaster."

"Wow, that was deep, I wasn't expecting that," Jason paused, "There's just one thing I don't get. Why is Alpha Squad called Alpha and not named after a natural disaster?"

"Alpha was the last squad to be created, so they probably couldn't think of another natural disaster to name it after."

"They could have gone with Hurricane and Earthquake."

"Hurricane and Earthquake are training squads."

"Training squads?"

"When new recruits come to the base they are put into either Hurricane or Earthquake Squad. These squads don't go on missions, they're just for training. When your training is considered complete you move into one of the active squads. Technically you should be in one of those squads but, because you're the Master of Darkness, you've been thrown right into an active squad."

"So I shouldn't be doing missions!? I should just be training!? Oh that's not fair! I would much rather be in training! It'd be much easier than being in Lightning Squad!"

Angel laughed, "We need to get inside, the lock down will start soon."

"What happens in lock down?"

"The grounds are cursed. Anyone who steps outside, gets burnt alive."

"That sounds awful!"

"Yeah it's nasty but it works. Everyone stays indoors and normally no one innocent gets fried."

"Normally?"

"Yeah well you never know."

"Great," Jason really hoped that he didn't suddenly decide to start sleep walking outside in the middle of the night.

* * * * *

Sophie's eyes fluttered open, but she couldn't see. She tried to move but she could only lift a finger.

"H…hello," Sophie stuttered.

"You're awake," Danny's voice echoed around the hospital room.

"What happened to me? Why can't I see? Why can't I move? Where am I?"

"You were stabbed with an iron dagger. Your eyes are covered. Rowan used magic to numb your body. You're in the hospital wing," Danny answered.

"Why are my eyes covered?"

"You still have Paris' powers. We don't want you to turn us to stone."

"Does Rowan have any idea how long I'll be a gorgon for?"

"Nope. We can't even work out how you managed to steal his powers. How did you do that?"

"I'm not really sure. What happened to him?"

"To Paris? He's in the cells."

There was silence then Sophie muttered, "Mr Jet wanted my blood, but Paris wanted to kill me…"

"Yeah that's been bugging me all day. If Mr Jet wanted you dead, he could have killed you in the forest so why did he wait and send Paris?"

"That is the question," Alexander muttered upon entering the room.

"Alex is that you?" Sophie asked.

175

"Yes, it's me, I've come to take over…"

"I'll be off then," and with that Danny got to his feet and headed out the room. However when he got to the corridor Alexander was in front of him.

"Damn vampires. Shouldn't you be with Sophie?" Danny asked bitterly.

"How did you survive the hell hound attack? It doesn't make sense. There's no way a mere illusionist could survive an attack by two hell hounds."

"And yet here I am!"

"What are you? You have clearly got illusionist powers but that's not what you are."

"What am I then? Look I get that you don't like me, but there's no need for you to question my identity. In fact if anyone's identity needs checking it's yours."

"What?"

"See I've never trusted you. I couldn't work out what it was about you I didn't like but there was just something. So I started to do some research. What I found out about you is very interesting. A lot of dead women." Alexander grabbed Danny and shoved him into a wall.

"I don't know what you've found out," Alexander hissed, "But…"

"Your reaction tells me you know exactly what I've found out," Danny smiled.

"You can believe the stories you've heard if you want to, but you don't speak a word of this to Angel. If you do…"

"You'll do what? Kill me? Try it. It only takes me two minutes to kill a normal vampire, I wonder how long it'd take me to kill a vampire mutant."

Alexander punched Danny's face. Danny smiled and returned the punch. They fought until Alexander had once again pinned Danny against the wall.

"My history, do you think the Colonel doesn't know it? If the Colonel thought my history was so important, he would have kicked me out or told Angel already," Alexander hissed.

"That just makes me distrust the Colonel."

"As much as I don't want to interrupt this cute little moment you two seem to be having," Skyjack mocked, "Could you get out of my way, I have patients to see to."

Alexander let go of Danny and turned to the pegacorn, "Sorry Skyjack."

"Yes well. Shouldn't one of you be guarding Sophie?"

"Yeah, he should," Danny muttered.

"Well then perhaps the pair of you should get back to where you're supposed to be," Skyjack pushed past them, "Lock down will be starting soon, if you have somewhere to be you better get there fast."

With that Skyjack left them and went into the hospital wing. Alexander followed. Danny quickly ran back to the Lightning Squad house. He made it just in time. As soon as he had shut the door, it glowed blue and locked. Outside the ground glowed red and all the windows slammed shut. Danny walked upstairs to Angel's room, but she wasn't there. He was about to head downstairs when he heard a voice muttering softly from the opposite direction. He headed down the corridor and found Angel knelt outside Paris' bedroom door. She had her wand in her hand and Paris' door was glowing dark blue. In Angel's other hand was a notebook, the pages were blank until, by magic, names started to appear.

"What are you doing?" Danny asked.

"I'm locking Paris' door. The captains will be coming tomorrow to search it, I don't want anything being moved."

"And the notebook?"

"This will tell me the names of all the people who have visited Paris' room. It should also tell me when and for how long they were there."

"I bet there will be a lot of late night visitors," Danny

muttered.

"Probably. You okay? You look annoyed."

"It's nothing."

"Which means it's something. What's up?"

"Alex," Danny sat down next to Angel.

"Ah, did you two get into a fight again?"

"Kind of."

"Why did you fight this time?"

"Nothing. It's just don't trust Alex, he's not what he seems. He's not…a good guy."

"Elaborate."

"Do you have any of Alex's files?"

"No, the Colonel has them."

"Don't you find that strange?"

"It is a bit. Is there something in those files you think I need to see?"

Danny sighed, "I don't know. I assume that the Colonel would know. I did some background research on Alex. He has a very bloody past. He even has links to the *Jack the Ripper* murder cases."

Angel was silent, "Does he have past affiliations with Mr Jet?"

"I don't know, it's hard to find out about him."

"Okay," Angel thought for a moment, "Find evidence. Continue doing your research and when you have got some solid evidence, I'll deal with this then. Right now, let's just deal with the Mr Jet issue."

"Okay," Danny agreed, "But don't keep Alex too close."

Angel didn't answer, instead she looked down at the notebook, "Looks like this is finished. You were right about the late-night visitors. Paris was certainly popular with the ladies, and with the gentlemen too it seems."

"Most of them aren't from the base, he probably just picked them up at a club or something. He must have had a pickup portal. That's the only way he could've got them onto the base."

"A what?"

"It's a new device being sold on the black-market. They're tiny portals that can carry two people. The idea behind them is, if you pick up a girl at a bar you can teleport her back to your place before she has a chance to change her mind, hence the name 'pickup' portals."

"That's," Angel muttered disgusted, "Wait, how do you know about them?"

"When we raided that goblins place a few months back, he was selling them. We confiscated a load, come to think of it, it was me and Paris who logged them into evidence."

"These portals, would they be able to break through the base's forcefield?"

Danny thought for a moment, "I don't think so, not unless Paris got the portal authorised. Authorised portals don't have to go through the forcefield's security."

"If this is the case, then we need to find out who authorised Paris' portal."

"First we need to find out if he had one."

* * * * *

Hiroshi, Jin, William, Jonathan and Ambroise arrived early the next morning to search Paris' room. Angel unlocked the room to let them in, then left them to it. Angel went to her messy office and sat herself down behind her desk. Angel's office was slightly bigger than her room and was pack full of stuff. Files sat in piles littering the floor and boxes filled with paperwork were stacked in a corner. A computer filled her desk and two battered chairs were sat on either side. On the desk was a crystal ball which contained the contents of the mind take. Angel connected the crystal ball to her computer and watched. Angel fast forwarded through the dead girl's memories. The dead girl had turned out to be Ellie Jones, a witch from Tsunamis squad. Angel had recognised her face, but it wasn't until she started watching Ellie's memories that she realised that they had joined the base at the same time. In fact they had been in the same training squad for a short while. Angel flicked through Ellie's memories feeling extremely uncomfortable. She was watching this girl's life through her eyes. Everything was from a first person point of view. It was as if Angel was living these memories. But these memories belonged to someone else. These memories were private. They were personal. They were not supposed to be watched and studied. Angel swallowed her feeling of discomfort, blocked out the voice in her head telling her it was wrong, and continued. She flicked through every birthday, every Christmas, every 'you-had-to-be-there' moment until, after hours of searching, Angel finally found what she had been looking for.

"I've brought food," Angel looked up to see Alexander in the doorway holding a plastic container full of food, "Sara made it. She was concerned when she didn't see you at lunch."

"Lunch? What time is it?" Angel muttered. Alexander entered and sat on the chair opposite Angel, placing the food on the desk.

"It's just gone three o'clock."

"Really!? I've been doing this longer than I thought."

"What have you been doing that's kept you so busy?" Angel turned her computer screen in Alexander's direction.

"Is this from the mind take?" he asked, "Did you find anything?"

Angel nodded and pressed play:

"Why is he coming here?" Ellie Jones whispered to Paris Surf.

"How should I know? He never tells me anything!" Paris hissed.

"How exactly are we going to get him onto the base? The borders are completely shut down!"

"I've sorted that."

"How?" Paris took out a small black circular object.

"What is that?" asked Ellie.

"It used to be one of those 'pickup' portals, but I've had it modified. If we attach this to the border, Jet can use this to get onto the base."

"Will this work?"

"Should do. I've been doing some test runs. It'll only manage two journeys though."

Angel hit the pause button and muttered, "That's what that crack in the border is. Hopefully, now that we know what it is, we'll be able to remove it. The Colonel and a group of experts are apparently working on it. I also found this." Angel skipped the memory forward then hit play.

Ellie was in her room, sat at her desk. She was writing an action report. By the side of her hand was a plain white warlock's card. For a few moments the footage showed nothing more than Ellie filling out the report, but then the warlock's card glowed dark orange. Ellie picked the card up and words appeared:

Be in the forest tonight.

Then the message vanished. Ellie took a pen and wrote on the card: **what time?**

For a moment there was nothing then the card glowed once more, and the words vanished. The card remained blank for a few minutes until it glowed again:

When Lightning Squad's night patrol begins.

"That's how Mr Jet is communicating with his followers," Alexander muttered as Angel hit the pause button, "A warlock's card."

"I have to hand it to them, they outsmarted us there. Warlock's cards can't be traced or detected."

"That warlock's card looks like the one you found in the forest."

"I was thinking the same. Do you still have the card from the forest?"

"Be right back," Alexander zoomed out of the room only to return seconds later holding the warlock's card. He handed it to Angel.

"They look very similar," Angel muttered, "I'll keep this and take it into evidence." Angel put the card in her pocket and then stuffed her mouth full of food. Alexander smiled as he watched Angel eat but then he noticed the personnel files on her desk, and his smile faded. The files of every Lightning Squad member lay open, each covered in highlighted scribbles and sticky notes.

"Are you going through everyone's files?" Alexander asked.

"Yeah. I just read through Paris' file and it's perfect. Completely perfect! I've read through all the reports, no one ever says a bad word about him! It's just…"

"It's not your fault, none of us saw this coming. We all trusted Paris. He was good at his job."

"Yeah well now he's in the cells and I have to try and work out if I have any more terrorists in my squad!"

"Have you read my file?" Alexander asked.

Angel paused, "I don't have your file. Actually I wanted to ask you about that. Why does the Colonel have your file?"

Alexander didn't say anything for a moment, "That's classified."

"Classified? Why would someone's personnel file be classified?"

"Ask the Colonel."

"I intend to."

"If the Colonel thought you needed to see my file, he would have shown it to you. Besides you know me well enough without my file."

"But I don't Alex, that's the problem," Angel sighed, "In fact I know practically nothing about you."

"I've lived for around two thousand years so admittedly I have not told you my entire backstory but believe me when I say that the person who knows me best, the person I've been the most honest and open with, the person who understands me best, is most definitely you."

"You say that but, you see, how do I explain this, I don't know why but I'm not, when it comes to situations involving you, I'm not the most objective. I don't want you to be, no matter what people say about you or what your history might be, I don't want you to be a bad guy. I'm not saying you are, what I'm saying is that, I trust you Alex however I probably shouldn't, at least not as much as I do."

Alexander nodded. There was a moment of silence. Alexander studied Angel for some time before he asked, "Do you think I'm a terrorist?"

Angel was silent than muttered, "No. But I also never thought Paris was one."

"True," Alexander lifted his hand and, after a moment's hesitation, gently pulled something from Angel's hair.

"What are you doing?"

"You had rice in your hair."

"Oh, that's gross."

"Are you aware that you inhale your food rather than eat it?"

"Oh I'm well aware. Werewolves aren't exactly taught table manners."

Alexander laughed. It was then that Angel realised that Alexander's hand was still lightly touching her cheek. If she had wanted to, she could have easily pushed it away, however she didn't.

"I'm not a terrorist," Alexander said sincerely, "I know you can't just take my word for it but, I want Mr Jet dead as much as you do. Perhaps even more."

"Why?"

"He did something to me in the past, something that he needs to pay for." Angel was about to ask more but her phone rang. Alexander quickly moved his hand away as Angel picked up the phone. She spoke briefly to Jin and then hung up.

"They've finished logging all of Paris' stuff into evidence," Angel explained.

"You should go look through it," Alexander got to his feet, "You may see something the boys have missed."

* * * * *

The evidence locker was a massive white warehouse run by goblins. Angel entered the warehouse and went over to the main desk, behind which two goblins sat. One of the goblins was a man with a long ginger beard that reached the floor and bright green eyes. He was typing away at a computer, looking highly irritated by something on the screen. The other goblin was a female with green skin and bleach blonde hair. She was reading a magazine, which she quickly put down as Angel entered.

"Afternoon," Angel greeted the goblins, "I've come to see the Paris Surf evidence."

"Can you show me some ID please?" asked the male goblin.

"Really? Francis, how long have you known me?"

"Just following procedure. Can you show me some ID please?"

"Yeah sure," Angel pulled out of her pocket her Lightning Squad ID badge.

"Okay, can you hold out your hand for me?"

"Why?"

"Just follow the procedure."

"Alright," Angel held out her hand, Francis placed a small square object onto her palm. From the object a blue light shone across Angel's body. Then a small needle pricked Angel's skin.

"Ow! What was that for!?" Angel exclaimed as Francis took the object away.

"DNA testing. We have to make sure you are who you claim to be," Francis plugged the square object into the computer.

"This is a bit much!"

"We have a lot of dangerous objects in here, we can't have any of them falling into the wrong hands," stated the female goblin.

The computer made a beeping sound, Francis smiled, "She checks out."

"Okay almost done. I just need you to sign here, here, here and here," the female goblin handed Angel a form.

"Are we done now?" After signing the necessary paperwork, Angel handed the form back to the female goblin.

"We're done. If you'd like to follow me, I will lead you to the Paris Surf evidence room."

"Finally," Angel sighed. Francis picked up his clipboard and led the way. The evidence locker was separated into many different rooms that each held different types of evidence. Angel followed the goblin through the maze of evidence rooms until they came to a small room with a blue door. The goblin pressed the electronic pad on the wall and the door swung open. Angel stepped inside to find the other captains, minus Axel, waiting for her. The room was completely white; white walls, white furniture, and a white floor. There was even a white computer hidden in the far corner of the room. Hiroshi and Jin were sat on chairs, flicking through some of Paris' old paperwork, whilst Jonathan, Ambroise and William stood by a long white table, discussing the objects that lay on it in detail. The captains looked up as Angel entered.

"When you are finished, press the blue button on the wall and a goblin will come to escort you back," Francis explained.

"Cheers Francis," Angel thanked the goblin as he left.

"What did you think of the evidence police?" asked Hiroshi.

"That procedure is ridiculous! It never used to be this strict."

"I think some evidence went missing a while ago," Jonathan explained, "They stepped up their security after that."

"It's still ridiculous! You have no idea how much trouble it was to log this stuff in!" Hiroshi exclaimed.

"Did you find anything interesting? And where's Axel?"

"Axel? No idea, probably sleeping. The stuff on the table over there are things that seemed a bit out of place, but apart from that there's nothing of real interest," Ambroise gestured to the table. After putting on a pair of gloves, Angel headed over to the table. The shapeshifter studied the array of objects that lay before her. Amongst Paris' things was a pickup portal as well as a white warlock's card.

"This is how Mr Jet is communicating with his followers."

"A warlock's card," Jonathan muttered, "Clever."

From her pocket, Angel pulled out the warlock's card that she had found in the forest and held it next to Paris'.

"I found this in the forest, I thought it might have belonged to one of the terrorists. Jonathan are they the same? They look the same but, magically, are they?"

Jonathan pulled out his wand and gently tapped each of the cards. The tip of his wand glowed purple.

"Yes, both cards are the same. They were created by the same warlock."

"How can you tell?" asked William.

"Everyone who uses magic has their own magic, err I guess you could call it a, fingerprint. Both these cards have the same 'fingerprint'."

"What the?" Angel muttered as the two cards glowed orange and words appeared. The words stayed on the card just long enough for Jin to write them down, before they disappeared.

"Mr Jet clearly doesn't realise we've found the cards."

"Or he does and he's trying to trap us," Angel mumbled.

Ambroise looked at the words Jin had written, "This looks like an address."

Jin typed the address into the evidence room's computer then exclaimed, "Oh that's not good. The address is for the warehouse that sends supplies to the Polar Base."

"The Polar Base? What do they want the Polar Base's supplies for?" Hiroshi asked.

"You don't think," Angel muttered, "That they're going to try smuggling demons up there."

William sighed, "It's only old McLean and a few workers there, it wouldn't be hard to sneak demons up. I think we need to inform the Colonel."

* * * * *

Alexander was stood in the graveyard waiting. The graveyard was the only quiet place on the base. It was a small green field in which rows of graves, housing the bodies of fallen D.D. Squad members, stood glistening in the sunlight. Woodland spirits ran across the gravestones, keeping the place clean and beautiful. A bat flew past Alexander and transformed into Araminta.

"Why did you want to see me?" Alexander asked.

"You're going to have to start checking in with me four times a day, like we used to," Araminta stated.

"Are you kidding me!?"

"No, these are orders from above. You're to be checked and monitored."

"How many years has it been? I haven't done anything!"

"Calm down, if you don't make a fuss and do as ordered, there won't be a problem. If you haven't done anything wrong, then this will prove it."

"These orders came from above? So they don't trust

me either."

"Can you blame them? Let's just take a look at your history."

"Which wasn't my fault! You all seem to have forgotten that part. I didn't choose to become like this! What happened wasn't my choice!"

"I know," Araminta said softly, "I know, but what happened, even though it wasn't your choice, did happen. We don't know exactly what they did to you or whether they can still influence you."

Alexander hissed, "Angel was asking to see my personnel file."

"I can get the Colonel to create a fake one for you."

"It has to be good. Danny, for some reason, is digging into my past as well."

"Why is he doing that?"

"Because he doesn't trust me, and he doesn't like me around Angel."

"About that, above don't want you near Angel either."

"I can hardly avoid her. I'm her vice-captain and we live in the same house!"

"Still keep your distance. Above don't like how close you two seem."

"In case you've all forgotten I left, they're the ones who brought me back here. They're the ones who made me her vice-captain and put me in the same house as her. I..."

"You ran away. When you realised who she was, you ran."

"Yes, yes I did. And they brought me back."

"So that you could take responsibility for this issue and deal with it. Not for you to fall even deeper..."

"Tell those above, that my life is mine. Me and Angel, that's something for me to deal with."

"Your life, Alexander, stopped being yours a long time ago. Look, my job is to protect you and Angel. Neither of you are...just do what I say and keep out of trouble."

There was a bitter pause before Alexander sighed, "We have one thing we might need to take care of. David Night is coming to the base. He knows who I am."

"I'll sort it."

"I think he knows something about Angel's past. I believe that's why he's coming here."

"What do you mean?"

"The Pied Piper showed Angel a memory. She was in it, so was David."

"Were you?"

"I don't know. If I was, Angel, she must not have seen my face."

"I'll deal with David. Those above might have already spoken with him, he's with them now."

"What about Danny? If he keeps digging…"

"I'll put a stop to it. No one can know about this. No one can know about you."

After a pause Alexander asked, "Why are they so interested in Angel?"

"I'm not sure. At first, I thought it was just because of her connection to you. Now I'm not so sure. Maybe it's because of Mr Jet. He's slightly fixated with her and now those above are as well."

"Yet she has no idea."

"And that's the way it's going to remain."

18

'MEMORIES'

Lightning Squad had been separated, then one by one they had been taken into an interrogation room. Jason hummed nervously as he sat, attached to a lie detector, waiting for his interrogation to begin. The interrogation room was smaller than the one the Pied Piper had been in. The walls were dark grey and there was a wooden table, with two chairs either side, in the middle. Jason didn't like it. He didn't like it at all. He hadn't done anything wrong, but the room was suddenly making him feel guilty. Guilty over useless things like for the time he had cheated during a mock exam and for when he had blamed his neighbours' cat for eating the last of the ice-cream. Sweat trickled down his forehead. He wanted to confess. He wanted to confess that he cheated and that he had eaten the ice-cream. The room was just too small. Too stuffy. Jason wanted to confess to things he hadn't done. He wanted to get out. He couldn't cope with the pressure! After a few moments, which felt like hours to Jason, Hiroshi entered the room and sat down opposite him.

"It's just a few questions. It won't take long," Hiroshi reassured, "Your name is Jason Dragonheart, correct?"

"No, I mean, yes," Jason stuttered.

"And you're the Master of Darkness?"

"Yes, well that's what they say I am, that's what I am, but I didn't realise I was, I know I am now, but I didn't know before, I mean, I should stop talking."

"How long have you known Paris Surf?"

"Err, I'm not sure how long exactly. Not long. About a month. Since I came to the base...which...was not long ago."

"What was your relationship with Paris?"

"Relationship? We weren't...I'm not...oh right you mean...yes...Paris was my friend. Well I guess he wasn't really, I thought we were friends. He helped train and tutor me."

"In your tutor sessions did Paris ever discuss Mr Jet with you?"

"No. Maybe. No. I don't think so. I don't remember. No. No I'm pretty certain he didn't. I think."

"Have you ever had any involvement with Mr Jet and his followers?"

"No. I've met him twice. So I suppose I have had some involvement with Mr Jet, but he killed my mum so we're not...I'm not on his side or anything," Jason rambled.

"Okay," Hiroshi got to his feet and opened the door, "We're done."

"We're done? Really? That's everything?"

"Yeah we're done, you're free to leave." Jason got to his feet and exited so quickly that he almost bumped into Angel as he did so.

"What did you do to him?" Angel asked as she joined Hiroshi in the interrogation room.

"Nothing why?"

"He looked terrified."

"Why? I only asked him a few questions. His was the shortest interrogation!"

"So what did you think of him?"

"He's definitely not working with Mr Jet," Hiroshi smiled, "When I asked him about his relationship with Paris, I think he thought I was asking if they were a couple!"

Angel groaned, "And he's the Master of Darkness!"

"Yeah he's certainly not like the legends! We didn't make a mistake, did we? Jason is just…"

"A useless idiot."

"Yeah. He seems like a nice guy but, you know if he ever got caught, he would definitely tell his captors everything."

"Yeah, I know. Hopefully one day he'll," Angel sighed, "How did the other interrogations go?"

"We're going to have to do some further investigation but for now your squad has been cleared."

"Anyone I should be keeping an eye on?"

"Not really. I'll send you the results and the video recordings of the interrogations. You may spot something we didn't."

"Any updates on the search warrant?"

"The Colonel put in a request, but he hasn't heard anything yet. The warehouse for the Polar Base is the Emperor's private property, there's nothing we can do about it until the Emperor agrees to the search."

"Have you started interrogating the people from Paris' room?"

"Jackson and Jin started questioning the ones from the base this morning. We're still trying to locate the civilians. Jonathan is questioning the trainee Paris was mentoring."

"I forgot he was mentoring a trainee."

"Yeah, she's only fourteen. We don't believe she's with Mr Jet, but we don't know what ideas Paris could have planted into her head."

"Has Captain Silas…" Angel's phone began to ring, "Yes. Right away sir."

"The Colonel?" Hiroshi asked as Angel hung up.

"Paris has been brought into one of the interrogation rooms. The Colonel wants me and Jackson to question him."

"Something tells me that this is not going to go well."

* * * * *

The guards brought Paris into the interrogation room. His face was hollow and pale. His body looked tired, but his eyes were full of determination. The guards sat him down opposite Jackson and Angel. The shapeshifter stared at the file in front of her. She felt uncomfortable. Although the room had been cleaned, there were still faint stains of blood on the wall from when she had killed the Piper. Angel was glad that her brother was taking part in the interrogation, as she didn't trust herself to be alone in this room once again. The Piper may have been dead but his memory vividly haunted Angel's imagination.

"How did you find your new roommate?" Jackson smiled. Paris didn't speak. "Exercising your right to remain silent, okay. See I'm actually here to offer you a deal."

Paris said nothing.

"The deal is simple; you tell us everything you know about Mr Jet's organisation and in return you don't get executed." Paris laughed. "What's so funny?"

"You really don't know, do you?"

"Know what?" Angel asked.

"This is all because of you. You and the Master of Darkness."

"Elaborate."

"Work it out. It's not hard if you think about it."

"I don't like riddles, so just explain it to me."

"Why do you hate Mr Jet so much?"

"Why do I…? Where do I start!? He wants to let

193

demons take over the world, he's killed thousands of innocent people including our mum."

"Correction. He killed his mum," Paris pointed at Jackson, "Not yours."

"What do you mean?"

"Your mum, Angel, your birth mum. She's very much alive."

"That's not the point of this interrogation," Angel snapped, "We found your warlock's card. What is Mr Jet planning to do at the Polar Base warehouse?"

"Oh maybe you're not as stupid as you look."

"What is Mr Jet planning?"

Paris was silent.

"Answer the question!" Jackson demanded.

Paris just started to laugh, "You're going to die. Angel Night, you will die."

"Yeah you said that before, it's getting a bit boring now," Angel hissed.

"On Halloween, you will die. Your death is coming. Your death is coming! The end is soon. The demons will rise," Paris sang.

"You're completely mad!"

"Your death is…"

"That's enough!" Angel shouted, "Now do you want the deal or not?"

"Why would I make a deal with a dead man?" Paris smiled.

"If you don't take the deal then you will *be* a dead man."

Paris just smiled, "Why don't you ask? Why don't you ask me about your mum? I've met her, you know. Come to think of it, so have you. I know everything about you Angel. Your age, who your parents are, even when and how you'll die!"

"You can tell me all that, after you tell me where Mr Jet is."

Paris started to laugh hysterically.

"Guards take him back to his cell," Jackson ordered. The guards led the laughing Paris away. For a moment Angel didn't know what to do. Angel had never thought about her birth parents. She had almost forgotten about their existence. She had been born, so obviously she must have had birth parents at some point. But why would Paris know them? Why would he mention her birth mum? Did he really know all about her? No, Angel quickly pushed this idea from her mind. Paris couldn't know. He didn't know. He was just trying to mess with her, Angel decided.

"Are you okay?" Jackson asked his sister.

"Fine. He was obviously just trying to mess with me. We should go to the others." Jackson and Angel left quickly and went to the observation room, where the Colonel and the other captains had been watching the interrogation.

"What was that all about!?" Axel exclaimed.

"I don't know," Angel muttered.

"He's not going to talk," The Colonel sighed, "Okay we're going to have to do this the old-fashioned way."

* * * * *

The Colonel and the captains watched as Axel pulled Paris' head out of the water barrel. They were in a long dark room which was stuffy and filled with numerous torture weapons. Strange horrific devices hung on the walls and disgusting odd contraptions stood around the room. A fire blazed in the corner and a thick layer of smoke filled the ceiling. Blood stains dyed the floor and a putrid odour hung in the air. The room was one of the only ones on the base that was without house fairies. None of them dared enter, for this was the torture chamber, a room that, while rarely used, was feared by all. Angel felt sick. She didn't agree with the Colonel's use of torture; she would have preferred to try and attack Paris' mind rather than break his body. Angel turned away as Axel began to beat Paris.

"Tell us what Mr Jet is planning and this all stops," Jackson negotiated.

Paris was silent. Axel grabbed Paris and dunked his head into the water barrel once again. Paris struggled until Axel pulled him out of the barrel and threw him onto the ground.

"What is Mr Jet planning?" Jackson asked once more.

Paris stayed silent.

"Fine. String him up lads," The Colonel ordered. Axel and William went to the side of the room and pulled down a chain. After tying up Paris' hands, Axel pulled the chain, making Paris rise until only the tips of his toes could reach the floor. Axel went over to the fire and picked up a metal poker, placing it in the flames.

"This is your last chance, what is Mr Jet planning?" Jackson asked once more.

Once again Paris remained silent. Angel noticed there was a smile tugging on the corners of Axel's lips as he pressed the hot poker against Paris' bare skin. Paris screamed. It was a loud and powerful scream. The captains, minus Axel, turned away. They were captains, brave men who had fought against some of the deadliest creatures in the world, but even they couldn't watch someone get tortured. It wasn't right. It wasn't what the "good guys" should do.

Angel felt as though the scream had ripped into her body. It was making her feel dizzy. Her chest felt tight and the world around her seemed to shake. She grabbed her head as strange images clogged her vision.

Images of a room. It was dark and smoky. Angel looked down to find that her body had shrunk. She was now the size of a child. Not only that but her hair was blonde instead of its usual blood red. Angel's uniform had also been replaced. She was now dressed in a blood-stained night dress. As the image became clearer Angel realised that she was strapped to a wooden chair. She tried to break free, but she couldn't. She tried to transform only to find that her powers no longer seemed to exist. The sound of heavy footsteps could be heard echoing around the room. Angel looked up to find a man stood in front of her. He was covered in blood and sweat. He lent forwards, holding a baton in one hand and with the other he gently stroked her tears, that had been running down her face without her realising it, away. Then he raised his hand and the baton swung down. The baton made contact with her jaw and her mouth filled with blood. The baton swung down again and again.

"Captain Night," the Colonel's voice cut through the vision.

"What?" Angel stuttered as she returned to her senses. The Colonel was now stood next to her.

"I said maybe you should ask Paris; he may be more willing to talk to you."

"Yes sir," Angel walked towards Paris.

"You okay, sis?" Jackson whispered to her. Angel simply nodded. She pushed Axel away from Paris. She stared at the former gorgon. His once smile-filled face was now bloody and broken. His sharp grey eyes gazed at her. There was no anger left in his expression, only exhaustion.

"Paris," Angel began.

"You're going to die," Paris sang, "You're going to die. On Halloween you will die. And then it all begins."

"What begins?"

"You do. See you're broken right now. They thought making you like this would make you more useful, but they were wrong. You need to be reset. You're soul needs to be cleansed."

"What do you mean?"

"The m…"

"Leave him Captain," the Colonel interrupted, "You're not going to get any useful information out of him. Axel continue."

Axel threw Paris to the floor and dragged him back to

the water barrel. Axel pushed Paris' head under the water and held him there. He pulled Paris up only to dunk him back into the water moments later, this continued for a few minutes then Axel threw Paris back to the floor. With a nod from the Colonel, Axel grabbed the hot metal poker and used it to beat Paris like a drum. Paris screamed. Angel's head burst with pain as her vision blurred and images of another place filled her mind once again.

Angel was dragged to the water barrel. The water clogged up her airways. Then she was pulled up by her hair and thrown down onto the floor. She hit the floor headfirst. There was a loud crack as her skull made contact with the stone. Angel felt something warm run down her forehead. She was bleeding. The shapeshifter was pulled up by her hair again and dragged to her feet. She was slammed into a wall and then…

Angel gasped as the images vanished. The noise of Paris being tortured had faded away like a distant soundtrack. All Angel could hear was the sound of her heart beating quickly. She looked down at her hands, they were shaking violently. Her body felt weak, as if at any moment her bones would crumble into sand.

Then Paris started screaming again.

Angel watched as Axel grabbed Paris and shoved him against the wall. Those two actions felt so familiar. Angel's heartbeat got louder. The room felt like it was closing in. It was as if she was suffocating. She couldn't stay here. Angel opened the door and ran out of the room. She stumbled from the torture chamber. Her legs were weak, she held onto the wall hoping it'd give her enough support to escape. She couldn't breathe. Angel stumbled into a bathroom. Once inside she went over to a toilet and threw up. After throwing up the entire contents of her stomach, Angel dragged herself over to the sink and splashed her face with cold water. The torture images wouldn't fade. They kept replaying. Over and over. Her body hurt. The pain was immense, it rippled over her body like a stone across a pond. Her heart felt like it would explode at any moment. Ba boom, ba boom. Ba boom, ba boom. It beat so loudly and so quickly that it pierced her ear drums. Tears ran down her face as the images consumed her.

Angel collapsed to the floor, unconscious.

A few moments later, Fern entered the bathroom.

Fern swore then dropped to her knees next to the shapeshifter, "Angel? Are you okay? I mean I can see that you're not okay but, what the hell has happened to you? Okay, okay, what can I do!?"

Fern tried to lift Angel up but couldn't, "This is why you shouldn't eat so much…not that I'm calling you fat! But if you lost a few pounds it'd make situations like this much easier. Okay, so how about you just stay there, and I'll get help? I guess I can't just leave you face planted on the bathroom floor. Err okay I'll lean you against the wall. Perfect! Right now you just stay there, and I'll go get…Roger! That's who I need! And I've just been talking to myself. Wonderful," With that Fern quickly left the bathroom. She ran down the dimly lit corridor, but then stopped.

"I can send a message, that'd be quicker," Fern pulled out her wand and was about to send a magic messenger spirit when Jackson headed down the corridor.

"Jackson!" Fern rushed over to him, "You're a wolf! Not the wolf I was thinking of but a wolf none the less!"

"Fern, why are you here?" Jackson asked.

"Well I left my wand here when I had my interrogation, so I came back to get it, then as I was on my way out, I heard some weird noises coming from the bathroom, and I found Angel, collapsed on the floor," Fern explained.

"Where is she?" Jackson quickly followed Fern back to the bathroom. Jackson knelt next to his sister.

"Angel? Angel! Can you wake her up?" Jackson asked.

"I can try," Fern flicked her wand. Freezing water splashed onto Angel's face, causing her eyes to open briefly, however they then rolled over, and she collapsed once again.

"That's not what I meant!" Jackson exclaimed. He grabbed Angel's head and placed it against his.

"What are you doing?"

"Wolf bond. I'm going to, if Angel lets me, enter her mind and see what's going on." Jackson pressed his forehead against Angel's and opened his mind. Her mind allowed him in, and Jackson could see exactly what she could. The images of torture filled the wolf's brain. After a couple of moments Jackson left Angel's mind and pulled his forehead away from hers.

"What's wrong with her?" Fern asked.

"I'm not sure. I think, she's remembered something," Jackson muttered.

"Remembered, you mean the childhood she can't remember? She's remembered something?"

"Perhaps. Open the door for me, I'm going to take her to the hospital wing." Fern did as Jackson asked. Jackson lifted his sister into his arms and carried her to the hospital wing.

"Rowan," Jackson called as he carried Angel into the private room where Sophie was sleeping.

"Jack, what the...? Put her on this bed," Rowan gestured to an empty bed, once Angel was laid on it Rowan turned to Fern, "Go get Skyjack, he's in the cafeteria."

Fern nodded and ran out of the room to fetch the pegacorn. Rowan turned to her husband, "What happened?"

"I think, watching Paris get tortured has triggered a memory, a really bad one."

"You've seen it?"

"Yeah she let me enter her mind. It's, Rowan it's really awful. She was being tortured. She was only a kid and she was getting...it was brutal."

"Angel!" Jason exclaimed in surprise as he entered. The Master of Darkness, who had a warm cup of hot chocolate in his hand, had just taken over Sophie's guard duty.

"Jason, can you pass me that needle and that blue vial from that shelf over there," Rowan asked. Jason mumbled his agreement, placed his cup down, went over to the shelf and picked out the blue vial and the needle, then handed them to Rowan.

"Thanks," the mermaid filled the needle with the blue liquid then injected it into Angel's neck. At that moment, Fern arrived back with Skyjack.

"What's happened?" the pegacorn asked.

"She was found unconscious," Rowan explained, "She has a fever, I need you to try and calm her body down." Skyjack pressed his horn to Angel's forehead. There was silence as the two healers continued working. Jason watched the pair work then picked up his hot chocolate. His rather loud slurping broke the penetrating silence. Fern then began to rant (and hit Jason violently) about how hot chocolate wasn't appropriate for this situation, but the witch was cut off by Skyjack who neighed loudly. The room fell into silence once more. Sophie somehow managed to sleep through this strange set of events and was completely unaware of how close she came to getting hot chocolate spilt all over her bed.

"Jackson," Rowan turned to her husband, "I think you should call your father. After what the Piper showed her and this, he really needs to be here."

Jackson muttered, "I'll go call him."

* * * * *

David Night was drinking tea with the Emperor of the Paranormal Empire. The pair of them, along with the head of the Emperor's guard and Lord Katar, were sat in the Emperor's private quarters. The room was warm with a royal flair and large brown leather seats. A fire glowed softly in the corner and portraits hung on the red walls. David Night (who looked a lot like Jackson) was tall with brown hair and brown eyes. He sipped tea from a teacup that seemed far too small for him as Anita (the head of the Emperor's private guard) spoke softly. Anita, who was dressed in her royal purple uniform, was an Indian fey with over twenty black belts to her name. Sat on a chair next to her was Lord Katar, the leader of the African Moon-Silver Elf clan and a member of the Elf council. He along, with leaders from the six other major elf clans, ruled and protected the Elf kingdom. His pointed elf ears were decorated with a golden cuff that matched his noble Moon-Silver red attire. The Emperor Marcus Cloelius Pompeius was a tall man with brown eyes and a head full of bouncy brown hair. He had a sharp clever looking face that was covered in unhealed battle scars. Dressed in a dashing grey three-piece suit, with light brown shoes shined almost as much as the simple gold crown that sat on top of his head.

"I hope that you understand how important it is that this information doesn't leave this room," the Emperor smiled.

"Given how important this information is, why tell me?" David asked, "Surely the less people that know, the better."

"Because I trust you. After all you're just as invested in this situation as I am."

"Most of Jet's research was lost in the fire," Anita explained, "We don't believe that he can restart his experiments, or at least it will take him a while to get back to the stage he was at."

"It's quite remarkable," David muttered.

"It is. If it wasn't for the fact he was working with the demons, I'd call the man a genius," the Emperor exclaimed, "We're looking into ways to reverse the effects but at the moment we're having no luck."

"There's one thing I don't understand. Why my daughter? Why was she chosen? Why is Jet so interested in her?"

"We don't know," Anita admitted, "Because the research and the whole facility burnt to the ground, we can't be sure exactly what Jet was doing. All our information comes from our source and our source, sadly, does not know."

"There is a lot we don't know," Lord Katar explained, "We..."

At that moment, David's phone started to ring.

"Oh, I apologise," David went to switch his phone off but then he realised it was Jackson (who only ever called in an emergency) calling, "Actually I'm going to have to take this."

"Of course," the Emperor smiled. David got to his feet and left the room. Once in the light corridor he answered the phone. He walked as he spoke to avoid the eavesdropping guards who were posted, in their full suits of silver armour, along each corridor. The werewolf alpha also had to avoid the bright blue servant spirits that dashed round the palace, never looking where they were going. As David answered, two spirits crashed into each other behind him causing a tray of tea (that had been intended for the Queen Dowager) to crash to the polished marble floor.

"Jackson, what's up?" David asked over the noise.

"It's Angel, something has," Jackson stuttered, "She's unconscious. And it'd be best for me to explain in person. Can you come to the base?"

"I'll be right there," David then hung up, walked around the wailing servant spirits, and returned to the Emperor, "I apologise but I need to leave."

"Is everything alright?" the Emperor asked.

"It's a family issue."

"Ah, well family must always come first. Go, it's alright

we can finish off here without you."

"Thank you, sir," David bowed and left the room.

"Do you think he'll keep his mouth shut?" Anita asked once the werewolf was gone.

"David is a good man, he'd never do anything if he believed it would cause me harm," the Emperor said carefully.

"That may be the case, normally sir, but this involves his daughter."

"I could hear his phone call from here," Lord Katar continued, his voice as smooth as honey, "His daughter is unconscious. It was his second eldest living son on the phone asking him to come to the base."

"She's not dying, is she?" the Emperor asked.

"The son didn't say."

"We need her alive. Anita call your asset at the base, tell them to watch the situation carefully. If David looks like he's going to talk, tell your asset to silence him."

"You don't mean…"

"Kill him? No! He is a friend and the head of the biggest wolf pack in the empire. Just tell your asset to make sure he keeps his mouth shut."

19

'DAVID NIGHT'

David Night arrived at the base thirty minutes later. He was quickly passed through security and escorted, by a rather chatty banshee, to the hospital wing. Jackson was waiting for his father to arrive. Upon meeting, the werewolves hugged briefly before getting to the heart of the problem.

"What happened to Angel?" David asked as the chatty banshee (called Bob) left the werewolves. Jackson pressed his forehead against his father's and opened his mind. Once he had seen the images, David pulled away.

'Don't speak,' David snapped telepathically, *'Talk through the wolf bond, we can't risk being overheard.'*

Jackson looked surprised but replied to David through the wolf bond, *'It's a memory, isn't it? She must have been a kid in that…who would do that to a kid!?'*

"What happened exactly?" David asked aloud before saying through the wolf bond, *'Don't say anything about Angel remembering aloud. It could put her in danger. What made her remember this?'*

Jackson, who had never felt this angry before, hissed aloud, "I'm going to kill whoever did this to her."

'Jack, talk through the wolf bond! And calm down!'

'Calm down! Pops, she was getting tortured!'

'It's awful Jackson, I completely agree. But us getting angry won't help this situation, so tell me exactly what happened,' David added sharply, *'Anything about Angel remembering say through the bond, the rest say out loud.'*

Jackson quickly explained what had happened. David growled slightly when Jackson mentioned the torture of Paris but made no other noise. The werewolf alpha remained silent until Jackson was finished.

"Okay," David said simply before adding through the wolf bond *'Does anyone know about Angel's memories?'*

'No. Not exactly.'

'Good, no one can know that Angel has remembered part of her past. I can't tell you the reason right now. I'll explain everything soon, but just know that Angel remembering puts her in serious danger.'

"What is Skyjack doing about the situation?" David asked aloud.

"I'm not exactly sure," Jackson muttered aloud then added through the wolf bond, *'Danger? Why? Do you know? What happened to Angel before you found her?'*

"Can I see Angel?" David asked, *'I have some idea. I need to do some research to find out if what I've been told is true or not.'*

"This way," Jackson led his father into the hospital wing and guided him to Angel's bed. Skyjack had his horn pressed against Angel's forehead. The tip of his horn was glowing a soft blue. Fern was sat with Jason (who had finally finished his hot chocolate) next to the sleeping Sophie's bed. Jackson quickly asked Skyjack for an update.

"She's settling down," Skyjack explained, "Nice to see you again David."

"Wow! You two look identical!" Fern exclaimed staring

at Jackson and David.

"Pops, this is Angel's friend and squad mate, Fern," Jackson introduced, "And that's Jason Dragonheart, the Master of Darkness. And the fairy with the blindfold on is Sophie Day, another member of Angel's squad."

"Dragonheart, it's been a long time since I've met anyone by that name," David muttered thoughtfully.

"You've met someone with my name before?" Jason asked.

"A long time ago. It's an honour to meet you," as David gently shook Jason's hand he muttered in surprise, "Huh, that's interesting."

"What is?" Jason asked nervously.

"It's nothing, just your scent, it's similar to someone I know."

"Is that bad?"

"No, it's just normally people with similar scents tend to be family, but that can't be the case here. Anyway it's nice to see that the Master of Darkness has returned," David released the confused Jason's hand and turned to Angel, "What happened to her exactly?"

"Her body went into an extreme state of fear, but I've been able to calm her down," Skyjack explained.

"Why was she like that?" Fern asked.

"It could be an aftereffect of the fight against Mr Jet's followers," Jackson announced suddenly, giving Skyjack a look, "She was pretty badly beaten up."

"It...yes...that seems likely. If she fought a warlock, this could be a delayed effect of a spell," Skyjack lied, "Angel was too busy after the fight, taking care of everyone else and running about for the Colonel, that she wasn't able to recover. I need to continue with my rounds. I'll send Rowan over to keep an eye on her." With that Skyjack left.

"So I guess for now we just wait and see," David muttered pulling a chair next to Angel's bed

"You two can go," Jackson dismissed Jason and Fern, "I'll watch Sophie. You two should go take a break, the questioning you went through earlier was pretty intense."

"But Angel," Fern started.

"I'll message you the moment she wakes up," Jackson promised, "Actually can you do me a favour, could you tell Roger and Ethan what's happened and ask them to come here?"

"And what exactly am I *saying* happened?"

"That Angel has collapsed due to a delayed spell.

"Would you like me to go tell the Colonel that?"

"Would you do that?"

"Sure, the Colonel doesn't scare me," Fern smiled, "And I'll drag the Master of Darkness with me, that way if the Colonel gets mad, Jason can turn into a demon and eat him! Come on demon-boy," Fern grabbed the protesting Jason's arm and dragged him out of the room.

"That witch is clever. She saw right through you," David muttered, "She didn't fall for the delayed spell story, will that be a problem?"

"No," Jackson explained, "Fern will play along with it until Angel wakes up, then she'll beat the truth out of us."

* * * * *

Fern dragged Jason to the Colonel's office and banged on the door, despite the protests from Helena the ghost.

"You can't do that!" the ghost screamed, "You shouldn't do that!"

"I know I shouldn't, but I'm going to anyway," Fern smiled before banging on the door again.

"I'm here, what's all the fuss about?" the Colonel's voice echoed down the corridor. Fern and Jason turned to see the Colonel stood behind them.

"Ah, sir!" Fern exclaimed, "Captain Night, the female one, has collapsed. The healers reckon that Angel was hit by a spell during her fight with Mr Jet's followers. They say Angel has been fighting off the effects of it since then, but those effects have now caught up to her. She's being treated in the hospital wing. She's unconscious at the moment. The healers are trying to work out exactly how much damage the spell has caused."

"Is she…? Hmm, okay, keep me informed," the Colonel muttered before walking straight past Fern and Jason, entering his office, and slamming the door in their faces.

"Rude. Come on Jason, let's go back to the house," Fern grabbed Jason's arm and pulled him down the corridor.

"You know, I am perfectly capable of walking by myself," Jason exclaimed.

"If you say so," Fern muttered, releasing her hold on Jason's arm. The pair walked silently through the Colonel's gothic manor house. The Colonel's manor was very dark; the walls were painted a deep green and the furniture was black. The floors were wooden, and they creaked under their boots. Not much of the inner personal rooms of the manor were visible, they were all locked away behind heavily wooden doors. The Colonel's office was on the ground floor. No one in the base's history had seen beyond that. What lay upstairs remained a mystery.

"Do you think Angel will be okay?" Jason asked as they stepped outside and walked past the building in which the hospital wing was situated.

"Yeah she'll be fine. She once got bitten by a zombie but managed to survive, so this is nothing."

"Why is the spell only affecting Angel now?"

"Are you stupid? Some spells don't affect you till a couple of days after you've been hit by it. Everyone knows that!"

"Hey, I'm not stupid! I haven't lived in this world for very long!"

"Well if you want to keep living in this world, you better start learning some common knowledge."

"Well, Paris was tutoring me."

"Then it's no surprise you've learnt next to nothing!"

"How well did you know Paris?"

"Clearly not well enough," Fern muttered, "I've known him for nearly ten years. We joined at the same time, but I was put into Hurricane Squad for training and he was put into Earthquake, so I never had much contact with him. We were then put into different active squads to begin with. I used to be in Wildfire Squad and Paris, I think he was put into Tornado, anyway I was moved into Lightning Squad and, I think about a year later, he was also moved up. It wasn't until then that I actually spoke to him. I never liked him."

"Ten years? You've been here a while. How long have you known Angel?"

"Six years or so. I was her mentor when she was a trainee, or at least I was to begin with, then they swapped things round and made Alexander her mentor instead. Ah, I forgot you never went through training! Every trainee gets a mentor, someone from one of the active squads. The mentors are meant to answer questions and help the trainee out."

"Oh okay, so Angel's been at the base for six years, then…"

"Yeah I'm pretty sure I just said that."

"Has anyone ever told you that you're really annoying."

"Yes, multiple times."

"That's nothing to be proud of."

"I don't know, being annoying is a skill. Not everyone can be as good at it as I am."

"Whatever! What I was trying to ask was how come Angel is captain when you've been here longer?"

"Oh I've never wanted to be captain, so I've never done the captain's exam. I probably wouldn't have passed even if I had done it, I've failed my broom flying exam sixteen times!"

"Sixteen times!"

"Hey! Flying on a broomstick isn't easy!"

Jason laughed, "How long has Angel been captain then?"

"Err, about three years. Yeah it must be about that. She did six months training then went into Wildfire Squad, then to Lightning and then she did her captain training, yeah so it must be about three years."

"Did you all go into other squads before going into Lightning Squad?"

"Yeah you see, Alpha, Lightning and Thunder are the top squads, so trainees can't be put straight into them. Trainees get put into another active squad then are transferred into Alpha or Lightning or Thunder if they're skilled enough. Unless you're the Master of Darkness, of course, then you just skip training all together and get thrown into one of the top squads despite the fact you have no skills at all!" Fern mocked.

"Hey! That's, I didn't ask to be put in this squad, and I have skills!"

"Yeah, name one?" Before Jason could think of an answer, the pair had arrived back at the Lightning Squad house. Fern opened the door and they went inside. They found Roger and Ethan with the other members of Lightning Squad in the operations room, where Alexander was explaining some new security measures that were being put into place. Fern barged into the room, interrupting Alexander mid-way through a sentence.

"Fern, you're late and Jason, shouldn't you be in the hospital wing, your shift isn't over yet," Alexander uttered annoyed.

"Roger, Ethan you need to go to the hospital wing," Fern announced, ignoring the vampire. "Angel has collapsed, and your dad is here. The healers reckon she got hit by a spell during her fight with Mr Jet's followers and is only now suffering the effects of it. She's unconscious."

Before Fern could say anymore, Ethan and Roger ran out of the room.

"If her dad has been called, is she…?" Elsa started to ask.

"She's not going to die," Fern explained, "Their dad was already coming to the base. Angel just happened to collapse on the same day."

"What kind of spell was she hit with?" Danny asked.

"I don't know, I wasn't there."

"What are the effects of the spell?"

"Err, I don't know. I just know that it made her collapse."

"Looks like you're going to be captain again, Alex," Clover smirked, "The lock up and now the hospital wing, it doesn't seem like Angel is fit for duty."

"I'm sure Angel will be back to full health in no time," Alexander reassured, "Now as I was saying, because of the recent attacks…"

"But until Angel gets better, you will be captain again, right?"

"There's only one captain of Lightning Squad and that's Angel," Fern snapped.

"Who isn't 'fit for duty' right now, but then has she ever been fit for duty?"

"That's enough," Alexander snapped, "I'm sure that, as soon as she wakes up, Angel will be returning as captain. I know the last few days have been very stressful for all of you, but this is not the time for us to be arguing and turning on each other. I won't hear any more on this subject. Is that clear?"

"Yes sir," the squad muttered in unison.

"Let's take a break," Alexander ordered, "Come back in ten minutes."

With that Lightning Squad, apart from Araminta, slowly left the room. Araminta stood up and walked up to Alexander.

"Is it time for me to check in?"

"Yes," Araminta pulled out a small electronic tablet from her pocket. She held the tablet up to Alexander's face. A blue light scanned his face causing the tablet screen to turn green, "Okay. You're clear. Your next check in is at midnight, don't miss it."

"I won't," Alexander muttered, "I don't know why you keep doing this, you're not going to find anything."

"I'm just doing what I've been ordered to do."

"I know, doesn't mean I can't moan about it. Do you know anything about what's happened to Angel?"

"No, however if David is here, you should keep away from the hospital wing. It'd be best if you two didn't run into each other."

* * * * *

Angel's eyes flickered open. She was in a hospital bed, she quickly realised, and there were four nervous looking werewolves staring down at her.

"Pops, why are you here?" Angel muttered.

"How are you feeling?" David asked.

"Alright. I guess. My head hurts."

"Skyjack reckons that you collapsed because of a delayed reaction to a spell, from when you fought with Mr Jet's followers," Jackson explained.

That's the cover story, so play along with it,' David whispered through the wolf bond.

"Oh, right, yeah that makes sense," Angel uttered aloud before asking through the bond, *'I wasn't hit with a spell when I fought with Mr Jet's followers. Why are you talking through the wolf bond?'*

'We can't risk being overheard,' David explained.

Before Angel could ask why, Roger suddenly exclaimed aloud, "You've been unconscious for six hours, we were starting to get worried."

'What happened?' David asked through the wolf bond, *'Jackson has shown us those visions you were having...what*

213

happened to you?'

'I'm not sure. I was watching Paris get questioned when I started feeling weird then I started having these strange visions, which you've seen. At first, I only saw them briefly, but then the visions kept repeating and I couldn't stop them. I remember running out of the room and trying to walk down the corridor. It was really hard to breathe and move, it was like I was stuck in quicksand.'

"Skyjack said the spell really messed with your brain," Ethan stated aloud.

"You're going to have to stay in the hospital wing for a day or so. Just so that Rowan can make sure that the spell didn't cause any other damage," David said aloud, he then continued through the bond, *'I think, actually after seeing your visions we all think that, those visions might be memories.'*

'How is that possible? I thought that the curse would prevent me from ever remembering anything. I thought I would have to try and get the curse removed.'

'Maybe because of what the Pied Piper showed you, your brain is starting to fight against the curse,' Roger suggested.

'It makes sense, but if what happened in those visions is true then…then…'

'Then you were tortured at some point during your childhood,' David finished the sentence.

Angel looked down at the numbers that were burnt onto her arm, *'Do you think that I got those when I was tortured?'*

'They might be…an experiment number…' David thought, the thought was meant to be a private one but because he was part of the wolf bond the others overheard.

'What do you mean?'

'I wasn't meant to share that, don't worry about it yet, that's something I need to look in to.'

'Why are we talking through the wolf bond? You never said why.'

'Because you remembering, that needs to remain a secret. You can't mention it aloud. I can't explain to you in detail yet. Once I find everything out for certain, I promise I will tell you but for now

you just need to trust me. Never mention the fact that you've remembered part of your past to anyone. It could put you in danger.'

'Danger? Why? Pops what is...Can you guys feel that?'

'Someone's trying to listen into our wolf bond!' Everyone leave the bond and close your minds. We'll have to discuss this some other time.' They all left the bond and closed their minds. For a moment, they all stayed silent as each of them tried to sense where the intruder was.

"That's funny," Angel muttered aloud, "I thought I heard someone."

"As did I," Roger said carefully, "It was probably just a healer passing by."

"How come you're here?" Angel asked David, "I thought you were visiting next week."

"I was already in Transylvania when Jackson called me and said you were ill, so I thought I'd move my visit forward," David explained.

"Ah that makes sense. I'm glad to see you, sorry to have worried you."

"Not at all, it's good to see that you're starting to feel better."

"Jackson what happened with Paris? Did they get anything out of him?"

"I don't know," Jackson admitted, "No one has told me."

"Ah okay." Angel fell into silence. Her brain was working overtime trying to process the fact that at some point during her childhood she had been tortured. She couldn't settle her emotions. She was angry. Angry that some unknown person had tortured her. Angry at herself for remembering something so painful. Angry at herself for not remembering more. Angel was upset. Upset at the fact someone had tortured her. Upset that her childhood had been so horrific. Upset that she had been put through so much pain. Angel was also curious. She wanted to know more. She wanted to know why. Why she had been

215

tortured and why remembering put her in danger. She wanted to remember everything but at the same time she hoped that she never remembered anything else. Angel wanted to cry. She wanted to scream and shout. But she couldn't. She couldn't do anything because some unknown force, for some unknown reason, was watching her. Angel had so many questions she wanted to ask. Why had she been tortured? Who were her birth parents and why did they let that happen? Why would remembering put her in danger? How had she escaped? Why had she arrived in the Night forest? Why did the witch call her Samantha? Was that her name? Who was the man in the Piper's memory? Angel had called her father to answer some of these questions but now he wouldn't be able to, because the answers couldn't be spoken aloud, nor could they be said in the wolf bond. So Angel was left without any answers, without an outlet to express her conflicting emotions, left to bottle up her feelings and to carry on as if nothing was wrong.

"You okay?" Roger asked.

"Yeah," Angel lied, "Just tired and hungry."

"I was waiting for you to say that," David smiled, "Whenever you're upset or angry, you always want food."

"She always wants food no matter what she's feeling," Ethan joked, "What do you want to eat?"

"Food," Angel said simply.

"What kind of food?"

"The edible kind."

"Sounds like I've come at the perfect time," Rowan smiled as she entered the room, holding two bags filled with food, "I also brought you a change of clothes."

"Ah yeah, I forgot I threw up a bit on these," Angel muttered sheepishly.

"No wonder you smell," Jackson joked.

"Hey! Patient! Don't bully me today!" Angel pulled the curtain around her bed and changed quickly. Rowan handed them each a container full of food. There was silence as the Nights devoured their dinner. The quiet was filled by the heavy feeling of uneasiness. Angel wasn't the only one tormented by the vast amount of unanswered questions, her brothers were feeling just as angry. They wanted to protect their sister; protect her from the memories, from the past and from the unknown force that lurked in the shadows. They wanted to kill the people who had harmed her; rip them to pieces and make them pay for their crimes. But they couldn't do that, for they didn't even know who they were angry at.

"How are you feeling Angel?" Rowan asked, breaking the tense silence.

"Alright. Any change with Sophie?"

"Sophie is recovering nicely. Hopefully we'll be able to discharge her soon."

"That's good news," Angel turned to Ethan and Roger, "Has Alex explained the new security measures to the squad yet?"

"He was doing that when we got the news about you," Ethan said, his mouth filled with food, "I imagine he continued after we left."

"You've only just woke up and you're already thinking of work," David shook his head.

"I'm just thinking about my squad. I've only just got back as captain."

"Alex can take care of things," Roger reassured.

"I know he can, but he hates it. And the squad hate it when he's in charge of training. Alex is my vice-captain."

"Ah the vampire?" Angel nodded then David continued, "You seem to get along with him well."

"I do. We work well together."

"I see," then David asked, "How long has the Master of Darkness been at the base?"

"Oh, did you meet him? Jason hasn't been here long, about a month," Angel added, "He's nice enough. A bit useless. He grew up in the human world so he's a bit of a pathetic Master of Darkness."

"Jason is great!" Roger smiled, "Me and Ethan are good mates with him. But yeah let's just say it's sometimes very hard to believe that he's the most powerful man on the planet."

"Hey, you know what I've just realised," Ethan exclaimed, "That this is the first meal we've all had together as a family since Rowan and Jack got married."

"Oh yeah!" Jackson exclaimed, "If only Tobias was here!"

"He would just bring down the mood."

"Have you told your parents about the marriage yet?" David asked Rowan.

"I told them yesterday," Rowan sighed, "It didn't go down well."

"Just give them some were-maids then they'll forgive you," Roger joked.

"Some what?"

"If you and Jackson have kids then we're going to refer to them as were-maids."

"You're not calling my kids that," Jackson protested.

"Were-maids is a cute name," David interjected, "I want a reasonably large litter of were-maid grandchildren and it'd be nice to gets some before I reach five-hundred."

"Pops," Jackson groaned.

"Well Jack, you're going to have to be the one to give me grandkids seeing as I'm unlikely to see any from the rest of you! You three can't even manage to get dates!"

"That's not, well, it's kind of true," Roger reluctantly admitted.

"Hey me and Roger aren't as bad as Angel. At least we've dated in the past, Angel has never dated anybody!" Ethan exclaimed.

"That's, yeah well hey you can't pick on me today, I'm ill!" Angel protested. The Night family laughed. The family joked and talked for most of the night. The subject of Angel's memories wasn't spoken of. As Angel looked round at her family laughing and smiling together, she realised how lucky she was that David had found her that day in the forest. If he hadn't, Angel dreaded to imagine what her life might have been like. When the other Nights finally fell asleep, Angel remained awake.

She whispered to herself, "So I was tortured, as a kid, I was tortured. Then I must have escaped. Escaped into the Night forest, where I killed a human child, tried to kill myself and then was cursed. This is so messed up!"

Angel hid her face in her hands and cried.

20

'NO ONE TOUCHES ANGEL'S SWORD'

The next morning Angel woke to the sound of David speaking. She opened her eyes to see him talking on the phone. The rest of the Night family were still asleep. Roger was curled up on the floor by Angel's bed, whilst Ethan slept across two chairs. Rowan and Jackson were asleep on one of the spare hospital beds.

"Yes, Edwin, yes I know this is a hard subject for you but you're the only one who can confirm it. Yes, yes, I know he could, but I haven't got time to go to China and find him. Yes. I know. This isn't easy for me either. At eleven? Ah, no, no, I'll be there. Thank you, Edwin," David hung up the phone, and turned to face Angel, realising she was awake he smiled, "Morning pup, how are you feeling?"

"Better. Who were you on the phone to?"

"An old acquaintance of mine, he wanted to meet with me today to discuss something."

"Is it something to do with me?" David didn't answer. "Are you going to meet him today?"

"I don't want to leave you."

"Go. I'm more than capable of looking after myself, and if I ever become incapable, I've got these idiots to take care of me. So don't worry and go to your meeting...but next time I come home, you better tell me everything. Danny?" Angel exclaimed in surprise as Danny entered the hospital wing.

"Angel, you alright?" Danny asked.

"Yes, what are you doing here?"

"It's my turn to guard Sophie. I wasn't sure if your brothers were planning to stay here during the day, so I thought I'd come and check."

"Oh, this is Danny. He's a friend of mine and a member of my squad," Angel explained to David.

"Is this your...?" Angel nodded, "Ah, nice to meet you sir." Danny bowed his head politely.

"You have the same scent too, how interesting," David mumbled, "Ah I'm sorry, I tend to think aloud, it's a bad habit of mine."

"Your daughter does the same. Angel, are you going to be here all day?"

"It'll depend on whether the healers let me go, for now Danny, just go back to the house, when I leave, I'll call you," Angel promised.

"I'll get going then, it was nice to put a face to the name sir," Danny bowed his head to David before leaving the hospital wing.

"Who just spoke? Hmmm, what time is it?" Roger mumbled. He had just woken up; his hair was messy, and he looked half asleep.

"Time you got up! I need to leave in a bit," David laughed.

"You're leaving? Already? Ethan. Ethan!" Roger hissed trying to wake his brother up. Angel picked up an empty water bottle, that had been on the table next to her bed and threw it. The bottle hit Ethan's nose.

"What the…? Who?" Ethan stuttered as he woke up, stunned.

"Oi, sleeping beauty, get up! Pops has to go," Angel smiled.

"Who just threw this at me?" Ethan asked. Roger pointed at Angel, who pointed back at her brother, "Pops, which of them threw this at me?"

"I don't know, I wasn't looking," David grinned, "Wake up Jack."

Grumbling Ethan turned in his chair and threw the bottle at his older brother. The bottle hit its mark; it bounced off Jackson's forehead and landed on Rowan's cheek. The couple woke up startled.

"Not like that!"

"What!? that's how they woke me up," Ethan sneezed.

"What's going on?" Jackson asked.

"Pops is leaving," Roger explained.

"Already?"

"I have a meeting," David stated.

"Do you want breakfast before you go?" Rowan asked, "I can…"

"No, don't worry about it," David stood up, "I have to get going if I'm late then I won't get another opportunity. Angel, please take care of yourself. If anything like this happens again…"

"I'll call you straight away," Angel promised.

"Make sure you don't do anything until you've fully recovered."

"We'll keep an eye on her, don't worry about it Pops," Roger reassured.

"I know. I know. You know I'm going to worry. My four little pups are all fighting against demons."

"So are you! We're just following in your paw prints," Jackson pointed out.

"Hmmm, yes but unlike you pups, I have years of experience and I'm not an idiot."

"We're not idiots!" Ethan exclaimed.

"Yeah, just because Ethan is an idiot doesn't mean the rest of us are," Angel teased.

"Hey!"

"Jokes aside," David said seriously, "Take care of yourselves and each other. I don't want to see any of you getting hurt or worse, so take care."

"We will if you do."

"Yeah, don't go off secretly fighting demons all by yourself anymore," Angel sighed, "You should take care of yourself too, the pack needs its alpha."

"If you're going to keep hunting demons, then at least take someone with you," Jackson insisted.

David smiled, "Aw, how did I get such great kids?"

"I know right? If it wasn't for Ethan, we'd be pretty incredible."

"Hey! Why are you all picking on me!?" Ethan exclaimed.

"Because Tobias isn't here."

"It's too early for this."

"Ethan, it's nearly eleven."

"Is it? Ah, I need to go," David realised, "I will see you all soon. Love you all."

"Love you," the Night siblings replied in unison as David left.

After a moment of silence Roger asked, "Is anyone else hungry?"

* * * * *

"I feel fine, can I go back to work now?" Angel asked when Rowan examined her four hours later. Angel had managed to persuade her brothers to return to their duties a few hours earlier and now she was desperate to do so herself. The shapeshifter wasn't very good at being a patient. She didn't like being in hospital and she didn't like leaving her squad after only just returning to them. It had been only a matter of days since she had been released from lock up. And Angel did feel physically fine; her body was back to normal and she was no longer overwhelmed by the past. Mentally she was still a complete emotional wreck, but she could cope with that.

"That's good. Hmmm, your readings are normal," Rowan muttered as she read through Angel's chart, "You're just going to have to be careful and make sure…ah Sophie you're awake!"

"Angel are you okay?" Sophie asked. The fairy was sat up in her hospital bed. Her eyes were covered in a thick bandage, so she was unable to see the ward around her, however she had recognised Angel's voice instantly.

"Yeah, I got hit with a spell and it messed with my system, but everything is sorted now. How are you feeling?"

"Well, apart from the fact I can't see, I'm fine. The stab wound doesn't hurt anymore."

"Oh, I brought you something that'll help with your eyes, I've got you Paris' sunglasses, they're specially designed so that you won't turn anyone to stone," Angel explained, "Rowan could you pass them to her?"

Rowan went over to a draw and pulled out Paris' sunglasses. She handed them to Sophie and started to untie the blindfold. Angel quickly turned her eyes away. Rowan did as well, leaving Sophie to cover her eyes with the sunglasses. The fairy did so. Paris' powers gave the world a grey tint that made the fairy feel rather disorientated at first but, after a couple of blinks, she soon got used to it.

"I've got the sunglasses on so you can look."

Angel turned back, "Until we can work out how to get rid of Paris' powers you'll have to keep those glasses on."

Rowan checked Sophie's readings and mumbled, "It seems that, apart from Paris' powers, you're back to full health. You can probably go back to work today but I would advise that you didn't do anything too extreme just yet. You'll have to come back here every few days for a check-up."

"You should probably go to the training centre," Angel advised, "Seeing as, at least for now, you're stuck with Paris' powers you should learn how to use them. Captain Phillip has dealt with a lot of gorgons, he might be able to help you out."

"How did you take Paris' powers? Your blood type also doesn't match up and you can heal yourself very quickly. What...?"

"Rowan leave it. She's only just woken up."

"But…"

"Angel!" Fern cried as she entered the hospital wing with Roger. She ran over to Angel and pulled her into a tight hug, "You're not dead!"

"Clearly. You're choking me!"

"Good," Fern pulled away, "You deserve it! You proper scared me! Collapsed like that. I thought I'd have to bury you. Oh Sophie you're awake too!"

"How are the patients?" Roger asked.

"Both seem to have recovered," Rowan explained, "They need to take it easy, but they should be able to leave the hospital wing today."

"Really? Then can I make a suggestion?" Fern grinned, "How do you two fancy a sparring session?"

"I said they need to take it easy."

"We will be. Only a light sparring session, just to get these two back into the swing of things."

"That sounds good," Angel muttered, "I'm really in the mood to hit something."

* * * * *

"Please don't kill each other," Roger called from the side as Angel, Sophie and Fern sparred. The training room they were in was a circular shape, with a magic circle painted in gold on the purple floor. The magic circle was a safe place where witches and fey could practice their magic without risk of damage or death. For the purpose of sparring, all three of them used wands to control their magic. Sophie and Angel fought Fern who, although in many other areas (broom flying especially) was a pretty useless witch, was an expert in wand sparring. Sophie's wand sent a purple ray of light at Fern, which she blocked with a green shield. Angel sent a white lightning fork at the witch but that too was blocked. Fern sent two rays of green light in their direction. Angel used her wand to send the spell in the opposite direction while Sophie rolled out of the way.

Rays of green, white, and purple dashed around the magic circle, lighting up the training room. Roger watched in awe as the magic trio fought against each other. The werewolf, who had no magical ability, always found magical fights enchanting to watch. Colours would spin across the room as the trio avoided being turned into frogs or chickens. The fighters were only using harmless spells (as they didn't want to kill each other) but they fought as if their lives depended on it. Blocking and attacking with such speed that Roger found it hard to keep track of who was winning. The sparring continued for nearly an hour until finally Angel and Sophie raised their hands and admitted defeat.

"Are you surrendering to me?" Fern asked as Angel stepped out of the magic circle.

"Today I am. But next time, next time I will wipe that smug smile from your face," Angel panted as she sat herself down on a bench and wiped her sweat away with a towel. Sophie did the same. Roger handed them both a bottle of water which they gulped down quickly.

"You two alright?" he asked.

"We're just tired," Sophie reassured.

"One day I'll beat her," Angel muttered.

"That's unlikely," Fern grinned, "I have never been

beaten before."

For a short while the quartet simply drank and discussed their fight; analysing their moves and suggesting areas for improvement. Then Angel suggested that Sophie and Fern should go find Jonathan (Captain Phillip) for he had dealt with many gorgons in the past and may be able to help Sophie master her new ability.

"Okay, that's a good idea," Fern nodded, "The last thing we need is Sophie turning everybody to stone. Though if you turn my sister into a garden gnome, I will be forever grateful."

"I'm not turning Clover to stone," Sophie muttered as she and Fern walked out of the training room.

Once they had left Angel walked into another training room. This room was small and set out like a boxing gym. The ring was occupied by Bob the banshee and an imp (who were in the middle of an intense round), so Angel went over to a punchbag in the corner of the room. She picked up a pair of boxing gloves and started pounding on it furiously. The emotions she couldn't express she poured into each punch. For a while Roger didn't say a word. He just stood back and watched as Angel's punches became more desperate. Roger wasn't sure what to do. Roger knew Angel best yet even he didn't know how to help her get through this. This was a situation he had never imagined. He had never expected her to regain some of her lost memories, in fact he had always dreaded the idea. Roger could remember the day Angel had arrived at the Night forest vividly. He could remember her broken bruised skin and how her pale skinny body had been covered in crimson blood. Roger shook away the memory and painted a smile on his face. Now wasn't the time to be haunted by the past, it was instead the time to help Angel get through the present.

"What did that punchbag ever do to you?" He asked.

"Nothing," Angel sighed, "It's just, it just keeps

running through my head. That and Paris."

"What's the capital of France ever done to you?"

"You know that's not what I'm on about."

"I know, I was attempting to lighten the conversation."

"It didn't work."

"You did have a slight smile, so I class it as a success."

"You're really weird."

"I know it's what makes me interesting. Now what is it about Paris that's getting at you?"

"It just bugs me. That he's a terrorist, and I didn't see it coming. Also…I think Paris let the witch onto the base. When I saw her in the forest, I found a warlock's card that said Samantha. After I found it, Paris turned up. Mr Jet's followers use the same type of warlock's card to communicate."

"So, the witch and Mr Jet might be connected somehow. And if that witch and Jet are connected, then Jet might have something to do with you getting tortured."

"There's something else, in his interrogation, Paris said that he knew my birth mum and that I've met her too."

"He was probably messing with you. Have you ever met another female shapeshifter?" Angel shook her head. "If you haven't met another shapeshifter, then you obviously haven't met your mum, unless your mixed heritage. Hey stop frowning! You look ugly when you frown."

"Thanks!"

"I'm sorry pup, I mean you don't look yourself, you look, no, yeah I'm digging a hole," Roger muttered with a smile on his face.

"Yeah you really are!" Angel laughed as she gently punched him. He grabbed her arm and pulled her into a head lock. The pair wrestled each other jokingly and ended up collapsed in a heap on the ground.

"Ugh I thought you were meant to be brother and sister," Axel swaggered into the room, "From where I'm standing you two look like a couple, well I guess you're not blood related."

"What do you want Axel?" Angel asked as she sat herself up.

"The Colonel wants to see you."

* * * * *

Angel found the Colonel, and the other captains (apart from Jackson and Jonathan), waiting outside of the torture chamber. The corridor they were in was dark and shadows danced up the walls. Except for a single fire imp (that played in the flames of the torches), the corridor was completely lifeless, there were no house fairies and no ghost dared enter. Angel felt nervous. She didn't like the idea of going back into the torture chamber. She feared the memories that might resurface if she did. Skyjack had given her a calming spell which would hopefully save her from collapsing a second time, but still butterflies banged in her stomach as she reached the door.

"Sir," Angel greeted, "How has the questioning progressed?"

"It hasn't. He hasn't said a word since you left," Hiroshi explained, "It'd actually be kind of impressive… if it wasn't for the fact, he was a demon worshiping traitorous lunatic."

"He is exhausted though," the Colonel explained, "Both physically and mentally. I want Captain Lu to attempt to enter Paris' mind. Captain Night I want you to act as the anchor."

"Anchor?" Axel asked.

"Jin will enter Paris' mind fully however I'll only enter his mind partially. If Jin gets into trouble, I can then pull him out," Angel explained.

"Ah I see. So an anchor can save a telepath from being trapped in someone else's mind!"

"But Angel you've only just got out of hospital,"

William pointed out.

"I'm fully recovered," Angel said quickly after seeing the Colonel's irritated expression, "Besides I've acted as Jin's anchor before so it's better that I do it."

"Good, now let's get on with it," the Colonel went back into the torture chamber, Axel followed.

"Angel are you well enough to do this?" William asked.

"I'll be fine besides I don't think the Colonel will take no for an answer."

"He's in a really bad mood. He won't listen to us. Jackson was against you being the anchor, so the Colonel kicked him out. I think the Emperor is pushing for results."

"Then we best get this over with quickly," Angel muttered. She took a deep breath and with a nervous heart entered the torture chamber. Paris was sat in the middle of the room. His body was broken, and his hair soaked in sweat. The determined gaze had vanished from his eyes and now he simply looked depleted. *He's a terrorist, he's working with Mr Jet*, Angel told herself as sympathy and the desire to save him bubbled in her chest. It was still hard for Angel to remember that Paris was no longer a member of her squad. Before his terrorism had become known, Angel would have died to protect him, as she would do for any member of her squad. However he was no longer a member of her squad, Angel quickly reminded herself, and no longer deserved her compassion. Jin sat down in front of Paris and Angel sat behind him, placing a hand on his shoulder.

"What are you doing?" Paris asked, "You won't...you won't be able to get into my mind...I won't let you in..."

Angel and Jin closed their eyes and opened their minds.

* * * * *

Angel's mind joined with Jin's and the pair met on a telepathic plane. It was a strange place filled with different colours and unique spiralling shapes. It was a bright and warm limbo between reality and the spiritual world. Upon meeting, Angel attached a white glowing rope around Jin's mental body, and the other end round her wrist, "Pull the rope, and I'll pull you out."

"I know, I taught you how to do this, remember," Jin replied.

"How deep are you planning to go in?"

"Hopefully not deep, I'm hoping the answers we seek will be near the surface."

Jin reached out (mentally) and tried to enter Paris' mind. Angel followed. The pair fell into a whirlwind of colours before they were greeted by a massive wall. The wall was crumbling, and looked battle worn. Its stone was grey and the gargoyles that sat watching from the arches made it clear that they were not welcome here. Directly in front of them was a large wooden door that was protected by a portcullis. Jin walked up to the door but a wave of red light burst from it, hitting him in the chest and sending him flying backwards into Angel. The pair stumbled to the ground as a second wave of red light attacked them. The world shook and then nothing. The realm of telepathy was still.

Angel pulled Jin to his feet. After quickly realising that they were not going to be able to enter via the main gate, they began to search for another entrance. Paris was weak and, while the entrance to his mind was still a force to be reckoned with, his outer defences were beginning to crumble. Jin (being the powerful telepath that he is) began to attack parts of the wall. He sent dark blue waves of light at the stone, each wave carrying a message of surrender. The message bounced off the walls until it found an area of the defences that was tempted by this idea. Once the weakest point was found, Jin began to direct his attack solely at that area. Angel watched in awe as Jin singlehandedly caused the wall to collapse. The stones tumbled to the ground, landing in a pile at Jin's feet. The telepath smiled and carefully climbed over the remains of the wall. Once he had assessed the situation on the other side, he called for Angel to follow which she swiftly did.

"Keep your guard up," Jin warned as Angel landed beside him, "This has been too easy."

They walked slowly, taking in the war-torn world around them. Everything was broken and decaying. The ground shook under their feet. It was covered in cracked photo frames and video reels that were ripped apart. The sky was red and the atmosphere cold. Doors lay ahead of them. Some had been flung open, by a strong force it seemed, whilst others were firmly shut. The inside of Paris' mind was a desolate place; empty, broken, without any warmth or love. Angel stared at a photograph that lay, ripped, and faded, at her feet. It was a photograph she knew well and loved. It was the group photo of Lightning Squad. Unlike the version that hung in the entrance to the Lightning House, this picture had the members faces burnt off. Angel sighed, tearing up slightly at the sight. She pushed all her thoughts away and turned her attention back to the job at hand. Jin was sat in front of the doors, eyes closed. After a moment, he raised his hand. Suddenly a door opened, and four glowing balls of light bounced through. They span around the sky and rolled across the rubble. Each ball was a different colour; white, grey, red, and pale green. Jin paused and watched the four balls, trying to judge which of them would hold the information he needed.

"The colours represent different emotions and thoughts, right?" Angel asked.

"Yes normally," Jin explained, "Grey is often linked to sadness however I don't think that's the case here. It doesn't look like sadness. This is something I haven't seen before. Notice that its fading, what is that? It's not his life force, a person's life force doesn't look like that."

The pair were silent for a moment, each deep in thought, then Angel exclaimed, "Fading…stone! Paris' powers! He's part gorgon but he's lost his powers! I think that ball represents the loss of his gorgon ability."

"You might be right about that. The green one, I've seen that colour before, it's peace. Paris has made peace with the fact he's going to die. He's prepared for it. Lights like that often appear in the minds of suicide bombers and martyrs. We don't need that one."

"Oh…the red one is hate and anger, right?"

"Pain and anger in this case, make sure that ball doesn't hit you.

All the anger and the pain Paris is feeling has been forced into it."

"Yes boss. What about the white one?"

"I think that's the one we need to catch. A white ball in this part of the mind normally means surrender. When people are questioned, the answers are normally right at the forefront of their mind even if they don't say them aloud."

"So you think the information is in that one?"

"If it isn't then we'll have to go in deeper." Jin reached out his hand and tried to call the ball over to him but it kept slipping through his fingers. It didn't want to be caught. It was teasing him. Jin held out both his hands and gestured for the ball to come towards him. Angel watched, once again, in awe of Jin's abilities as the ball slowly landed in his hands. Jin pressed his forehead against it. He pulled his head away, smiled, then passed the ball to Angel who pressed it to her forehead. All the answers entered Angel's mind. Once she was done, Angel handed the ball back to Jin, who pushed it together until it became a tiny ball of light which he could put into his pocket.

"This is far too easy," Angel muttered.

"I know...let's..." before Jin could finish he was hit in the stomach by the red ball of light. All of Paris' pain and anger crashed into Jin, forcing him to his knees. Suddenly, a large cage dropped from the sky and trapped Jin inside. The ground shook violently and the world around them began to crumble. Inside the cage, lightning forks hit Jin's body repeatedly. He doubled over in pain as the lightning struck his skin. Angel tried to run over to him, but her legs sank into the ground like it was quicksand. The shapeshifter struggled and began to pull the rope that was around Jin's body. The rope not only connected Angel and Jin together but also connected Angel to the real world. If she pulled the rope both she and Jin would be transported out of Paris' mind and back into their own bodies. However before she could finish the process a large ogre-like creature crashed through one of the doors, that led to Paris' deeper mind, and started attacking them.

The ogre lifted Angel out of the quicksand. She landed heavily on a pile of rubble. Angel ducked as the ogre swung its sword in her *direction. Angel mentally created a sword and a shield. The ogre and Angel fought against each other. The battle wasn't productive for either party. Angel was trying her hardest to keep the rope out of the direction of the ogre's sword. If the ogre cut the rope, then Angel would be transported back to her body but Jin would remain trapped in Paris' mind. The ogre clearly knew this as it kept aiming its sword in the rope's direction. The ogre pushed Angel to the ground, she pulled herself up quickly, throwing away her sword and shield. She glowed white and transformed into a dragon. The dragon roared, fire burst from its mouth burning the ogre into pieces. The world around them began to fall apart. Strange disfigured monsters crawled out of the darkest corners of Paris' mind. The sky began to cry fiery tears. Angel fought against the monsters, desperately trying to reach Jin who was collapsed on the ground still getting hit by lightning forks. Angel flew over to the cage, killing monsters and avoiding meteorites as she did so. When she finally reached him, Jin was barely conscious. Angel transformed back into herself, glowed bright white, and pulled the rope as the world around them melted into a hellish chaos.*

* * * * *

Angel gasped as she was forced back into reality. She was back in her own body, sat on the floor of the torture chamber. Jin was sat in front of her. His body convulsed as his soul returned, then he slumped and collapsed into Angel's lap. His body was boiling, and blood dripped from his lips.

"How did you do it!? That's not possible my mind is protected! You evil bit…" Paris continued to scream abuse in Angel's direction, but she ignored him.

"Hiroshi take Jin to the hospital wing," Angel ordered, "He was hit pretty badly." Hiroshi and Ambroise carefully lifted the unconscious Jin up and carried him out of the room.

"Did you get the answers we need captain?" the Colonel asked.

"Mr Jet sent Paris a message to go guard the Polar

warehouse. Mr Jet told him that this was a crucial factor in his 'master plan'. Apart from on the night of the attack Paris has only met with Mr Jet once. The night I was made Captain. Surf thought he should have got my job, so he and a few others went out and got drunk. Paris was annoyed so left the others then he 'bumped' into Mr Jet. Instead of arresting him, Paris found the idea of power more appealing so swapped sides. He doesn't know who any of the other terrorists are, he only knew the girl, who we did the mind take on, because she had been converted at the same time. When they met in the forest, they were told not to reveal their identities," Angel said without taking a breath.

"That's," the Colonel started.

"Oh, and you know how my sword, my favourite sword Ted, yes I named my sword, don't judge me, had been stolen and that I found it in the hands of one of the terrorists, yeah well it was Paris here who nicked it!"

"Well done Captain! You and Captain Lu have done an excellent job," the Colonel applauded, "Well done indeed, I'll arrange a meeting with the Emperor in the morning and get a search warrant for the warehouse."

"You will die Angel Night!" Paris screamed, "You will die! You will die on Halloween."

"Yeah well, you'll be dead by then so it's not like you'll be able to enjoy it," Angel got to her feet.

"Knowing you will die will send me to my grave happy."

"You know what, I don't care. I don't care about you or your grave! I would happily leave you down here to rot and not even bother with an execution."

"Then why don't you?"

"You see the thing is, you stole my sword. No one steals my sword. In fact no one touches my sword."

"You'll execute a man because he touched your sword?"

235

"Oh no you'll be executed for being a demon worshipper."

Angel then punched Paris' face, breaking his nose, and knocking him to the ground.

"That," she smiled, "Was for touching my sword."

21

'NEEDLES!'

JASON

"Ouch," I gasped as Rowan stuck a huge needle into my arm. Due to the threat of another Mr Jet attack, everyone at the base had been ordered (by the Colonel) to get a medical examination to ensure they were fit for duty. Meaning that I was forced to come face to face with my worst enemy…Needles!

"Wimp," Rowan laughed as she drew the blood from my veins.

"Hey, I thought nurses are meant to be nice."

"I'm not a nurse."

"Fine, I thought healers were meant to be nice!"

"Yeah, about that, I'm not officially a healer."

"I beg your pardon," I spluttered. Not that I wanted to offend Rowan when she had a huge needle in her hands, but I was slightly concerned that I wasn't being treated by a professional.

"Well I'm a princess so I can't be made an official healer."

"So how come you work here?"

"The Colonel keeps quiet about me being here," Rowan removed the needle from my arm and emptied my blood into a vial, "My parents don't exactly know I'm here."

"Are they really that bad?"

"Well I guess they're not the worse parents in the world, but they are very strict and have some rather old-fashioned views. What about your parents? You haven't spoken about them since you arrived."

"My mum was a nurse. She really wanted me to become a doctor."

"Did you want to be a doctor?"

"No. To be honest I never really thought about what I wanted to do in the future. I was too busy getting in trouble and accidentally setting people on fire. Don't look at me like that. It was an accident! See I was messing about with a mate of mines lighter and it slipped or something."

"You sure? Maybe you were using your powers before you came to the base, you just didn't realise it."

"I was already using my powers, that might explain the crazy building incident. Oh, I was on a school trip and half of a building decided to collapse…when…no way! It happened when I got mad!" I realised. Thinking back to the incident, that occurred when I was seven, the museum had only started to collapse after Billy Broker (a small but large boy who had bullied me during my primary school years) had stolen my chocolate bar. Needless to say I had been distraught by this so, as all intelligent seven year olds do, I had a tantrum, and then the museum had started to collapse.

"That was probably your powers breaking through. When your emotions are high your powers feed off the energy, making your powers both stronger and harder to control."

"It would explain why some of my dates went wrong too."

"You sure that wasn't just you?" Rowan smiled cheekily.

"Hey! No but sometimes odd stuff would happen. See I get panic-attacks easily and I don't always like meeting new people. So I'd get really nervous. see what happened was, well one time a water pipe burst, another time I think I gave the girl an electric shock...oh and once the girl got hit by a bus! Don't worry she's fine, she was in a coma for three months, but she's fine now."

"And you didn't think that there was something strange going on!?"

No I hadn't. Despite all the strange and unexplainable events that had happened during my time in the human world, I had never considered that there might be something strange going on. And I certainly never considered that these weird events were happening because I was a supernatural being! I just thought I was incredibly unlucky!

"Now I just have to give you this injection," Rowan lifted another big needle filled with a green coloured liquid. Why is it never a small needle!?

"You've been living in the human world," Rowan continued as I stared down the needle, "So you've been vaccinated against human illnesses but not paranormal ones. You were vaccinated in the human world, right?"

"Yeah...Ah!" I exclaimed as the needle was stabbed into my skin and the liquid pushed into my blood.

"You really don't like needles, do you?" Rowan grinned as she took the needle away.

"No, no I don't, and you wouldn't either if you were sat in my position."

"I love seeing how pathetic people get around needles, it's great fun."

239

"For you! Ouch that really stung! Is everyone having this done?"

"The blood tests yes but not the vaccination. Normally you get that when you first arrive at the base, as a trainee, but with everything that's happened your vaccination got forgotten. Right now I just have to put this in you," Rowan held up what looked like a small microchip.

"What is that!?" I exclaimed louder than I had intended.

"It's a teleportation chip. Everyone at the base has one of these implanted into their arm. You need it so that we can teleport you out of danger. Let me implant it, then we can give you a demonstration of how it works, okay?"

"Okay." No, not at all, not one bit of this is okay! Rowan gently took my arm and with a small surgical knife she cut into it. I stayed cool, calm, and collected on the outside whilst completely freaking out on the inside! I didn't like this. I didn't like this at all. Just nope! The needles were like cuddly teddy bears compared to this! She was cutting me open and putting this microchip, which I still didn't completely understand what it was for, into my arm!

"Done," Rowan dripped water onto my arm. The water sunk into my skin and pulled the broken parts together. I could see, if I squinted my eyes and put my arm next to my face, a small black square under my skin.

"Jason, are you okay?" Rowan asked.

"Perfectly, completely, totally."

"Are you sure because you've been staring at your arm for about five minutes."

"I'm good. What is this for again?"

"Come with me," Rowan smiled as she led me out of the hospital wing. As we headed down the navy corridor, we bumped into, well actually I walked straight through, Helena the ghost, who had been floating by the door to the library, looking glum. She screamed at me for walking through her, which I apologised for repeatedly, then she started to laugh, which was just as scary as her scream!

"Well look who it is!" Helena shrieked after realising it was me who had walked through her, "Not dead then. It's a shame, I would quite like to have you as my death companion."

I wasn't quite sure how to respond to that.

"Where are you going?"

"It's none of your business Helena," Rowan said firmly as the ghost followed us further down the corridor.

"None of your business Helena, do this Helena, do that Helena! No one cares about poor dead me! No one! Everyone just forgets us ghosts. Do this Helena, do that Helena, don't go into that room Helena! Keep your mouth shut Helena!" the ghost continued to moan as she followed us into a small room. The room was grey and empty apart from a couple of computers and Willow. The telepath was sat behind a computer desk, softly discussing something with a house fairy. Upon seeing us arrive, the fairy quickly vanished.

"Jason," Willow smiled widely, "Here to test your teleportation chip?"

"Yeah," I muttered, "I think."

"Hello Helena," Willow greeted the ghost politely.

"Willow, nice Willow, she respects me! She greeted me; the others just ignore me!" Helena continued to mumble to herself.

"Come on I'll show you how the chip works."

"Jason if you just stand here," Rowan pointed to a spot right next to the computer desk. I did so, feeling slightly nervous. Willow sat down at the computer with a smile on her face that I didn't like the look of. Rowan stood behind her and whispered something in her ear.

"Right, you ready Jason?" Rowan asked.

"For what?" I answered.

Rowan just smiled as Willow pressed a button. My

world began to spin. I couldn't feel my legs or my arms. It was like my whole body was turning to jelly! My knees felt as though they were giving way and my eyesight blurred. Everything went purple and then, with a POP, I fell to the ground. I laid on my back for several moments trying to work out what had just happened. As my senses returned, I realised that someone was laughing, someone with a very high-pitched laugh.

"Look at him, he flopped like a fish!" Helena squeaked.

"What did you just…what the!?" I exclaimed. I had just sat myself up when I realised, I was not where I was meant to be. I had started by the computer now I was lying on the floor of the corridor! I had moved! I had moved without moving! I wasn't sure whether I was supposed to be thrilled by this experience or terrified. My mind raced from one emotion to the next. This was insane! I had moved. I had teleported!

"What did you do!?" I laughed as Willow and Rowan came out of the room and into the bright corridor.

"The teleportation chip, this is what it does. We can move you out of harm's way and teleport you home," Willow smiled.

"That's awesome!" Then it hit me. My stomach rumbled and my head span. I felt dizzy and hot. Really hot. It felt as though someone had thrown me into an oven. I crawled across the floor, grabbed the nearest bin, and threw up the contents of my stomach. Once my belly was empty, I stopped and sat myself up. That was embarrassing, really embarrassing. Above my head I could hear the soft sound of the house fairies, laughing at me! Even the nice friendly fairies were laughing at me! I really wished that the ground would swallow me up, and Helena's mocking did not make the situation any better.

"Haha the Master of Darkness gets portal sickness! Sickly little master!" sang Helena.

"Are you okay Jason?" Willow asked, "Portal sickness

is very common. You'll get used to it after a few more test runs."

"A few more, you mean I have to do that again!?"

* * * * *

I fell flat on my face.

"Ouch!" I exclaimed. I was outside the squad house, fight training with Roxy and Willow. The downside to this 'wonderful' plan was that both girls had telepathic powers, so every time I went to move, they were two steps ahead of me. It was mid-afternoon and the crispy March wind tickled the back of my neck. I was tired. It had been a long day for me. I had tested out my teleportation chip (10 times), had thrown up (also, sadly, 10 times) and now all I wanted to do was relax, not have fight training!

"Oh, come on Jason put some energy into it," Willow teased from the side lines as I pulled myself up ready to face Roxy again. I swung my sword, but it was automatically blocked by Roxy. I pushed Roxy back and she was forced to break hold. I swung my sword again, but it was once more met with great ease. This fight was going nowhere. Roxy was blocking my every move! She suddenly leapt forwards and I had seconds to react as her sword came bearing down on me. I blocked but my feet weren't properly balanced, which was exactly what Roxy wanted as with a smile she twisted her sword and kicked me in the chest. I fell to the ground. Roxy smiled happily at my defeat as I lay flat on my back in the mud.

"What is the point of this?" I moaned, "Your telepathic, you know my moves before I even make them!"

"You need to learn to block your mind," Roxy laughed.

"I thought I was!"

"You've started to. There are parts of your mind you've already blocked from me. Now you need to learn to block all of it."

Willow got to her feet, she went over to one of the

weapons sheds and dragged out a large Roman shield. I was almost certain it belonged to Alexander, so I wasn't planning on touching it. The last thing I wanted to do was get on the bad side of that vampire.

"What's that for?" I asked.

"It's a shield! What do you think it's for!?"

"Actually, it's not for Jason to defend himself with," Willow added, "Well at least not physically."

"You've lost me," I muttered as Roxy nodded with a knowing smile.

"Okay, me and Roxy are telepaths, so we can enter people's minds, however you can block us out with a mental shield," Willow explained.

"A mental shield? What's one of them?"

"To say you're the Master of Darkness, you're a real idiot," Roxy laughed.

"That's a bit offensive."

"A mental shield is exactly what it sounds like, it's a shield that you create in your mind to block out telepathic attacks," Willow explained.

"Ah okay. How do I get one of these shields?"

"You don't get one, you have to create it yourself."

"Okay, so what, you want me to imagine a shield in my head or something?"

"Not just a shield, create a defensive cuboid," Willow sighed, "No let me rephrase, the historical explanation will only confuse you. Okay I want you to use the shields to create a big box which you can hide inside."

"Okay, I think I can do that," I nodded.

"Close your eyes and relax."

I closed my eyes however the relaxing part was a little bit more complicated. How could I relax!? Paris was in the cells, Mr Jet was still at large, and I hadn't had my lunch, so all I could think about was how much I fancied a cheese sandwich!

Relax. Anyone else have that problem that when you're

told to do something you automatically want to do the opposite, because I have that problem! So when Willow told me to relax, I straight away wanted to run around in a circle dancing an Irish jig! I'm not sure why that was the first thing that popped into my head, it's a bit odd really, moving swiftly on. I took a deep breath and allowed myself to fall deep into my mind. My mind was a simple place. It was bright white with doors of different colours leading off into different areas of my mind. For example the red door led to my angry memories, the blue door to my sad ones, the orange door led to a room where I had saved the memories of my favourite foods and the black one led to a dark scary prison in which my demon was locked away, or at least that was what Willow and Roxy had told me. I had never actually spent much time "*in*" my mind, so I wasn't one-hundred percent sure where everything was.

Use the shields to create a big box that you can hide inside. Not the most helpful advice I've ever received. How was I meant to create a shield? How did I make them into a box? What was I supposed to do? Why hadn't they given me a diagram? Or a 'how to build a mental shield' guidebook!?

'*Okay calm down Dragonheart!*' I thought to myself, '*You're standing with two telepaths, if you don't calm down, they'll hear your stupid panic-attack!*'

I mentally slapped myself. At that moment I felt something in my pocket. I pulled out a red crayon and a folded piece of paper. I unfolded the paper to find, to my surprise, a diagram! The diagram showed several shields lined up next to and on top of each other, creating a cuboid like shape.

But where do I get the shields from? I wondered to myself.

You draw them with the crayon, you idiot! Came Roxy's mental reply.

The sound of her voice in my head made me jump and

realise that the two telepaths were listening to everything I thought. I knelt down and began to draw a shield. I started off by drawing the outline and then slowly I added in the details, making it look more realistic. Well as realistic as it was going to look, I was drawing with a red crayon, so it was hardly going to be a Da Vinci painting!

When I had finished the shield, to my surprise, it became real. A real solid shield! I smiled and drew several more. Once I had finished drawing, I studied the diagram and followed it as carefully as I could. I slowly placed the shields around me in a rectangle formation. Once I had put them in place, the shields remained standing. Not only that but they also joined together so that I had an impenetrable wall made out of shields. Of course, if I was to do this in the 'real' world it wouldn't work, but inside my head anything goes! I finally placed the last shield above my head. Inside the shield was much bigger than I'd thought it'd be, in fact my entire mental world fitted inside, which either means that I have a very small mind, or the shields were really big! It was a very strange experience. When I opened my eyes, and returned to reality, Roxy and Willow were smiling at me.

"Did I do it?" I asked surprised.

"Yeah," Willow smiled, "I can't read or enter your mind."

I turned to Roxy, "Is it time for a rematch?"

Roxy smiled and raised her sword. I swung my sword down; it was met with Roxy's. I pushed back and forced Roxy to break the hold. She twisted her sword and jabbed forwards. I jumped out of the way. We circled around each other each trying to guess the others next move. Roxy attacked first; our swords crashed together. After Roxy shoved me with some force, I stumbled backwards. Roxy kicked my knee causing me to fall to the ground. I quickly defended myself as her sword came bearing down on my head. I pushed myself up and broke the hold. I swung my sword and the blades met with great force. I twisted my wrist and forced Roxy's sword from her hand.

"Give up?" I asked my sword pointing at her chest. Her answer was interrupted by a loud squeaking sound. "What's that?"

"Means the Colonel is going to give an announcement," Willow pointed to a set of speakers that hung on the outside of the Lightning Squad house.

"This is your Colonel speaking," the Colonel's voice echoed around the base, "The Emperor and I created this base nearly three hundred years ago. Back then it was a small organisation and now we are the most successful unit in the paranormal military. I never expected that I'd have to give this kind of announcement."

"Stop being dramatic and just get on with it," Roxy muttered, "We all know what's coming."

I didn't have a clue what was coming. I was about to ask Roxy what she meant by that, but the Colonel began speaking.

"Paris Surf has been found guilty of demon worshipping, attempted murder and terrorism. For the crimes he has committed against the Empire and against you, his friends, and teammates, he has been sentenced to death. I know this news will be distressing to many of you," the Colonel continued, "Many of you believed Paris to be a friend, but he destroyed that friendship when he betrayed you all. I will not keep you any longer however I wish to see all members of Lightning Squad in the conference room in five minutes."

With that the announcement ended.

"Sentenced to death," I muttered in shock.

"Knew it," Roxy hissed, "Come on, we best not keep the Colonel waiting."

* * * * *

"I know that Paris' sentencing will have hit you the hardest," the Colonel said. I was sat with the rest of

Lightning Squad, including Sophie who had finally been discharged from the hospital wing, in the Captain's conference room. I was still in shock. Sentenced to death, that couldn't be real. It couldn't be, it just sounded so strange, so medieval. I looked around at the rest of the squad. They all wore their best poker faces but even I could tell that they were not okay with this situation.

"The Emperor has ordered this personally. He is declaring war on Mr Jet and his followers," the Colonel explained.

"How is Paris to be executed?" Ethan asked.

"Bleed out."

"What?" I had to ask as I had no idea.

"Oh yes I forgot that you've lived in the human world," the Colonel explained, "Basically the prisoner is strapped to a board and the executioner slices them across the body and the prisoner bleeds to death."

"That's horrible! That's just horrible!"

"Yet it's the Emperor's favourite method of execution," Alexander muttered bitterly.

"It's terrible!" Just the idea made my stomach turn. It was disgusting! How could anyone do such a thing. I couldn't imagine. I didn't want to imagine it! It was sick. I had forgotten, until that moment, just how dark and dangerous the world I had fallen into was.

"Yeah the citizens tried to ban this form of execution, but you can't mess with the Emperor."

"Enough of that tone," the Colonel snapped, "You make it sound like we live under a dictator."

"We do," Alexander muttered under his breath, just loud enough for me to hear.

"Anyway because Paris was a part of the military the Emperor wants to show that no one is given special treatment, if you betray the Empire then you will pay for it. He has planned for Paris' execution to take place tomorrow morning; however he doesn't want it to be an actual executioner who…completes the task. Instead he wants Paris' captain to do the execution to show that we are stamping out the terrorists in our squads."

All eyes turned to Angel who had turned a ghostly shade of white.

"That's not happening," Roger exclaimed, "Angel has barely recovered."

"It's the Emperor's order!"

"I don't bloody care who ordered it, my sister is not doing it!"

"Why should she do it!? We have official executioners, don't we? Get one of them!" Ethan snapped.

"This is an order from the Emperor!" the Colonel shouted getting to his feet.

"Where is the execution being held?" Araminta asked changing the subject.

"The execution house in the city, all the squads will assemble there at eleven-hundred hours. The execution will happen within the hour. It'll be a quick but forceful gesture against Mr Jet and his terrorist organisation."

"What about that search warrant?" Angel asked quietly, it was as if it was difficult for her to get the words to leave her lips.

"The Emperor has signed the search warrant. We have also been given permission to go to the Polar Base if we do find anything."

"What search warrant is this?" asked Sue.

"You're just checking up on one of the storage warehouses," the Colonel said lightly, "Nothing to really worry about, just a routine check. You'll go to the warehouse at fourteen-hundred hours tomorrow. Go fully armed just in case."

"Armed?" Elsa asked confused, "I thought it was just a routine check?"

"We're not taking any chances. Right, now I know this is a lot to process but I need you to pull yourselves together and erm, yes well, I shall leave you be. I'll join you at the execution," with that the Colonel left the room.

"This is ridiculous," Danny hissed, "Why does it matter who kills Paris? It makes no sense!"

"Can't you just say no?" I asked innocently.

"It's the Emperor's order Jason! If she refuses, then she becomes guilty of treason! And if she is found guilty of treason not only Angel but the whole Night werewolf pack will be arrested and potentially executed!"

"Why?"

"Because that's the messed up way this Empire works! Treason is a capital offense, the worst one there is! You don't deny the Emperor, not if you want to live. Also the people prefer Angel's dad to the Emperor, and there's no way that he isn't aware of this. If Angel was to refuse, he could use it as an opportunity to get rid of the potential competition!"

"Danny stop! Everyone go back to the house," Angel ordered, "Go back home and rest up. Tomorrow is going to be a long day."

"Angel? Are you…?" Fern began to ask.

"Squad dismissed," Angel muttered before she ran out of the room.

"I'll go check on her," Roger excused himself as he exited.

"Do as Angel said," Alexander continued, "Go home. Get some rest and try to mentally prepare yourselves for tomorrow."

* * * * *

The next day came far too quickly for my liking.

The squad travelled to the city in a battered old truck. No one could offer me an explanation as to why we weren't teleporting but instead using a horrifically uncomfortable small truck. The road we were taking was bumpy, so we ended up falling on top of each other. I was squashed next to Ethan and I spent most of the journey tumbling into him. I don't think it had really hit me that I was on my way to the execution of someone I had considered a friend. That I was going to an execution. I don't think I had properly processed the fact that Paris was going to be executed. And executed by Angel. Angel was sat in the front of the truck with Alexander who was driving. She hadn't said anything the whole journey, she just stared out of the window, lost in her own thoughts. I couldn't even begin to imagine what was going on in her head. I crashed into Ethan, landing face first into the werewolf's belly, as the truck stopped.

"Ouch," the wolf squeaked.

"Sorry," I muttered pulling myself up, "You should really get seat belts for this thing."

"Let's go," Alexander got out of the truck. I climbed out and found myself on an old fashion cobbled street. There was a grey church at one end and rows of small cottages on either side. The people looked as if they had stepped out of a black and white photograph. They wore long Victorian style clothing; women in long dresses and men in full suits with a top hat. I have to admit I was slightly tempted to steal one of the hats…they just looked so cool! A horse and cart clattered down the street which made me jump back in surprise. That was when I noticed the huge old miserable building behind me. It was tall and towered over the rest of the street, its long shadow covering the road. Its sandy stone columns and heavy wooden door stared down at us. While the building gave off a grand air, it also made me feel extremely uncomfortable. The butterfly pit at the bottom of my stomach started fluttering fiercely.

"That's the court and execution house," Willow explained, "Welcome to Gallows Way."

"What?" I squeaked; the name sent shivers running down my spine.

"That's the name of the street, Gallows Way. Prisoners

are brought here from the prison, which is down there," Willow pointed to another building that could only just be seen in the background. It was like the court and execution house but much bigger and more terrifying. A high metal fence ran around the outside of it and guard towers were posted at each corner. The building, while it had similar architecture to the courthouse, lacked the grandeur, it was instead simply terrifying.

"Scary, isn't it?"

"Jason, Willow, stop talking," Araminta called, "We need to get a move on."

"Coming!" Willow muttered as we began to walk up the steps and into the execution house.

The entrance room was lit only by candlelight. Dark daunting shadows stretched across the floor and strange cold paintings littered the walls. The walls were red and white columns were posted, like prison guards, around the room, giving the place a regal vibe. A freezing chill raced up my spine as two figures walked towards us. When the figures finally stepped into the light, I realised that they were not the revengeful ghosts I had expected them to be. To my surprise, one was a nun dressed in a long plain dark blue dress, whilst the other figure was a priest, dressed, like the nun, in a dark blue habit.

"I didn't think paranormals would be religious," I muttered to Araminta.

"Many paranormals are. Some believe in the same religions that humans believe in, but most follow the paranormal religion," she explained.

"The paranormal religion? You have your own religion?" Araminta nodded.

"Sister, Father," Angel greeted the nun and priest respectfully.

"I am Sister Odetta," the Nun bowed her head, "And this is Father Paul. Captain Night please come with us. The rest of you go down that corridor, one of the sisters will be waiting there to take you through."

"Right," Angel turned to us. Her face was sickly pale, and she looked as though she was about to faint, "Alex is in charge of you until I come back. You do as he says, okay? Right, see you when this is over."

With that Angel followed Father Paul and Sister Odetta out of the room. We followed Alexander down a long corridor. Despite the candles that floated above our heads, the corridor was incredibly dark. So dark in fact that I ended up crashing into Fern.

"What the hell!?" Fern hissed, "What was that for? I haven't even done anything to you today!"

"Sorry I'm not really used to the dark," I spluttered.

"Ha! The Master of Darkness isn't used to the dark!"

"Hilarious Fern."

"Hold out your hand."

"Why?"

"So I can plant it in the ground and grow a sunflower, what do you think!?"

"I don't know that's why I'm asking."

Fern grabbed my hand and pulled out her wand mumbling, "I try and be nice and this is what I get."

She flicked the tip of her wand and sparks flew onto my hand. They tickled like a thousand feathers stroking my skin. The sparks joined together and formed a blue ball of light in my hand. I went to thank Fern, but she had skipped off down the corridor. Now that I could see, I realised that the walls of the corridor were red and covered in horrifying paintings, that I quickly wished I hadn't seen.

The corridor was not helping my anxiety. I was already in a terrible state and the corridor was just making it worse. Before leaving the base, Rowan had given me medication that was supposed to help me keep calm, however it wasn't working. I was anything but calm! I was stressed and anxious and terrified and...I couldn't even list all the things I was feeling I was so worked up! I was about to watch someone get executed...executed! I felt faint. From out of nowhere, Araminta appeared by my side. She gently helped me walk down the rest of the corridor. When we finally reach the end of, what I had thought was an endless, corridor we were greeted by a nun and a large wooden door.

"IDs please," the Nun said. We all quickly pulled out our Lightning Squad ID badges. Once the Nun checked our IDs, she opened the door and led us out into the bright morning sunlight. We were led into a garden. There were flowers growing and birds singing. It would have been picturesque, if there hadn't been a huge execution stage in the middle of it. I turned my eyes away from the stage. I couldn't look at it. I knew full well that if I did, I would have thrown up. I kept my eyes firmly faced down as Araminta guided me through the crowd of people.

Around the stage was coliseum styled seating. Rows upon rows of seats led up to a golden box, in which sat the Emperor. The seating was only on one side of the execution stage, on the other side stood the execution house. The Nun led us to our seats, were we sat nervously. The seats were made of stone. I felt as though I had been transported back in time to the Roman era and was awaiting a gladiator fight. I didn't like it. I didn't like it at all. I kept staring down at the ground. I was vaguely aware of the fact that people were staring and pointing in my direction. This was the first time the "legendary" Master of Darkness had been seen in public, so apparently people were very excited to see me. I, however, was not excited to see them. In fact I didn't see them as I never raised my head.

I don't want to be here.

I don't want to see this.

Those two sentences kept rattling around my head.

I couldn't watch this.

I didn't want to watch this.

I didn't want to be there.

No matter what Paris had done, I couldn't watch him get executed. I felt sick. I could feel the panic rise up from my stomach. It banged on my chest so hard that I felt as though my heart was going to explode. I couldn't breathe. I felt dizzy. The world seemed to spin around me. I could hear people talking but I couldn't hear a word they were saying. This was too much. This was wrong!

I needed to escape.

I needed to get out.

I couldn't do this.

I didn't want to do this.

"When the Emperor starts speaking," Araminta muttered, "Everyone will stand up, that's when I'll grab you and race you over to that door over there. That door will take you out of here. Just head to the little blue room which is at the end of the corridor we've just come through. Once this is over Angel will meet you there. This is her plan. She doesn't want you to see this. She doesn't want any of us to see this."

Panic had gripped my tongue, so I simply nodded. I was extremely grateful that Angel had created an escape plan for me, but I couldn't express it. I couldn't even process it properly. I just knew that I wanted to escape. That I needed to escape.

"Good. Damn!" Araminta cursed as a group of people carrying pens and notepads took their seats, "The press is here. Fantastic…"

The gathering fell silent as a drumbeat sounded across the gardens.

The execution was about to begin.

22

'THE END OF PARIS SURF'

"Perhaps you would like to pray before we go on," Father Paul suggested to Angel. The priest and Sister Odetta had led the shapeshifter down a long dark corridor and were now stood in front of a small wooden door.

"I'm not religious," Angel snapped, sounding harsher than she meant to.

"Fair enough but I would suggest that confession may be helpful."

"I don't need confession. I just need to make a phone call. It will only take a minute."

"We'll leave you to it," Sister Odetta led the Priest away, leaving Angel alone. She pulled out her phone and called David, but her call went straight to voicemail.

"It's Angel again. I tried calling you last night, but you didn't pick up, and you're still not picking up. Pops, I'm about to become an executioner, a murderer. Pops, I don't know what to do. I don't know…the Emperor has ordered this so I can't refuse. But I don't want to do it! I don't want…Pops what do I do!?" Angel exclaimed on the brink of tears.

"Captain Night," someone called.

"Shi…I'm going to have to go and kill…when you get this the execution will probably be over, even if that's the case can you still call me back. Please." With that Angel hung up the phone.

She leant her head against the wall. What was she going to do? How could she escape? The answer Angel knew too well. She couldn't. To defy the Emperor's order would be treason. To be accused of treason would lead to both herself and her family being investigated and, should anything the Emperor considered treasonous be found, all executed. And Danny hadn't been wrong, while the Emperor and David Night were friends, they were also in a bitter competition for the public's affection. Over the last hundred years, David had become a respected and beloved public figure, more so then the Emperor. There were even rumours, whispered in the shadows of the taverns, that David wanted the throne. While Angel knew this wasn't true, she was also highly aware that her refusal could cause a political dispute between the Emperor and her father…one that could end in bloodshed.

Perhaps that's why the Emperor ordered it, the thought plagued the back of Angel's mind, *perhaps the Emperor wanted to test her, and the pack's, loyalty.*

Angel knew that there was no way of getting out of it, but still she tried to think of an escape plan. She had been thinking about it all night yet couldn't find an answer. She had screamed, she had cried, she had thrown up, she had got angry but still no answer had revealed itself. Angel sighed, tapping her head against the wall. She was going to have to kill him. Angel felt sick. She went over to a bin, retched but didn't throw up. She had nothing left in her stomach.

Angel had killed before but killing a person in a battle

or fight was different to executing them. Not only that, but this wasn't some evil monster, this was Paris. He had been a member of her squad, a friend, family. To Angel, Lightning Squad was a family. A big, messed up, family. And now she was about to kill one of its members.

"Captain Night," Sister Odetta called, "I'm afraid it's time, please come with me." Sister Odetta led a reluctant Angel into a small room. The room was brightly lit and was filled with weapons. Sat on a bench by a window was a short man with a black beard and a bottle of beer in his hand. His eyes were blood shot and Angel could tell that the bottle in his hand wasn't the first drink he had had that morning.

"Captain Night this is Derek Clarkson, he's the head executioner. He'll show you what to do," Sister Odetta introduced.

"So this is the Captain then, I was expecting you to be a guy, not a little girly!"

"And I was expecting you to be sober," Angel snapped, "Seems we're both disappointed." Derek got to his wobbling feet, he walked over to a box in the corner of the room and pulled out a thin fencing sword. He handed it to Angel and pointed to a model of a person that was stood in the opposite corner of the room.

"I take it you know how to hold a sword girly," Derek spluttered.

"No I became Captain by creating daisy chains and playing hopscotch," Angel hissed sarcastically, she took the sword from Derek and flicked it gently bringing it to a stop by his neck, "Happy?"

"You mock me but when you kill him, you'll understand exactly how this feels! This is a show to them! We are entertainers!"

"Derek!" the nun interrupted.

"Just run it through," Derek muttered before collapsing in a heap on the bench. Angel raised her sword and quickly brought it down, slicing across the model's chest.

"Hey, look at that, the girly is a natural! A natural kill…"

"That's enough!" Sister Odetta snapped, "Captain Night will you please follow me, it's time."

"Go and put on a good show, the Emperor is watching after all!" Derek spat.

Sister Odetta led Angel out of the room and into a pale corridor where they were joined by Father Paul. He led them down a flight of steps and to a door, in front of which were two armed guards. Angel showed them her ID and they let her pass. The shapeshifter was greeted by another flight of stairs before she found herself in the cells. It was dark and a freezing chill ran through the air. Angel's footsteps echoed as she walked through the rows of damp musty cells. The smell was disgusting but not as horrifying as the smell in the base's cells (it lacked the putrid odour of rotting zombie flesh). Lit only by candlelight, it was difficult for Angel to tell where the cells began, and the shadows ended.

"Those," Father Paul pointed to a row of cells to Angel's left, "Are prisoners waiting to go on trial. The ones to your right are the prisoners waiting to be executed."

Angel looked at the prisoners waiting to be executed. There were a lot of them, each as beaten and bruised as the next. They ran up to the bars of their cells as Angel approached, reaching out their thin arms, they tried to grab her. They screamed at her, some screamed abuse while others begged her to save them. Angel shut out their cries, continuously reminding herself that they were criminals who had committed serious crimes and followed the priest to Paris' cell.

Paris was sat on the floor, his eyes staring at the candle that hung on the wall opposite. His body was bruised and his face haggard. He no longer looked like the carefree playful young man Angel once knew. Paris looked up as she arrived, a sinister smile illuminating his face.

"Are you here to kill me?" Paris asked, his voice was emotionless.

"Yeah wasn't exactly how I had pictured my morning either," Angel replied.

"Paris Surf," Father Paul said solemnly, "Before your sentence is passed is there anything you wish to confess?"

"Do you really have the guts to kill me?" Paris got to his feet and walked over to the bars. His face was only centimetres away from Angel's, "If you do, you'll never find out who your parents are, where you came from…or the identity of the witch who's haunting you."

"Who is she? Did you let her onto the base? Is she working with Mr Jet?"

"Help me escape and I'll tell you."

"That's not going to happen."

"Then you'll never know."

"No I will. I just won't find out from you."

"Paris Surf before your sentence is passed is there anything you wish to confess?" Father Paul repeated.

"Confess!" Paris laughed, "Yes I confess that I'm rather looking forward to seeing your demise, Angel Night."

"You should be thinking about your own demise, not mine."

"Oh Angel, you'll soon come to realise that in this world death is only the beginning."

"What does…" Angel's question was interrupted by the sound of drums. The noise sent the prisoners crawling back in fear. This was the sound of the execution march. This was the soundtrack to Paris' death. Two guards unlocked Paris' cell while the Nun and the Priest dropped to their knees and began to pray. The guards grabbed Paris' shoulders and pushed him forwards. Angel followed. They made their way up the large staircase, into the blinding sunlight that engulfed the execution platform.

Angel couldn't bring herself to look at the crowd. She didn't want to see how many citizens had shown up to enjoy such a horrific form of entertainment. Angel could feel her stomach turn. Vomit tickled her tongue, but she swallowed it down. Angel's eyes remained fixed on her boots as Paris was strapped to a wooden board and a sword was placed in her hand.

The Emperor and the crowd stood up as the execution march ended. Out of the corner of her eye, Angel noticed someone slip out of the crowd and disappear out of the execution garden. How Angel wished she could have done the same. The crowd sat down as the Emperor raised his hand.

"This man is guilty of terrorism, demon worshipping and attempted murder," the Emperor's powerful voice echoed around the execution gardens, "After hundreds of years of war, the paranormal empire is finally at peace. This man and the terrorist known as Mr Jet wish to destroy this peace. Demons have no place in this empire! Let today stand as a warning, anyone who threatens the peace of the empire will be annihilated. Proceed!"

Damn, why was his speech so short!? Angel thought.

Her hands were shaking as she raised the sword. She closed her eyes, took a deep breath, and swiftly ran Paris through. Angel dropped the sword. The blood on the blade splattered onto Angel's boots as the sword clattered to the ground. Angel opened her eyes. Paris stared at her and smiled.

"This is not the end," Paris hissed, "This is not the end Angel Night. We shall be seeing each other again soon. Just you wait. Oh and look the next player in this game has arrived."

Paris coughed up blood and his head flopped forwards.

And that was the end of Paris Surf.

"The next player," Angel muttered, she followed Paris' gaze. His cold dead eyes were staring out into the crowd.

Staring at one member of the crowd in particular.

"Mr Jet!" Angel yelled.

Mr Jet smiled, got to his feet, and zoomed out of the crowd. Angel transformed into a vampire and chased after him. Angel followed Mr Jet out of the execution gardens into a courtyard, where the vampire stood waiting. The courtyard was small; there was a water fountain in the middle which took up most of the space and a cherry blossom tree grew peacefully next to it. There were three exits, Angel quickly noted, one was the way they had come, the other led to the main road and the other led into the execution house. Angel pulled out her gun and aimed at Mr Jet. She approached him carefully, not daring to get close.

"It's lovely to see you again Samantha," Mr Jet smiled.

Angel pulled the trigger, the wooden bullet flew straight through the air and hit Mr Jet right above the heart. The vampire steamed as the wood cut into his skin. Mr Jet grunted, pulling the bullet out of his body, and throwing it to the ground.

"It seems the time for pleasantries has passed," Mr Jet said with a light and playful air, "What a shame, I do enjoy our little chats."

"Yeah, well I don't," Angel shot Mr Jet again but this time he held up his hand. The bullet froze mid-air, it then turned around and aimed for Angel. She ducked as the bullet hit the tree behind her. She went to fire again, but, with a flick of Mr Jet's wrist, her gun flew from her hands. Mr Jet clicked his fingers and the roots from a nearby tree shot into the air and wrapped around Angel's body.

"How did you do that!? Vampires can't have magic!" Angel exclaimed as she struggled against the tree roots.

Mr Jet simply smiled, "They're all lying to you Samantha. The Colonel, the Emperor, your father. They're all lying to you. Ask them. Ask them the identity of the witch who haunts you. For they all know."

"So do you it seems. Does she work for you?"

"Something like that. But that isn't really the point, is it Samantha? The point is your leader, your commander, your family and even your vampire lover…"

"Who?" Angel asked genuinely confused.

"Alexander!"

"Oh. Just say that then! He's not my lover. Hang on, why am I explaining this to you?"

"The point is," Mr Jet snapped, "They're all lying to you, so that they can use you. They all…"

"No the point is," Angel interrupted, "The only reason I let you keep talking, was so that you'd be distracted long enough for me to break free of these tree roots."

With that Angel escaped the tree roots, transforming into a large white dragon as she did so. The dragon spat fire at Mr Jet, causing the vampire to be trapped in a circle of flames. The dragon dived down, transforming into a white lioness as it hit the ground. The lioness pounced forwards but before it could devour the vampire, Mr Jet threw a glowing orange object in its direction. The object hit the lioness' forehead, the creature stumbled to the ground and was forced to transform back into Angel.

"Nice trick," Angel muttered as she spat out blood, "But what are you going to do now? You're stuck, unless you want to burn."

Mr Jet smiled. He jumped through the flames and then rolled across the water fountain he had landed in, dousing down the fire.

"I did not think of that," Angel muttered before she got to her feet and followed Mr Jet through the flames and into the fountain. Mr Jet grabbed hold of Angel and pushed her under the water. Angel pulled out her knife and sliced wildly at Mr Jet's legs. The vampire stumbled backwards. Angel transformed into water and swam up behind Mr Jet. She then transformed back into herself and stabbed the vampire's back. Mr Jet hissed, swinging round, cutting Angel with his sharp vampire nails. Angel went to punch Mr Jet, but her fist was caught by the vampire. His hand glowed orange and Angel began to feel a violent pain spread through her hand. Angel tried to shapeshift into a stronger creature however she found, to her utter horror, that she was unable to. Mr Jet smiled as he tightened his grip, crushing the bones in Angel's hand.

Angel yelled out in agony.

Her cry was so powerful that it lifted the water from the fountain into the air. The water slammed into Mr Jet, pushing him backwards off the fountain and onto the cobbled ground. The vampire hit the ground heavily. Angel raised her unbroken hand and the flames, that had once circled the vampire, attacked Mr Jet. He raised his arms and a forcefield grew up around him, protecting him from the blaze.

"How can a vampire have magic?" Angel asked.

"How can a shapeshifter transform into other paranormal beings?" Mr Jet replied with a question, as his forcefield extinguished the flames. "Have you never wondered Samantha, why your shapeshifting abilities are so unusual? Or why you're more powerful than your peers?"

"Ah, is this the part where you imply that you know the answers to all these questions, and you say that if I join your little demon worshipping squad, you'll tell me?"

"You mock but deep down you are slightly curious."

"Not really," Angel transformed into a phoenix and dived at Mr Jet. However the vampire raised his hand and Angel was once again hit by the strange orange glowing object. Like before, Angel was forced to transform back into herself. She collapsed to her knees. Mr Jet smiled. He walked forward and pressed his hand against Angel's forehead.

"This isn't over Night. In fact it's far from it but until we meet again," Mr Jet whispered as Angel fell into unconsciousness.

* * * * *

Angel stood outside an old manor house.

The manor house was crumbling and falling apart. The roof had caved in slightly and the windows were smashed. It looked like it belonged in a horror movie. Its walls were grey and uninviting. The house was in a forest, close to a small lake. Unlike the forest at the base, this place was silent. Not even the sound of a fluttering bird could be heard.

"Where am I? How did I get here?" Angel wondered aloud.

She looked around, there was miles of dark green forest in every direction. As Angel stared at the mass of leaves, she noticed a little girl skipping across the undergrowth. She hopped over the rocks by the lake. The girl was small with brown hair that fell in curly locks and pink cheeks. She wore a pale pink dress and shiny red shoes. The child ran over to Angel.

"Hello," the little girl smiled, "Are you here to play?"

The girl didn't wait for an answer. She ran up to the old house and pushed the decrepit door open.

"Kid, what are you doing here?" Angel asked, "Hey! Hey kid, where are we?"

"Come on Angel it's time to play!" the girl squeaked.

"How do you know my name?"

"Come on they're waiting!"

"Who is waiting!? Kid!" Angel jogged after the girl and up to the door of the house. The girl skipped inside, and Angel reluctantly followed. Once she was inside the door slammed shut behind her. Angel felt in the darkness for the door handle but there was none.

She was trapped!

Candles suddenly flickered into life and Angel could see the interior of the house she had stupidly walked into. In front of her was a large staircase which led off in two different directions and there were shut doors on both sides. The walls were painted a dark colour, what that colour was Angel couldn't tell as the paint was so faded that it had lost its natural shade. The floor was wooden and dead animal heads lined the corridor. Suddenly Angel felt something tap her back. She jumped and span around. The little girl was stood behind her.

"This way Angel," the little girl grabbed Angel's hand and dragged her into a room. The door once again slammed shut.

"You're going to die Angel Night," the little girl sang.

"What!?" Angel turned to the girl, but she had vanished, "Kid! Hey kid! Where did you go?"

The room was completely empty. The walls were bare and spiderwebs decorated the ceiling. Angel banged against the door desperately trying to open it. She tried to transform but found herself unable to. Her powers were gone. She was trapped in this unknown place without her powers to save her.

"You know a lot about curses, don't you?" said a voice. Angel turned around and found that the room was no longer empty. A table and two chairs had appeared. Seated in one of the chairs was the Pied Piper of Hamlin.

"You, but you're, this isn't real, this can't be real!" Angel exclaimed. Angel walked over to the table and sat opposite the Piper, "Are you a ghost? What are you even doing here?"

"You were cursed by a memory loss spell, correct?" the Piper asked distantly.

"That...wait you said that before!"

"Clearly the curse never fully settled, which must be why your hair never returned to its natural colour."

"Yes you said that before as well."

"Ah, it seems that we have run out of time," the Piper sighed, "For showing you that memory and for what I am about to make you do, I am truly sorry."

"What is this?"

Suddenly the Pied Piper vanished.

"Piper! Where are you!?" Angel got to her feet.

"He's gone," said the little girl who had suddenly reappeared.

"What is going on here? What is this place? Who are you!?"

"They all have things to say to you."

"Who? Who has things to say to me?"

"Only one way to find out," the girl smiled and skipped through

266

an opened door. Angel ran after the girl. However as she ran through the door, she found herself strapped to a chair.

"What the...?" Angel struggled but the straps merely tightened. Smoke filled the room and a fire suddenly coughed into life. Angel looked down; her uniform had been replaced with a blood-stained nightdress.

"Oh no, no," Angel gasped as from a darken corner a man with heavy footsteps walked forwards. Angel couldn't see the man's face, however the baton in his hand was clearly visible. Before Angel had a chance to scream, the baton hit her face. Angel spat out blood. She closed her eyes as the baton continued to bare down on her body. Then it stopped. Angel opened her eyes as the man tipped her chair backwards. Angel fell, but instead of hitting the floor, the chair went straight through it.

And landed in the lake. The chair sunk to the bottom of the lake, hitting the riverbed softly. The straps turned into seaweed and Angel was able to break free. Angel swam to the surface. She took a deep breath, allowing the cool water to heal her aching body.

"This isn't real. This can't be real," Angel muttered to herself as she swam to the sandbank and pulled herself onto dry land.

"Samantha." Angel looked up and came face-to-face with the witch. She knelt in front of Angel. She grabbed Angel's face and whispered in her ear, "You can't escape. You can't run."

"Watch me," Angel got to her feet and ran as fast as she could. As she ran the witch's voice echoed around the forest.

"Samantha. I'm coming for you."

Angel ran as the voice got louder and louder. Then suddenly everything went silent. All Angel could hear was her own heart beating. Angel stopped running as the world began to spin. When the world stopped spinning Angel found herself once again inside the haunted old manor house. This time she was in a dark empty room. Angel sat down, her body aching too much for her to stand. As she did so another young girl entered the room. Angel recognised her instantly.

It was herself.

A younger version of herself.

"Hello, can you hear me?" Angel asked her younger self.

She didn't reply. Instead a man appeared behind her. He shoved her to the floor. There was a loud crack as her skull made contact with the stone floor. Blood ran from the girl's forehead. The man grabbed the young Angel's hair and pulled her to her feet. He then slammed her into a wall.

"Let me...her go!" Angel yelled as she ran over to the man, pulled him away from her younger self and saw his face for the first time.

"Alex?"

The man was Alexander.

Dressed in his Lightning Squad uniform (black trousers and a black polo shirt with the Lightning Squad logo printed on it), the vampire stood staring at Angel. His eyes were red and his gaze menacing. The younger version of Angel vanished, leaving the real Angel alone with Alexander. There was silence. Angel didn't dare speak; she didn't want to prompt the madness of this nightmare.

"Angel, what you saw...was it you getting cursed?" Alexander asked suddenly.

"What? Oh this is so messed up," Angel stumbled backwards.

This wasn't Alexander. Angel knew that for certain. This was some kind of strange illusion. It spoke with Alexander's voice and wore his skin, but it lacked the emotion and feeling of the real thing. The words it spoke were mere recordings. Repeated conversations, lacking the original context and meaning.

"Angel, some memories are forgotten for a reason. If these memories are painful then maybe its best that you don't remember them."

Angel laughed and took a defiant step forward, "You're not him. This isn't real."

"Have you read my file?"

Angel laughed bitterly then suddenly the fake Alexander raced forwards and grabbed her neck. He pushed her backwards, up against the wall. Angel tried to break free but found herself both unable to shapeshift and unable to escape. Alexander grabbed her head and tilted it so that the juiciest part of her neck was within biting distance. The vampire lent forwards pressing his mouth against her skin.

He whispered, "I'm not a terrorist. I know you can't just take my word for it but, I want Mr Jet dead as much as you do. Perhaps even more."

"Don't trust Alex, he's not what he seems," said a familiar voice. Angel yelled out in frustration and was finally able to push Alexander (who had suddenly become still) away. She stumbled across the room to find Danny stood in the opposite corner.

"You're here too!" Angel exclaimed. Like Alexander, Danny was dressed in his Lightning Squad uniform and wore an emotionless expression.

This was not Danny.

This was simply a phantom figure masquerading as reality.

The fake Danny sighed, "I did some background research on Alex. He has a very bloody past. He even has links to the Jack the Ripper murder cases."

Danny and Alexander continued to talk. Their words overlapped each other and echoed around the room. The room span as the words got louder and louder.

"Stop it! Stop it! Stop it!" Angel screamed.

There was silence until...

"Excuse me...what are you...this is crazy! I'm dreaming...this is a nightmare! I'm human!"

"Jason!?" Angel cried as Jason appeared behind her.

"The point is your leader, your commander, your family and even your vampire lover. They're all lying to you," Mr Jet said as he appeared from the darkness, "Have you never wondered, Samantha, why your shapeshifting abilities are so unusual? Or why you're more powerful than your peers?"

Angel sank to the floor, grabbing her head as the voices got louder and louder. The fake Jason spoke quickly whilst the fake Mr Jet spoke with a steady pace. Their voices interrupted the continuous chatter from the fake Alexander and Danny. What was going on? What was the point of this? Was there a meaning behind all of this? Whatever it was Angel didn't understand it. The ghosts of the men she knew continued to repeat their words as Angel slowly began to *fall into insanity.*

"You really don't know, do you? This is all because of you. You and the Master of Darkness." Paris laughed as he suddenly appeared next to Alexander. Upon his arrival, the others disappeared leaving the shapeshifter alone with the man she had just murdered. Angel stumbled to her feet. The room was silent. Paris stared at her. He was no longer beaten up and battered, he instead looked the same as he used to; full of life, mischief, and charm.

"Your mum, Angel, your birth mum. She's very much alive."

"Paris," Angel sighed, "What is this? Is this you? Is this some kind of ghost enchantment?"

Paris just started to laugh, "You're going to die. Angel Night…you will die."

"Is that your new catchphrase?"

"On Halloween you will die." Suddenly blood began to drip from Paris' chest. A line of blood grew across his body. His heartbeat seemed to echo around the room and Angel could hear it getting slower and slower. Paris took a step forward, grabbing Angel. He collapsed and died in her arms. Angel pushed him to the ground. His blood stained her hands.

"It's nearly time to go," the little girl announced appearing from the shadows.

"Go where?" Angel asked as Paris disappeared, "Who are you?"

"You killed me. Don't you remember?"

"What?"

"You killed me!"

* * * * *

"Angel!"

When Angel opened her eyes, she found Jason staring down at her.

"Jason, are you real?" Angel mumbled.

"Yes! I am! Angel! Hi! Can you see me?" Jason asked.

"What are you doing here?"

"Well, see I followed your plan. When the Emperor was about to speak, and the crowd all stood up, Araminta

270

helped me sneak away. But I couldn't find the blue room and well I got lost! I was trying to find my way back when I saw you and Mr Jet. He tapped you on the head and then you collapsed. I ran to you. Mr Jet smiled at me, said 'bye Jason' then disappeared. I started shouting 'Angel' and then you woke up," Jason stuttered quickly.

"Right. Ah!"

"Your hand is broken."

"Really? Is it Jason? I hadn't noticed!" Angel exclaimed as she cradled her broken hand.

"No need to be rude. Should I go and find help?"

"Don't bother, you'll only get lost," Angel pulled out her wand with her other hand. She flicked her wrist and blue sparks floated from the tip of the wand to her hand. There was a horrible grinding sound as Angel's hand healed itself.

"Oh that's cool! A bit gross but in a cool way!"

"You said Jet disappeared. How long ago was that? And in which direction was he headed?"

"It was a while. Well not a while exactly but it was a couple of minutes ago, like maybe five, possibly six."

"Forget it. He'll be long gone anyway..."

"What happened? How come Jet was here? Did he save Paris?"

"No."

"That means you...oh," there was a pause, "Are you okay?"

"No, no I'm not. I just executed...I just murdered someone! Not just someone...Paris! I've never...I'm not okay Jason," Angel sighed close to tears.

They fell silent until Jason asked, "Why did he come then? Mr Jet, if he wasn't here to save Paris, why did he come?"

"I think he was just here because he could be. It shows just how powerful he thinks he is. He's just appeared right next to the Emperor and got away."

"Like a publicity stunt?"

"Exactly."

"What did he do to you? I just saw him touch your head and then…"

"He has magic!"

"But he's a vampire. Vampire's don't have magic, do they?"

"No, no they don't. I've never heard of a vampire with magical powers. I've heard of vampires with seer abilities before and I've even met one with elemental powers. But in these cases the vampires have been from mixed heritage backgrounds."

"Mixed heritage?"

"Ah it means that they had powers before they were turned. It's rare though, normally if a vampire bites a paranormal, the paranormal just dies. Vampires rarely go after paranormals anyway. Human blood tastes better, apparently."

"Perhaps Mr Jet used to be a warlock," Jason suggested.

"It's a possibility I suppose. Why didn't he kill me? He had the perfect opportunity too, so why didn't he? He must want me alive for some reason," Angel muttered, "Come on, we need to get back and report this."

As Angel got up, she felt a burning pain in her arm. She looked down at her wrist. It was covered in blood. Angel turned to the fountain and dipped her arm in the water. As the blood washed away, Angel found that the name Paris Surf had been tattooed onto her skin.

"You are working fast today witch," Angel muttered.

"What is that!?" Jason exclaimed.

"It's something you need to forget about," Jason was about to protest but Angel cut him off, "Jason, I don't have the time or energy to explain this to you today. Let it go. I will explain it some other time, until then you don't breathe a word about this to anyone, understand?"

Jason nodded. Angel muttered her thanks as she watched as the name faded into her skin. Where it would remain forever waiting for her to look at her reflection and see the monster within.

23

'THE HAZARD TEAM IS LESS IMPRESSIVE THAN IT SOUNDS'

JASON

As me and Angel headed back to the courthouse, we ran into a rather scary looking fairy. She was well armed and raised her sword in our direction as we approached.

"Captain Night. What happened to Mr Jet?" the fairy asked.

"He got away," Angel muttered, "The Emperor?"

"Safe. Your Colonel escorted him back to the palace. How exactly did Mr Jet escape?"

"We fought. He won and got away."

"And left you alive? I see."

"What is that supposed to mean?"

"Did anyone see you fight with Mr Jet?"

"I did," I stuttered, the scary fairy turned to me.

"And who are you?"

"The Master of Darkness."

Upon hearing this the fairy sheathed her sword and bowed her head, "Ah I apologise sir."

"No need to…"

"How did Mr Jet get into the courthouse?" Angel interrupted, "I thought you had security covered."

"As did I," the fairy admitted.

"It seems you have a leak. You might want to sort that out."

"Worry about your own squad not mine." At that moment a stretcher walked past us. On the stretcher was a bloody corpse. A corpse with ginger hair. Paris! Before I could see the body clearly, Angel covered my eyes with her hand. I took a number of deep breaths. I had to suppress both my desire to vomit and my urge to scream. I couldn't freak out. Not now. Not in front of Angel. And especially not in front of the scary fairy with the sharp sword! But I wanted to freak out. Paris was dead. Not only was he dead but he had been executed. Executed by Angel. Angel had killed Paris with her own hands. The same hands that now covered my eyes!

Jason calm down and save your mental breakdown for when we get back to the base, Angel's voice boomed into my mind. I quickly calmed my thoughts after that.

"What are you doing?" the fairy asked.

"The Master of Darkness is half-demon. And while we've locked Jason's demon up well, it still gets restless at the sight of blood," Angel lied. I knew she was lying, not because of some special sixth sense, but because she had stood on my toe, the moment I went to correct her statement.

"Really? For a moment I thought you were trying to hide the body from the Master of Darkness."

"Not at all. If Jason wants to stare at corpses, then he is welcome to do so. However not in a public place where we would be unable to control his demon self." With that

Angel removed her hand from my face. The stretcher and Paris' body had vanished by the time I opened my eyes.

"Thinking about it, I don't remember seeing you at the execution," the fairy turned to me, her eyes studying me carefully.

"Yes, well you also didn't see Mr Jet. Perhaps you should get your eyes tested," Angel retorted. Before the fairy could respond, Alexander ran over to us.

He grabbed hold of Angel's shoulders, "Angel! Are you alright? What happened? What happened to your face? And what happened to your hand?" Although Angel's hand was no longer broken, it was still a horrid blue colour.

"Ah, Mr Jet broke my hand. It's healed, just a bit sore. What's wrong with my face?"

"It's scratched, and you have a weird red mark on your forehead."

Angel slapped my arm, "Why didn't you tell me?"

"I thought you knew!" I exclaimed.

"If I had known about it, I would have healed it already!"

"Angel this mark on your forehead is really strange," Alexander took Angel's face in his hands and studied her forehead, "It looks like a symbol."

"What kind of…?" The fairy coughed. Alexander broke away from Angel and turned to face the scary fairy.

"Anita. I didn't see you there," Alexander said coldly.

"Clearly," the fairy, Anita, smiled bitterly, "My team are going to do a search of the courthouse. So you three should re-join your squad and wait for further instructions."

"Do a good job," Angel sneered as she grabbed my arm and pulled me past the fairy.

Once we were back inside the courthouse, I asked, "Who was that scary fairy?"

"Anita is the head of the Emperor's private guard,"

Alexander explained, "She also once tried to kill Angel."

"She did what?"

"It's a long story but the short version is…" Before Alexander could tell me, he was interrupted by the sound of Fern's voice.

"Hey! That's not fair he started it!"

"You punched him! And broke his nose!" cried another loud voice.

"I think I know where our squad is," Angel sighed as she pointed to a door, "Why can you always hear them before you see them?"

She opened the door and stepped into the chaos within. Fern, Willow and Elsa were arguing. Ethan and Roger were stuffing their faces with food. Sue, Roxy, and Clover were crying. Sophie was sat quietly in the corner, fading in and out of visibility. Danny was sat watching the situation amused and Araminta was missing. The room was small with blue furnishings and walls. It was elegantly dressed and looked like a noble gentlemen's study. The squad looked rather out of place in such a grand setting.

"What's going on!?" Angel exclaimed.

"Fern broke a reporter's nose!" Elsa cried.

"Fern!"

Fern grinned, "I know! Isn't it awesome! I didn't realise my right hook was so good!"

"No Fern it wasn't awesome. That guy was a reporter! This incident is going to end up all over the morning papers and you're going to get sued!" Elsa hissed.

"A reporter? As in a reporter for a newspaper? You have newspapers here!?" I asked.

"Yes of course we do you idiot!" Fern looked at me like I was the stupidest person on the planet (which I probably was in that moment).

"Why did you punch him?" Angel asked.

"Because he insulted you, and Jason. I didn't care when he was insulting Jason. What he said was actually rather amusing and not completely unfounded, however then he insulted you. So we had an argument and I broke his nose!"

"Fern."

"He said you were a…"

"I don't want to know. You can't just go around punching people. Especially not reporters and not when you're on duty!"

"So what I take from that is, I can punch whoever I like as long as I'm not on duty and they're not a reporter."

"Fern!"

"Alright, it was just a joke!"

"Where is Araminta?"

"She went with the Colonel," Elsa explained, "They should be returning soon."

"What happened to your face?" Roger asked getting to his feet and walking up to Angel.

"Nothing, it's just a scratch," Angel brushed her brother away.

"Did you fight Mr Jet? Alone!? You could have been killed!"

"But I wasn't and that's all that matters right now," Angel turned to Clover, Sue and Roxy and asked gently, "Why are you crying?"

"Why do you think!? Paris just…You just killed Paris!" Clover exclaimed, "Even though he was a terrorist, he was…he…"

"We're not all as cold hearted as you! We can't just feel nothing!" Sue cried. I had expected Angel, or one of the werewolves, to refute this claim but, to my surprise, none of them did. Roger looked like he was about to, but Angel raised her hand to silence him. She then walked over to where the three crying girls were sitting and knelt in front of them.

"You're right. You're not as cold hearted as I am. You all have big warm hearts that embraced Paris as a friend.

So of course you're upset. Of course you want to cry. But here isn't the place to mourn. We're surrounded by reporters and investigators who might easily mistake your tears for treason. So dry your eyes and put on your brave faces. Later, later when we're back home, I'll unlock Paris' room and you can go in there and mourn him, okay?"

As Angel wiped the tears from the girls faces, I suddenly realised just how much Angel cared for the members of her squad. Although Roxy, Sue and Clover constantly spoke back to Angel and questioned her leadership, Angel didn't seem to bare any grudges against them. Instead she dried their tears and spoke words of comfort. I have to say I was rather impressed. Angel was a lot cooler than I had realised.

"What happened to your hand?" Sue asked.

"Ah Mr Jet broke it," Angel explained, she then stood up and addressed the squad, "Currently we're not allowed to leave the courthouse. Until we hear from the Colonel, I want you guys to stay in this room and rest."

"What about the reporter Fern punched?" Willow asked.

"I'll deal with it. Don't worry," Angel then turned to me, "Jason can you do me a favour? There's a first aid box on the wall in the corridor, can you go get me it?"

I nodded and quickly left the room. It was only when I was outside of the room that I realised that Angel hadn't told me which corridor. Did she mean the corridor on my right or the one on my left? I didn't want to look like an idiot and go ask her, so I took the corridor to my right and began my search for the first aid box.

After twenty minutes, three dead ends, five wrong turns, and a bathroom break, I finally found the first aid box and began to head back to the room. However when I got back, I found Angel sat on a table in the corridor having a serious conversation with Alexander. Here I found myself in an awkward situation. I didn't want to interrupt their important conversation, nor did I want to eavesdrop, but I also didn't want to walk away as then I might end up completely lost. While I debated what to do I accidentally, and it really was an accident, ended up overhearing their entire conversation.

"Jet has magic!" Alexander exclaimed.

"And it's powerful, really powerful. He could very easily take out a warlock," Angel muttered, "You've not heard of a vampire having magic before?"

"No never."

"He also had something. I'm not sure exactly what it was. It was an object. It was orange and glowed. I got hit by it multiple times and each time I was forced to transform back into this form."

Alexander swore then grabbed Angel's head and began to stare at the mark on her forehead.

"I thought I recognised this symbol. Angel, you know how shapeshifters used to be considered enemies of the empire and they were…"

"Massacred."

"Yes well during that time the government created weapons that would force a shapeshifter to involuntary transform. It looks like you got hit by one. You currently have the symbol of the former Emperor marked on your forehead," seeing Angel's bemused expression Alexander explained, "The weapons were designed to brand a shapeshifter, so they could be tracked down even if they escaped."

"Great! Can I get rid of it?"

"Luckily you only got branded lightly, from a distance people won't notice. I might know someone who may be able to remove it. I'll talk to them and see if they can do anything."

"Thanks. I thought all anti-shapeshifter weapons were destroyed."

"If only. The government claimed they got rid of them

all but to be honest I wouldn't even be surprised if there were a few at the base."

"Oh thanks Alex! Now I feel really safe!"

"If Mr Jet has one of those, if he has anti-shapeshifter weapons, then why didn't he kill you?"

"I've been wondering the same thing. He clearly needs me alive for some reason."

"You need to be extra careful. Anti-shapeshifter weapons are extremely dangerous."

There was silence. I was about to use this opportunity to make my entrance but before I could, Alexander asked softly, "Angel, this may be a very stupid question but, are you okay?"

To my surprise, Angel grabbed Alexander's shirt, pulled him forwards, rested her head against his body and burst into tears. The vampire wrapped his arms around her and held her close. At this point I felt even more awkward than I had done before! I really wanted to leave however I didn't dare move. I didn't want Angel and Alexander to hear me and think I had been purposely eavesdropping. As I really hadn't been! I just wanted to hand Angel the first aid box and go rest, why was that turning out to be so difficult!?

"I killed him, Alex. I didn't even hesitate I just…I killed him. And everyone saw…I…am I a monster Alex?"

"No," the vampire said firmly taking Angel's face in his hands, "You're not a monster. You're…This isn't your fault."

"I killed him Alex. I did that. It doesn't matter that he was, I killed him to save myself and the pack, what kind of person does that make me? I killed a person to save myself!"

"He was a terrorist…"

"He was still a person! Not a zombie or a demon…a person. A person who I shared a house with for nearly four years," Angel buried her face in the vampire's chest once again.

I sniffed back my own tears. I have never been very good around crying people. Other peoples' tears always make me cry! So as I stood there, holding the first aid box, I felt my eyes prickle with sadness. Pity also rose in my chest. Angel hadn't had it easy. Be accused of treason or execute Paris, those had been her only options. I was still internally having a massive panic-attack over the fact that Paris had been executed; I didn't want to process it or admit that it had happened. I wanted to forget all about it. However my panic was suppressed by Angel's sorrow. How could I panic when the person who had been made to complete the task was sat there calling herself a monster. I didn't think Angel was a monster. She was just a person who made a hard and terrifying decision, the outcome of which she would have to deal with for the rest of her life.

When Angel eventually calmed, Alexander held her face in his hands once again and wiped her tears away. He lightly ran his fingers against the scratches on Angel's cheek, "You should heal these before they scar."

Angel nodded. She glowed white and the scratches on her face quickly healed.

"That's better. You should put a bandage on that hand too. You may have healed it but if it…"

"I know. That's why I sent Jason to get me the first aid box…actually where is Jason?"

Finally! My chance! I was just about to make my entrance when…

"Jason what are you standing there for?" Araminta asked as she and Rowan walked down the corridor.

"I wasn't standing here. I was getting a first aid box," I replied.

"Jason why are you speaking so loudly?"

"I'm not speaking loudly." Actually I was speaking louder than usual in the hopes that Angel and Alexander would hear and break away from their, easily to misinterpret, position.

"You are. Are the others in the room?"

"Araminta you're back," Angel greeted as she walked up to us, taking the first aid box from my hands, "Jason, what took you so long?"

I wanted to retort that I had been there ages, waiting for her and Alexander to finish having their little moment, but I gulped down my bitterness and replied, "I got lost."

"What do you need that for?" Rowan asked gesturing to the first aid box.

"My hand. Fight with Mr Jet. Don't worry it looks worse than it is," Angel muttered as she wrapped her hand in a bandage, "Rowan, why are you here?"

"The Colonel wants us to head to the Polar warehouse. I've been assigned to go with you as an onsite healer, just in case."

"Are we free to leave?"

"We are. There's just one slight problem. Outside is swarming with reporters."

"Damn it! Right, no matter what happens don't let Fern anywhere near them, otherwise those poor reporters are going to end up in therapy for the rest of their lives!"

* * * * *

"Master of Darkness is it true that Mr Jet killed your mother?"

"Is it true you plan to rid the world of demons?"

"Where's the Mistress of Light?"

"Captain Night how did Mr Jet get into the execution today?"

"Why have you stayed hidden for so long?"

"Is it true you don't have a sister?"

"Captain Night is it true that Mr Jet knew about the Master before we did?"

We had to push against the mob of reporters all

shouting their questions and flashing their cameras in my face. I did not enjoy this one bit. The reporters were rude and kept demanding that I give them answers. But I didn't have any answers to give! I didn't know why I didn't have a sister and I certainly didn't have a plan to 'rid the world of demons'! Only three weeks ago I was a nice normal boring human! Admittedly not all the questions were directed at me, some were directed at Angel who just acted cool and completely ignored anything that was asked. Fern, however, had had enough. She took out her gun and fired twice into the sky. The reporters fell silent as they all turned to look at her, giving me and Angel time to jump in the back of the truck. Fern was the last member of the squad to get in. She sat down with a massive smile on her face.

"Please tell me you didn't shoot one of them," Angel exclaimed.

"What? No! But I've just seen the guy whose nose I broke, it's put me in a good mood," Fern grinned.

"Alex get us out of here," Angel ordered. The truck rumbled into life and slowly we pulled away from the courthouse.

"Glad that's over," I muttered, "Where is the Polar warehouse?"

"It's a couple of miles out of the city," Angel added, "There isn't normally many people there, just a couple of security guards."

"Do they know we're coming?"

"Jason, for all we know this warehouse could be filled with Mr Jet's followers, do you honestly think I'd call them before hand and tell them to put the kettle on?"

"Ah I guess not. What happens if we find something?"

"Then we'll be taking a field trip to the Polar Base."

* * * * *

My bum had gone numb by the time we reached the

Polar warehouse. It was a very uncomfortable truck!

As the truck finally came to a stop, Angel explained, "Right, so I haven't been completely honest with you guys. This isn't a routine check. There's actually a high possibility that this warehouse is filled with Mr Jet's followers. So get your weapons bags and put your bulletproof vests on."

We quickly did as Angel ordered then clambered out of the truck. I was extremely nervous! I didn't like this situation at all. Also my bulletproof vest wasn't particularly comfortable which was making me panic even more.

"Okay guys listen up…" Angel started but she was interrupted by gunfire. From one of the warehouse windows someone had started shooting at us. We quickly took cover behind the truck. Guns, shooting…I really didn't want to be here! This was not for me. My training hadn't prepared me enough for this! I didn't want to be…before I could fall into the terrifying realm of panic, Angel slapped me hard across my sensitive little belly. That quickly brought me back to my senses.

"Where is he?" Elsa yelled to Angel.

"Far left window," Angel then shouted at Sophie, "Turn him to stone!"

Sophie smiled, she jumped to her feet and made eye contact with the shooter. She took off her sunglasses causing him to turn to stone. The gun shots stopped, and it all went quiet. I sighed in relief and tried to sneak away back to the truck, however Angel grabbed hold of the back of my shirt and stopped me from escaping.

She then ordered, "Everyone get with your partner. You guys take the back entrance, you guys take the front. When you get inside, you four will head to the second floor and I'll take the side entrance. Ready, let's go. Jason, you're with me."

Before I had time to panic, Angel led me to the big metal doors that led into the warehouse. She tapped some numbers into the keypad and the doors opened. The warehouse was smaller than I had originally thought. It looked…well like a warehouse! It had rows of shelves stacked high with boxes and large metal containers balanced on top of one another. It was lit by sharp electric lights and the ground was grey concrete. The squad quickly split and went off in different directions. I followed Angel as she led me through the rows of containers and wooden boxes.

"Hey what are you doing here?" a man shouted in our direction.

"I'm Captain Night of Lightning D…" before she could finish, Angel was rudely interrupted. The man pulled out a gun and started shooting at us.

"Get down," Angel shoved me behind a box.

"Don't any of them have manners!?" I exclaimed, "Why do they always start shooting at us?"

"Because they're not nice people Jason!"

"Oh yeah."

"Cover me."

"What?" Angel didn't answer instead she shapeshifted into an ant and clambered over the boxes until she was behind the shooter. She transformed back into Angel and pressed her hand against the man's head. The man glowed yellow and then collapsed to the floor.

"What did you just do?" I asked standing up from my hiding spot.

"He's unconscious and paralysed," Angel explained briefly before she began to walk away. I swiftly followed. I could hear gunshots in other areas of the warehouse.

Then I suddenly felt something heavy land on my shoulders and sharp claws dig into my skin.

I yelled out in pain.

Angel turned around and fired two shots at the creature on my shoulders. It screeched then leapt onto Angel. The creature was so ugly! It was small with thin arms and legs that twisted into disgusting shapes, and a face that looked like it had lost a fight with a cricket bat. I raised my gun and fired repeatedly. One of the bullets hit its mark. The lime green creature screamed and dropped to the floor. Angel pulled out her sword and cut off the creature's head.

"You alright?" I asked. But before Angel could answer, someone started shooting at us, again! This time the guy had a massive machine gun. We dropped to the floor as the bullets rained down on us.

"Stay here," Angel ordered. She glowed white and transformed into a bat. The bat flew above the towers of boxes unnoticed. I watched as bat Angel landed behind the mad guy with the machine gun. Angel transformed back into herself and once again placed her hand against the man's head. The man dropped to the floor. I crawled out from behind the boxes and stood up, half expecting to be attacked again.

"You alright?" Angel asked.

"Fine," I gasped.

I was far from fine. I was an emotional wreck! Gunshots, strange creatures, more gunshots…this was too much for me to handle. I had never wanted to be a soldier. I didn't like guns. I didn't even like shooting computer games! I just liked being at home watching cute cat videos whilst eating ice-cream. I wanted to scream and run far away from this terrifying labyrinth of gunfire, but I didn't dare. Whilst the gunmen scared me tremendously, the thought of Fern's mocking if I ran away terrified me even more. My plan had been to just follow Angel and let her do all the scary fighting stuff whilst I watched and provided cheers of encouragement, but even that wasn't going so well. I really wasn't suited to all this fighting nonsense. I just wanted us all to sort out our differences over a nice hot cup of tea and a chocolate biscuit!

"Clear," came a yell, which sounded like Fern.

"Clear," someone else called.

"Clear," Angel shouted. The rest of the squad made their way over to us.

"Let's open one of these boxes and find out what they're hiding," Angel went over to one of the boxes and pulled out her knife. She prized the box open. Ethan and Roger held their noses.

"There is something not right in there. It's messing with the wolf senses," Ethan complained as Angel pulled the box apart. Inside was a large silver bag which Angel cut open. Mixed in with a load of vegetables was a black eel like creature. It was fat yet long. Its black body was stretched and, almost lovingly, curled around the potatoes. Its sharp green eyes were clouded over, and its dead stare gazed at the miniature carrots in disgust. Its scales were shiny and covered in squashed tomatoes.

"What is that?" I asked.

"That's a snake demon, one bite and you're screaming in agony. It's dead," Angel muttered.

"Just to make sure," Fern kicked the demon's belly. Its skin broke causing its insides to spread across the floor. It was gross. Its guts were pink and covered in thick black slime. It was sickening. For a brief moment I thought I was going to throw up, but the moment past and I was able to (somewhat) adjust to the disgusting sight before me.

"Is it just me or are those guts moving?" I asked. As I had been trying not to vomit on the dead demon, I had noticed that its sticky fat guts were wriggling…this had made me want to throw up even more, so I quickly shut my eyes and covered my mouth.

"They're its babies," Angel pulled out her gun and everyone, minus myself as I hadn't realised what was happening, fired at the five baby demons. Only when all the demons were dead, did the squad stop shooting.

"If that had got to the Polar Base," Roxy said slowly, "The babies would have killed everyone there…How many demons are in here?"

"I haven't a clue," Angel pulled out her phone and dialled the Colonel, "Sir, we were right. There are demons in with the food. We have no idea how many are contaminated. We need a hazard team down here. Yes sir," Angel hung up.

"What's happening?" asked Roger.

"The Colonel is sending a hazard team. He's also coming to see for himself."

"What about us?"

"We have to stay here and wait."

It took half an hour for the hazard team to arrive and then it took them another three hours to finish their examination. During that time myself and the rest of Lightning Squad were made to sit patiently in a corner. I rather enjoyed this peaceful time. It meant I had chance to have a nap and had time to stare distantly off into nowhere, an activity I rather enjoy doing. Fern, of course, was not happy about being left in a corner for three hours and she felt the need to let the head of the hazard team know of her feelings, which led to her being forcefully removed from the vicinity.

"What even is the hazard team?" I asked Roger who had been dozing next to me.

"The hazard team are another unit. They clean up after us most of the time, they make sure that infected areas are wiped down. We normally just call them the 'clean-up crew' as that's basically all they do," Roger smiled.

"Well the hazard team is certainly less impressive then it sounds," I muttered, "Why are they here?"

"They're here to clean up. Get rid of the bodies and disinfect the warehouse."

"It's taking forever, why won't they let us help with the whole demon disposing part, that's kind of our job!" By *us* what I actually meant was the rest of the squad minus myself, there was no way I was going to go dispose of demons! I wanted to stay as far away from the demons as possible. It was bad enough that I had one inside me, I wasn't about to go around hunting for more!

"Because they don't like us. They seem to think they do all the hard work, yet we get all the praise."

The Colonel, who had been talking to the head of the hazard team for what felt like forever, finally came over to us.

"What's the situation sir?" Angel asked, getting to her feet.

After a slight pause the Colonel replied, "You're going to the Polar Base."

24

'POLAR BASE'

JASON

Despite its name, I hadn't expected the Polar Base to be on the actual North Pole! Yeah, those stories of Santa living on the North Pole with cute elves and reindeer are all wrong! Instead there's a miserable looking base full of paranormal beings who kill demons for a living…I know, it ruins your entire childhood! The Polar Base was a small grey building which was right next to the north 'pole' itself.

We used a teleport to get there. This was the first time I had teleported properly, and I hated every second of it. It felt like I was riding a roller-coaster backwards while upside down and spinning. I wobbled as we landed in the gloomy base and ended up falling flat on my face. Everyone laughed at me which I thought was a bit mean…it wasn't my fault that I'd never properly teleported before! As I looked up, I came face-to-face with a giant rat head! I screamed and jumped, so did the giant rat.

"I'm sorry to startle you," it stuttered, "I'm Marvin McLean."

"Lieutenant Colonel McLean, it's an honour to meet you," Angel extended her hand, "I'm Captain Angel Night."

"Captain Night, yes," McLean took Angel's hand and shook it.

"I'm sorry for our sudden arrival."

"Oh its fine. We don't get many visitors. The last guest we had was the other Captain Night. Please follow me I'll take you to the main building," McLean stuttered. We followed him as he pattered down a corridor.

The Polar Base was very grey.

The floors were grey, the walls were grey, the ceiling was grey, in fact everything was grey! We followed the rat man until he pushed open a heavy metal door which led into a bright white room. This room was round with computer monitors covering the walls. There was a round black table in the middle of the room, around which sat four people.

The first was a small Asian woman with black hair, body piercings and a metal robotic arm. The next was a skinny blonde-haired man whose extreme paleness made it obvious that he was a vampire. Sat with them was a pair of identical twin brothers. The brothers were tall, black, and muscular with long dark hair and miserable faces. I couldn't work out what species the pair belonged to, I had initially thought werewolf, but Ethan had told me that wasn't the case.

"This is my science team, that's Becks, Angus, Joel and Fredrick," Mclean introduced.

Angel nodded her greeting then asked, "Are any of you armed?"

"Of course not!" Becks (the woman with robot arms) cried, "This is a peaceful base. We don't carry guns. There are other ways to solve the world's problems then through violence!"

"Oh great, they're hippies," I heard Fern mutter under her breath.

"Are you aware that demons have been smuggled on to your base?" Angel asked sharply. There was silence, "So you knew and none of you thought to report it?"

"If we had reported it, we would have been shut down," said Joel, I think, it could have been Fredrick. I couldn't tell them apart!

"What happened to the demon?"

"We released the poor animal," Beck said softly.

"Released it!? Are you mad!?"

"The animal had been locked up."

"It wasn't a trapped hedgehog. It was a demon! Do you not know the difference?"

"We're scientists, don't question our intellect," Angus snapped.

"You let a demon go. Have any of you been vaccinated against the demon plague? I'll take your silence as a no. How can you not be!? I thought you were a Lieutenant Colonel!?" Angel snapped at McLean.

"I'm the Lieutenant Colonel of the science division," McLean shrugged.

"Why would we be vaccinated?" asked Fredrick, I think, it might have been Joel, "Vaccinations only make our bodies weaker."

"I thought you were scientists!"

"Now listen here you hippies!" Fern snapped, already bored of the conversation, "You'll do whatever Cap here tells you to do otherwise I'll lock you out in the freezing cold!"

"How dare…" Becks started but Fern interrupted.

"Metal arms here clearly wants to be the first person to freeze to death," Fern went over to Becks, forced her to the floor before grabbing her hair and dragging her towards the door.

"Get off me!" Becks yelled.

"Are you going to be a good little hippy and do as Captain Night says?"

"Fine!"

Fern let go of Becks' hair and smiled, "See that wasn't that hard? Anyone else?" She turned to the others who quickly shook their heads, "There you go Cap."

"This is going well," I whispered to Araminta, "We've only been here five minutes and Fern has already attacked one of the locals."

* * * * *

"Hold still," Rowan stabbed a needle into Becks' neck.

I turned away not wanting to look at the needle…I really hate needles…they give me shivers just thinking about them! We were in a small medical room. The room was grey with four white hospital beds. The room was too small; the shelves of medicines and the medical equipment overpowered the space, meaning that there was hardly any room for us (or any sick people) inside. Rowan had gotten to work straight away, vaccinating all of the base's workers. They had protested (a lot!) but Fern's terrifying stare had quickly silenced their complaints.

"Done," Rowan placed a piece of cotton wool over the needle puncture.

"Thank you," Becks hissed bitterly before walking off.

"That ungrateful…Does she realise that I just saved her life?"

"She's one of those hippies," Fern said as if that explained everything, "Do you think they really let that demon go? They might have kept it."

"Working with Mr Jet? That's a possibility," Rowan muttered packing up her medical equipment.

"What would happen if Mr Jet took over this base?" I asked.

"Nothing good," Angel said walking into the room, "Which is why we won't let that happen. I've sent the guys to the supply room to look through all the boxes. The others are doing a sweep of the base just to double check the security."

"What do you think Mr Jet is planning?" asked Rowan.

"I'm not sure. He boxed the demons alive, he wanted them to get here, to do what?"

"To kill everyone?" I suggested.

"There are much easier ways to kill people. Also he could have done it by now. The workers are still alive. If Jet wanted the base, he could have taken it ages ago. There's something else going on here."

"What do you want us to do Cap?" Fern asked.

"Fern, I want you and Rowan to watch over the workers. Keep a close eye on them, see if anything seems strange. Jason, me and you are going to talk to McLean."

I followed Angel down a grey corridor to a small office which was filled with books. Angel knocked on the door. McLean jumped at the sound.

"Captain Night, sorry I didn't hear you. Please, please sit," McLean stammered, as he gestured for me and Angel to sit opposite him.

There was no sign of technology in the office. Shelves, covered in papers and tattered old books, towered high above McLean's head. A large map of the paranormal world hung on the only shelf-free wall and a dusty candle lamp lit up the shadows. Boxes covered the ground making it almost impossible for Angel and me to walk through. Ink from a quill dripped over the edge of the desk into a puddle on the carpet. There were two old and unstable chairs on the opposite side of McLean's desk that were also covered in books. Angel gently removed the books so that we could sit.

"You seem busy," Angel nodded her head towards the large pile of paperwork that littered McLean's desk. I didn't say anything. I was too busy staring at McLean's rat head. I know it's not polite to stare but it was really hard not to. It was a giant rat head! With massive whiskers and everything!

McLean smiled, "Got to keep things up to date."

"Why didn't you kill the demon?"

"The reason me and my workers stay up here is because we don't believe in the war against the demons. We believe that even they should be free to live their lives."

"They've killed thousands of our people!"

"And we've killed thousands of theirs. It's a vicious circle. Don't get me wrong I don't want them to take over. I just think that they should be allowed to live in their world."

"And we should be allowed to live in ours. Look I haven't come here to argue, I've come for the incident file."

"The what?" McLean asked confused.

"The incident file, you know, the official paperwork you have to fill out if there's been a problem. You should have filled one out when you found that demon."

"Ah, I don't use those. I have a logbook, just let me…" McLean rustled through some papers then pulled out a large brown book, "Here we go. Everything that has happened is written in there."

"How long have you been up here?" I asked staring at the book.

The book was massive.

It was really heavy too! Paper stuck out of it and its cover was almost falling off. It was tattered and broken, yet the joy in McLean's eyes made it clear that the book was something to be treasured.

"I came out here in 1764 to do research on the ice caps," squeaked the rat man. My mouth dropped open. 1764!? That was nearly, nearly…that was a long time ago! A really long time ago! McLean didn't look that old…but then again it was hard to tell. I had never met a rat-man before.

"Lieutenant Colonel, what exactly is it that you and your workers do up here?" Angel asked.

"We look after the portal. We make sure it's stable and that nothing gets through that isn't meant to."

"Your workers aren't with the military, are they?"

"No, they're scientists. I handpicked them from the top universities."

"You guys have universities!? This is…this probably sounds very stupid," I trailed off. Newspapers, universities, what else does the paranormal empire have? Do they have theme parks? Do they have movies? Do they have reality TV? A long list of questions popped into my mind.

"The demon you found," Angel gave me a sharp look, "They said you released it?"

"Ah yes, I opened the portal and sent it back to the underworld."

"What size was the creature?"

"It was small, its stomach had shrivelled up."

"What did it look like?"

"It looked like a cat, but with a longer body and webbed feet."

"Did you say everything is in here?" Angel asked pointing to the book.

"Yes, everything."

"Good, thank you for your time," Angel got to her feet. We left McLean's office, shutting the door behind us. We headed down the corridor.

"This isn't good," Angel muttered.

"What isn't?" I asked.

"The demon he described; I've met that kind before. They're small but deadly."

"Then it's a good job they released it."

"There's more. When these demons give birth, the babies suck all the blood and minerals out of the mother, causing the mother to shrivel up."

297

"You think that the demon was a mother?"

"I'm sure of it. The babies would have been small, they could have got out of the box without being seen."

"You mean," I gulped as anxiety began to bubble in my chest.

"The babies, they're still on the base."

25

'TROUBLE'

Blood, guts, dead demons, and potatoes painted the floor of the supply room. Danny slid to the floor exhausted whilst Alexander finished off the last demon. Roger and Ethan transformed back into their normal forms and collapsed to the floor. Jason and Angel stared at the chaos opened mouthed as they entered the room.

"What happened?" Angel asked.

"Well basically," Roger started.

"Open box and BANG there's a huge demon! Then shoot, shoot, shoot and finally the thing is dead. Then open another box and OH SNAP it's an even bigger demon who isn't very pleased when you try to shoot it. So it goes CRASH BANG GROWL and tries to eat us! So we cut off its head and everything is fine. But then there's another demon and another and another and another! And like man they just won't die! Then finally they do and yeah," Ethan explained with extravagate hand gestures and loud sound effects.

"What he said," Roger nodded unable to think of a better explanation.

"Right. Okay," Angel muttered, "Err how many?"

"All the boxes that have arrived recently had a demon inside," Ethan gestured around the room, "As you can tell."

"What about before then?"

"Nothing. Judging by the boxes, this started about a month ago."

"A month, why a month? Why now, what's changed in a month?"

"Oh lemons," Jason muttered. Jason wasn't sure why the word 'lemons' had popped into his head, but he suspected that it had something to do with all the fruit that was rolling across the floor.

"What is it?" Angel asked.

"It's me."

"What?"

"That's what's changed."

"I'm not following," sneezed Ethan.

"This started a month ago, right? Well it's only been a month since Mr Jet killed my mum and…"

"The Master of Darkness entered the paranormal empire. Jet's been planning this from the start. Damn it! We've been set up!" Angel ran out of the room. Jason looked at the others who shrugged and followed Angel down the corridor. She led them to the white room they had been in before. Once inside, Angel rushed to the phone on the wall.

"Captain Night, number 7354, come in," she said quickly but her voice was met only with static. Angel slammed her hand and the phone down, "Damn! Mobile phones?"

"No signal," Danny muttered staring at his phone, "Your telepathic link with Jin?"

"Nothing. It's like his mind is blocked. I can't even

reach Roxy and we're in the same building! The wolf bond is blocked as well," Angel pulled out her wand and tried to send a messenger spirit, but the spell crumbled into blue dust, "Messenger spirits are blocked, how is this possible?"

"Guys look at this," Roger beckoned them over. They crowded around the computer screen. The scanner was flickering. One moment it seemed as if the base was surrounded then moments later there would be nothing.

"What in Jupiter's name?" Alexander muttered under his breath.

"Interference?" Angel asked.

"I have no idea," mumbled Roger as he tried to fix the scanner.

"Right stay here, I'm going to teleport outside and find out what's going on." Angel glowed white. She disappeared only to reappear less than a second later.

"That was quick."

"I didn't go anywhere," Angel muttered. She tried to teleport once again, only to reappear seconds later. She collapsed to the floor and coughed up blood.

"Angel!" Roger exclaimed kneeling next to his sister.

"I still haven't gone anywhere," Angel hissed getting to her feet, "My teleportation powers, they're not working! Something is stopping me from teleporting. It's like there's some kind of forcefield."

"What's going on?" asked McLean walking into the room.

"We were hoping you could tell us," Angel gestured to the computer screens.

"That's not right, not right at all," McLean muttered. He hurried to the computer and started pressing buttons, "That's not good."

Then everything went black. The screens faded and the lights disappeared. Angel could no longer see Roger despite him being stood right next to her. The entire building was in shadows.

"Is it dark for everyone else or have I gone blind?" Jason asked from somewhere in the darkness.

"The powers gone!" McLean squeaked.

"Is there a backup system?" Angel asked, flicking her wand, and sending a pale white ball of light into the air. The ball of light glowed, illuminating the room.

"I...I...Yes I think there is one...just a minute," the rat man hurried to a cupboard, "Something's wrong."

"Really? I never would have guessed that! What's wrong with the power?"

"I...I...I..."

Angel went over to McLean and the power box. She stared at the wires and, after realising she had no idea how to fix the problem, she punched the power box. To her surprise the red safety lights came on.

"Everyone alright?" asked Angel, "The power box has been eaten! The wires, something has taken a massive bite out of the wires! This is the only power we've got."

"Teleportation is down," Roger muttered, "And communications are down."

"So we are stranded on a floating iceberg!" Danny summed up.

"Well actually the North pole isn't..." McLean started.

"Shut it!" Danny snapped at him before turning to Angel, "What's the...?"

Danny was interrupted by a roar.

* * * * *

The lights had just gone off. Clover and Elsa stood unsure what to do. After a few minutes of darkness, the red safety lights flickered into life.

"What just happened?" asked Elsa.

"They're the safety lights, we should get back to the others," Clover whispered. The darkness was unnerving. The shadows followed them wherever they went. A single red light swung back and forth, as cold gusts of Arctic wind whistled and broke the silence. Clover and Elsa walked slowly down the corridor.

"It's quiet," muttered Elsa.

"Very," Clover replied, she pulled out her torch, "Worried?"

"The quiet is disturbing."

"Why do we always end up in situations like this?"

"I don't know."

"I blame Angel. We never had this much trouble with Jackson."

"I can remember when she first joined Lightning Squad, she never used to listen to Jackson despite him being Captain."

"It's a shame the Colonel created Alpha Squad. I liked having Jackson in charge."

"I don't know, I quite like having Angel as captain. She's very good at her job and our squad's success rate has massively improved."

"I…"

Then there came a noise. It sounded like someone, or something, was breathing heavily.

"Hello?" Elsa asked, "Is anyone there?"

There was no reply.

"Identify yourself!"

Still there was no reply.

Then suddenly a large demon raced towards them. It had twenty-two small eyes and its skin was stretched so thinly that Elsa could see the red veins and green bones that lay beneath. Elsa shot at the demon, but her bullets bounced off its body.

"Clover go get Angel!" Elsa yelled.

Elsa jumped on to the demon's back and stabbed into its thin skin. The dagger slashed across one of the demon's veins, causing burning black blood to drip onto Elsa. She screamed as the acidy demon blood melted her cold dead skin. She jumped off the demon and ducked as it slashed its claws in her direction. Elsa rolled across the floor and stabbed the demon in its belly. The demon roared. It grabbed the vampire and threw her down the corridor. As Elsa pulled herself up, she noticed that Clover was stood watching her.

"What are you doing? Go get Angel," Elsa yelled.

But Clover didn't move.

"What the hell is…?"

Elsa didn't get a chance to finish her sentence for the demon slashed its claws in her direction. Elsa ducked out of the way. She then ran forwards and climbed onto the demon's back. She stabbed the demon repeatedly. The demon roared and slammed its back into the wall. Elsa fell to the floor. Acidy blood poured onto the vampire. Elsa crawled away from the demon.

"Don't just stand there, help me," Elsa pleaded to Clover.

"Of course I'll help you," Clover knelt quickly and stabbed a wooden stake into Elsa's heart.

"Fern…was right…about…you…" Elsa gasped as she crumbled into ash.

Clover smiled and blew the ashes of Elsa across the corridor. She stood up and walked over to the demon, trampling on Elsa's remains as she did so. Clover raised her hand, it glowed red. The demon stumbled backwards in fear.

"Good boy," Clover smiled, "The rest of your dinner will be joining us shortly."

As if on cue, someone shouted, "Elsa! Clover!"

Clover clicked her fingers and the wooden stake burnt into nothingness. The murder weapon vanished just as Angel and the men of Lightning Squad arrived at the scene.

"What's happened?" Angel asked racing over to Clover.

Clover put on a terrified expression and answered, "There's a demon, it killed Elsa, she's…"

Angel turned to Alexander, "Get her to Rowan and tell the others to get armed."

Alexander nodded. He grabbed Clover's wrist and they zoomed away. Roger and Ethan transformed into their wolf forms and attacked the demon. Jason just stared. He had never seen a huge demon in person before, so it took him a moment to recover from the shock. By the time Jason had returned to his senses, Danny had climbed onto the demon's back and had cut open its neck. However the demon didn't die. Instead it healed itself quickly then slammed its body against the wall, knocking Danny to the floor.

Angel transformed into a phoenix and attacked the demon. Her beak pecked at the demon's eyes and her flaming wings scorched its skin. The demon stumbled backwards and began to claw at the phoenix. Its sharp claws slashed across the phoenix's chest. The phoenix fell to the floor and transform back into Angel. Angel stumbled to her knees, her chest bleeding.

"Jason shoot at its eyes!" Angel ordered.

In quick succession Jason fired his gun at the demon's eyes. The bullets dug deep into its eyeballs. Danny did the same. The pair continued to shoot until the demon went blind. The visionless demon stumbled backwards. The two werewolves pounced on top of it. Angel glowed white and transformed into a fire nymph; a small red creature whose footsteps scorched the floor. The fire nymph ran up the demon's body, setting it alight. Roger and Ethan jumped off the demon as it burst into flames. The demon crumbled into ash. Angel transformed back into herself and collapsed to the floor. She glowed white and began to heal her wounded body.

"Angel," Roger exclaimed as he raced over to his sister.

"I'm fine," Angel reassured as Roger helped her to her feet.

"I'm good too, thanks for asking!" Ethan muttered as

he transformed back into his usual self, and then sneezed repeatedly, "It's really hard being allergic to dogs when you're a werewolf!"

"Idiot," Roger smiled punching his brother affectionately.

"Nice shooting Jason," Angel complimented.

"Thanks," Jason squeaked, panic had stolen most of his vocabulary but stuttering he forced out the words, "That didn't look like the demon McLean described."

"No it didn't. Can you hear that?"

"What?"

Angel dropped to the ground and placed her ear to the floor, "It sounds like there's something below."

"There are cells beneath us, right?" Roger asked kneeling next to Angel.

"I believe so. It sounds like there's something down there," Angel muttered, she looked up and noticed the pile of ash on the floor, "Elsa."

"Where?" Jason asked confused.

Angel pointed to the pile of ash, "There."

"What…but that's…wait…"

"She died Jason. Elsa. She died."

* * * * *

All of Lightning Squad, Rowan and the workers from the Polar Base were cramped into the small medical room. They stood in an uneasy silence.

Angel cleared her throat, "Elsa…Elsa has died. She was killed. Err I'm afraid I can't give you time to mourn her as the base is currently under attack. We have absolutely no idea how many demons we are up against. We also have no back up and no means of communication, we are completely on our own."

"What do you want us to do captain?" asked McLean firmly.

"We need to get the communications working, is

anyone here good with technology?"

Becks raised her hand, "I spent two years at a technical college."

"Okay, I need you to see what you can do. Fern will assist you."

"What!? Why me!?" Fern exclaimed.

"Because Fern as well as being the most annoying member of this squad, you're also the cleverest. So put your personal differences aside and work hard with Becks!"

"Yes Cap."

"There have been noises coming from the cells. There's a high possibility that it's a demon. I want to lead a team down there to check it out. Roger, Ethan and Jason, I want you to come with me."

"Why me?" Jason squeaked, on the verge of having a major breakdown.

"Because you're the Master of Darkness...and half demon. The best thing to fight a demon with is another demon. Don't worry Jason, I'll protect you."

That didn't make Jason feel any better.

"I'll go too. I know the cells, I used to manage them when they were in use," Angus explained, "I may be of some help."

"Okay. Do you have any weapons here? I know this is a science base."

"We have an armoury," Joel explained, "We've just never used it."

"Alex, Clover and Danny go with Fredrick and Joel and bring all the weapons here. This room will act as our base."

"Some of the weapons are very outdated," Fredrick muttered.

"I don't care. Just bring them all here," Angel turned to Roxy and Willow, "From here can either of you sense if there's demons outside?"

"Not from here, but this room is right in the centre of the base," Roxy explained, "If we were by the main door, we might be able to. That's only if the demons use the same telepathic frequencies we use. If they don't then our powers won't be able to sense them."

"Right, you two head to the main door. If you can't sense them then just open the door slightly and look."

"Can't we just look out of a window?" Jason asked.

"This base doesn't have windows."

"What!?"

"I know, it's ridiculous. We need to know if there are demons outside. We need an escape route. Are the main doors the only way in and out of the base?"

"Yes," McLean nodded.

"Wait so this place doesn't even have a fire exit!?" Jason exclaimed, "That's so stupid!"

"We didn't think we'd need one."

"Of course you didn't," Angel muttered, "If necessary, we'll just blow up one of the walls and escape that way. Though if we have no teleports, I'm not quite sure where we'll be escaping to."

"Angel can't you just walk through walls and see for yourself?" Araminta asked.

"No, I tried but there's something stopping me. I can't walk through walls and I can't teleport us out of here."

"What about your telepathic link to Jin?" asked Sophie.

"Can't reach him," seeing that Jason was about to ask, Angel explained, "Jin, that's Captain Lu, and I have what's called a telepathic link. It means that we can mentally communicate. Normally no matter how far apart we are, we can talk to each other."

"But you can't reach him?"

"No. Whatever forcefield Mr Jet has put on this base is blocking it."

"Paris knew about your telepathic link," Sophie said suddenly, "He also knew about your wall walking and teleportation powers."

"He must have told Jet, who must have created a forcefield specially designed to block those powers. Sophie, I want you to go with Roxy and Willow to the main doors."

"What do you want me to do?" Rowan asked.

"I want you and Sue to turn this room into a proper medical bay. Araminta, you and McLean need to collect all the classified documents that we can't let Jet have and bring them here."

"Yes Cap," Araminta nodded.

"Look this isn't going to be easy but I swear I will do everything I can to get you all out of this alive. I am so proud of all of you. You guys are the bravest, smartest, loudest, and greatest squad the paranormal empire has. We can win this," Angel smiled, "And when we do let's all go for a drink at Bertie's."

"Only if you're paying," Fern called cheekily.

"If we survive this then I'll pay for two rounds!"

26

'DEMONS TASTE LIKE CHICKEN!'

JASON

The cells were dark, lit only by a single red lightbulb that swung like a washing line in the wind. Skeletons sat lonely in several of the cells and dried blood covered the icy floor. I didn't like it! I still couldn't really understand why Angel had felt the need to drag me down to the cells with her. I was a panicking emotional wreck; I was hardly going to be of any help. Also the cells were cold! Really cold, and I'm not a fan of the cold…nor am I a fan of warm weather. I like nice middle temperature weather, sorry am I rambling? I feel like I'm rambling.

"Jason calm down," Angel said softly, her breath visible, "I'm not going to let you get hurt. You're going to be fine, so stop panicking and if you can't stop then can you at least block your mind, your rambling is giving me a headache!"

"Sorry it's just, this place smells!" I moaned, "A lot!

310

And it's cold! Really cold!"

"I've not been down here for a long time," Angus mumbled.

"When was the last time you were down here?"

"1862."

"That's certainly a…" Suddenly the floor began to shake violently. I stumbled to the ground. This is it, I thought, this is the end. I closed my eyes and prepared myself for the endless sleep. My entire life flashed before my eyes, there were a lot of cat videos.

"Is everyone alright?" Angel asked once the shaking had stopped. She grabbed hold of my elbow and forced me to my trembling feet.

"What was that!?" I squeaked, hitting a pitch I didn't realise I could reach.

"It came from below," Angel pressed her ear to the ice-covered ground.

"There's something under there," Roger muttered, he sniffed the ground and wrinkled his nose in disgust, "Not friendly, I'm guessing."

At that moment I noticed something in the corner.

"Aww, I think there's a cat in here," I said kneeling down to get a better look at it, "Come here kitty."

"Jason that's not a…" Before Angel finished her sentence, a demon pounced on top of me. It looked like a cat, but it definitely wasn't a cat! Rather than soft silky fur, the cat-demon had sticky blubber that clung to my face and suffocated me. I couldn't see. I couldn't breathe. Just as I was about to have a nervous breakdown, Roger (in his wolf form) ripped the cat demon from my body. Roger clawed at the cat-demon, pulling its body apart.

"Jason are you okay?" Angel asked as she helped me up.

"I'm fine," I stuttered, "Mentally scarred for life but fine!"

Another cat demon ran up behind Angel and sunk its

sharp fangs into her ankle. Angel transformed into a fire nymph and burnt the cat-demon into ashes. As she transformed back into her natural form, Ethan was attacked by a third cat-demon. The cat-demon pounced onto Ethan's back. Ethan struggled as he tried to avoid getting his ear bitten off. I tried to pull the demon away, but it held fast. Its skin stuck to my fingers.

"This is gross!" I exclaimed.

"Jason set it on fire!" Angel yelled as she fought against a fourth cat-demon.

"Fire? Ah yeah, I can do that!" I closed my eyes and pictured fire. When I opened my eyes, I found that my hands and the cat-demon were on fire…as was Ethan!

"Jason! Stop! You're burning me!" Ethan cried.

"Sorry," I clicked my fingers and the flames extinguished.

"You burnt a hole in my coat!" Ethan exclaimed as he brushed the cat-demon remains off his back.

"Sorry."

"Is everyone okay?" Roger asked transforming back into his natural form.

"Fine apart from the third degree burns I have on my back!" Ethan hissed.

"I said sorry!" I exclaimed.

"Was that all of them?" Angus asked.

"I hope so," Angel muttered, she knelt down and began to heal her bitten ankle, "Angus are the cells as big as the base?"

"The cells cover…" Before Angus could finish a large demon crept up behind him and bit off his head.

The demon was huge.

It had a large pig-like face and sharp claws. Its body was covered in scales and its eyes were blood red. From its mouth sprang a pair of milk white fangs. I stumbled back. I was not okay! This demon was terrifying and was staring straight at me! I couldn't do this. I was going to die! There was no way I was going to make it out of these cells alive. These three sentences rattled around my head as Angel gently pulled me back.

"Oh this isn't good. Not good at all. We've met this kind of demon before," Roger explained whilst backing away, "They're very hard to kill. They're bulletproof, fireproof and swords can't break through their scales."

"How did you kill the last one you met?" I asked.

"It got squashed by an avalanche."

"Oh."

"Jason, turn into a demon," Angel muttered backing away from the monster, "Right now."

"I can't do it on demand!"

"Why not?"

"I don't know how!"

"Well learn how and quickly!"

And that was when I began to panic. I had never released my demon on purpose before. What was I supposed to do? How was I supposed to release it? It wasn't like I could just press a button and transform into a demon. I would have to unlock all the locks in my mind and then let it take over. But what if I couldn't get it locked up again? What if I ended up becoming a demon forever? What if I accidentally ate someone!?

"Jason, I apologise in advance if this doesn't work," Angel said before stabbing me in the stomach.

I fell to the ground.

Blood poured from my belly. I had never felt so much pain before. I pressed my hands against the stab wound, trying to stop the blood from pouring. Tears rolled down my cheeks.

I wanted to scream but I couldn't get the words to leave my lips. I stared at Angel. She was watching me closely, a small smile tugged at the corner of her mouth. How could she be smiling!? I was going to die! My body trembled. My vision went blurry. This is it, I thought for the second time, this is the end.

Then suddenly the pain stopped.

I pulled myself to my feet and stretched my aching body. My body seemed larger and heavier than usual. It took me a moment to get used to it. My stomach rumbled. I was hungry. I was really hungry. It felt as though I hadn't eaten in weeks. I could smell something.

Something delicious!

What was it? Where was it coming from? I followed the smell until I found the pig-faced demon staring up at me.

Huh, I thought, how did this demon get so small? It was huge a moment ago.

And when did it start smelling so good!?

The pig-faced demon pounced on top of me. I grabbed it between my fangs and threw it into a wall. It slashed its claws in my direction. I span around and bashed the demon with my spiked tail. The pig-faced demon slumped to the ground. I stabbed my fangs into its flesh. Its blood tickled my forked-tongue.

Surprisingly it tasted a lot like chicken!

Once I had finished my meal, bones, and all, I turned to the others. Angel, Roger, and Ethan were staring at me. Horrified expressions covered their faces. I took a step towards them, but they backed away. Ah, I thought, they're probably just surprised to see me eat a demon.

Wait I just ate a demon!

And I liked it!

Wait I had a tail!? And fangs!?

I looked down to find bird-like claws where my feet should have been. I raced over to a patch of ice and stared at my reflection. In the ice, a large demon stared back at me. It looked like a black Chinese dragon, only it had bird-like legs and sharp claws. Spikes ran from the top of its head all the way to the end of its powerful tail. Its eyes were blood red. I stumbled backwards in surprise. My body trembled once more, and I found myself sinking. My body gave way. I collapsed to the icy ground. I shut my eyes as the world span.

"Jason? Are you okay?"

"Am I still a demon?" I asked.

"No, you're back to being you." I opened my eyes and found Angel staring down at me. I looked down at my body. No tail. No fangs. No spikes. I was back to normal! "Did I just turn into a demon?"

"Yes," Angel nodded.

"Oh right good. Oh good. I turned into a demon. A demon! I turned into a demon, that means I just ate a demon."

"Jason are you okay?"

"I just turned into a demon!"

"Yes."

"And I just ate a demon!"

"Yes."

I placed my head into my hands and mumbled, "I might have a massive panic-attack."

"Could you have it when we get back to the base? We don't really have time for it right now."

"Okay. Wait, you stabbed me!"

"Yes," Angel nodded sheepishly as she pulled me to my feet.

"Why?"

"Because I could hear your internal panic-attack from the other side of the room! We really needed you to turn into a demon."

"So you thought stabbing me would be the best way to bring my demon out!?"

"Yeah."

"It hurt!"

"But it worked."

"I thought I was going to die!"

"But you didn't."

"What did the demon taste like?" Ethan asked.

"It…tasted like chicken."

"Really? Huh I thought it'd taste like pork. Was it tasty?"

"It…" I stuttered, "It was…it was really tasty."

"I'm not sure if I'm disgusted or fascinated by this situation," Roger stared at me.

"Stop staring, you're freaking me out."

"Guys save your questions for when we get back home, and for after Jason's had his mental breakdown," Angel walked over to Angus' headless body.

"Poor guy," Ethan muttered, "He seemed like a decent fella."

"He seemed…" before Angel could finish her sentence, we were attacked, again! At first it looked like a puddle of black paint but then it grew and stood up. The demon was featureless. It had no eyes or nose, just a pair of long thin arms. It pointed at me.

"Why is it pointing at me?" I asked.

"Take a step towards me," Roger said. I did so, the demon's pointed finger followed me.

"What does it want from me?"

"Well you did just eat it's friend," The demon suddenly leapt forwards. It pushed Roger to the ground and grabbed hold of me.

* * * * *

I fell backwards but instead of hitting the ground, I fell into a strange shadowy world. Angel and her brothers vanished. I was alone. I got to my feet and stared at the barren plane I had landed in. There was nothing for miles and miles. A grey sandy desert was all that could be seen. There were no stars, just a jet black sky.

"Where am I?" I asked aloud.

"You are in my mind," came a reply.

I turned around to find the strange faceless demon stood behind me.

"In…in…did you just say…did you just say I was in your mind?"

The demon nodded.

"Oh…that's…wait you can talk!?"

"You can hear me. You can understand me."

"Yes."

"Only a Master can understand the language of the demons. You belong with us."

"Ha! No. No I don't think so."

"We're connected. You and me. Both of us creatures of darkness."

"If you say so. Now if you wouldn't mind showing me the exit…"

"Your powers, they've been locked away. Someone locked them up. When you were a child, a baby, all alone. Crying for your sister."

"What are you…I don't have a sister."

"The Master of Darkness always has a sister. The Master of Darkness and the Mistress of Light are bound together. There can't be one without the other. Just you wait, she'll enter this world soon."

"If you say so."

"Let me unlock your powers. It's time for the Master to return to full strength."

"Why…why would…?"

"I do not wish to harm you. I am your friend."

"I don't think so."

Before I could finish my sentence, the demon raced forwards and pressed its hand over my heart. Images of caves of blood and slime echoed into my mind. I saw demons fighting each other and rotting bodies stumbling across a sandy wasteland. There was a long black river of acid that bubbled and spat at me as I walked past. Snake-like demons slithered over broken bones and featherless vultures flew across the crimson sky. As I stumbled through the monstrous abyss, I suddenly realised…

I was in hell!

"I don't want to be here. I don't want to be here," I muttered, "Demon take me back! Take me back!"

* * * * *

317

I opened my eyes. Angel, Roger, and Ethan stared down at me.

"I'm back," I gasped.

"Back? Jason you didn't go anywhere," Roger helped me to my feet.

"I did. I went…I went to hell. Where did that demon go!?" Roger, Angel and Ethan just looked at each other, none of them seemed to want to answer.

Finally Roger coughed, "It went into you."

"Pardon?"

"It went into you."

"Jason save it for your mental breakdown later. Just tell us what the demon did to you," Angel said sharply.

"Right, well the demon said I was in its mind. It said my powers had been locked away and that it was going to unlock them for me. It said that we were connected and that it was my friend…which I thought was a bit weird. Oh then it said that the Master of Darkness can't be without the Mistress of Light and that I do have a sister. I think that's what it was saying, to be honest I was a bit confused by the whole thing. Then it showed me hell."

"That's…what is that?" Angel stared at a shadow under the ice.

"There's something beneath us," Roger whispered, "And there's something in here with us." Roger pointed to a dark figure that was hiding in the corner of one of the cells. Angel shone her torch in its direction, but it slipped away from the light. Angel walked into the cell.

"Was that a gorilla?" I asked following the shapeshifter.

"Where did it go?" asked Angel to no one in particular.

At that moment the large gorilla-like demon pushed Angel to the ground. The demon had spikes instead of fur and fifteen small eyes. Angel struggled against the demon as its spikes pierced her skin. She reached for her sword, but the gorilla-demon squashed its body against hers, making it impossible for her to move.

"Jason a bit of help here would be appreciated!" Angel yelled. Without thinking, I raised my fist and released my fingers. The gorilla-demon exploded into tiny pieces. Angel got to her feet.

"Why didn't you do that earlier!?" she exclaimed.

"I didn't know I could," I stared at my hand in wonder, "How did I just do that? I didn't plan to do it."

"You didn't overthink it, you just did it. That demon, maybe it really did unlock your powers."

Before I could respond, Roger raced into the cell quickly followed by another gorilla-demon. The demon grabbed hold of me and shoved me to the ground. I was about to pull myself up when the demon decided to sit on top of me. I gasped as the demon squashed the air out of my lungs. Roger transformed into a wolf and pounced on the gorilla-demon. They rolled across the ground.

Angel transformed into a chimera; a strange creature that had a lion head at its front, goat head sticking out of its back and a snake head attached to its butt. The goat head blew fire at the gorilla-demon. The fire bounced off the demon's body. The chimera and the gorilla-demon fought against each other. The gorilla-demon picked the chimera up and threw it across the cell. As it landed, the chimera transformed back into Angel.

"Jason stop staring and blow it up!" Angel hissed.

"Right," I muttered as I got to my feet. I released my fist and the gorilla-demon crumbled into nothingness.

"You should have done that to begin with," Roger muttered transforming back into his usual form.

"Sorry I was distracted by, Angel what did you just turn into?"

"A chimera," Angel explained.

"I was distracted by how ugly the chimera was."

"Jason that chimera was me, are you calling me ugly?"

"I...no...that's not what I...It's just that the chimera isn't your most attractive form. I mean...Err...I don't know what I mean."

"She's just messing with you," Roger laughed.

Angel smiled, "You're even easier to tease than…hey where's Ethan?"

"Guys!" Ethan yelled from the corridor. We ran out to join him. In the middle of the corridor was a massive slug-like demon. It had wrinkled purple skin and large fangs.

"Oh that is disgusting," Roger muttered, "Jason please blow it up."

I released my fist and the slug-demon exploded. However the exploded pieces then joined back together, and the slug-demon returned to life.

"What the…?" I released my fist again and once more the slug-demon exploded only to stick itself back together.

Suddenly the ground began to shake. From under the ice, tall human shaped figures push their way up to the surface. They had grey scales, fish-like faces and mouths full of sharp fangs.

"I'll take the slug," Angel ordered, "You guys deal with those."

Angel transformed into a dragon and attacked the slug-demon. I exploded the fish-faced demons, however as I killed one, two more would pull themselves to the surface. I was about to explode my seventh demon when one jumped onto my back. I fell face first to the ground. The demon dug its teeth into my back. I yelled out in pain. I reached for my sword and stabbed it into the demon. The demon screeched and rolled off me. I got to my feet and blew it up, just as it was about to take a bite out of my ankle.

As I continued to fight against the fish-faced demons, Angel battled against the slug-demon. Dragon Angel blew fire in the demon's direction, but the fire bounced off its skin. Dragon Angel then attacked the demon with her claws. She scratched at the demon, cutting into its wrinkled body. The slug-demon coughed up toxic slime and spat it at dragon Angel. Angel fell to the ground, transforming back into herself as the toxic slime burnt her dragon scales. She raised her hand and water soaked her body, washing the toxic slime away.

"Jason!" Angel shouted at me, "Let's swap. You deal with this thing and I'll deal with the fish."

"I can't deal with that thing!" I exclaimed.

"Just turn into a demon and eat it!"

"How!? I still can't transform on demand!"

Angel sighed heavily before slicing me through the middle with her sword as she passed me. Like before intense pain rippled up my body. I collapsed to the ground. My vision went blurry.

Then it stopped.

My demon had taken over.

I turned to the slug-demon. It didn't smell tasty like the demon before had. It smelt like old socks. I sighed and then attacked the slug-demon. I hit it with my tail knocking it over. I then pounced on top of it and ripped it apart. It tasted disgusting! It was slimy, and its skin stuck to my fangs. Once I was certain the demon was dead, I jumped to the ground and gobbled up the fish-faced demons. These demons were very tasty! They tasted just like tuna. When I had eaten my fill, I collapsed to the ground and transformed back into myself.

"Nicely done mate!" Roger smiled, pulling me to my feet.

"Can I sleep now?" I muttered feeling exhausted.

"Not yet. What did that slug taste like?"

"Don't just don't," I stuttered feeling sick to my stomach.

"Is your stab wound healed?" Angel asked.

"Yeah, thanks for that."

"Don't mention it, really don't mention it because if the Colonel finds out that I've stabbed the Master of Darkness twice…"

"You will be in lock up for life," Ethan laughed. Suddenly a tentacle burst from under the ice. It wrapped around Ethan's body and threw him across the cells. It bashed Ethan into the walls, his head cracking open as it made contact with the stone. The tentacle then dragged the werewolf under the water.

"Ethan!" Angel yelled. She ran over to a hole in the ice and jumped into the water. A few minutes later Angel dragged a bloody Ethan up to the surface. Roger lifted Ethan into his arms, gently placing him down on solid ground.

"He's not breathing," Angel muttered. She pressed her hands against his chest. They glowed white as she performed CPR on her brother. After a while Ethan coughed up water. I was expecting him to wake up but after spitting out water, Ethan's body went limp.

"He's breathing," Angel pressed her hands against her brother's head. A soft white light ran down his bloody body. At that moment another tentacle burst out of the ice. It wrapped around Angel's legs and dragged her under the water. As Angel's body disappeared into the freezing ocean below, me and Roger were attacked by a small army of demons. They came in different shapes; some were like the fish-faced demons we had fought earlier, some looked like orcs whilst others crawled out of the ice with naked slimy bodies and faces filled with fangs.

"Stay here and protect Ethan," Roger ordered. He transformed into a wolf and began to attack the demons.

I stood next to Ethan, exploding any demon that came close. The problem was that some of the demons just wouldn't die! Every time I exploded them, they just healed themselves and began to attack us again. One larger demon grabbed hold of Roger and threw him across the corridor. Roger stumbled to his feet. The wolf raced forwards and pounced onto the demon, knocking it to the floor. He sliced the demon's face. Its acidy blood burnt

Roger's paws, but the werewolf didn't stop until the demon was dead. Roger then transformed back into himself and ran over to me.

"If only it was a full moon," he hissed as he picked up Angel's fallen sword.

"Why? What difference would that make?" I asked as I clicked my fingers and a circle of black fire surrounded us, sending the demons stumbling backwards.

"Oh you don't know. When it's not a full moon, werewolves can transform whenever they like into giant wolves, as you've seen. However on a full moon, werewolves are forced to transform into horrific half-man/half-wolf monsters. Put simply, on a full moon we transform into proper werewolves," Roger shouted as he fought against a demon.

"Ah, a proper werewolf would be handy right now."

"If I stabbed you would you turn into a demon?"

"Probably."

"Then I'm sorry about this."

But before he could stab me, another large demon burst from under the ice, catching Roger in its mouth. The demon had a muscular body with blue skin and large webbed feet. Its face looked like a shark and its mouth was filled with sharp black teeth. It had piercing red eyes and a sinister gaze. Roger transformed into a wolf as the demon threw him into the air. The demon opened its mouth and Roger dropped inside. The wolf struggled as the demon's teeth snapped and chewed down on his fur.

I needed to turn into a demon. Ethan was unconscious, and Angel had been dragged under the ice by a demon. The only person who could help Roger was me. I ran and picked up Angel's curved sword. Just as I was about to stab myself with it, I felt a sharp pain in my stomach. The pain was so intense that I collapsed to the ground. I coughed and spluttered. My body shook, and a dark mist covered my vision. Lightning forks sprang from my fingertips, they bounced around the cells frying any demon that got in their way.

The pain vanished as suddenly as it had arrived. I looked down at my body and found that my demon had taken over. I ran forwards and jumped on top of the demon, forcing it to drop Roger. The demon slashed its claws. Hot blood ran down my face. I bashed the demon with my tail. The demon caught my tail between its teeth.

I howled in pain.

My cry was so loud that it caused the room to shake. The demon stumbled backwards. As it did so two bullets flew through the air and burst the demon's eyeballs. I turned to see a bloody Roger slump to the ground, a gun in hand. As the demon wandered around blindly, I jumped onto its back and dug my fangs into its neck. The demon screamed and threw me to the ground. It was about to pounce on top of me when a white dragon burst through the ice distracting it. I used this to my advantage and wrapped my spiked tail around the demon's neck. My spikes dug into its flesh. Its blood dripped onto the ice. The dragon blew fire at the demon's face and scratched at its blinded eyes. I unwrapped my tail and took a step backwards. I then coughed up thick black mist. The mist wrapped around the demon.

It sank into its scales.

And the demon exploded.

I stumbled backwards. I fell to the ground and transformed back into myself. The dragon transformed back into Angel. She picked up her fallen sword and ran over to me. She was soaking wet and blood coated her body. Angel held out her hand and helped me to my feet.

"Are you okay?" she asked.

"Yeah, I think. I just transformed without being stabbed," I muttered.

"Good for you. That mist thing was pretty impressive."

"Yeah, I have no idea how I did that!"

"Roger!" Angel exclaimed as she noticed her brother. We ran over to him. Roger was covered in blood. One of his arms was missing and his stomach was cut open. Angel pressed her hands against Roger's chest. Water ran from the hole in the floor and covered Roger's body. The water sank into his wounds causing Roger to cry out in pain.

"I'm sorry. Just hold on," Angel muttered, "We need to get you to Rowan."

Angel stood up and pulled out her wand. She flicked her wrist, Roger and Ethan rose into the air surrounded by pink lights.

"We need to l…"

Before she could finish, the ice broke once more, and hundreds of demons began to crawl to the surface. Angel grabbed hold of my wrist and dragged me back to the entrance, Roger and Ethan flew alongside us. Once we were at the top of the stairs, Angel flicked her wand again. Roger and Ethan flew out of sight.

"Where did they go?" I asked.

"To the medical bay," Angel muttered, she shoved her wand into her boot and raised her hands. A bright white light burst from her fingertips and covered the entrance to the cells. As the demons raced towards us, they crashed into the white light.

"Is that a forcefield?"

Angel nodded, "The two of us can't stop them. Even if you turned into a demon. There are just too many of them. I need you to head to the medical bay and tell the others. If they've got the teleportation systems working, then leave. That's an order."

"What are you going to do?"

"I'm going to stay here and hold them off for as long as possible."

As Angel spoke the demons crashed against the forcefield. Angel yelled out in pain as the forcefield began to strain. Her hands trembled, and blood began to run from her ears. I stared at Angel. Her coat had been lost long ago, her blood-stained shirt was ripped and soaking wet from being dragged into the freezing ocean. Her right hand was still blue from where Mr Jet had broken it, her forehead was branded and the demon bite on her left ankle hadn't healed. Angel's skin was bruised, and her face was a ghostly shade of white.

"You'll die," I realised, "You're too injured to keep the forcefield going."

Angel smiled, "Maybe you're not as stupid as you look."

"This isn't the time to joke!"

"Jason, please just do as I say."

"I…" My words were lost as I became distracted by Angel's blood. I was vaguely aware that Angel was speaking but I didn't hear a word she said.

I couldn't tear my eyes away from her blood. The crimson liquid glowed as it ran down her arm and dripped onto the forcefield. I looked down at my own bloody hands. Unlike Angel's that seemed to shine, my blood was so dark that at times it seemed black. Without thinking, I raised my hand and pressed it against Angel's.

Her beautiful bright blood and my bleak black blood mixed together. The mixed blood spread across the forcefield causing it to change colour. A ring of black light surrounded the white light. As the ring of black touched the ring of white, the forcefield expanded dramatically. It engulfed the cells, evaporating any demon that it encountered. The forcefield stroked the ice. The ice grew. It covered the holes in the ground then rose, submerging the cells in an icy cage. The entrance to the cells completely disappeared. All that remained was a block of black tinted ice.

"What did you just do?" Angel asked, placing her hand against the block of ice that used to be the entrance to the cells.

"I have no idea. How…how did I just do that? I wasn't planning, it just…just happened," I stared at my hands in wonder.

"Add this to the list of things you need to have a mental breakdown about."

"I…yeah…I will…do you think that will hold?"

"For now…Come on we need to get to the medical bay."

As we ran towards the medical bay, Danny and Alexander ran to meet us.

"Are you okay?" Danny and Alexander asked in unison.

"Later. I need to find my brothers," Angel gasped as the four of us ran to the medical bay. Angel swung the doors open as we arrived. Ethan and Roger lay on hospital beds, attached to monitors. Rowan was trying to sew up Roger's wounds while Sue was trying to stop Ethan's head from bleeding. Angel ran over to them. She grabbed her brothers' hands and a soft white glow embraced both werewolves.

"What happened?" Rowan asked.

"Ethan, sea demon. Its tentacle grabbed him and threw him around, then dragged him underwater. He was underwater for too long, so I had to perform CPR, and Roger…Roger was…" Angel stuttered.

"Eaten," I explained simply.

"Angel," Roger whispered, opening his eyes slightly.

"Roger," Angel smiled as tears pricked her eyes.

"Stop. Stop trying to heal me. You're just wasting your energy."

"What are you…?"

"You can feel it, the wolf bond, I'm dying Angel."

"Don't say…"

"Angel, it's okay," Roger placed his only remaining hand against Angel's face wiping away her tears, "It's okay…you know that I love you right? The day Pops brought you home. That…that was the best day…of…my

327

life…"

"Stop it!"

Roger looked over to Rowan, "Rowan, look after Jack for me. He's not as strong as he looks. Make sure you…you give Pops…a big litter of were-maids…"

Rowan sobbed as she nodded.

Roger turned his gaze towards the rest of us, "It…was…an honour to fight alongside you please…look after…protect…my Angel…"

"Stop it," Angel begged, "Please!"

Roger smiled faintly, "A…Angel."

Roger's head flopped. His hand went limp.

"Roger? Roger!? Wake up, I was healing you, wake up!"

I stared at Roger. He was dead. Roger Night was dead. The loveable werewolf who was kind to everyone, loved food and a good laugh was dead. I looked at Roger's once playful eyes and saw nothingness. Tears ran down my face. I stumbled backwards. The world seemed to spin. Araminta hugged me close but I didn't even register her existence.

All I could see was the corpse lying on the hospital bed.

27

'SOUL SUCKERS'

A long-held beep echoed through the silence.

Roger's heartbeat had disappeared from the monitor. Angel pressed down on Roger's chest in a desperate attempt at CPR. Her hands glowed a bright white as Angel's healing magic sank into Roger's body. But Roger's heartbeat didn't return. Rowan pulled Angel from her brother's lifeless body.

"Stop now Angel. He's gone," Rowan whispered.

"No he's…" Angel grabbed her chest as pain flooded into her heart.

"Angel!"

"The wolf bond, it hurts. Why can't I feel him anymore?"

"What's happening?" Danny asked as Angel doubled over in pain.

"Angel and the rest of the wolf pack are connected through the wolf bond. They can communicate and feel each other telepathically. Which means when one of the

329

pack dies, they all physically feel it," Rowan explained.

Suddenly Ethan's heartbeat started to drop rapidly.

Rowan rushed over to him. Rowan pressed her hand against Ethan's forehead. A soft blue glow ran from her fingertips and embraced the werewolf's body. Ethan's heartbeat continued to drop. It dropped until a second long-held beep joined Roger's. Ethan's heart had stopped beating. Rowan quickly started to perform CPR, but Ethan's heart didn't start beating. Angel pulled herself up, pushed her sister-in-law away and cupped her hands around Ethan's head. As her brother's blood trickled onto her fingertips, Angel's entire body began to glow a violent white.

"Angel what are you doing?"

"Ethan hasn't faded yet. The wolf bond, Roger's gone but Ethan hasn't yet. He's still here," Angel gasped. The white glow engulfed Ethan's body. It wrapped around his wounded head and spread down to his broken toes. Angel slammed her hands onto Ethan's chest.

Beep.

Beep.

Beep.

Ethan's heart began to beat. Tears ran down Angel's face as she slid to the floor. She tried to sit herself up but found that she couldn't. Without saying a word, Alexander knelt beside her and rested Angel's body against his. Danny was not amused by this, but he held his tongue. This wasn't the time to start an argument.

Rowan quickly examined Ethan, "You put him in a coma."

Angel nodded, "He won't wake up until he's completely recovered."

"If he can't recover…"

"He will."

"But if he can't…"

"He will! He has too!" Angel snapped, she then turned

her attention to Roger, "Why didn't it work...Roger, why didn't it work on you?"

"There was nothing you could have done," Rowan cried as she spoke, "He was too far gone."

"What happened to the demons? You said you were attacked," Araminta asked pulling away from Jason.

"Dealt with. It turns out if you stab Jason, he'll turn into a demon and eat your enemies for you," Angel looked up and noticed McLean, Fredrick, and Joel for the first time. "Angus died. I'm sorry."

McLean nodded as tears tickled his whiskers.

"Did you get all the important documents and the weapons?"

"The documents are in my backpack and the weapons," McLean gestured to three wooden boxes.

"Is that all you have?"

"Clover is bringing the last one," Danny explained.

"Danny do me a favour, go tell Clover about...and go get Fern and Becks. We need to find out what's happening with the communications."

"On it," Danny quickly left the medical bay.

Alexander helped Angel to her feet. Angel stumbled to Roger's bed. She planted a kiss on her brother's forehead then covered his body in a white sheet. She paused; a few stray teardrops fell to the floor. Angel wiped her eyes and walked over to the boxes of weapons.

"Most of the weapons are very old and rusty," Joel explained, "But they might still work."

"We can make use of them," Angel took out an old-fashioned pistol and bullets, "I'll take this, I lost my gun in the cells. The rest of you, go through the boxes and take whatever you can use."

At that moment Danny, Clover, Fern and Becks entered the room. Fern opened her mouth to speak but, for the first time in her life, she found that she had nothing to say. Her mind had gone blank. She couldn't even find the words to ask if Angel was okay. Instead Fern just stared at the bodies of her fallen friends in complete silence.

"Are you getting anywhere with the communications?" Angel asked.

"We have a theory but nothing practical. And the theory is more about how the demons got here rather than about the communications," Fern explained, "See we were wondering how the demons got onto the base. The big ones. The small ones obviously came in the supply boxes, but the big ones couldn't have got here that way."

"So how do you think they got here?"

"Well you know there's one of the gateway portals here, and that these portals can only connect..."

"What are gateway portals?" Jason interrupted.

"Gateway portals are the doorways between the different worlds in the empire. So for example, to get from Atlantis to the fey realm you'd need to use one of these portals. Normally these portals can only take you to places within the empire, however if someone managed to re-loop the portal you could in theory..."

"Open it up in the underworld," Angel finished.

"Bingo!"

"Re-looping a portal, how did they do it? Jet surely doesn't have that kind of power."

"Jet doesn't but he does," Fern pointed at Jason.

"I do? But I didn't do anything! I didn't re-loop the portal! I didn't even know these portals existed until a minute ago!" Jason exclaimed.

"According to the legends a Master of Darkness can create portals to the underworld..."

"But I haven't created a portal!"

"I wasn't finished! Jason's soul and his powers are connected to the underworld. If Mr Jet got a hold of some of Jason's soul, he could extract some of Jason's powers and use them to open a portal."

"The death cloud," Alexander muttered, "That's how he got Jason's soul."

"But if Mr Jet needed Jason's soul, he could have got a Soul Sucker to take it from him easily," Clover interjected, "Why do it himself?"

"Because a Soul Sucker would have killed Jason. Jason needs to be alive. The portal will only stay open if the Master of Darkness is alive," Fern explained, "So in other words if we kill Jason then we'll no longer have to worry about demon attacks."

"What!?" Jason stumbled backwards horrified.

"It was a joke. Don't worry we won't kill you, unless absolutely necessary. To re-loop the portal Jet would've also needed powerful fey blood. A person's soul once removed from their body tends to fade. The fey blood would stop Jason's soul from fading."

"That's why Jet went after Sophie, he needed her blood," Angel muttered, "Can we destroy the portal?"

"Yeah it's like the easiest thing in the world, all you need to do is blow it up," Fern said, Becks nodded in agreement.

"So I need to get to that portal…"

"I? I think the correct pronoun is we. You'll need help disabling the portal."

"Disabling it? I thought I just needed to blow it up."

"You do but if you want to get the communications and teleportation systems running then you'll need to disable the forcefield first. The same system that's re-looping the portal is also blocking your teleportation powers."

"Fine," Angel hissed, "Jason, Becks and I will head to the portal."

"What about me?"

"Fern, you'll stay here. If blowing up the portal doesn't bring back the systems, then we'll need a new plan."

"Sophie and the others haven't returned yet," Danny

pointed out, "We don't know how many demons are out there."

"This place only has one exit, so we'll probably bump into them on the way. If it turns out that there are no demons out there, then we'll escape that way. The rest of you be ready, the moment we get the teleportation system working we're leaving."

"I shall come with you," McLean squeaked, "I've been looking after the portal for nearly half my life. I know it best, so I may be of some help. Also we have snowmobiles in the shed outside. If we use those, we'll get to the portal faster."

"Okay," Angel nodded, "We need to go. The rest of you, be careful and protect each other. Alex I'm leaving you in charge."

Fern pulled Angel into a tight hug, as did Rowan. Becks and McLean said their goodbyes to Joel and Fredrick. Jason was attacked by hugs from both Sue and Clover. As Jason pushed them off, he was attacked once again. This time it was Araminta, who hugged him close and whispered "be careful" into his ear. Angel smiled as she watched Jason get repeatedly dragged into hugs by the three girls. The Master of Darkness, despite his strange and foolish personality, was rather popular amongst the Lightning Squad ladies. If Willow and Roxy had been there, Angel was certain, Jason would have been suffocated by all the affection. To her surprise, Angel also found herself attacked by an unexpected hug from Danny.

"This is unlike you," Angel muttered.

"Be careful," Danny said pulling away.

"I'm always careful."

"Liar."

Angel smiled and turned to her brothers. It didn't seem real. Roger and Ethan were normally such a lively pair yet here they were, laying still and silent in hospital beds. A hundred and one emotions danced in Angel's tormented heart. Putting Ethan in a coma had been Angel's only way of saving him, but she was well aware that it was not the safest situation for her brother to be in. As for Roger, Angel couldn't process it. Roger had known her best, had cared for her the most and had given her more love then she could reciprocate. And now he was dead. First the traitorous Paris, then the wonderful Elsa, the brave volunteer Angus and now the loveable Roger, how many more was she going to lose today?

Angel didn't hear Alexander walk up behind her. As the rest of Lightning Squad noisily said their goodbyes and chose their weapons, the vampire gently placed a hand on Angel's back and whispered into her ear.

"I'll take care of them."

"Ethan can't…"

"He won't. I'll make sure he's guarded. I promise you. I'll keep him safe."

"Thank you."

"Stay alive. No matter what, stay alive."

"You too."

"Too late for that. I'm already dead, remember?"

"Well then don't die again. I can't lose anyone else…especially not…" Angel didn't finish her sentence. She didn't need to. Alexander already knew how it ended. Angel turned to face the vampire. Upon turning the shapeshifter found that Alexander was much closer to her then she had expected, "Don't die. That's an order."

Alexander paused, painted on his signature dashing smile, and said simply, "Yes Cap."

Angel nodded then stepped away from the vampire. She stared at the rest of her squad. At her family. Each of them as brave and as brilliant as the next. No one else, she told herself, she couldn't lose anyone else.

"Time to go," Angel called reluctantly, "Look after each other and we'll see you all soon."

With that the four of them left the room. There was

silence until Danny suddenly cried out in pain and collapsed to his knees.

"Danny?" Rowan asked, "Can you hear me?"

"Sophie's in trouble," Danny gasped, "Didn't you hear her?"

"We didn't hear anything."

"Sophie screamed. No. She wasn't just screaming. She said something."

"What did she say?"

"Soul Suckers."

* * * * *

Willow, Sophie, and Roxy ran as fast as they could down the corridor until they reached a door. The Soul Suckers followed, their movements graceful and deadly. They stood seven feet tall and were covered by shapeless large black cloaks. They had long white thin arms and long fingers with black nails. In their hands they each held a Scythe. Roxy pushed open the door and the trio found themselves in a dome shaped room.

The room was large and messy. A chandelier, lit by only candles, swung gently as a cold breeze whistled round the room. Papers and books were scattered across the floor whilst Bunsen burners, warming vials of bubbling coloured liquid, littered the tables. Willow slammed the wooden doors shut. The trio had been attacked before they could reach the main door. The Soul Suckers had just appeared from the shadows. There had been no warning or dramatic entrance, they had just appeared silently and had begun chasing them down the dark corridors.

"How the hell did Soul Suckers get here!?" Roxy screamed.

Before anyone could answer, the soft sound of footsteps could be heard resonating round the room. The girls raised their weapons as the sound of laughter cascaded down from the roof and whispered into their ears. Then the room went silent. Roxy looked up and screamed. Hanging onto the chandelier was a clown-faced Soul Sucker, a scythe in hand. It smiled widely, blood pouring from its eyes. It laughed loudly as its scythe sliced the chandelier, causing it to fall to the floor. Sophie watched as the Soul Sucker's cloak fell empty on top of the glittering glass mess. The Soul Sucker had disappeared.

Suddenly the door opened, and a group of Soul Suckers floated inside. Roxy shot at the Soul Suckers. Her bullets fell through the Soul Suckers bodies and landed uselessly on the floor. Sophie raised her hand and sent a Soul Sucker flying backwards.

Willow jumped on top of a table and kicked a Soul Sucker. It stumbled backwards. She picked up a test tube filled with bubbling purple liquid and threw it at the Soul Sucker. The liquid caused the Soul Sucker's cloak to burn. It slashed a scythe in her direction. Willow avoided the blade but fell from the table and landed heavily on the marble floor. She rolled out of the way as the scythe was once again swung in her direction. As she got to her feet, Willow pulled out her knife and threw it at the Soul Sucker. The knife stabbed into the Soul Sucker's forehead. The Soul Sucker slumped to the ground, thick black blood oozing from the knife wound. Before Willow could catch her breath, the Soul Sucker stood up and pulled the knife from its head. Willow dived out of the way as the knife was thrown in her direction.

Roxy ran across the room, a Soul Sucker close behind. She grabbed a Bunsen burner and threw it at the Soul Sucker's head. The Bunsen burner bounced off the Soul Sucker and fell to the floor with a clang. Roxy ran towards the door but was blocked by the clown-faced Soul Sucker. Roxy stumbled backwards.

The Soul Sucker grabbed hold of Roxy, it pulled her close and whispered in her ear, "Roxy... come to me..."

Sophie's fey ears could hear the Soul Sucker's soft tones from the other side of the room. She jumped into the air and shrank to a fairy's natural size. She flew across the room and landed in front of the clown-faced Soul Sucker. She grew and took off her sunglasses. The Soul Sucker turned to stone. After putting the sunglasses back on, Sophie grabbed Roxy and pulled her from the Soul Sucker's grasp, just as the Soul Sucker burst from its stone prison. Roxy's eyes were clouded over.

Sophie slapped Roxy, "Snap out of it! You are an incredibly powerful mind witch. Your mind is yours. Don't let someone else take over!"

I am a mind witch. My mind is mine. I can fight this. I can beat this, Roxy told herself, *my mind is mine. My mind is mine!*

Just as Roxy was about to break free of the Soul Sucker's telepathic hold, Sophie was thrown across the room. Sophie landed heavily on top of a bookshelf. She watched as the clown-faced Soul Sucker once again grabbed hold of Roxy. Sophie jumped down from the bookshelf and took off her sunglasses once more. She turned to stone any Soul Sucker that looked in her direction. However the Soul Suckers quickly broke free and chased after her.

Roxy stood in front of the clown-faced Soul Sucker, unable to control her own mind. The clown-faced Soul Sucker pulled out a gun from within its cloak and Roxy copied, pulling out her own gun.

Sophie clicked her fingers and Roxy's gun quickly flew from her hands. The clown-faced Soul Sucker growled and, using unrecognisable words, ordered the other Soul Suckers to attack. Sophie was quickly surrounded by Soul Suckers. The fey clicked her fingers and a ring of fire rose up around her. The Soul Suckers doused down the flames with their cloaks and grabbed hold of Sophie. They dug their nails into her skin, pinning her to the floor.

"Roxy!" Sophie shouted, "You're not a puppet! You're the master of your own mind!"

The clown-faced Soul Sucker handed the possessed

Roxy a gun and smiled, "Don't listen to her. You want to join me. You are one of my children. You must join me in the end. This is your calling Roxy. This is what you want. Come to me."

The clown-faced Soul Sucker pulled a second gun out of its cloak and placed it next to its head. Roxy copied, pressing her gun against her head. The gun felt cold against her skin. Roxy was terrified. She didn't want to die, but she couldn't stop herself. Her hand shook as she tried desperately to gain control. A war raged inside her mind. Her powers battled against the Soul Sucker's. She was losing. Roxy took back every mean word she had ever said about Angel, as she desperately wished the shapeshifter would come and save her.

Please, I'm sorry for everything, just save me, Roxy pleaded, *I don't want to die. I don't want to die like this. Please save me!*

"Come to me, my child, come to me," the clown-faced Soul Sucker's soft voiced trickled into Roxy's ear.

"Roxy fight it!" Sophie shouted.

The clown-faced Soul Sucker pulled the trigger.

And Roxy copied.

Sophie screamed as Roxy Ash dropped to the floor.

Dead.

The clown-faced Soul Sucker then turned to Sophie. It lifted her up. Its cold hands grabbed her face, forcing their eyes to meet. Sophie's eyes glowed grey as she attempted to turn the Soul Sucker to stone. However the Soul Sucker didn't get trapped in a prison of stone, instead its skin absorbed and stole Paris' powers. Before Sophie realised what was happening, Paris' gorgon powers were gone. Her eyes returned to their original purple colour. Sophie grabbed her dagger and stabbed it into the Soul Sucker's chest. Instead of blood, hot toxic gas escaped from the stab wound. Sophie choked as the gas hit her face. The clown-faced Soul Sucker laughed and stabbed its fangs into Sophie's neck.

A soft whisper echoed into her head, "Give in. Let go. Come to me. You want to come to me."

Sophie screamed and sent a telepathic warning message into the mind of the only person who would be able to hear it.

Danny.

From the other side of the room, Willow watched as the Soul Sucker bit into Sophie. Willow ran across the room, narrowly avoiding a scythe as she did so. She jumped onto the clown-faced Soul Sucker's back, pushing both it and Sophie to the floor. The trio sprawled across the marble floor as the other Soul Suckers began to circle them. Sophie's eye's glowed dark purple as she slammed her hand down.

The room trembled as her palm hit the floor. A purple light exploded from Sophie's body and pushed the Soul Suckers backwards. Willow grabbed Sophie's hand and the pair ran towards the exit. The Soul Suckers, who had swiftly recovered from Sophie's attack, followed them. As Sophie and Willow reached the door, Alexander, Joel, Fredrick, and the rest of Lightning Squad entered.

Araminta was the first to react. She pounced on top of one of the Soul Suckers, knocking it to the floor. She swung down her sword, but it was blocked by the Soul Sucker's scythe. The pair fought. Their blades crashed against each other. Araminta jumped onto one of the tables. She picked up a flaming Bunsen burner and threw it at the Soul Sucker. The Soul Sucker stumbled back as its cloak began to burn. Araminta cut off the Soul Sucker's head. The vampire smiled as the Soul Sucker's headless body fell to the floor.

However her smile soon faded as the Soul Sucker's headless body lifted itself up, doused down the flames and placed its head back onto its neck.

Upon entering the room, Joel had been immediately attacked by a Soul Sucker. The pair had fought but Joel had quickly lost. Joel's sword clattered to the ground, swiftly followed by his head.

Fredrick had lasted longer.

His swordsmanship had saved him from his first attacker but had distracted him from his second. For as Fredrick disarmed one Soul Sucker, a second sneaked up behind him and cut off his head. Clover laughed as she watched the twins die. She raised her hand, it glowed red and the Soul Suckers quickly left her alone. Clover kicked Fredrick and Joel's heads out of the way, sending them rolling across the bloody floor. The witch then headed towards Roxy's body. After checking that her squad-mates were distracted, Clover knelt next to the body.

"What a shame," Clover whispered into Roxy's ear, "I was hoping to kill you myself."

Clover gently placed her hand against the gunshot wound. She let Roxy's blood dye her fingertips then brought her fingers to her lips. Clover smiled as she licked Roxy's blood from her fingers. The sweet taste satisfied the witch greatly. Clover pulled out her wand and pressed it against Roxy's heart. Her wand glowed red as it sucked up Roxy's powers and what remained of her soul. Once completed Clover walked away from Roxy's body. She silently slipped past Danny who had been pinned to the ground by three Soul Suckers and headed towards the bodies of the fallen twins. Clover quickly repeated the task on Joel and Fredrick's bodies. Clover then returned to her shadowy hiding place, where she watched as the fight continued.

Fern (as always) was not happy.

She fought, back-to-back with Alexander, against four Soul Suckers.

"Why don't they just die like normal demons!?" Fern hissed as she flicked her wand and set the Soul Suckers on fire. One of the blazing Soul Suckers stepped forwards, grabbed hold of Fern, and pulled her into a burning embrace. Fern cried out in pain as the flames stroked her skin. She flicked her wand, water poured over her and the Soul Sucker, extinguishing the flames. Fern pushed the Soul Sucker off of her and picked up a fallen scythe. She stabbed the blade into the Soul Sucker's chest. The Soul Sucker pulled out the scythe with ease and laughed.

"Don't laugh I'm trying to kill you," Fern snapped. Alexander zoomed behind the Soul Sucker and snapped its neck in half. The Soul Sucker dropped to the floor.

Fern smiled, "Nicely done grandpa."

"Stop calling me that. What the…?" Alexander backed away as the Soul Sucker pulled itself up, its neck still broken.

"Oh that is disgusting," Fern exclaimed. She picked up her sword and with a clean slice cut off the Soul Sucker's head. Even then the Soul Sucker's body didn't fall, it just picked up its head and placed it back on to its neck.

"Oh sugarplums," Fern cursed under her breath.

On the opposite side of the room, the clown-faced Soul Sucker and Sophie fought against each other. Sophie raised the Soul Sucker up in a mist of purple and threw it into a wall. Her throw was so powerful that the wall broke as the Soul Sucker hit it. Sophie was about to use her magic to fix the broken wall when a second Soul Sucker grabbed hold of her and hurled her through it.

As Sophie landed outside in the snow, the clown-faced Soul Sucker stabbed her in the back with its scythe. Sophie screamed in pain. Her scream caused the dark sky to light up with purple lightning forks. The lightning forks hit the clown-faced Soul Sucker. But still it didn't die. Sophie crawled away, her back bleeding heavily. Before she could get far, the Soul Sucker grabbed hold of her ankle and dragged her back. It turned her over and pressed it scythe against her neck. The Soul Sucker lightly cut into her skin. Sophie could feel warm blood trickle down her neck.

At that moment the clown-faced Soul Sucker was

suddenly grabbed by two strong grey hands. The hands dragged the Soul Sucker backwards and attacked it. Whilst the battle between the two demons continued, Sophie pressed her hand to her back and began to heal her wounded body. She then stood up and walked carefully over to the fight.

The new creature had a wolf-like face and stood on two legs. It had a tall grey muscular body and spikes piercing out of its back. The creature wrestled against the Soul Sucker, pinning it to the ground. The Soul Sucker slashed its scythe across the creature's chest. The creature's blood dripped onto the snow. The creature then dug its teeth into the Soul Sucker and ripped it into pieces. Once it had completely devoured the Soul Sucker, the creature turned to Sophie.

Sophie stared into its sharp brown eyes, only to find that there was something familiar about them.

"Danny?"

The creature shuddered and its body shook as it stumbled backwards, falling behind a pile of snow. Sophie walked over to where the creature had fallen to find Danny lying in its place.

His chest ripped open.

28

'ZOMBIES'

JASON

Seven demons had been surrounding the Polar Base. Upon us opening the main doors they quickly attacked. Without asking for my permission, Angel stabbed me in the back. I transformed into a demon and killed the seven demons with ease. To be honest repeatedly turning into a demon was really starting to freak me out. It was a strange experience. When I transformed my demon didn't take over my mind, not exactly. I was still Jason. I still had control over my own thoughts however I also gained a love of demon flesh.

And demons tasted so good!

They were so yummy and full of flavour and I'm beginning to freak myself out again! For while eating demons is tasty and enjoyable in my demon form, when I return to normal, I find the idea rather disturbing.

Moving swiftly on...

Once I had got rid of the demons, the four of us started our journey to the gateway portal. I shared a snowmobile with Becks while Angel shared one with McLean. We soon arrived at the temple that housed the portal. It was beautiful. It was completely made of ice! The dome roof, the walls, the pillars, even the large doors that greeted us were all carved out of ice! McLean pulled out a key from his pocket and unlocked the doors. It was dark inside the temple. Angel clicked her fingers and small white balls of light rose into the air.

The temple was just as beautiful inside. Large columns stood like guards protecting the carved ice statues of the gods and the goddesses that stood proudly in the temple's centre.

"Where's the portal?" asked Angel.

"Follow me," McLean said quietly.

We followed the rat man as he led us to the back of the temple where we were once again greeted by large ice doors. McLean pulled from his jacket a round metal disk. He slotted the disk into the lock and turned it anticlockwise. There was a great grumble as the doors slowly came to life and opened. I stood there and stared. The portal was massive. It looked like a large oval mirror. Encased in a golden frame was a twisting cascade of colours.

Next to the portal was a strange contraption. It looked like a computer. A computer powered by steam and magic. Becks ran over to it.

"Someone has definitely been messing with the portal," Becks muttered. Connected to the computer were three vials; one held a bright white fluid, the other dark purple liquid and the third held a thick black substance. The three vials were wired up to the computer and were glowing.

"The black stuff is Jason's soul, the purple stuff is the fey blood," Becks explained, "But I have no idea what the white liquid is."

"If you can get the teleportation system back up, then there's something I need you to do," Angel said softly, "Anyone whose teleportation chip is not registering them as alive, I need you to teleport them to the hospital wing at the D.D base."

"Yes, I think I can do that."

"And this is," Angel handed Becks a piece of paper, "Ethan's teleportation chip ID. I want you to teleport him there as well."

McLean and Becks worked quietly while I stared at the portal. I was too distracted by the portal's grandeur that I didn't notice Angel walk up behind me.

"It's beautiful, isn't it?" Angel whispered.

"It is," I agreed.

The portal glowed light blue and swirls of colours twisted around inside the golden frame. The portal hummed softly as it calmly lit up the dark temple. I turned to face Angel which was when I realised that the shapeshifter was staring intensely at the floor. "What are you doing?"

"It's too easy. There were only seven demons outside the base, if this place is so important then where are the demons?" Angel dropped to the ground. She pressed her ear against the icy floor. She knocked on the ice. Nothing then BANG! A noise from under the ice echoed around the portal room. Angel sat up quickly.

"They're under the ice," Angel hissed, "How far down does the portal go?"

"What do you mean?" McLean asked.

"Does the portal go below the ice?"

"No. It shouldn't do."

"I think they've expanded it. Look at the ice around the portal, its…"

Suddenly there came a loud cracking sound.

Angel gestured for silence and for me to follow her. I raised my gun as we slipped like ghosts out of the portal room. It was dark and so very quiet. The soft sound of us breathing was all that could be heard. In the centre of the temple was a large hole from where something had pushed its way out from under the ice. Angel flicked her wand and lit up the temple. We searched for a demon but found nothing.

Then I felt something warm drip onto my shoulder.

I looked up to find a massive demon hanging from the ceiling. It had a dragon-like face, with beady red eyes and sharp black teeth. Its long twisted neck connected to a strong scaled body. It hissed its forked tongue in my direction, saliva running from its lips and dripping onto my shoulder. Angel shot at the demon. Her bullets flew uselessly off the creature's scaled body. We rolled out of the way as the demon dived at us. I scrambled behind a pillar. I raised my fist and released it, in an attempt to explode the demon, but my powers didn't work.

"Jason are you actually doing something or are you just waving at it!?" Angel shouted as the demon crashed its body against the pillar she was hiding behind.

"I don't know!" I exclaimed.

I'm pretty certain that Angel then shouted some form of abuse in my direction however the demon roared so loudly that I didn't hear what she said. The demon slammed its body into the pillars. The ice cracked and groaned. I skidded across the floor as chunks of ice dropped from the ceiling. Angel transformed into a white tiger and attacked the demon.

The tiger pounced onto the demons back and clawed at its armour of scales. The tiger clambered onto its dragon-like head where it scratched at the demon's eyes. The demon screeched and threw its head backwards sending the tiger flying. The tiger hit a wall, transforming back into Angel.

I clicked my fingers and threw black fire at the demon. The demon did not like that at all. It stumbled backwards as the flames licked at its scales. At that moment Angel, in fire nymph form, ran up the demon. Her fiery footsteps set the demon's scales alight. Angel jumped to the ground, transforming back into herself, as the flames engulfed the demon. The fire melted the icy floor. The ice finally gave in and the demon plunged into the ocean below.

I walked over to the hole in the ice. At that moment the demon's claws sprang out of the water, grabbed my waist, and pulled me down into the watery grave below.

"Jason!" Angel yelled.

The demon's claws cut into my skin. Its grip was tight and unmoving. I tried to set my hands alight, but the water kept putting out the flames. As I struggled against the creature's grip, I noticed something. I could see the portal under the water, and it was surrounded by demons. However the demons weren't swimming out of the portal, they were swimming into it.

That's strange, I thought, they're swimming in the wrong direction.

Then I began to feel lightheaded and sleepy. I was about to die, I realised. I didn't even have the energy to panic. I was just too tired. Too sleepy. I don't really remember what happened next.

I vaguely recall someone slicing off the demon's claw and grabbing hold of me. However my next clear memory is of breaking to the surface and feeling the cold Arctic air stroke my skin. It wasn't until that moment that I realised that I really love breathing! Breathing is the best! Breathing is just so great and so underappreciated!

"I'm glad you love breathing so much," Angel laughed, "But how about showing some of that love to the person who just saved you?"

"Did you just read my…oh my god you have a tail!" I exclaimed as I noticed that where Angel's legs should have been there was a long white tail, "You're a mermaid!"

"Shapeshifter, remember?" Angel smiled pulling herself

out of the water. I stared open mouthed as I saw Angel's mermaid tail properly for the first time.

It was amazing!

Angel transformed back into her normal self and her awesome mermaid tail vanished. She held out her hand, which I took, and pulled me out of the water. I shivered. I was freezing cold and tired. Angel pressed her hand against my chest and suddenly I was filled with warmth.

"What did you just do?" I asked.

"Magic," she replied simply.

"Obviously. Hey, there was something weird going on down there. The demons were swimming into the portal, not out of it." Angel cursed loudly as she ran back to the portal room, I quickly followed.

"Where's the portal going?" Angel demanded as she reached the computer.

"Err, just give me a minute," McLean muttered as he calculated the machinery, "How very odd."

"What's odd?"

"The portal keeps changing. Most of the time it's going to the underworld but sometimes it changes to Atlantis."

"Damn it! We've been set up!"

Suddenly the sound of breaking ice echoed around the portal room. I turned as a grey hand pushed its way to the surface.

The hand flexed as it felt the breeze for the first time in centuries. Then there was a second hand, then a third and then a fourth. Soon there were over two dozen hands flexing and rolling their wrists in the cold artic air. Each single hand gained a partner. The two hands then pushed the rest of their body out of the ice. We were quickly surrounded by an army of undead creatures. They stood and looked like humans, but they most certainly were not human! They had rotting flesh that hung to their rusted bodies like old rags. The eyeballs, of the creatures that had eyes, were bloodshot red and they were dressed in battered clothing. Purple veins bounced out of their skin. Their teeth were black and their lips crusty.

"Not again. Not again." I heard Angel mutter. She had gone pale and was stumbling backwards. That's when I realised what these demons were.

"They're zombies, aren't they?" I gulped as Angel nodded, "You've dealt with zombies before, right?"

"Once. It didn't end well. Whatever happens don't let them bite you."

I raised my hand, released my fist and a zombie crumbled into pieces. I was about to congratulate myself when the zombie picked up its broken flesh and stuck itself back together.

"Fire," Angel whispered, "That normally stops them."

"But you won't be able to use fire in here," McLean explained, "The portal room is protected against it."

"Jason?"

"You know this'll be the fourth time today that you've stabbed me," I muttered.

"Well learn how to turn on demand and then I won't have to stab you," Angel hissed as she stuck her sword into my side.

I doubled over in pain and transformed into my demon self. The transformation was much quicker than it had been the last three times. The zombies attacked the moment I transformed. I swung my tail in their direction, knocking the zombies to the floor. The only issue I found with having such a large demon body was that I couldn't see when zombies snuck up behind me. I constantly had to spin around in order to make sure that zombies weren't trying to bite my behind.

Angel had been grabbed before she even had chance to transform. A zombie had taken hold of her wrist and dragged her into its arms. Angel struggled and threw the zombie over her back. The zombie landed with a crack as its arm broke. Angel pulled out her sword and chopped off the zombie's head. As she did so a second zombie rugby tackled her to the floor. Angel quickly transformed into water and trickled away from the zombies. She headed to Becks. When Angel reached her, she quickly transformed back into her natural form. She swiftly saved Becks from a zombie and then dragged her to the computer.

"No matter what happens you stay here and work," Angel ordered as she raised her hands. A forcefield rose up around Becks, shielding her from the zombie attack.

While Becks worked quite happily without fear of interruption, I was being attacked by six zombies. They kept jumping onto my back. Every time I shook them off, they'd just jump straight back on again! One of the zombies had a sword which it kept poking into my belly - which I didn't think was very nice! I slammed my demon body into a wall. The three zombies on my back fell to the floor. I then sliced my claws in their direction. The zombies stumbled backwards and fell through one of the holes in the floor.

Out of the corner of my demon eye, I noticed McLean fighting against a zombie. The rat man was a better fighter then I had expected. He fought with a small dagger which he quickly used to slice off a zombie's arm. The arm flopped to the ground and wriggled in spasms. The zombie threw a lazy punch, with its only remaining arm, in McLean's direction. The rat man grabbed the zombie's fist, twisted the creature into a wall then cut off its head. A second zombie grabbed McLean and threw him to the floor, but the rat quickly jumped to his feet.

While this was occurring, I was getting repeatedly harassed by zombies. They climbed onto my tail and tried to sink their rotten teeth into my skin. I grabbed a zombie between my fangs and threw it into the air. I grabbed a second and then a third repeating the process. I had attempted to eat the zombies however their flesh tasted so disgusting that I couldn't swallow it.

It was just too chewy!

I stumbled backwards as more and more zombies clambered on top of me. I threw myself to the floor and rolled over, squashing the zombies as I did so. I then jumped to my feet. However I landed on a thin patch of ice which broke under the weight of my demon body. As I fell into the icy water, I involuntarily transformed back into myself. I swam up to the surface. As I pulled myself out of the water and on to dry land, a zombie jumped onto my back pushing me to the floor. Just as the zombie was about to bite me, a white tiger caught the creature between its teeth and dragged it away from me.

"I've done it!" Becks yelled above the noise.

"You've done what?" Angel shouted as she transformed back into her normal form.

"I've fixed the communications! I think."

Angel jumped over a zombie's body and ran (dragging me along with her) through the forcefield. Becks flicked several switches and handed Angel an old-fashioned phone. A red light flashed, and a voice could be heard.

"Polar Base, this is Captain Hardwick we've been…"

"Will, its Angel, get all the squads and all the other military units to Atlantis. There's an army of demons heading there," Angel explained quickly.

"What's going on?"

"I don't have time to explain, just get to Atlantis!"

"Angel…"

Then the line went dead.

"I've teleported the deceased and your brother to the hospital wing at the base, at least I hope that's where I teleported them too.," Becks muttered.

"Can you teleport everyone to Atlantis?" Angel asked.

"Including the folks at the Polar Base? I might be able to hack into the system and get you into the main hall of the palace if I reboot…"

"Great, do that!" Angel interrupted as she pulled out a

small circle object from McLean's bag that had been left on the desk.

"What is that?" I asked.

"A bomb."

"A what!?"

"A bomb. I found it in one of the boxes from the Polar Base's armoury. Let's hope it works. McLean get in here!" Angel shouted. The rat man quickly entered the forcefield.

"What's your plan captain?" he asked.

"I plan to throw this into the portal. Once we get the…"

"Done it!" Becks smiled, "Everyone has teleportation chips, so it was easy. I've done it. I think." As she spoke a second set of zombies pushed their way out of the ice.

"I'm going to throw this into the portal. The moment I do, I need you to get us out of here," Angel said, staring at the zombies.

"Yes Cap," Becks nodded gravely.

"How are you going to get to the portal?" I asked, "There are zombies everywhere!"

"I'll work something out. You three stay in here. No matter what happens just stay in here. This forcefield, even if the portal explodes and the teleportation doesn't work., it might still save you. So stay here."

"But what about you?"

"I'll be fine," Angel smiled.

Before anyone could stop her, Angel exited the forcefield and ran through the chaos of zombies. The zombies attacked Angel. They grabbed onto her legs and sliced their swords in her direction. But Angel didn't stop. She kept running towards the portal. As she got closer, more and more zombies attacked. They grabbed her ankles, forcing her to the floor. Angel kicked and struggled, desperately trying to avoid getting bitten.

When she got close enough, Angel pressed the timer on the bomb and threw it into the portal.

"Now Becks!" Angel shouted.
Becks quickly pressed a button…
As the portal exploded!

29

'FRED THE DEMON'

JASON

We landed with a loud crash. My body hit a strange green table then fell onto a hard mosaic floor. As I pushed myself up, Angel landed on top of me, her back (she had a very bony back by the way) squashed into my face. I couldn't see the others, but Fern's loud voice told me that they had also arrived.

"Get off me!" Fern shouted, "Danny! You have three seconds to…hey! Danny? Hey! Guys, I think Danny might be dead!"

"I'm not dead," I heard Danny groan.

Angel pulled herself off me. She stumbled over to Danny, who had landed on top of Fern. Rowan, who had landed on top of a bookshelf, quickly joined them and the pair healed Danny's bloody chest. I looked around. Willow and Clover had landed right in the centre of the green table, squashing the lovely flower centre piece. Sophie,

Becks and McLean had landed in a heap on a small pink stairway that was covered in strange light blue flowers. Alexander and Araminta had landed close to me. Araminta walked over to me and held out her hand. I took it and she pulled me to my feet. My body ached so much! It was like someone had run me over with a bus a few hundred times…just, you know, without the dying part!

"Are you alright?" Araminta asked.

"Yeah. You have gills!" I exclaimed as I noticed the fish gills that were attached to the vampire's cheeks.

"Of course I have gills. We're underwater."

"What!? Then how am I breathing?"

"Because you also have gills."

"What!?" I touched my cheek. She was right! I had gills. Fish gills!

"We're in Atlantis," Araminta explained, "Luckily for us, Atlantis has a protection spell which gives any airbreather gills upon entering the kingdom."

"But why don't I feel wet? And how come I'm standing not swimming?"

"Magic Jason!"

"This is so weird!" I said touching my gills, "Aww it's a seal!"

Right next to me was an adorable grey seal. It had large brown eyes that stared up at me and whiskers sticking out of its chubby cheeks. It was treading water, its little flippers flapping against the waves. It was strange to see the creature swimming so close to me, especially given that I couldn't even feel the water that surrounded me. To me it felt as though I was on dry land. Had I not just survived a zombie attack (the thought of which was occupying a rather large part of my mind), I would have probably freaked out about the fact that I was breathing thousands of miles below the surface, that I had gills, and that I was stood next to a seal. However I didn't, instead I simply stared at the seal in awe of its adorableness.

"Oh it's so cute!"

"I'm not cute!" the seal barked.

"You can talk?"

"Of course I can talk, you idiot!"

"Have I suddenly gained the ability to talk to animals! Oh that's so cool! I've always wanted to have a conversation with a duck! Wait," I recognised that voice, "Sue!? You're a seal!"

"I'm a Selkie! Human on land, seal in water. I did explain this to you!" Sue (the seal) snapped.

"That's so cool! Rowan, you have a tail!"

"I'm a mermaid. Of course I have a tail," Rowan, who had a green mermaid tail, laughed as she helped Danny to his feet.

"Is everyone okay?" Angel asked as she helped Fern up. It was at that moment I noticed that Angel's shoulder was bleeding.

"Angel, did you get bit?" I asked, "Your shoulder is bleeding."

As Angel desperately tried to get a better look at her injury, Alexander asked, "Bit by what?"

"A zombie." Alexander was by Angel's side in an instant. He examined the wound carefully.

"It's okay. It's not a bite. You must have been cut," Alexander dropped his head onto Angel's shoulder in relief.

"Jason don't scare me like that!" Angel exclaimed as she slapped me.

"Hey, I was just asking! Loads of zombies were attacking you," I stuttered.

"Zombies?" Sophie rushed over to Angel, she pushed Alexander away and grabbed Angel's arms. She studied the shapeshifter closely, then took hold of her face, "Are you okay? Did they hurt you? Are you having flashbacks? Do you need anything? Are you…?"

"Sophie I'm fine," Angel reassured.

Sophie nodded then pulled Angel into a tight hug. Sophie's sudden outburst of questions had surprised me. Since joining Lightning Squad I had rarely heard Sophie speak, in fact that had probably been the most I had ever heard her say. People had told me that Sophie and Angel were close friends but, until that moment, I had never seen them together. The fey continued to study Angel long after the hug ended.

"Where's Roxy?" Angel asked stepping away from the fairy.

"Dead," Sophie explained, "Soul Sucker. Joel and Fredrick too."

Angel swore and covered her face with her hands.

There was silence.

Before I had time to process Roxy's death, Fern asked, "Why are we at Atlantis?"

"That's exactly the question I was going to ask," came a booming voice.

We all jumped at the sound.

We turned around to find that we weren't alone. In fact we were far from it. There was a semi-circle of mermen guards pointing tridents in our direction. Behind them were twenty important looking mer-people, who were stood in front of two large coral thrones. Sat on one of the thrones was a mermaid with a long scarlet tail. Her shirt matched the colour of her tail and she wore a golden band around her long ginger hair. On the other throne sat a merman. He had a purple tail and long grey hair which was covered by a crown.

"Have you just been sat there watching us this whole time!?" Fern exclaimed, "That's just creepy! You should…"

"Fern," Angel warned sharply.

"Father," Rowan bowed, facing the thrones. Father? Then it clicked. The man and woman in front of us were Rowan's parents, the King and Queen of Atlantis! I was stood in front of royalty, and not just any old royalty, mermaid royalty!

"Rowan darling! Drop your weapons that's my daughter!" the Queen exclaimed as she rushed over to Rowan. The Queen hugged her daughter, but Rowan didn't hug her back. Instead she just stood there awkwardly, waiting for the embrace to end.

"Did the Colonel send you?" the King asked.

"Not exactly," Angel explained, "Demons were smuggled up to the Polar Base. We were sent there to deal with the situation. However when we got there, we found that the gateway portal had been re-looped. Mr Jet was using the portal to send an army of demons to Atlantis."

"The demons. They have taken most of the lower town."

"Is that where your portal is?"

"Yes."

"Have any reinforcements arrived?"

"No. No one has been able to teleport in or out. You're the first to arrive. How were you able to get in?"

"Becks did something technical," Angel explained awkwardly, she then turned to Becks, "Do you think you'd be able to get this portal working?"

"Err possibly. I might be able to reroute the portal, but I won't know for sure until I see it in person," Becks muttered.

"Which would mean going through the army of demons."

"Angel you know how you blew up the portal at the Polar Base," I thought aloud, "Does that mean that no more demons can get into Atlantis?"

"It should do...which means that the portal room should be pretty empty. Demons aren't known for being clever. They'll probably just head straight into the city, not thinking to guard the portal. You said no one can teleport in or out, right?" Angel asked the King.

"That is correct," the King replied.

"Is this place protected against teleporters?"

"No. We rarely get teleporters in Atlantis, apparently it's hard for them to use their powers underwater."

"Hard but not impossible."

"Mr Jet might have put up another forcefield," Alexander warned, "Like he did at the Polar Base."

"He might, or he might not have expected us to make it out alive," Angel muttered. She glowed white then with a POP she vanished. Moments later she reappeared.

"How did you teleport!? No one has been able to get in or out. How did you do it?" the Queen asked aggressively (the queen was a very scary mer-lady).

"I can't teleport out of Atlantis, but I can teleport to other parts of the city," Angel panted.

"You can teleport us to the portal," Alexander said catching Angel's train of thought.

"Yes, there were a few demons there, so I'll teleport myself and..."

"Your highness," at that moment a merman crashed into the room, he bowed to the King before saying, "The demons have almost reached the palace."

"Right," Angel turned to us, "Alex, I need you and the squad to buy me some time."

"Yes Cap."

"Danny, me and you are going to teleport to the portal room. We'll get rid of any demons, then I will teleport back here for Becks and McLean. Once you two have begun working on the portal, I will teleport back and forth taking your highnesses, the council, and any other survivors to the portal. Sue, I want you to stay here and just swim around the palace, make sure we don't miss anyone."

"Yes cap," Sue the seal barked, "But Angel are you sure you're going to be able to teleport that much? Teleporting underwater is…"

"I'll be fine. If you find any survivors tell them to head to the palace. I'll take everyone from here first, then I'll try to teleport into the city and find others. We need to save as many people as possible."

* * * * *

We reloaded our weapons then headed down to the lower town. The buildings in Atlantis reminded me of pictures I had seen of Ancient Greece. They were built with white stone and coral, with tall columns and large archways. Once Atlantis would have been beautiful, however now it was a wasteland. Demons had rampaged through the city, knocking down buildings and killing people as they went. The sound of screaming pierced our eardrums. We found survivors being chased by a gang of ugly demons.

The demons had skinny milk white bodies with sharp black fangs and long tails. Dressed in rags, these demons were quick and deadly. Upon seeing me, one of the demons picked up a wooden stick and swung it repeatedly at my face. Each time I blocked the stick with my sword. After realising that the stick wasn't an effective weapon, the demon threw it to the ground and pounced on top of me. I stumbled backwards and fell. The demon knocked my sword from my hands and scratched at my face. Just as it was about to take a nice big bite out of my ear, I opened my fist and the demon exploded.

"Nice trick," Alexander complimented as I got to my feet.

"I've gotten quite good at…"

"Watch your back," Alexander said as another demon tried to kill me. Alexander quickly blocked the demon's sword. The vampire kicked the demon's chest then cut off its head.

"Nicely done," I nodded as I tried not to throw up at the sight of the headless body. I was trying to stay calm and collected in front of the super cool vampire, even

361

though on the inside I was panicking. I was fighting against a demon army in a city that shouldn't exist! This was a lot to try and process!

"Oi you two!" Fern ran over to us, "Stop talking and start helping!"

"Right," Alexander zoomed off leaving me alone with the mad witch.

"Get down!" Fern yelled, she grabbed my collar and dragged me behind a pillar, just as a fire ball whizzed past.

"How can it throw fire!? We're underwater!" I exclaimed.

"Magic Jason! Magic!" Fern snapped, "The gills, the underwater fire, the demons, it's all because of magic!"

"I know but..."

"Magic Jason! It's very obvious and the fact that you didn't realise it yourself just shows how much of an idiot you are!"

"You know I really don't like you."

"The feelings mutual," Fern muttered as she turned to stare at the demon that had thrown the fire ball.

It was huge.

It had two stumpy legs, dusky pink skin, and one large eyeball. I dragged Fern down as a second fire ball was thrown in our direction. Fern pulled out her wand. She peaked around the pillar and flicked her wand towards the demon. A purple lightning bolt hit the demon's fat belly. The seabed shook as the demon stamped its heavy feet in anger. I opened my closed fist and the demon exploded into tiny pieces.

"You should have done that to begin with!" Fern snapped.

"Well I...Oh no," I muttered as the tiny demon pieces began to stitch themselves back together and the demon returned to life.

It roared loudly.

"Oh well done Jason, you've made Fred angry!"

"Who the hell is Fred!?"

"Oh that's what I named him."

"You named the demon?"

"Yep."

"How do you know it's a guy?"

"I don't. I just thought it looked like a Fred."

"I don't think he likes his name," I pushed Fern out of the way as the demon charged at us.

We ran down the street as fire balls chased us. We slid down an alleyway and came out by a large pool of water. The demon raced after us. Fern flicked her wand and the water burst upwards hitting the demon. The fireballs hissed into steam. The demon roared as it was pushed backwards into a wall. Fern flicked her wand again and sent a large electric blast at the demon. The demon's body shook and twisted as the electricity ran over his flesh. The demon screamed. Fern flicked her wand once more and from the tip a soft purple mist floated towards the demon. The mist floated into the demon's gaping mouth, muting the creature.

"Why is there a pool of water…?" I began to ask but instantly regretted.

"Magic Jason! Once again!" Fern exclaimed, "It's a pool that links the outside sea world to Atlantis. It's so that the normal fishes can come and play with the magical ones!"

"I was just…never mind! What are we going to do about the demon?"

"Yes…why Fred will you not just die?"

"I wish I could just blow it up," I sighed, "But my powers don't work on it."

"Your powers don't but this might," Fern pulled out an object from her pocket.

"What's that?"

"A bomb. It's filled with really powerful magic."

I stared at Fern, trying to resist the urge to strangle her,

"You're telling me that all this time you had a bomb in your pocket!"

"Yeah. Maybe I should have mentioned it earlier."

"You think! If you had, we could've dealt with this demon ages ago!"

"Alright calm down. Here's the plan. You're going to run up to the roof of that building and throw this at Fred. All you have to do is press the red button. After you do, we'll have about a minute to get to safety, this thing is pretty powerful," Fern explained as she handed me the bomb.

"And while I do that, you're going to distract it, right?"

"It has a name."

"Fine," I hissed, "While I do that, you're going to distract Fred?"

"Exactly," Fern smiled as she raised her wand. Fred was lifted upwards. Fred fought against the magic, roaring silently in frustration. Fern then dropped the demon. Fred hit the sandy seabed with a bang.

While Fern continued to beat up Fred, I ran up to the roof of a nearby building. I think the building had once been a house. It was hard to tell. The orange coral furniture inside had been so badly ripped apart that it was difficult to make out what it had once been. I waited for the demon to get close. I carefully held the bomb, not wanting to set it off accidentally. Internally I was panicking. I had a bomb in my hands. A bomb! A real life, powerful, scary bomb! And I was going to have to press the big red button! I was both terrified and slightly excited. When Fred got close enough, I pressed the red button and threw the bomb at the demon. I ran back downstairs, grabbed hold of Fern, and jumped into the pool of water.

BANG!

Tiny demon pieces rained across the seabed. We swam up to the surface and climbed out of the pool of water. Rotting flesh splattered the walls of the remaining buildings and thick black blood coated the sand.

"Oh this is disgusting!" Fern cried as she cleaned the demon remains from her glasses.

"Yep," then for some reason we both burst into an uncontrollable fit of laughter.

30

'THE FALL OF ATLANTIS'

Araminta was pushed to the seabed as a wolf-like demon jumped on top of her. It stood on four spindly legs and had large white fangs. The demon bit into Araminta's arm. The vampire hissed as she reached for her knife. She grabbed hold of the handle and in one fluid movement she stabbed the demon's heart. The demon whimpered and flopped. Araminta pulled her arm from the demon's fangs and pushed the dead weight off her.

Willow was forced into a headlock by a large red two-headed demon. Willow elbowed the demon's ribs and wriggled from its grasp. She ran towards her fallen gun, but the demon got there first. It punched her then grabbed her waist and threw her to the ground.

As the demon picked up a broken piece of stone, Willow crawled towards her gun. She grabbed hold of it and fired twice.

The demon fell to the ground dead.

A bullet in both its foreheads.

"You alright?" asked Araminta as she helped Willow to her feet.

Willow nodded, "I hate demons!"

* * * * *

Sophie and Alexander stared at the demons in front of them. The demons were orcs. The humanoid demons had dark grey skin, crimson eyes and were dressed in battered chainmail. The orcs cut open their victims in such an elegant manner that it was almost artistic.

"They're getting closer to the palace," Willow shouted as she ran over to meet them, "They must have realised we've been sending survivors there."

Sophie nodded, "You ready for this?"

"Ready?" Alexander grinned, he zoomed behind an orc and swiftly broke its neck, "I've already started."

Sophie and Willow quickly joined Alexander on the battlefield.

Sophie's eyes glowed as she sent demons flying out of her way. As she did so an orc sneaked up behind her and grabbed her waist. It threw the fairy over its shoulder. Before Sophie could get to her feet, the orc slammed a mace into her back. Sophie fell to the ground. The mace crashed into her back once again.

Sophie screamed.

Her powerful scream knocked over every orc within a three-metre radius. Sophie pulled herself to her feet. The orc that had attacked her was about to do the same but the fey raised her hand. A bolt of purple lightning flew from her fingertips and hit the orc's chest.

The orc screeched as it turned into a pile of ash.

Willow killed four orcs with ease however her fifth was turning out to be a bit of a problem. The orc swung its sword in her direction. Willow blocked but the orc was too strong. Willow was forced to break hold and stumble backwards. She tried to land a kick but missed. The orc swung its sword again. Willow took a step backwards, as she did so she tripped over a fallen merman guard. Willow fell to the ground; her sword flew from her hand. Out of the corner of her eye Willow noticed the guard's spear. As she rolled out of the way of the orc's sword, she grabbed the spear and stabbed it into the orc's belly.

The orc fell dead.

As Willow got to her feet, however, a sixth orc sneaked up behind her and stabbed her in the back.

Alexander killed seven orcs in a matter of minutes. The vampire fought quickly and with great skill, defeating any orc he encountered. One attempted to attack the vampire with a mace, but Alexander simply zoomed up behind the orc and chopped off its head. As he did so he noticed Willow fall to the ground.

A dagger sticking out of her back.

"Will!" Alexander rushed over to Willow. Sophie quickly joined them.

"We need to get her to Rowan, now!" Alexander ordered.

"There's too many of them," Willow gasped, "Unless reinforcements arrive, we can't win this, not alone."

"Maybe we don't have too," Sophie muttered as an idea popped into her head, "Maybe we don't have to fight at all."

"What do you mean?"

"During one of the sea wars, the former King created a device, a switch, that when activated would wash away Atlantis. The entire kingdom was washed away, then once the war was over Atlantis was rebuilt."

"If the device still exists, and Becks gets the portal working, we could get everyone to safety then wash away the entire kingdom," Alexander muttered.

"The demons included."

* * * * *

Angel and Danny teleported to the portal room. The portal room was elegant and grand. It had a mosaic floor, light blue walls that were covered in royal portraits and a coral balcony from which the entire city was visible. The portal was encased in a frame made of gold and coral.

The portal glowed a soft pink and hummed quietly as three demons stood guard in front of it. One of the demons was a large monster, with three snake heads and a long-spiked tail, while the other two were orcs.

"I'll take the big one, you deal with the other two," Angel ordered. Angel transformed into a water dragon and fought against the larger demon.

As she did so Danny pulled out his gun and shot at the orcs. One fell dead in a matter of moments while the other swung its mace at Danny. The mace hit Danny's hand, knocking the gun to the floor. The orc swung down its mace once more, but Danny ducked out of the way. Danny rugby tackled the orc to the floor. The orc struggled from Danny's grasp, dropping its mace as it did so. Danny grabbed hold of the mace and slammed it into the orc's head. Dark grey blood splattered onto the wall as the orc fell dead.

"Nicely done," Angel muttered as she transformed back into herself.

"The other demon? Oh," Danny stared at the bloody demon corpse.

"I forgot how powerful my water dragon form is."

"You're rather impressed with yourself, aren't you?"

"You know what, I am. I thought that demon would be much harder to kill. Right I'm going to go get Becks and McLean. See you in a sec," with that Angel disappeared, only to reappear moments later with McLean and Becks.

Becks went over to the computer by the portal, "The portal itself hasn't been damaged, however it has been hacked. The portal currently will only allow things from the polar portal to enter. It won't allow anyone from this side to pass through or change its destination."

"Can you fix it?"

"Now that the polar portal no longer exists, I should be able to change the portal's destination. The problem is that when the polar portal exploded some of its power backfired and fried this portal's ability to bring people in…"

"But will we be able to portal people out?"

"That system, it's been hacked so we can't use it at the moment but, it looks okay. It's not damaged so I should be able to get it working. But it'll take time. At the Polar Base all I did was get the base's teleportation system up and running, I didn't touch the portal so I'm not sure…"

"We'll buy you as much time as we can. If you can't get it working, then see if you can get rid of the forcefield surrounding the kingdom. If we can get rid of that then I'll just teleport everyone out."

"Angel that could kill you! Teleporters aren't supposed to teleport from the sea kingdom to land," Danny exclaimed.

"I'm well aware of that Danny, however if Becks can't get the portal working then we won't have a choice. McLean?"

"Yes?" the rat man stuttered.

"Does that computer have a scanner? If it doesn't can you make me one? There may be survivors that can't make it to the palace. If I know where they're hiding, I can rescue them."

"I'll see what I can do."

"Good. I'm going to get the others."

Angel repeatedly teleported to and from the palace. After teleporting the King and Queen, she teleported all the council members, their families, the palace servants, the citizens who had made it to the palace as well as the guards. As she teleported Sue, Angel collapsed to the floor.

"That's everyone from the palace!" Angel panted.

"You okay?" Sue asked.

"Yeah. Teleporting underwater is just really hard work."

"Angel you've teleported over a hundred times! It's a miracle you're still alive! Are you sure you can keep doing this?"

"I'll be fine. We need to save as many people as possible, that's our job."

"Our job is demon disposal, not saving the bloody world," Danny muttered.

"Funny how often the two seem to go hand in hand."

A few moments later McLean scurried over to Angel and handed her a strange electronic tablet, that was a mixture of technology and coral.

"The red dots are Atlantis soldiers, the blue dots are citizens and the green dots are your squad," McLean explained.

"McLean you are a genius!" Angel smiled, "Look at all the blue dots! McLean help Becks. I'm going to go save people."

Angel teleported quickly. Popping around the sea kingdom, grabbing the survivors and teleporting them to safety. At times she had to carry more than one at once. It was exhausting but Angel didn't stop. There were people who needed her. Aquatic children hiding in coral cupboards. Old mermaid couples too tired to try and escape. Young Atlantis soldiers unprepared for the fight they faced. Angel saved them all. Then she teleported her squad and finally her task was done.

"I've done it! I've got the portal working. We can get everyone out of here!" Becks shouted as Angel teleported back to the portal room for the last time.

"Becks you are a genius!" Angel smiled, "Let's send the injured and the children through first. Araminta, take Willow through now."

"The King and I should use the portal first," the Queen

announced, "That would be…"

"Willow is injured," Angel walked over to where Willow lay. She pressed her hand against Willow's forehead and a soft healing glow travelled down the telepath's body."

"Save your strength. I'll be fine," Willow gasped.

"I know you will. Araminta take her through. McLean send the rest of the injured and the children through after."

As Araminta carried Willow through the portal the Queen cried, "How dare you give orders in my kingdom…"

"Sophie has an idea," Alexander interrupted, "A way to get rid of the demons but we need to discuss it with your Highnesses first."

Sophie quickly explained her idea.

"Does this device still exist?" Angel asked the King.

"It does. The switch is in the war room at the palace," the King explained.

"Let's send everyone through then we'll use that switch to," the Queen interrupted Angel with a slap.

"This kingdom has stood for over five hundred years! Once we go through the portal, we can get the Emperor to send the paranormal army here and they can get rid of the demons," the Queen exclaimed.

"We don't have time! If the demons realise this portal works…Transylvania is not prepared for a demon attack of this scale. Thousands would die in a matter of minutes! We can rebuild Atlantis, but we can't bring people back from the dead."

"I mean we can," Fern interjected, "We can get grandpa here to turn us all into vampires."

"Even vampires can die Fern," Alexander countered.

"Yeah but…"

"Not now Fern!" Angel snapped, "Look I understand that this situation is difficult for you. But look at your kingdom. The demons have ruined most of it already. You'd have to rebuild anyway."

"But where will our people live?" the Queen asked.

"Me and my squad will personally take care of that. Look we don't have time to argue."

The Queen was about to protest but the King interrupted her, "She's right. Okay Captain, we'll do as you ask."

"Thank you. Now if you tell me how to work the device, I will wait till everyone has gone through the portal then teleport to the switch and wash away Atlantis."

"But if you're here to press the switch, won't that mean you'll also get washed away?" Rowan asked, "Angel what you're suggesting is a suicide mission! The magic used to wash away Atlantis will kill you along with the demons!"

"That won't happen," the King explained, "The switch has a timer setting. We'll have enough time to return to the portal room and escape."

"We'll?" Angel asked.

"I'm coming with you. The switch can only be used by the King of Atlantis."

"Okay. Here's the plan. Rowan, you, and your mum are going to go through the portal in a minute then we'll send the rest through. Lightning Squad you'll leave once everyone, including the soldiers, have gone. Becks and McLean, I'm going to have to ask you to stay until the end. I need you here in case something goes wrong with the portal. Jason, I want you to stay as well to protect Becks and McLean while I teleport the King to the palace."

"Jason!? Why!? He's an idiot who can barely protect himself!" Fern cried.

"Hey! That's just rude!" Jason exclaimed.

"See what I mean! He's…"

"Jason is a demon!" Angel interrupted, "Yes he's a bit of an idiot, no offense Jason, but he's also a demon. And the best weapon against a demon is a demon."

"Can you stop calling me an idiot!?" Jason exclaimed, "It's really starting to hurt my self-esteem. And saying 'no offense' doesn't make it less offensive! Also…"

"Look we don't have time to deal with your self-esteem problems right now Jason. I promise when we get back to the base, we can have a serious discussion all about it. But right now we need to get everyone out of here."

It didn't take long to get everyone through the portal. Fern had been extremely unwilling to leave Angel behind with only Jason for backup. So much so that the only way they had been able to get the witch to leave was by having Danny throw her over his shoulder and drag her through the portal. The demons must have sensed that their dinner was escaping as all too soon they started banging against the portal room door.

"How long will that door hold?" Jason asked nervously.

"Hopefully long enough for us to escape," Angel muttered, "Your highness, are you ready?"

"Yes," the King nodded.

Angel took the King's hand and with a pop they had arrived back in the palace's war room. The King went over to a wall and pressed his hand against a stone. The stone moved and revealed a strange device that looked a bit like a computer screen. The King pressed his hand against the screen and a blue light scanned his face. There was a beep and the blue light vanished. The King then pulled out a key and placed it into a lock in the wall. He turned the key. The computer grumbled as a panel in the wall lifted revealing a big red button.

The King glanced out of the window, taking one final look at his beloved kingdom.

Then he pressed the big red button.

"You have seven minutes to evacuate," the computer said as a countdown came up on the screen.

"Let's go," Angel grabbed the King's hand and they teleported back to the portal room.

"Did you do it?" Jason asked.

"Yes, now we need to…"

Before Angel could finished the demons broke down the door. Angel raised her hands, creating a forcefield around both the King and the portal. The demons bashed their bodies against the forcefield and scratched at it with their claws. Angel's hands shook as she tried to keep the forcefield going.

"McLean, Becks, your Highness leave!" Angel ordered, "I can't hold this for long!"

"What about you?" the King asked.

"Me and Jason will stay behind to hold them off."

"Captain…?"

"Now!" Angel shouted as the forcefield began to shake.

"Yes cap," Becks dragged McLean and the King towards the portal.

"How long will this forcefield hold?" Jason asked.

"Not long. I've teleported too much…I haven't got much power left. In a minute I'm going to drop this forcefield and create a smaller one in front of the portal. We just need to hold them off for less than seven minutes."

"How will we know when the seven minutes are up?"

"I've set an alarm on my watch. It'll go off once six minutes have passed."

"So once it goes off, we'll have a minute to get through the portal?"

"Exactly. Jason are you okay?"

"Not really. I'm actually on the verge of having a massive panic-attack. I feel a bit faint and like I can't breathe. You see I'm actually having a really bad day. I know you guys see me turning into a demon as a good thing, but I don't actually…Ow!" Jason cried as Angel stabbed him once again.

"Sorry Jason but you were rambling."

"You know that…" Jason transformed into a demon

before he could finish his sentence.

Angel dropped the forcefield, creating a smaller one in front of the portal. Demon Jason attacked the larger demons leaving Angel to deal with the others.

Angel transformed into a water dragon. The water dragon (a beautiful white and blue creature whose body glided through the waves with the grace of a ballet dancer) and demon Jason fought side by side. They ripped demons apart and squashed orcs with their powerful tails.

Suddenly Angel's powers gave out. She involuntarily transformed back into her natural form. She tried to transform once more but found herself unable to.

"This is not the time powers," Angel hissed as she pulled out her gun. Angel fired two shots at an orc, it fell dead. Seconds later another orc slammed a mace into her back. Angel stumbled to her knees. She twisted around quickly and shot the orc in the head.

She pulled herself to her feet as an axe was thrown in her direction. She dodged the axe but was unable to avoid the sword that sliced her arm. Angel fired at the demon, but the bullets flew off the demon's scaled body. Angel pulled out her sword as another demon swung its axe in her direction. She blocked the axe whilst also trying to avoid another orc's mace.

I can't survive this without my powers, Angel quickly realised.

Crying out in pain as she did so, Angel forced her body to transform once more. This time her powers didn't fail her. She transformed into a water dragon and floated across the fight. She grabbed demons between her teeth and stabbed her fangs into their rotting flesh. As she successfully killed her twenty-ninth demon, a tentacle wrapped around her dragon belly. Dragon Angel looked up to find a kraken staring right back at her. The kraken's tentacle tightened as it threw dragon Angel into a wall. Dragon Angel fell to the ground and transformed back into Angel.

As Angel tried to get to her feet, the kraken slammed its body into the ceiling causing the roof to crumble and fall on top of her legs.

Jason, in demon form, had been happily enjoying himself. The orc demons lacked taste, but the larger demons had been quite delicious. Slightly chewy but enjoyable none the less. Demon Jason had just been about to devour another demon when the kraken swam past him.

It was at that moment that Jason remembered that they were underwater.

The kraken's ability to swim confused him greatly as he, as well as the other demons, walked and fought the same way they would have done if they were on land. Although he knew that the answer to his question would be magic, Jason still felt a strong urge to ask Angel about it anyway. Demon Jason turned and noticed Angel lying limp under a pile of rubble.

Demon Jason roared Angel's name and raced towards her. As he did so a large three headed shark-like demon tried to stop him. But demon Jason didn't stop. He slammed his spiked tail into the shark demon and scratched it with his claws. The shark demon struggled and bit into his side. Demon Jason roared out in pain and slashed his claws, slicing off one of the shark demon's heads. Demon Jason kept on slashing his claws until the shark demon finally fell dead.

He then swiftly made his way to Angel. He nuzzled Angel's small head; her response was nothing more than an inaudible murmur. Demon Jason carefully dragged the rubble from Angel. He gently placed her into his mouth and carried her into the forcefield. Once inside the forcefield demon Jason transformed back into normal Jason.

"Angel!? Angel!?" Jason yelled.

He grabbed Angel's body and tried to shake her awake. As he did so blood from his wounded side dripped unnoticed onto Angel's skin. Jason's blood ran down Angel's arm into her sword wound. The blood sank into Angel's injury.

The wound glowed black as Jason's and Angel's blood mixed together.

The glow faded as Angel's eyes snapped open.

She sat up quickly, which she soon regretted as the pain in her lower body intensified.

"Angel? Are you okay?"

"Yes. No. I don't know. Did you put me in your mouth?" Angel asked.

"Err yes. Yes I did."

"That's gross! That's so gross!"

"But it saved your life," said a third voice.

"Your Highness!?" Angel exclaimed as she stared at the King of Atlantis, "What are you doing here? I thought you'd left!"

"This is my kingdom. I should fight for it until the end."

"While that is a noble idea, it's also an extremely stupid one! If you die…"

"If I hadn't been here who would have kept the demons distracted long enough for the Master of Darkness to pull you from the rubble?"

"Well thank you for that," Angel looked at her watch, "Less than two minutes. You two should leave."

"What about you?" Jason asked.

"I need to stay and keep this forcefield going. I'll go through right before the kingdom collapses."

"But Angel…"

"Jason don't worry. This isn't a suicide mission. If I could leave now I would, but the forcefield would collapse and the demons would get through. I'll join you soon. So please just go. Now!"

Angel shoved Jason through the portal.

"Now you your…" Angel cried out as a trident cut

through her stomach. She stared in horror as the King withdrew the trident, his eyes clouded over.

This was not the King.

This was a demon using the King's body. The King tried to stab Angel again, but she twisted out of the way.

"Your Highness you need to fight this."

"The King isn't here right now," the King's lips moved but it was not his voice that spoke. This voice belonged to a demon. It was cold and emotionless, like Angel was talking to an answer machine.

"Then I'll just have to take you instead," Angel tried to grab the possessed King, but he wriggled out of her grasp.

He aimed the trident at her, sending a large wave in her direction. The wave knocked Angel to the floor. The King stabbed her again and again. Angel yelled out in pain as she grabbed the King's arm and pulled him to the floor. She pulled herself on top of the King and punched him.

"Your Highness?"

"The King isn't here right now," the possessed King threw Angel off and returned the punch.

At that moment the one-minute alarm on Angel's watch went off.

"Fantastic," Angel muttered spitting out blood.

Angel pulled out her wand. With a flick, a magic rope wrapped around the possessed King's body. Angel dragged herself and the King towards the portal. But the King merely laughed and broke free of the rope.

He grabbed Angel, pulling her into a tight embrace. His hands ran down Angel's body and unsheathed her sword from her belt. The possessed King then pushed Angel to the floor and stabbed her sword into his own chest.

He then grabbed Angel once more and the two of them fell through the portal.

The water cascaded into the portal room.

The water crushed and drowned the demons.

It dragged down monuments and destroyed family

homes. Corpses of Atlantis citizens were washed, along with dead demons, across the seabed. The waves wild white horses swiftly trampled a once historic kingdom.

Soon all that remained of the mystical city of Atlantis was a pile of blood-stained sand.

31

'THIS IS ONLY THE BEGINNING'

Jackson was having a dreadful day.

He had been in a meeting with the Colonel when Roger's body had teleported into the hospital wing, quickly followed by the injured Ethan. He didn't have time to process the loss of Roger as Captain Hardwick had received a call, moments later, from Angel saying that an army of demons was heading to Atlantis.

This led to several failed attempts to enter Atlantis and many long hours of waiting around for news. Finally survivors had started arriving at the gateway portal in the Emperor's palace. Jackson, Alpha Squad, and the other squads from the base were there to greet them and get the injured to the hospital. Jackson was helping an injured family of water sprites into a pool of water when he heard someone shout his name. He looked up and saw Rowan stood close by. Jackson ran up to her and pulled his wife into a tight embrace.

"Are you okay? Is everything...?" Jackson's questions

were stopped by a kiss. Jackson returned Rowan's kiss desperately, allowing the warmth of his wife's body to ease his weary heart.

Someone cleared their throat loudly behind them and the couple quickly pulled apart. The Queen of Atlantis stared daggers in Jackson's direction.

"Your Highness," Jackson bowed his head politely to his mother-in-law.

"To say your sister isn't blood related," the Queen snapped, "She acts just like the rest of you Nights. Rude, arrogant with no respect for laws or regulations."

"Angel? Where is she? What happened?" Jackson asked quickly.

"She'll be here soon," Rowan reassured, "She's going to come through last. Jackson…are you okay?"

Jackson wanted to lie.

He wanted to say that he was fine, but he couldn't get the words to leave his lips. Instead he simply shook his head. Rowan pulled him close, despite the Queen's protests, and Jackson sobbed into his wife's shoulder.

* * * * *

On the other side of the room Alexander stepped through the portal. He was quickly greeted by Araminta.

"Willow?" Alexander asked.

"She's been transferred to the hospital wing at the base," Araminta explained, "Angel did a decent job healing her, so she should pull through."

"Is the Colonel here?"

"He's over there, with the Emperor. Were you the last one?"

Alexander nodded. His eyes fixed on the Emperor.

"Are you going to keep staring or are you going to say hello?" Araminta asked.

"Neither. What about Ethan?"

"Also at the hospital wing. As is Roger."

"Has David…?"

"He's been informed."

The two vampires fell into silence as the minutes passed. The portal suddenly became active again as McLean and Becks stepped through.

"Angel?" Alexander asked quickly, not even allowing the pair to catch their breath.

"She's still there. Demons broke through the door. She said she'd stay with Jason to hold them off," Becks explained. Alexander swore louder than he intended and scratched his head in frustration.

"You two should go get checked out by the healers," Araminta said after giving her fellow vampire a sharp look, "Where's the King?"

"He was right…Oh where is he?" Becks looked around in surprise, "He was right behind us."

"Did he press the switch?"

"He did."

"How long do they have?" Alexander asked.

"Seven minutes."

The next seven minutes were the longest in Alexander's prolonged life, and he wasn't the only person who had started to grow restless. The Queen paced the portal room and Jackson itched his body as his anxiety rose. The Colonel and the Emperor quickly joined the anxious party as they waited for someone to pass through the portal.

After what felt like a lifetime, someone finally did. Jason fell through and landed flat on his face. Araminta raced over to him.

"Are you alright?" she asked.

Jason nodded, looking around, "Where am I?"

"You're in Transylvania…"

"Where is the King?" the Queen shouted at Jason.

"He's…oh! He was right behind me! he'll be here soon, they only…only have two…min…"

"Jason you're bleeding!" Araminta exclaimed.

"Am I? Oh yes I am," Jason muttered as he collapsed to the ground.

"Jason!"

"Get him to the hospital wing," Alexander ordered. Araminta quickly carried Jason away.

A few moments later Angel and the King fell through the portal.

The Colonel ordered the portal to be shut down as strong waves followed Angel and the King through. Angel rolled away from the King. Her body was covered in blood.

Alexander was by her side in an instant. He gently lifted Angel into his arms. Alexander's soft touch was a welcome relief to the intense pain that was racing through Angel's body.

"Angel! Angel are you okay?" Jackson asked as he dropped next to his sister. Angel stared at her brother, nodded, and smiled slightly. She then turned to Alexander whose eyes were searching her body intensely.

"Your eyes are red," Angel muttered raising her hand to Alexander's face.

"What?" the vampire asked.

"Your eyes are red. Ah, it must be all the blood. Sorry this must be really difficult for you."

"Why are you worrying about me right now!? You're covered in stab wounds and you're not healing. We need to get you to the hospital wing."

"Husband!" the Queen screamed as she turned over the King's body and found Angel's sword sticking out of his chest.

"Don't touch him. He's been possessed. We need an exorcist," Angel spluttered, "Rowan! Your father is possessed. Don't let her touch him."

"Nonsense! Oh he's still breathing. Darling? Darling, who did this to you?"

The possessed King raised his hand and pointed at

Angel.

"He stabbed himself. He's possessed. Look at his eyes!" Angel cried.

"Liar! He isn't possessed, your highness, your highness!" the Queen screamed as the King took his last breath and passed away.

Rowan pressed her hand against his neck trying to find a pulse. There was none. She desperately tried to do CPR, but it was too late, he was gone. Rowan got to her feet and stumbled backwards, tears running down her face. Jackson raced to her side and pulled his wife close. The Queen screamed and burst into hysterical tears.

"You need to get away from him, the demon might not be," Angel muttered.

"You murderer!" the Queen yelled.

"I didn't kill him, he was possessed. He stabbed himself," Angel gasped as she pulled herself, with some help from Alexander, into a sitting position. The Queen rushed over to Angel, dropping to her knees in front of the shapeshifter. She grabbed Angel by her collar and yelled in her face.

"Liar! Was this your plan from the start!? It was, wasn't it? You planned this. You planned to kill the King and destroy my kingdom!" the Queen slapped Angel's face.

"Mother that's enough!" Rowan shouted, "If Angel says that father stabbed himself then he did."

"You! My own flesh and blood! You've been bewitched by them. You're no longer talking sense," the Queen turned to the Emperor, "With your permission, I would like to have this...this thing placed under arrest."

"I don't," the Emperor began but then Anita, who had been watching the scene closely from the shadows, whispered something into his ear. The Emperor paused for a minute, then smiled, "I give my permission."

"You can't do this!" Alexander shouted as the Emperor's guards surrounded him and Angel. The vampire got to his feet and pushed the guards out of the way. Jackson joined him.

While the pair fought against the Emperor's guards, Angel's eyes didn't leave the Queen. Angel watched as a slight smile tickled the corner of the Queen's mouth. Before Angel had chance to contemplate the meaning of the smile, the pain her body had gone through finally caught up with her and she fell unconscious.

* * * * *

Jason woke up in the hospital wing, craving mint ice-cream. His vision was fuzzy at first, but it soon returned to normal. Jason was then able to clearly see Araminta who was stood, talking to a healer, by his bed.

"Jason. Are you okay? Can you hear me? Can you see me?" Araminta asked quickly.

"Mint ice-cream! Huh...what...what happened?"

"You fainted. The healers have sorted out your injury. Jason are you okay? You've been through a lot today."

"It's been a really long day," Jason sighed, "You know I've been stabbed like five times! I've turned into a demon. I've ate other demons. One demon went into me, which personally I think is really disturbing! That same demon showed me its mind and took me to hell. Did I mention that I've eaten demons!?"

"You did yes."

"And turning into a demon isn't fun. Well it's kind of is but it's also really weird! I suddenly crave flesh, like I really crave it! And it's really tasty! That's weird isn't it? I shouldn't find demon flesh tasty, but I do!"

"Turning into a demon must have been a strange experience for you."

"No kidding! I have a tail! Not right now but when I'm a demon I have a tail. Which is really handy for knocking demons out of the way but also rather hard to control. It gets in the way, you see, and the zombies kept trying to bite it, now that's a sentence I never thought I'd say! The zombies were trying to bite my tail. Zombies are awful! They smelled, and I couldn't eat them, they just tasted horrific!"

"Jason are you aware that you're talking really quickly and rambling on slightly?"

"Yes I am. You see I'm currently on the verge of having a mental breakdown and a rather large panic-attack. Angel said I was free to have one once we got back to the base. What happened to Angel? Did she get back okay?"

"She's been arrested," Willow called from the bed opposite Jason's. Willow was pale and weak, but her wound was healing well.

"Willow! You're okay!"

"Yeah, I am, but could you decide whether you're having your panic-attack internally or out loud please. Your internal one is giving me a headache."

"Don't read my mind then!"

"I can't help it! You're too loud!"

"Well I'll try and panic quietly. Did you just say Angel's been arrested?"

"Yeah. The King of Atlantis died with Angel's sword sticking out of his chest."

"What? But Angel wouldn't have…"

"No she wouldn't," Araminta agreed, "Angel says that the King was possessed and stabbed himself. Jason, what exactly happened?"

"Possessed!? I don't know. See it was a bit weird. Angel sent the King through first along with Becks and McLean. But then he suddenly turned up behind us and said he'd never left. Angel then ordered me to go through, well actually it was more like she shoved me through, the portal and the King was supposed to come with me. But he didn't."

"So the King could have left Atlantis but he, on two occasions, chose not to?"

"That sounds dodgy to me," Willow muttered, "Also Angel has no motive. Why would she kill the King? And why would she do so with her own sword? Do you think…do you think this was Jet's plan all along?"

"Maybe but it seems a bit farfetched."

"Where is Angel?" Jason asked, "She was badly injured. The roof collapsed on top of her and she'd teleported so much that her powers were fading."

"She collapsed when she arrived. She's in there," Araminta pointed to a door on the opposite side of the hospital wing, "It's a private room. There are guards blocking the entrance and no one, except selected healers, is allowed in."

"What about Ethan?"

"He's in another private room. His family is with him."

* * * * *

Alexander stood and watched as Jackson wept over Ethan's comatose body. Rowan was talking quietly with a fellow healer. Alexander couldn't hear what they were saying, but then he wasn't really paying attention. His thoughts were elsewhere. He couldn't get the Emperor's face from his mind. Alexander was certain that the Emperor had originally intended to refuse the Queen's request to arrest Angel, so what had Anita said to change his mind so quickly.

"How is he?" Jackson asked as the healer left the room.

"Well to be honest the situation is a bit complicated," Rowan said as she sat down opposite her husband, "On paper Ethan's injuries are practically beyond repair. Most of his bones are broken and he suffered an intense blow to the head. He also…he also drowned. However…"

Before Rowan could continue David and Tobias Night entered the room. Tobias was a tall skinny man with a mock of brown hair and sharp facial features. Unlike his brothers, the oldest Night sibling had an unfriendly pair of green eyes and his face continuously wore an unamused scowl.

"Pops what happened? What did the Emperor say?" Jackson asked.

"He," David paused for a moment.

While the pause lasted no more than a few seconds, it was long enough for Alexander to deduce that whatever the werewolf leader was going to say next would be a lie.

"He said that there's nothing that can be done," David explained, "Although he doesn't believe Angel is guilty, after everything that has happened to Atlantis he doesn't want to go against the Queen. She has a sharp temper and powerful followers. She could quite easily break up the empire if she wished."

"But that's just…"

"This is a political issue Jackson," Tobias snapped, "There's nothing that can be done."

"I'll talk with my mother," Rowan sighed, "I might be able to get her to stop. I'm really sorry about this."

"It's not your fault," David reassured, "How's Ethan?"

"I was just explaining that Ethan's condition is complicated. To put it bluntly Ethan should be…should be…"

"Dead?"

"Yes. However Angel has created something rather incredible. Ethan is currently in a magically induced coma and while his mind sleeps the rest of his body is healing. Angel attempted to do the same to Roger but he…he passed away before it could be completed."

"Will he wake up?"

"Hopefully. To be honest we've never seen anything like this before. It's very different to other magically induced comas. Ethan won't wake up until he's fully healed that's for sure."

"However if he doesn't heal?"

"Then he probably won't wake up. I think. Like I said

none of us healers have seen anything like this before. We need to discuss it with Angel."

"Did you ask the Emperor? Can we see her?" Jackson asked. David shook his head. Jackson got to his feet and kicked a chair in frustration. At that moment Skyjack entered the room.

"I've just been to see Angel," Skyjack said quietly.

"How is she?"

"Her condition is still very unstable. She's been stabbed multiple times. Her legs have been crushed. A roof collapsed on top of her I'm told. She also teleported repeatedly underwater which is an extremely dangerous thing to do. She's not self-healing but she is responding well to treatment."

As Jackson started to ask more questions about Angel's condition, Alexander silently slipped from the room. Before he got far, he heard someone call his name.

The vampire turned to find David Night stood behind him.

"Did you think I hadn't seen you?" David asked.

"Why did you lie?" Alexander countered, "What did the Emperor actually say to you? I have to say you're very calm to say your daughter has been arrested for a crime that, if she's found guilty, could lead to her execution."

"What are you implying?"

"I'm not sure, what am I implying?"

David was about to say more but he was interrupted by Anita who shouted Alexander's name.

"Let's finish this conversation another time," David whispered to Alexander before returning to the room Ethan was in.

"What did you say to the Emperor?" Alexander asked Anita, "He wasn't going to arrest Angel but then you said something and changed his mind. What did you say?"

Anita smiled, "Would you like to see her? Angel. Do you want to see her?"

"No one is allowed to...you won't even let her family..."

"I'll let you. I'll let you see her."

"Why? Why would you?"

"Worry about that after you've seen her. I won't give you this opportunity again."

* * * * *

When Angel opened her eyes, three days later, Alexander was sat next to her bed. The vampire's eyes were closed but he wasn't sleeping.

He was contemplating every possible outcome and questioning everything that had happened. Lightning Squad had been set up. That he was certain of. The question was when had the set up started. From Paris' interrogation or from Mr Jet entering the base? Or had this all started when Lightning Squad had received the order to find the Master of Darkness? The vampire's forehead wrinkled as he tried to find the answers.

Angel stared at Alexander silently. His red eyes had faded and now the vampire simply looked tired. Alexander normally looked calm, collected, and youthful (despite his old age) however in this moment he just looked tired. For a while Angel just stared, enjoying the luxury of being alive and being able to see Alexander's face. There had been a moment back at Atlantis when Angel had thought she'd never see the vampire again. This thought had scared her more then she'd ever admit.

Memories of Atlantis flooded back to her, as did the images of the zombies, the demons and Roger...Angel sighed deeply. The sound awoke the vampire from his thoughts. He opened his eyes to find Angel staring up at him.

"Angel?" Alexander asked, a slight smile of relief tickling his lips, "How are you feeling?"

"What is this?" Angel gestured to the chains wrapped around her body, "Did they arrest me?"

Alexander nodded, "Your father has spoken to the Emperor but at the moment there's nothing that can be done, apparently."

"Pops? Where is he?"

"With Ethan. Ethan's okay. He's still in the coma. You've managed to confuse all the healers with that. They can't, your family, they're not allowed to see you."

"Why not?"

"I don't know. I'm not really sure what's going on. The situation is…" the vampire sighed.

"That bad? Is everyone else okay? Willow, how's she doing? And Jason? Is he okay? Danny? Have you contacted Roxy's family? And what about…?"

"They're fine. Jason, Willow, the rest of the squad, they're all fine. Roxy's family are here, Clover is taking good care of them. Ah, Fern's in lock up though. When she found out that you'd been arrested, she decided to let the Queen know how she felt about the situation."

"Why can't that witch ever keep her mouth shut? Ah!" Angel gasped as a wave of pain rippled from her legs upwards.

"Does it hurt? I'll go get a healer," Angel grabbed Alexander's arm before he could move.

"Don't leave."

"I'm just going to get…"

"Don't leave. I'm okay."

"Angel you're not okay! You were stabbed, your legs were crushed, Jet broke your arm, you teleported…"

"You don't need to list my injuries. I'm well aware of them."

"Are you? Do you have any idea how serious your condition has been? When they first brought you here, all the healers thought you wouldn't last the night. You have no idea how worried I thought I was going to…" Alexander sighed, took Angel's hand from his arm and held it.

"Sorry."

"Why are you apologising? You didn't ask to be injured."

"I know but still, I'm sorry."

"Don't be just…You need to start taking better care of yourself. Seriously do you have any idea how many times you've terrified me this past month?"

"It's only been a month, everything that's happened. Jason arriving, Rio, the Pied Piper, lock up, the memories, the attack at the base, Paris, the execution, the Polar Base, and Atlantis, it all happened in a month! It's no wonder Jason was panicking. There's been so much going on that I didn't actually get a chance to train him."

As Angel spoke tears ran down her face.

It had been a long and painful month. So much had happened in such a short space of time. Everything had happened so quickly. Too quickly, never allowing Angel, or the rest of the squad, time to breathe. Alexander wiped the tears from Angel's cheeks.

"To say he's an idiot, Jason's adapted to this chaos rather well," Alexander joked.

"We shouldn't call him an idiot. I think I technically owe him my life."

For a while neither of them spoke.

Angel closed her eyes. She exhaled as she contemplated the long month that had claimed four of her squad members lives. Three, she corrected herself. Paris was a terrorist therefore unworthy of her sorrow.

Memories of Elsa, Roxy and Roger surfaced. Looking back Angel found that she didn't have many memories with Elsa. The vampire had always been kind, nice and had never caused any problems. She always did her job and did it well. But this meant that she had often gone unnoticed. In most of Angel's memories Elsa was faded into the background, like an extra in a movie.

Roxy on the other hand had caused Angel many

problems over the years. Her love of gossip, her big personality and her sharp criticisms had irritated Angel immensely, but they had also been her driving force. The need to prove Roxy wrong and gain her respect had been something Angel had always strived for. As despite her flaws, Roxy's heart had always been in the right place and her criticisms not always unfounded.

The memories of Roger flooded Angel's mind. There were too many of them. Roger had named her. He had been the one who had taught her to read and to write. He had been the first to make her laugh and the first to love her. Angel opened her eyes, blinking away the memories of Roger. Alexander was watching her, his hand still resting against her cheek. He stroked her skin softly and waited until Angel worked up the courage to ask:

"Alex, where's Roger?"

The vampire didn't answer. He simply got to his feet and walked over to the guard stationed at the door. After a few minutes of conversation, Alexander returned.

"I'll take you to him," he said.

The guard brought over a wheelchair and Alexander carefully lifted Angel into it. The guards followed close behind as Alexander pushed Angel down a dark corridor and into the morgue. The guards waited outside as Alexander pushed Angel into a small room.

Inside the room were three metal tables. On one lay a pile of ash, the remains of Elsa, whilst the bodies on the other two were covered by white sheets. With shaking hands, Angel pulled back one of the sheets, under which lay Roxy. A gunshot wound penetrating her skull. Angel's tears fell to the floor as she gently placed her hand on Roxy's cheek. After a few moments, Angel turned to the final table and pulled back the sheet revealing Roger's body.

Angel rested her head on his chest and sobbed.

"I'm sorry," Angel cried, "All of you. I failed you all.

I'm so sorry."

* * * * *

The final gong sounded as the last coffin was placed into the ground. The sun was slowly setting around the graveyard. The graveyard was a pretty place. White and red roses grew between the graves and a small building stood in the centre.

The Colonel, stood in the middle of the newly made graves, cleared his throat.

"Today we stand here to remember those who fell in the battle at the Polar Base and at Atlantis," the Colonels voice was emotionless, "They fought bravely, and they will be remembered. So as I read the list of the dead, I ask you all to think of them as they once were. From our team at the Polar Base: Angus O'Neil, Fredrick Reed and Joel Reed. And from our own Lightning Squad: Elsa Sunday, Roxy Ash and Roger Night. We must also remember the hundreds of Atlantis citizens who lost their lives in this battle."

There was a howl from the Night wolf pack, who had arrived earlier that morning, when the Colonel mentioned Roger.

Then there was silence.

Jason looked down at his shoes. He felt awful. He had never been to a funeral before. The other members of Lightning Squad were feeling just as miserable. Clover and Willow looked grim and depressed. Fern was twisting her wand absentmindedly between her fingers; sparks were flying off and gently floating to the ground. Araminta was stood very still with her eyes closed. Sue was standing away from the others, unable to look at the graves. Whereas Sophie stared at the graves, incapable of pulling her eyes away from them. Danny was lent against a tree carefully studying the others around him whilst Alexander was watching the graves with a bowed head. Angel was sat, chained to her wheelchair, next to David, Tobias, and

Jackson, with two Atlantis guards watching closely. Rowan was stood with them; she was tired and pale. This was the second funeral she had been to in the last two days. The day before at the Emperor's palace there had been a funeral for her father, it had been a small and official affair.

The gong sounded once more, and the ground covered the coffins. Everyone saluted in unison, the wolves howled, and the funeral was over.

David turned to Angel, "Me and the pack are going to take Roger's coffin home. We'll bury him next to the others."

Angel nodded, "Take care of him. Once the investigation is over, I'll come see him."

David hugged his daughter and then he, Jackson, Rowan, and the rest of the pack left. Angel watched as they carried Roger's coffin away. She kept staring long after the wolf pack had disappeared from view.

She was too distracted with thoughts of Roger that she didn't notice Jason walk up next to her.

"Are you okay?" Jason asked.

"Jason, yes I'm fine. How are you? I heard you fainted."

"Ah yeah. I got bit by a demon but I'm alright now."

"Good…have you had your mental breakdown yet?"

"Yes, well it's kind of still on going. It started the moment I woke up in the hospital wing. Well actually that's not true. First, I started thinking about mint ice cream…that happens every time I wake up in the hospital wing…it's a bit weird. Anyway when I stopped thinking about mint ice cream, I then began my mental breakdown."

Angel laughed, "You're a bit odd, you know that, right? But a good kind of odd. You're nice and human-like. I'm also…err…proud of you."

"Sorry could you say that a bit louder, I didn't quite hear you."

"I'm not saying it again. But the Polar Base and Atlantis, you handled both incredibly well."

"But I panicked the entire time!"

Angel laughed softly, "Yes you did. But do you know what your panic-attacks have taught me?"

Jason shook his head.

"They taught me that it's okay to panic. It's okay to be scared and to have no clue what you're doing. As long as you keep going. As long as you keep fighting. You just fought a massive battle and yes, you did freak out the *whole time*, but you did it. You survived. That's pretty incredible. You also saved my life! You're clumsy, naive and an idiot, yet you saved my life. You've impressed me Dragonheart."

"Thanks."

"Your panic-attacks also made me realise that I must be a saint! I mean there were so many times, when you were panicking, that I wanted to hit you, but I didn't. If that's not saint-like behaviour, I don't know what is!"

"Thanks!"

Angel smiled, "Seriously though, I think that one day you're going to be a brilliant Master of Darkness."

"Really!?"

"Yeah. You'll still be an idiot though!"

"Hey that's not…"

"Angel Night!"

The crowd split in two as the intruder's voice echoed around the graveyard. Anita stood with a group of the Emperor's guards. They pushed their way through the grieving crowd towards the Colonel.

Anita shouted, "Angel Night show yourself."

"I'm right here," Angel called, the two guards grabbed her, "What the hell? Get your hands off me!"

"Angel Night you're under arrest for the murder of the King of Atlantis."

"You have got to be kidding me!?"

"The arrest warrant has been signed by the Emperor

himself, see," Anita handed it to Alexander, who had stood protectively in front of Angel.

"Don't do this," Alexander warned.

"Bring it out," Anita ordered.

Two guards brought forward an orange glowing straitjacket. Angel glanced at Alexander. His face confirmed her fear. This straitjacket was one of the anti-shapeshifter weapons that should have been destroyed long ago.

"Are you crazy?" Alexander exclaimed, standing firmly between the guards and Angel, "That thing kills shapeshifters!"

"Move Alexander or I shall arrest you as well."

"Then you better do that," Alexander hissed. Danny, who had been watching the situation closely, swiftly punched one of the guards and the rest of Lightning Squad quickly joined in the fight.

"You can stab me again, if that'll help you get out of here," Jason offered.

Angel shook her head and shouted at Anita, "If you want to arrest me, you're going to have to catch me first!"

And with that Angel Night vanished.

EPILOGUE

The Kingdom of the Elves was one of the most beautiful, elegant, and peaceful places in all the known worlds. Its steep hillside tumbled down to soft sandy beaches that rolled into the deep blue sea. On the top of one of the towering cliffs the small town of Aelgifu stood. The town had houses made of incredible white stone; its colour glowed, never fading, enchanting anyone whose eyes landed upon it.

Normally the sound of children playing and laughing in the sunlight would be heard echoing from the busy marketplace.

However today there was silence.

From the roof tops, thick black smoke rose into the sky, casting a dooming shadow upon the kingdom of peace.

Ailward, head of the elf council's private guard, scanned his surroundings searching for some sign of life. Ailward was tall, with shoulder length brown hair and a sharp face, his green eyes saw more than most.

"What are your orders, sir?" asked Edward, Ailward's second in command, a short skinny elf whose long ginger hair was swaying in the light breeze.

"We move in." Edward nodded and the pair kicked their horses into a swift trot. As the horses reached the town gates, they were met with a horrid smell. The sight in front of their eyes was one that would haunt their dreams for the rest of their days.

There had clearly been a battle, swords and arrows were sprawled across the bloody pools on the ground. Children lay broken in the mud; their bodies had been ripped open and their bloody organs now painted the buildings. One child, a boy with large chocolate brown eyes, was dangling on a washing line between two houses; his heart had been ripped out. The adults had been rounded up, their heads taken from their necks and their bodies broken into a mass of decomposing porridge.

On one of the walls, painted in blood, was a message.

The message read:

This is only the beginning...

MASTER OF DARKNESS

Lightning Squad shall return in *The Dragonheart Chronicles Book 2:* Mistress of Light

ABOUT THE AUTHOR

Hi, I'm K.T. Kaye.
As well as being an author, I am a theatre actor and
performer. I started writing Master of Darkness when I
was eleven, as I was bored of the books in my local library
and wanted to go on adventures of my own. I used to have
panic-attacks when I was younger, so I wanted to create a
character who suffered from them too yet still managed to
be a hero.

Printed in Great Britain
by Amazon

53765076R00246